PRAISE FOR BRIAN FREEMAN

"Reads like a whirlwind . . . brilliantly crafted . . . highly recommended for those who enjoy their psychological thrillers infused with plenty of smarts and nonstop action."

—Bookreporter on *Thief River Falls*

"Freeman does a masterful job creating a nightmare scenario of never-ending darkness, roads that go nowhere with bogeymen at every intersection. A disturbing yet compelling thriller."

—*Booklist* on *Thief River Falls*

"This is a thriller that will keep you up all night. And even the most perceptive crime novel fan will be stunned by the cliff-hanger conclusion."

—Pioneer Press on *The Crooked Street*

"Excellent . . . A cleverly constructed, page-turning plot and fleshed-out primary and secondary characters make this a winner."

—*Publishers Weekly* on *Alter Ego* (Starred Review)

"Freeman's latest psychological thriller is sure to seize readers and not let go . . . Gripping, intense, and thoughtful, *The Night Bird* is a must-read."

—*Romantic Times* on *The Night Bird* (Top Pick)

"If there is a way to say 'higher' than 'highly recommended,' I wish I knew it. Because this is one of those thrillers that goes above and beyond."

—*Suspense Magazine* on *Goodbye to the Dead*

"Writing and storytelling don't get much stronger . . . and thriller fiction doesn't get much better than *The Cold Nowhere*."
—Bookreporter on *The Cold Nowhere*

"My discovery this year has been the Edgar-nominated crime writer Brian Freeman . . . Fleshed-out characters, high tension, and terrifying twists put Freeman up there with Harlan Coben in the psychological crime stratosphere."
—*London Daily Mail* on *The Burying Place*

"*Spilled Blood* is everything a great suspense novel should be: gripping, shocking, and moving. Brian Freeman proves once again he's a master of psychological suspense."
—Lisa Gardner, #1 *New York Times* bestselling author, on *Spilled Blood*

"Brian Freeman is a first-rate storyteller. *Stalked* is scary, fast paced, and refreshingly well written. The characters are so sharply drawn and interesting we can't wait to meet the next one in the story."
—Nelson DeMille, #1 *New York Times* bestselling author, on *Stalked*

"Breathtakingly real and utterly compelling, *Immoral* dishes up page-turning psychological suspense while treating us lucky readers to some of the most literate and stylish writing you'll find anywhere today."
—Jeffery Deaver, #1 *New York Times* bestselling author, on *Immoral*

INFINITE

Also by Brian Freeman

Stand-Alone Novels

Thief River Falls
The Deep, Deep Snow
Spilled Blood

The Frost Easton Series

The Crooked Street
The Voice Inside
The Night Bird

The Jonathan Stride Series

Funeral for a Friend
*Alter Ego**
Marathon
Goodbye to the Dead
The Cold Nowhere
Turn to Stone (e-novella)
Spitting Devil (e-short story)
The Burying Place
In the Dark
Stalked
Stripped
Immoral

INFINITE

BRIAN FREEMAN

THOMAS & MERCER

Text copyright © 2021 by Brian Freeman
All rights reserved.

Published by Thomas & Mercer, Seattle

www.apub.com

Amazon, the Amazon logo, and Thomas & Mercer are trademarks of Amazon.com, Inc., or its affiliates.

ISBN-13: 9781542023863 (hardcover)
ISBN-10: 1542023866 (hardcover)

ISBN-13: 9781542023870 (paperback)
ISBN-10: 1542023874 (paperback)

Cover design by Rex Bonomelli

Printed in the United States of America

First edition

For Marcia

One world at a time.

—Thoreau, on his deathbed

CHAPTER 1

"We're very sorry for your loss, Mr. Moran," the cop told me as he handed me a white foam cup filled with coffee. He already had his own coffee in his hand, and he was eating a powdered doughnut that left a dusting of sugar on his mustache like fresh snow on a lawn.

I said nothing. I felt dazed and numb, as if I were in a coma from which I wasn't sure I would ever awaken. The chill made me shiver. They'd taken away my soaked, dirty clothes and wrapped a wool blanket around my naked body, but it didn't help. A policewoman who lived nearby had offered to wash and dry my clothes and bring them back to me before morning. The deep cuts on my arms and legs had been disinfected and bandaged, but I felt a stinging pain regardless. I kept coughing, and when I did, I could still taste the river.

It tasted like death.

"Feast or famine," the cop said.

He was probably about forty years old, with a round face and not much brown hair left on his head. He had a large mole in the seam of one of his nostrils, which was the kind of thing you couldn't stop looking at. He was plump, clean, and dry, a cop who spent his nights at a desk. Two other cops, young and fit, had found me in the field, with rain pouring over my face along with my tears.

Where was I?

What town was this?

I didn't even know. The police had driven me here, but I remembered none of it. I only remembered shouting Karly's name as they dragged me away. She was still down there in the water.

"Feast or famine," the cop said again. "That's been us this season. May and June were dry as a bone. Been driving the farmers crazy. Land's hard as a rock. We get a storm like this, and all the water just runs off into the creek. The banks ain't made for that much rain that fast."

He was right. My grandfather grew up in the flatlands of North Dakota, where the waters rose every spring with the snowmelt, and he used to warn me about rivers. *Never trust a river, Dylan. Give a river even half a chance, and it'll try to kill you.*

I should have listened.

"Sorry about all the paperwork at a time like this," the cop continued. I thought his name was Warren, but I couldn't even lift my head to study the nameplate on his shirt. "I know that's the last thing on your mind, but somebody dies, we have to jump through a lot of hoops. That's the law. Like I say, I'm really sorry."

"Thank you." I barely recognized my voice. It didn't even sound like me.

"Can you tell me your wife's name again?"

"Karly Chance."

"You and she didn't have the same last name?"

"No."

"How old was she?"

"Twenty-nine."

"And you?"

"I'm thirty-two."

"The two of you live in Chicago?"

"Yes."

"What brought you down to this part of the state?"

Dylan, let's go away for a few days. I know you're upset and angry, and you have every right to be, but we need to start over.

4

"I'm sorry. What did you say?"

"I said, why were you down in this part of the state?"

"We took a weekend away from the city," I replied. "A friend of Karly's has a place in Bigneck."

"What do you do in Chicago, Mr. Moran?"

"I'm the events manager for the LaSalle Plaza Hotel."

"And your wife?"

"She works for her mother. She's a real estate agent." I added a moment later, "She was."

Warren popped the last bite of doughnut into his mouth and then rubbed his mustache clean with a napkin. He kept scribbling notes on the yellow pad in front of him, and he hummed to himself as he did. I looked around the police interview room, which had chipped cream-colored paint on the walls and no windows. Warren sat on one side of a rickety oak table that was old enough to still have cigarette burns in the wood. I sat on the other side, swaddled in the blanket like a newborn. I couldn't trust any of my senses. When I breathed, all I smelled was the dankness of water in my nose. Every time I closed my eyes, I was back inside the car, as the river flipped us like a carnival ride.

"You got a way to get home to the city?" Warren asked me. "Family or friends or somebody who can pick you up?"

I didn't know what to tell him. I had no family, not really. My parents died when I was thirteen. That's the clinical way I describe it to people, which is easier than saying that my father murdered my mother and then killed himself right in front of me. After that, I moved in with my grandfather. Edgar's ninety-four now and doesn't drive. We get along, but we don't get along, if you know what I mean. It's always been that way.

As for friends, the childhood friend who had always bailed me out when things got bad was Roscoe Tate, and he died four years ago after bailing me out. Literally. That was the night I met Karly. I was covered in blood, my arm broken, my leg broken. Roscoe was dead behind the wheel, his neck snapped. I thought I must be dead, too. I stared through the car's shattered windows and saw an angel staring back at me, her dress billowing in the wind, her hand reaching in to hold mine. Her quiet voice murmured that help was coming, that I was going to be okay, that she wouldn't leave me.

That was Karly.

And now she was gone. Another car accident.

"I really don't have anyone," I told Warren.

"Oh," the cop replied, his mustache wrinkling. "Well, we can figure something out. Don't you worry, we'll get you home."

"Thank you."

As we sat there, the door to the interview room opened. The deputy's face bloomed with surprise, and he jumped to his feet, brushing sugar from his sleeves. A fifty-something woman, trim and small, stood in the doorway. Her size didn't diminish any of the authority she conveyed. Her blond hair was pulled into a tight bun behind her head, leaving wispy bangs on her forehead. She had polite brown eyes and a calm, neutral expression on her mouth. Her uniform was slightly damp, as if she'd come in from outside, but the creases were crisp.

"Sheriff," Warren exclaimed. "Sorry, I didn't realize you were coming in."

The sheriff gave her deputy an impatient look that said he shouldn't have been surprised at all by her arrival at four in the morning. A river had flooded, and a woman had died in her county. Out here, that was a big deal.

"I'll take over, Warren."

"Yes, ma'am."

Warren made a quick exit with a sympathetic nod to me. The sheriff sat down and opened a file folder with a small stack of papers inside. With a glance at the top page, I saw an incident report from the Chicago police. I was pretty sure my name was on it.

"Hello, Mr. Moran," she said. "I'm Sheriff Sinclair. You have my deepest condolences on the death of your wife."

"Thank you."

I realize there's nothing else for people to say in these circumstances, and it makes them feel better to say it. *I'm sorry for your loss.* But as the one who just lost everything, I can tell you, it doesn't help at all.

"I wonder if you could take me through the details of the accident."

"I've already done that, Sheriff."

"Yes, I know you've been through it with my men, and I know how difficult this is, but it would be very helpful if you could tell me again." So I did.

I replayed it all like a horror movie that you can't stop watching. How the two-lane road vanished, swallowed up by inky black water overflowing the banks of the river. How we plunged into the mud-thick current, which wriggled and surged like a sea creature. How we shimmied on the surface like a dancer struggling to do a pirouette, and then the front end lurched downward, and sludgy water filled the car.

"That's a terrible thing," Sheriff Sinclair said when I was finished. Her eyes never left me the entire time I was talking. Somehow I had the idea that I was strapped to a polygraph in her mind, with probes tracking my heartbeat with every breath I took. She reminded me of my mother, who'd also been a cop and who'd been able to tell when I was lying as a child just by looking at my face.

"Do you know how fast you were going when you went into the water?" the sheriff continued.

Dylan, slow down.

"I'm sorry, what?"

"Do you know how fast you were going when you went into the water?"

Dylan, please. Slow down.

"No, I don't know. Too fast, obviously. I didn't see the flood in time to stop."

7

"The car sank immediately?"

"Yes."

"And you were both trapped?"

"Yes."

"How is it that you managed to get out of the car but your wife didn't?"

I twitched. In my head, the car jerked through a somersault under the water. Our bubble of air spilled away. The window near me broke into pieces, and something shot through the space like a javelin.

"A tree trunk came through the car," I explained. "I was able to pull myself out. I was trying to get Karly out, too, but the car shifted and ripped her away from me."

"Did you dive back down to find her?"

"Of course I did."

"At what point did you give up?"

"I didn't *give up*, Sheriff," I snapped back at her. "I lost consciousness. At some point, the current must have thrown me clear. When I came to, I was on the riverbank, and the police were there."

"I see." The sheriff pushed some of the papers in the folder with her fingers. Her tone stayed neutral, but I heard an accusation in her voice. "I have a few other questions, Mr. Moran. Had you been drinking before the accident?"

"No."

"Nothing at all? No liquor, no drugs?"

"Your deputies tested me. The test was negative."

"Yes, I know. Although to be clear, it took them some time to get the test done, so the results aren't necessarily reliable. I ran your name through the system. It's routine in cases like this. You've had a history of problems with alcohol, haven't you? I'm seeing two DUIs in your record."

"Those were years ago. Yes, sometimes I drink too much, but I wasn't drinking tonight."

"Okay."

Sheriff Sinclair twisted a pencil around in her fingers. Her eyes were still focused on me, as if she were taking the measure of this man in front of her. I've always felt that women make rapid judgments about the men they meet, for better or for worse. They decide if they're solid or not solid in a matter of seconds.

"You have a temper, don't you, Mr. Moran?"

"Excuse me?"

"I'm seeing arrests for assault in your past, along with the drunk driving. Bar fights, that kind of thing. Your record suggests that you can be a violent man."

"I've made mistakes a few times when I was drunk," I acknowledged. "I deeply regret the things I did."

"Ever hit your wife?"

"No. I have *never* laid a finger on Karly or any other woman. Ever."

"What about verbal abuse? Threats?"

"Absolutely not."

"How were things between the two of you?"

Dylan, I'm sorry, I'm sorry. I made a stupid mistake. Can you ever forgive me?

"What?" I asked.

"How was your marriage?"

"Our marriage was fine," I lied. Which was a foolish thing to do. People knew what had happened. Karly had told her mother about it. I'd told one of my coworkers. And yet I couldn't say out loud to this police officer that my wife had cheated on me.

"Your wife came from money, didn't she? She's a Chance, as in Chance Properties?"

"Chance Properties is her mother's real estate agency, yes. Karly worked for her mother. I'm not sure what that has to do with anything, Sheriff."

"I just want to understand what happened. You were driving too fast. Some might say recklessly. You have a history of alcohol abuse and violent behavior."

My face reddened. I could feel the heat of the flush. "What the hell are you saying? Are you implying that I drove my car into the river deliberately and then left my wife there to die?"

"I'm not implying anything."

"Well, you seem to think I'm the kind of man who would do that."

"I have no idea what kind of man you are, Mr. Moran. I'm not saying you were to blame for the accident. It's simply my job to get the facts."

I leaned across the table. The blanket slipped down my bare shoulders and I shrugged it back. My voice rose, but with the static of a radio station that's going out of range. "You want the facts? The *fact* is, my wife is dead. I loved her. I did everything I could to save her, and I failed. If life handed out second chances, I'd be back in the water right now trying to get to her. Is that clear enough for you, Sheriff?"

Her face softened just a little. "It is. I'm sorry, Mr. Moran."

"I'd really like to be alone," I said. "This is all too much. I don't even know where I am."

"Yes, of course."

Sheriff Sinclair closed the folder in front of her. She rolled the pencil back and forth on the table, then slid it inside a pocket. She stood up and went to the door, but as she opened it, she turned around and studied me again.

I knew what was coming.

"One more question, Mr. Moran. According to my deputies, you were mostly incoherent when they found you."

"Is that a surprise?"

"No. Of course not. But they said you kept talking about seeing a man on the bank of the river near the scene of the accident. You kept asking why he didn't help you. Why he didn't try to rescue your wife."

My throat went dry. This was the part no one would understand.

"I don't remember saying that," I replied.

"*Did* you see someone near the river?" the sheriff asked.

I closed my eyes and inhaled sharply. I felt my lungs screaming for air again, my chest ready to burst as my face breached the surface. I gulped in a breath, and as I prepared to dive back down, I saw him.

A man.

A man stood barely ten feet away on the riverbank at the edge of the rapids. When the lightning flashed, I saw him clearly. There was no mistaking what I saw, and it didn't matter that what I was seeing was impossible. All I could do was shout to him. Beg. Plead.

That man was my lifeline. I needed him. He could save Karly.

Help me! My wife is drowning! Help me find her!

"No," I told the sheriff, keeping my voice steady. "No, it was night. It was raining. I didn't see anything."

A strange little wrinkle of concern crossed her forehead. She didn't believe me, that was obvious, but she couldn't understand why I would lie about something like that. Instead, she gave me another polite smile and left the room and closed the door behind her. It was quiet now. I was alone with the chipped cream-colored paint on the walls and the stench of the river in my head.

Yes, I was lying, but I couldn't tell her the reason.

I couldn't tell her about the man I'd seen, because I had no way to explain it to myself. You'll think I was imagining things, and I probably was. I was panicked and oxygen deprived, and it *was* night, and it *was* raining.

On the other hand, I know what I saw.

I was the man on the riverbank.

It was *me*.

CHAPTER 2

After the accident, I couldn't go home. It was too soon. Karly and I lived near River Park in a two-story Chicago apartment house, where I'd grown up with my grandfather. Edgar lived upstairs, and our place was on the first floor. When I walked in, the rooms would smell of Karly's perfume. Photographs of us would be hung on the walls and in frames adorning the fireplace mantel. Her clothes would be in the closet, her shampoo in the bathroom. I'd see her handwriting on little poems she'd scrawled and left for me on the fridge. In the apartment, my wife of three years would still be alive, and I couldn't face the fact that she was dead.

One of the police deputies drove me as far as Bloomington-Normal, and I took a train from there into the city. I walked to the hotel where I worked, which was on Michigan Avenue across from Grant Park. I booked a room and got out of the lobby before the staff could fawn over me with their sympathy. I spent the next two days and nights in a kind of hibernation. The phone rang; I ignored the calls. People knocked on the door; I didn't answer. I ordered room service and had them leave the trays outside, and then I put them back in the hallway later, having eaten almost nothing at all.

Did I drink?

Yes, I drank a lot.

I know what you probably think of me. Dylan drinks. He gets into fights. He is a bad man. I can't really disagree with you. It's been that way since the death of my parents, but that's not an excuse for how I've led my life. It simply is what it is. My vices cling to me like boat anchors. Karly told me once that I was always doing battle with another side of myself and that one day I would have to make the choice to cast him aside. But I've never known how to do that.

Sometime during my second night in the hotel, I had a nightmare that I was still under the water. I was a blind man, with no compass to guide me, swimming deeper into an abyss of darkness. The heaviness weighed on my lungs, like a balloon about to be popped. Somewhere beyond my reach, I could hear Karly's muffled voice calling to me, begging for rescue.

Dylan, come find me! I'm still here!

I awoke tangled in the blankets. I was bathed in sweat, gasping as I stared at the ceiling. My blood was still poisoned with alcohol, leaving me dizzy. The hotel room spun like a carousel. I got out of the ultraplush bed and went to the window. Grant Park stretched out below me, the glow of lights lining the street that led toward Buckingham Fountain. Behind the park, Lake Michigan loomed like the stormy backdrop of a painting. Normally, I loved this view, but now I saw nothing but my own reflection in the glass, going in and out of focus.

Dylan Moran.

I stared at that face and saw a stranger reflected back from the window. I couldn't see inside the person who was staring at me. It was as if I had broken into pieces and left part of myself with that other man on the bank of the river. And yet, for all that, the reflection was still me. My face.

My black hair is bushy and a little unkempt. My dark eyebrows are thick, arching like the hunched shoulders of a gargoyle. My face is full of sharp angles, a tight jawline, pointed chin, hard cheekbones, fierce little nose. Karly would joke that she had to be careful when she caressed my face because she might cut her fingers. I wear heavy stubble on my lip and chin, mostly because I can never seem to shave it completely away, so I stopped trying. It's like a shadow that goes with me everywhere.

I'm not tall. My driver's license says I'm five ten, but my doctor knows I'm barely five nine. I stay in good shape, running, boxing, lifting weights, doing all the things that a short, skinny kid does to make himself look tougher. I want everyone to know you don't mess with Dylan Moran, and you can see that in my eyes. They are ocean-blue eyes, intense and angry. I've spent too much of my life angry about something. It never seemed to matter what it was.

It was funny. Not long after we got married, Karly was digging around in Edgar's apartment, helping him straighten things up, and she found a photograph of me when I was about twelve years old. This was before everything happened with my parents. Before the high school years when Edgar and I argued over grades and girls and smoking and drugs. I didn't look all that different back then, not physically. I still had the same messy haircut, and I was already about as tall as I was ever going to be. But Karly looked at that photograph and then over at me, and I could see what she was thinking.

What happened to you, Dylan?

Back then, I had a big smile and a wide-eyed innocence. I'd been a happy kid, but that young kid was long gone. He'd died in the bedroom with my parents. Staring at my reflection in the hotel window, with the park and the lake hovering behind my face, I said the same thing out loud.

"What happened to you, Dylan?"

Then I put a half-full bottle of vodka to my lips, drank what was left, shouted a profanity at the city about a dozen times, and threw the glass bottle against the wall. It broke into razor-like pieces that sprayed across the bedsheets. I sighed with disappointment at myself. It always happened like this, again and again. I went and gathered up the shards, and then I sat down by the side of the bed and squeezed the glass fragments in my fists until blood oozed through my fingers.

For the rest of the night, I stayed right there, until the blood dried and I finally fell asleep.

The first wave of grief can't go on forever. You may feel dead, but eventually you realize you're still alive, and you have to figure out how to go on.

On the morning of the fourth day, I picked out a suit from the closet in my hotel room. My assistant manager, Tai, had arranged for some of my work clothes to be sent here from my apartment. She was efficient that way. I took a shower, put on the suit, knotted a tie tightly against my neck, and left the room. I wasn't really ready to go back out into the world, but I didn't have a choice.

I took the elevator to the lobby. The LaSalle Plaza was one of downtown's grand old hotels, dating all the way back to the White City days of the Chicago World's Fair. You could feel turn-of-the-century ghosts here, passing you with a brush of silk. The lobby glistened with marble floors, a chambered ceiling, and elaborately decorated archways of glass, brass, and stone.

I'd worked at the LaSalle Plaza since I was a college student at Roosevelt University. I started as a bellman and worked my way up. The previous events manager, a man named Bob French, hired me as his assistant, and he stuck with me even when my behavior outside the office got me into trouble. Six years ago, Bob left to run the events program at the Fairmont in San Francisco. He invited me to go with him, but I couldn't imagine a life outside Chicago. Bob did me the favor of telling the hotel managers that they shouldn't hire anyone but me to fill his shoes, which was a big leap of faith given my age at the time and my tendency to leave the hotel and head straight to the Berghoff for drinks rather than going home. Ever since, I'd tried to prove they made the right call, which often meant fourteen-hour days and long weekend nights. Karly told me more than once that my work was my life. She didn't say it as a compliment.

My first stop wasn't in my office but in the hotel ballroom. Karly and I were married here; it was the hot ticket for Chicago weddings. The two-story space was a kind of miniature Versailles, all done up in gold leaf, with chandelier sconces on the walls and cherubs flying above the rounded doorways and murals painted on the ceiling. I hovered in the back, watching the maintenance team set up chairs and a riser for an evening event. Normally, I could rattle off every ballroom event for weeks at a time, but the accident had erased certain details from my memory. I saw a large marketing poster on an easel near the door, and I walked across the stone floor to remind myself who had booked my ballroom for the night.

The poster showed a photograph of an attractive woman in her forties. She had long brown hair that glinted with blond highlights and was swept over her head like a cresting ocean wave. She was white, but the faint almond shape of her eyes suggested Asian blood somewhere in her past. Her eyes were golden brown, staring intently at the camera, with lips creased into a dreamy smile that offered only a hint of teeth. She wore a black long-sleeve knit top, and she leaned forward with her arm on a desk. Her fingers were bent as if in midcaress. The whole effect of the picture was intimate and erotic, as if she were beckoning you to come closer.

Above the photo was her name and the title of her talk:

DR. EVE BRIER
AUTHOR—PSYCHIATRIST—PHILOSOPHER
"MANY WORLDS, MANY MINDS"

I tried to remember who she was, but I came up empty. We hosted conferences and speakers here all the time, but I had no recollection of

16

booking space for Eve Brier. Based on the photograph, I didn't think I would have forgotten her. And yet there was something familiar about her, too. Her face stirred . . . what? What was it? It wasn't really a memory, but I felt as if we'd met somewhere.

"Hello, Dylan."

The voice came from behind me. I turned around and saw my assistant manager, Tai Ragasa. Her face was exquisitely sad. She came and put her arms around my neck and held me tightly. Her closeness made me uncomfortable, but I opted not to push her away. She hugged me for several beats longer than was appropriate, and then we broke apart. Tai wiped away a tear and reached out and took hold of both of my hands. I could feel the sharpness of her long fingernails.

"I don't know what to say," she told me.

"I know."

"It's so horrible."

"Yeah."

"Are you sure you should be here?"

"No, but I was going crazy on my own."

"Of course."

Tai led me to a row of chairs at the back of the ballroom. We sat down next to each other. The maintenance men worked around us, calling out to each other in voices that echoed in the high space, their cleaning equipment banging on the furniture. I tried to pull my hand away, but Tai wouldn't let go.

"What can I do?" she asked.

"Nothing."

"Everyone in the hotel has your back. I mean, if you need anything, we'll all be right there to help you."

"I know."

"You really don't need to be here. I'm serious. I've got everything under control. We can manage."

"I appreciate that."

"Just focus on yourself," she said.

"Thanks."

She kissed me softly on the cheek. Her clean, floral smell enveloped me. When she backed away, her ebony eyes held on to mine, and a few strands of her black hair clung to the buttons of my shirt.

"If you ever need to talk, I'm here," she murmured. "I'm sure you're not ready yet, but any time you want to—"

"I'm not. I'm definitely not ready."

"Okay."

The speaker on her radio buzzed. I heard one of my staff reaching out to her with a catering question. In our jobs, we had to be in constant contact with vendors inside and outside the hotel. Successful events were about a million details, laid out in order, one by one. Tai gave me a look of apology as she answered the call, but I was glad to have some space.

I'd hired Tai six years ago, right after I got promoted myself. Like me, she went to Roosevelt and was enrolled in their hospitality master's program. As a boss, I chose people based on my gut, and my gut said she was smart and would be running the whole hotel someday. She was twenty-eight now, with a conservative Catholic family back in the Philippines. Tai had a deeply religious streak herself, but it was tough to stay conservative in a metropolis like Chicago. In the past few years, she'd discovered tequila and hip-hop music and tight dresses that emphasized her bony curves.

She was a wisp of a thing, a five-foot-nothing dynamo in high heels. Her black hair was very long and straight and parted in the middle. Her dark eyes twinkled below wicked eyebrows, and her lips were always bright red. Her cheeks dimpled when she smiled, which was often.

If I were posting about our relationship on Facebook, I would say it was complicated. I liked mentoring her. I liked that she flattered me by telling me how good I was at my job. I liked the snarky little jokes she whispered about couples getting married in the ballroom. To me, she was a younger sister, and as an older brother, I tended to confide my secrets to her. Most recently, I'd told her about Karly's one-night affair, and like any good sister, Tai was quick to assure me that I was right and Karly was wrong.

All of this seemed safe to me because I had no romantic interest in her. Karly didn't see it that way. From the moment they met, she didn't like Tai at all. Karly had a habit of making up words to suit what she wanted to say, and she invented one for Tai. *Manipulatrix.* In Karly's dictionary, that was a dominant, controlling woman who got what she wanted by pretending to be submissive. To Karly, who was strong in her own right, that was the worst kind of sin.

"So what can I do for you, Dylan?" Tai asked when she put away her radio. She took my chin with her long fingers and turned my face so I was looking at her. "I want to help with anything you need."

"I don't even know yet," I replied, which was true. "Just hold down the fort here, okay?"

"Absolutely."

"I thought I could go back to work, but I don't think I can. Not yet."

"No one would expect you to be ready so soon," Tai said.

I checked the time on my watch. "I need to go. I've got to meet Edgar at the Art Institute in an hour. It drives him crazy if I'm late."

"Does Edgar know? I mean, about Karly?"

"I called to tell him, but I don't know whether he really understood what I was saying. Plus, his short-term memory is shot."

"Sure."

I stood up from the chair. So did Tai, and she wrapped me up in another embrace that went on too long.

"Are you staying in the hotel again tonight?" she asked.

"Probably. I can't go back to the apartment yet."

"I'll call you before I head home."

"You don't need to do that."

"I just want to make sure you're okay."

She squeezed my shoulder, and I gave her an empty smile of thanks. I turned away, but then, as an afterthought, I remembered what I wanted to know.

"By the way, who's Eve Brier?"

"What?"

I gestured at the poster near the ballroom door. "She's the speaker at the event tonight."

"Don't you know her?"

"No."

"Well, that's strange," Tai replied.

"Why?"

"She told me she picked the hotel on your recommendation."

"On *my* recommendation? She said she knew me?"

"Definitely."

I took another look at the photograph of Dr. Eve Brier and felt the same sensation that her eyes were sending me an invitation. *Come closer. Get to know me.* Yes, she looked familiar, but I had no recollection of meeting her.

"Maybe I ran into her somewhere and gave her my sales pitch," I speculated, although I didn't think that was true. "Who is she?"

"She's some kind of new age self-help guru," Tai explained. "She left me a copy of her book, but I haven't looked at it. Whoever she is, she's very popular. We're planning on a big crowd for her talk."

"'Many Worlds, Many Minds,'" I said. "What does that mean?"

"Apparently, she applies a theory from quantum mechanics in physics to her psychotherapy practice. It's about how we're all part of an infinite number of parallel worlds. Every time we make a choice, a carbon copy of ourselves makes the opposite choice in a different universe."

"Parallel worlds?" I said skeptically.

I couldn't wrap my brain around the concept. Maybe that's because I was focused on the other two words she'd used.

Carbon copy. Like a double. A twin. A man in a storm.

"That's what she says," Tai replied. "When Eve was signing the contract for the ballroom space, she told me that an entirely separate universe had already been created in which she *didn't* sign it."

"What did you say to that?"

Tai winked. "I said to make sure that she lived in the universe where she paid the bill."

CHAPTER 3

On my way to meet Edgar at the Art Institute, I stopped in the museum's south garden, near the Fountain of the Great Lakes, where the water flowed from clamshells over the bodies of five beautiful bronze women.

This place was flush with memories for me.

I'd sat with Karly here once on a spring afternoon, holding hands among the honey locust trees and listening to the bubble of water. We were still in our early days then, when we knew we were in love but before we'd shared all our stories. Karly wore a long-sleeve green sweater and a plaid skirt that made her look, to me, like some kind of Irish rebel. A woman for all seasons. Her skin was ivory pale, with a few freckles. Her eyes had a way of changing color with the light, and that day, in the cool April shadows, they were a sad country-song kind of blue. A single brass stud adorned the top of her left ear. Her blond hair, jaggedly chopped off at the shoulders as if she'd done it herself to show the world she could, smelled like a fresh sprig of rosemary.

I remembered that particular day well, because that was when I'd told her what my father had done to my mother. She knew what had happened, of course, but not the details, not what I'd actually seen from the corner of the bedroom. Other than Roscoe, I'd kept that secret to myself. I'd told Karly I had something important that I needed to share with her, and although I didn't say what, I was sure she'd already guessed. That moment from my childhood was a gaping hole in what she knew about me. Even so, as we sat together by the fountain, I found myself struggling to talk. Somehow, I couldn't switch on the clickety-clack of my mental projector and go back to when I was thirteen years old, my eyes wide, smelling the smoke and seeing the blood on the floor. There are simply places in your past you don't want to visit again.

Karly gave me space. She didn't push me, hoping I'd tell her without prompting. When that didn't work, she told me one of her own stories to get me started. Most of Karly's stories had to do with her mother.

"Did I tell you that Susannah's first business failed?" she said. She always called her mother Susannah, not Mother or Mom. "Before she started Chance Properties, she went bankrupt. Not many people know that."

"Oh, yes?"

I didn't know why Karly had chosen that story for that moment, but she always had her reasons.

"Yeah, this was years ago. She and her best friend split from one of the big commercial houses and went off on their own. Small time, just the two of them, but you know Susannah, she had big plans. They were pretty overextended. Her partner—Bren was her name. I liked her a lot. We had a little apartment on Devon back then, and Bren would always bring me takeout from Superdawg when she came over to meet with Susannah."

"How old were you?" I asked.

"Eleven, twelve, something like that. Like I said, I really liked Bren. The two of them were the same age, and their relationship went back for years, but Susannah was definitely the boss. I guess Bren just kept trying to please her, but even as a kid, I already knew that was a no-win game. Anyway, the business was only a year old when Bren screwed up. I mean, it was a big screw-up, but Susannah signed off on it, too, so it's not like it was all Bren's fault. They closed on a series of commercial properties south of Milwaukee, because Bren had inside information about a big corporate headquarters relocating out of Chicago. This came right from the CEO. It was solid. But as it turned out, the tip was just a ploy to get the city to shell out more tax breaks. Susannah and Bren wound up holding the bag. They'd been played. They lost everything."

Karly stopped. She studied the women in the sculpture pouring water, which was meant to symbolize the flow of the water from Great Lake to Great Lake. A cardinal landed on the very top of one of the women's heads and trilled about what an amazing spring day it was.

"Bren came over that day, and Susannah laid into her," Karly finally went on. "Blamed the whole debacle on her. She said they were ruined, that Bren was a failure, that she should never have trusted her to do anything right. It was one of Susannah's most impressive performances. And Bren just sat there and took it. I mean, she walked into our apartment knowing what she was going to get, but she came over anyway. She even remembered Superdawg for me, too."

I watched Karly steel herself. I didn't understand the emotion I saw in her face, but I knew there was a twist to this story. Bren was important to her, and that was why she'd picked this moment to tell me about her. While I was struggling with my own past.

"Karly?" I asked softly. "What happened?"

"That night, Bren killed herself. She cut her wrists in the bathtub."

A little strangled gasp of air escaped my throat. "I'm so sorry."

"She actually left a note *apologizing* to Susannah. Can you believe that?"

"I'm so sorry," I said again.

"I love my mother, Dylan, but you have to understand that there are times when I hate her, too. She can be so thoughtlessly cruel. To be honest, I'm always afraid that I'll turn out like her. That she's in my genes and I can't escape my destiny."

"I understand."

Because I did. I knew exactly how she felt. I'd spent my life afraid of turning into my father.

Karly wiped her eyes and waited. I knew what she was waiting for. She'd done her part to help me pry open a locked door. To give me a safe space. If she could share her pain, her fears of who she was, then I could share mine.

In the long silence that followed, I gathered my strength. I said, barely louder than a whisper, "My mother was packing a bag."

Karly didn't need an explanation, didn't need me to tell her what this was about. She reached out and took my hand, and her eyes held on to me with the fiercest, deepest of stares. My breathing got ragged; my heartbeat got faster. I could still see it all in my head, because it was always there. My father, drunk out of his mind, his face beet red, wearing an old leather biker jacket he'd had for years. Me, watching the two of them, my knees up to my chest as I sat in the corner. I could see it. I just needed to drag out the words so Karly could see it, too.

"My mother was packing a bag," I said again. "She was in a hurry. She was getting us out of there, and she wanted to be gone. We were going to live with one of her friends on the force for a while. That's what she told me. A cop friend, a man. I had no idea she was having an affair with him. My father knew, though. He knew."

I remembered the things my father had said about her, the names he'd screamed in her face, but I couldn't repeat them. Not to anyone. They were too vile.

"Her gun was on top of the dresser," I went on. "I don't know why she left it there. I guess she was rushing, and she didn't think. My father was shouting at her, and she just kept putting clothes in the suitcase as he got madder and madder. Until he grabbed the gun. I saw him do it, like it was slow motion, you know? He hesitated with the gun in his hand, but not for long, maybe a few seconds. Then he cocked it and fired. The blood flew, all over their bed and the wall. Mom collapsed, dead, just like that. My father looked at her body in a kind of shock, like even he couldn't believe what he'd done. And then he looked at me."

I felt Karly squeezing my hand, as if I were dangling from a bridge and she was the only thing to keep me from falling.

"He saw me in the corner. I knew what he was thinking. I read his eyes. Me next. Kill me, too. I saw him raising the gun and aiming it right at me, but I was frozen. I couldn't move. Something must have shifted inside him, watching me. He kept bending his elbow up until the gun was under his chin. Then he gave a little whimper. I remember that so clearly, this whimper, like a dog when his master dies. And then he fired."

Karly was bawling. Not making a sound, but crying so hard she could barely breathe. Not me. Back then, I was cried out.

"I should have been able to stop it," I said.

She threw her arms around my neck and told me what people had been telling me for years. "You were a kid. You were just a boy. What could you have done?"

Yes, what could I have done?

I'd asked myself that question every day since I was thirteen. I'd never been able to find an answer, but it wouldn't have mattered if I had. No matter how much you wish or pray, there are no second chances. All you can do is make peace with your mistakes. Unfortunately, there's no manual to tell you how to do that.

Now, years later, I felt as if I were living in a kind of infinite loop. They'd all died because of me. My mother. Roscoe. And Karly.

Every time. Every single time it was the same.

I should have been able to stop it.

Edgar and I met every Thursday at lunch in front of Edward Hopper's classic *Nighthawks*. My grandfather and I didn't agree on much, but we agreed that this was our favorite painting in the Art Institute.

For years, when I stared at Hopper's three customers in the late-night diner, I would see myself as the lonely man with his back to the artist, the one whose face you couldn't see. That was me, alone in Chicago. Then, after I met Karly, I began to see myself as the other man, seated next to the redhead in the slinky red dress. I liked being that man. I liked his cigarette and his hat and his suit, and most of all, I liked the woman with him.

As I stood there, I heard the thunk of my grandfather's cane on the wooden floor of the gallery. Edgar came up beside me, his right foot dragging as it had since his ministroke seven years ago. He wore a Cubs cap backward on his head, along with a V-neck Hanes white T-shirt that exposed his curly gray chest hair, baggy tan shorts, and black, well-shined dress shoes with black socks. Yes, Edgar had his own sense of style, and he didn't care what anyone else thought about him. He didn't acknowledge me. Instead, he exhaled with a sigh of satisfaction as he stared at Hopper's painting.

At ninety-four, the fact that my grandfather was still alive was sort of a miracle. He'd been a heavy smoker his whole life, existing mostly on a diet of Chicago dogs and Budweiser. We used to be the same height, but he'd shrunk over the years and was now three inches shorter than me. He didn't leave the apartment much anymore, and Karly and I had hired a nurse to stay with him several days a week, which he hated. But every Thursday, regardless of rain, wind, cold, or snow, Edgar still hopped a bus and headed downtown to meet me at the Art Institute. I was never sure if he was really here to see me or *Nighthawks*.

"Did I ever tell you that I'm the reason this painting is here in the museum?" Edgar asked.

This was our routine. He asked me the same question every week and told me the same story. I didn't know if he'd forgotten that I'd heard it a thousand times, or if he didn't care.

"I was six years old," Edgar continued, listening to himself talk as he adjusted the volume on his hearing aid. His voice carried to the entire gallery. "My parents had taken me to Chicago to see the Christmas windows at Marshall Field's. We were at the corner of State and Randolph, and I saw this man with a huge white beard near the store. I was absolutely sure it was Santa Claus. I took off running, and I collided with a man who was just about to cross the street. Knocked him completely off his feet! Well, don't you know, at that moment, a grain truck went screaming through the intersection. If I hadn't knocked that man down, he would have been killed for sure. And do you know who that man was?"

I smiled. "Who was he, Edgar?"

"His name was Daniel Catton Rich. He was the director of the Art Institute. That was Christmas of 1941, and the very next year, Rich acquired *Nighthawks* directly from Edward Hopper. It's been here ever since. If it weren't for me, who knows where that painting would be?"

Edgar shuffled on his feet, looking pleased with himself, as he always did.

I let him study the picture awhile longer, because I was hesitant to raise the subject of Karly. I didn't know how he would react. When the crowd around us had thinned, I finally said in a low voice, "Edgar, do you remember my call? Do you remember what I told you?"

My grandfather took off his Cubs hat and scratched his scraggly gray hair. "About what?"

"About Karly. About what happened."

I didn't see any recollection in his eyes. Facts had a way of coming and going in Edgar's mind without hanging around for very long. He put his hat back on and stared at the painting again. His brow wrinkled in frustration, as if he knew I'd told him *something* important and he should remember what it was.

"She died," I reminded him, my heart breaking as I said it.

He thought about this for a long time without replying. After a while, I wondered if he'd even heard me. Then he pursed his lips to tell me what he thought.

"You're better off without women," he announced, with a dismissive sharpness in his tone. "Nothing but backstabbers. My wife left me for another man when I was fifty. Never saw her again. Good riddance."

"Edgar," I sighed, not wanting to hear another diatribe. Not today.

"She said she didn't know who the hell I was anymore! What does that mean? I was the one putting food on the table, that's who I was. Someday you're going to realize you're lucky, Dylan."

I squeezed my eyes shut. My fists clenched as I struggled to control myself.

I'd like to tell you that this was Edgar's age talking, but in fact, he'd been this way most of his life. He was a cantankerous son of a bitch and the king of mean jokes. Pick any "ist" you like, and that was Edgar. Narcissist. Racist. Misogynist. I never met my grandmother, but I was sure he didn't treat her well, and that's what led to her packing up and leaving for California without even a note.

All that anger Edgar felt covered up a lot of pain. And guilt, too. People were always blaming him for what my father did, and on some level, I'm sure Edgar blamed himself, too. When your son murders his wife, you can't help but ask yourself what you did wrong. Plus, with my parents both dead, Edgar was stuck raising a teenager on his own. He was already in his seventies when I moved into his apartment. I didn't make it easy on him, that's for sure. I was hurt and angry, and I hated the world and him, too. I made sure he knew it.

We made a hell of a family tree. Edgar. My father. Me. But I wasn't going to stand there and let him tell me I was lucky because Karly was dead.

"I'm going to walk around a little," I said in a clipped tone, swallowing down my desire to shout at him. I just needed to get away, or I'd say something I'd regret.

"Yeah, whatever. We'll get a hot dog later, right?"

"Right."

"Is Karly coming?" Edgar asked. "She's a keeper, that one."

This time it really was Edgar's age. He'd already forgotten.

"No," I replied, not wanting to say it again. "No, Karly can't make it today."

"Too bad. You don't deserve a girl like her, you know."

"Yes, I know."

I left my grandfather in front of *Nighthawks*. He didn't need me to stay with him. He'd be there for hours some days, staring at the painting and telling everyone who came up beside him the story of Daniel Catton Rich.

I had nowhere in particular that I wanted to go. I just needed to breathe, but that was hard to do in here. It was a crowded day inside the museum, with tourists crushed in front of the standards like *American Gothic* and *Water Lilies*. I wandered from wing to wing, barely stopping, my chest heavy. When I went into the men's room to wash my face, I turned on the faucet at one of the sinks and realized that just the sound of water was enough to make me hyperventilate. Even the barest trickle crashed through my head. I had to turn it off and grab the counter for balance, and my reflection stared back at me, still as opaque as a total stranger. I staggered back out of the restroom in a sweat.

Faces stared at me wherever I went. That was how I felt. I imagined eyes on me everywhere. The people, pushing around me, blocking my way, all looked at me as if they were murmuring under their breath, *"He's the one. His wife died."* Even the paintings haunted me. Warhol's Elizabeth Taylor flirted with me from behind her red lips and blue eye shadow. The younger of Renoir's two sisters studied me curiously from under her flowered hat. They were so close, so vivid, so bright that I expected them to come to life.

I know what you're thinking. I was in the midst of a panic attack. That's the explanation for what happened next. My grief, my anger over Edgar, my hyperventilation, my face in the mirror—it all came together, and I began seeing things that weren't there. Maybe you're right, but that's not how it felt.

It felt real.

As real as it had been when I was drowning in the river.

I was in the room with Seurat's enormous pointillist masterpiece *A Sunday Afternoon on the Island of La Grande Jatte*, ten feet wide, nearly seven feet tall. I'd seen that work a thousand times, probably more. I could tell you the details from memory: the long pipe of the man in the muscle shirt, the monkey with the perfectly curved tail, the parasols all in different colors. It was one of the museum's most famous works, and I couldn't get anywhere close to it because of the crowd, so I stood at the back of the gallery, eyeing the painting over the heads of thirty or more people clustered in front of it. They made a kind of *Grande Jatte* themselves, different ages, races, heights, sizes, clothes, all frozen in wonder by the art.

Then my gaze drifted to one man with his back to me. What drew my attention was his jacket.

It was a leather motorcycle jacket, weathered and black, with parallel seams down the backs of the sleeves. The jacket was just like the one my father had been wearing that night when I was thirteen. That night when my life became Before and After. For years, I'd kept that jacket in a closet, unable to touch it but also unable to throw it away. After Karly moved in, she finally convinced me that the day had come to get rid of it. I burned it. It became ash. It no longer existed.

So it was a shock to see the man in front of the painting wearing a jacket of the exact same style.

Except, more than that, I realized that this was *my father's jacket.*

When I looked closely, I could see the chocolate-brown bloodstains. They were soaked into the leather, a permanent reminder of the night that changed my life. Believe me, I'd memorized the pattern of the blood spray long ago, like the paintings I saw in the museum. I would never forget it.

The man in the coat glanced back, revealing his face. When he did, my knees buckled beneath me. I couldn't stand; I had to grab for the wall to hold myself up. Our eyes met as dozens of people came and went between us. He looked at me; I looked at him. He reacted. He *recognized* me. I watched his steely blue-eyed gaze grab on to me like a predator spotting prey.

The encounter lasted only a second, and then he turned casually away and disappeared into the next gallery.

But I'd seen him. I'd seen *myself.*

My profile. My face. Just like at the river. That was Dylan Moran studying *La Grande Jatte* and wearing my father's murder coat. The shock of it left me paralyzed, but *he* didn't look surprised to see me at all. It was as if he'd been waiting for that moment, waiting for me to find him.

I shook myself out of my coma and pushed off the wall. I headed across the exhibit floor, weaving through people in my way, who didn't understand the impatience of the crazed man pushing past them. My doppelgänger had disappeared, but I rushed after him into the next hall, where I stopped to pick him out in the crowd.

Where was he?

Where was I?

But the man I'd seen wasn't in the room. He'd already vanished.

I continued to the next gallery, and then the next, and finally I ran down the stairs to the first floor of the museum and all the way out to the busy traffic on Michigan Avenue. I collapsed on the steps near one of the green lions facing the street. It was a summer afternoon, warm and perfect. People surrounded me everywhere, but there was no Dylan, no man in a biker jacket, no identical twin taunting me.

I sat on the museum steps and breathed in and out like a piston. I thought about Edgar, his memory failing, his mind drifting around in time, unable to distinguish what was real and what wasn't.

Maybe the same thing was happening to me.

Maybe this was what it felt like to go insane.

CHAPTER 4

"Your blood pressure is elevated," Dr. Tate told me. "So's your heart rate. But that's not surprising. All of your other vitals are normal. As far as the scans go, I don't see any physical abnormalities in your brain that would explain what you're seeing. No tumors, no aneurysm. So that's a good thing."

"I'm just crazy," I said.

The doctor gave me an affectionate smile. "I wouldn't go that far, Dylan."

She got up from the rolling chair and went to the sink in the examining room to wash her hands. When I heard the water, I twitched a little. I'd come to her clinic on Irving Park just east of the river without an appointment, but I knew that Alicia Tate would always fit me in. She'd known me since I met her son Roscoe in sixth grade. After my own mother was killed, she became a kind of surrogate mother to me. As with Edgar, I didn't make it easy. I could appreciate everything she'd done for me now better than I did as a hostile teenager. I also appreciated that after Roscoe died in the accident, she didn't blame me for his death.

That made one of us, because I definitely blamed myself.

I picked up the picture of Roscoe that sat on her desk. Four years later, I could still hear his voice in my head, and I missed him more than ever. The photograph didn't show him smiling. Roscoe rarely smiled;

he was serious, both as a boy and as a man. That didn't serve him well in school, where the other kids picked on him because he was bookish, small, and black. I wasn't much bigger myself, but Edgar had taught me to be a dirty fighter, and I beat up the largest of the bullies who taunted Roscoe. They didn't bother him after that, and Roscoe and I became best friends. That fight was also the last time I ever felt like he needed any help from me. Instead, Roscoe was the one who became my rock through my many ups and downs.

The photograph showed him in his priest's frock and collar. Roscoe was a straight-A genius who could have been a doctor like his mother, but he'd chosen to serve God in a South Side Catholic parish instead, where he railed against guns and gangs with every breath. I wore a tough shell around me, but my best friend—five foot four, skinny, and mostly bald, in his Goodwill sweaters and old-fashioned glasses with Coke-bottle lenses—had been a far tougher man than I'd ever be.

Alicia sat down in front of me again. She noticed the photograph in my hand. "I still talk to him, you know. It makes me feel better to do that. You can, too."

I put the photo back on her desk. "These days, I'd be concerned that he might start talking back."

"I really don't think you're crazy, Dylan."

"Then what's the explanation? I'm obviously having hallucinations, but they don't feel like hallucinations. I've seen *myself*. Twice. Looking as flesh-and-blood real as you are right now. This other Dylan *interacted* with me. He saw me, gave me this strange stare, as if he wasn't surprised to see me. How is that possible?"

Alicia took my hand. Her skin had an antiseptic smell. "The first time this happened was at the river, right? When you were in the midst of a horrific, stressful event that no human being should ever experience? Nearly drowning and losing the love of your life?"

I nodded.

"The second time was at the museum today? And 'you' were wearing a leather jacket that doesn't exist anymore—the jacket your father was wearing when he murdered your mother? In other words, *another* horrific, stressful event in your life that no human being should ever experience?"

I nodded again.

Alicia looked at me as if I were a child. "Do I really need to explain this to you, Dylan?"

"Okay, it's a mental breakdown. I get it. Of course I do. Grief, loss, stress, shock. My mind is misfiring."

"Exactly."

"But why a manifestation like this? Why am I seeing other versions of myself?"

"That I can't tell you. The brain reacts to trauma in unusual ways."

I thought about the poster of Dr. Eve Brier in the ballroom at the hotel. She was a stranger to me, but I could still picture her face in my memory with unusual clarity. "Well, there's a speaker at the LaSalle Plaza tonight who believes that we're living in the midst of infinite parallel universes. So I guess there must be a lot of other Dylan Morans out there. Maybe they're paying me a visit."

"Are you talking about the Many Worlds theory?" Alicia asked.

I chuckled in surprise. "You've heard of it?"

"Of course. Most scientists have."

"Is it legit?"

Alicia shrugged. "Many physicists believe it is."

"Parallel universes? How the hell does that work?"

"Well, this isn't my field, but as I understand it, the math of quantum mechanics creates a strange paradox. According to the math, particles have the ability to exist in two different states at the same time. However, whenever we look, we only see one state. That's the problem."

"Let me guess," I said. "This is about Schrödinger's cat."

"I'm impressed, Dylan," she replied with a smile.

"Hey, I watched *The Big Bang Theory*."

"And you're correct. Erwin Schrödinger used the story of the cat to explain the paradox. There's a cat in a box with a vial of poison that may or may not be released depending on whether a single atom decays. Until an observer opens the box to check, quantum theory suggests that the cat is simultaneously alive *and* dead. Except we all know that's absurd. Well, a Princeton scientist named Hugh Everett came up with an answer: when the box is opened, the universes split. One observer sees a cat that is alive, and in a parallel universe, another identical observer sees a cat that is dead. That's the Many Worlds theory."

"That sounds insane," I said.

"Not according to the math of quantum mechanics. And the math is pretty solid. That's why we have things like the atomic bomb."

I shook my head. "Well, I'm not a cat in a box, so what do I do? I've lost everything, and now I can't even trust my own mind."

"Try not to obsess about it," Alicia suggested. "I can't really explain why this is happening to you, but I suspect the hallucinations will go away as you deal with your grief."

I wanted to believe her, but I kept seeing my doppelgänger in the museum. His face. *My* face. The way he looked at me. "You know what really scared me about that other Dylan?"

"What?"

"It was what I saw in his eyes. I felt this cloud of menace from him. He was capable of anything. And he was *me*."

"Dylan, he's not you. He's not real."

"Is that the way I look to other people? Dangerous?"

"No. Not at all."

"The sheriff called me a violent man," I pointed out.

"Well, you're not."

I picked up the photograph of her son from her desk again. "Are you sure about that? Be honest with me, Alicia. We both know I'm the reason that Roscoe's dead."

I'd finally sobered up.

With my bail paid, it was four in the morning, and Roscoe was driving me to his mother's clinic, where Alicia was waiting to take x-rays and give me something for the pain. I was sure Roscoe had been asleep when I called. I knew he'd already had a long day, because there had been another shooting near his parish. There was always another shooting in Chicago. But he told me not to worry; he would be there for me. And he was.

I hadn't said much on the drive. Roscoe didn't push me to talk, not at first. We cruised through the green lights on Montrose, and fall leaves blew in the air and slapped across the windshield. The car was warm and quiet on a cool October night. Roscoe wore his white priest's collar, which fit loosely on his skinny neck. He always wore the collar when he talked to the police. He said they didn't like to argue with a priest.

"Are you going to tell me what happened?" he asked finally, when it was obvious I wasn't going to open up. He eyed me from behind the wheel, his expression calm and serious, the way it always was. The city lights reflected in his glasses. Even at this late hour, he looked smoothly shaved, except for the neat beard around his mustache and chin.

"Come on, buddy," he went on. "Talk to me."

"I drank too much. I got in a fight."

"You've been sober for months. Why fall off the wagon now?"

"It's been crazy at work. I just wrapped up a week-long conference. I wasn't ready to go home, so I went to a bar in Mayfair."

"Is that all?"

It took me a long time to answer. "Okay, it's also the anniversary."

"There we go."

"If I went home, I'd think about it, and I didn't want to do that tonight."

Roscoe shook his head. "Why didn't you call me?"

"I needed to deal with this myself."

"No, you didn't. How many times have I told you that? Anyway, it doesn't matter. You were alone, and you'd been drinking. Then what happened?"

"There was this man at the bar," I said. "He was being a shit to his girlfriend. I told him to knock it off."

"I'm sure that went over well," Roscoe said.

"Yeah. He threw a drink in my face. The girl said I should mind my own business."

"So you hit him?"

"No. I said thanks, I needed a shower. That was that. The two of them left. I finished my drink and headed out of the bar like fifteen minutes later. But they were still on the street, screaming at each other. I tried to ignore it. I was waiting at the bus stop, and I wasn't going to do anything."

"But?"

"But he hit her, Roscoe. He just hauled off and slugged the woman in the face. I lost it. I went over there and threw him to the ground. I got down on my knees and began beating the hell out of him. The two of us went at it until the police got there."

Roscoe didn't say anything for a while.

He eased the car to a stop, because Montrose was closed ahead of us. Overnight construction was underway. Weird, when you add up all the things that make a difference. The little choices that change everything. If some bureaucrat had picked a different night for the construction, Roscoe would be alive. If we'd taken Irving Park east instead of Montrose, he'd still be alive.

More than anything, if I'd kept my cool outside that bar, my friend would still be alive.

Roscoe turned onto a leafy side street a couple of blocks from Horner Park. We drove past matchbox homes and old three-story apartment buildings. Cars were parked on both sides, blocking our view. He drove slowly and kept looking over at me, focused on me and my story. He should have been paying more attention, but it was the middle of the night on a deserted street.

"I'm him," I said.

"Who?"

"My father."

Roscoe sighed as he pulled up to a stop sign. The only thing that I remembered from that intersection was a house for sale at the corner. A gold stone apartment building with a sign mounted on the lawn.

CHANCE PROPERTIES

I remembered it because it made me think about chance. Chance ruled everything. Chance determined who lived and who died.

"I'm him," I said again. "My father lost control that night. That's what happens to me."

Roscoe took a loud breath. I had no way of knowing it was practically his last one. "Why?" he asked me.

"What?"

"Why did you attack that man? Why did you go after him?"

"Because he hit that girl."

"Exactly."

Roscoe eased his foot onto the accelerator and started across the intersection. He was distracted, and he forgot to look right. If he had, he would have seen the headlights of the truck coming down the one-way street and barreling through the stop sign. I was off in my own world and didn't see it either.

"Buddy, you're not your father," Roscoe told me.

That's the last thing I remembered until I woke up and saw Karly's face.

CHAPTER 5

This was where we'd met.

The ash tree on the corner still bore the scars of the accident. The truck hit us so hard that it drove Roscoe's car over the curb and wrapped it around the tree trunk. I ran my fingers over the jagged crevices in the bark, which were the only remaining evidence that something violent had occurred here.

I hadn't really intended to come back to this place, but Alicia's office wasn't far away. The day had turned dark, and rain began to spit on my face. I looked up at the old apartment building at the corner of the intersection. That was the building that had been for sale back then, with Karly as the listing agent. It was one of her first properties. She was twenty-five years old, determined to get a top price to impress her mother. She'd been working late out of a vacant apartment, and she'd fallen asleep, when the noise of the accident awakened her. That was when she rushed downstairs to find me in the car, broken and bleeding.

This beautiful stranger promised not to leave me, and she kept her promise.

Karly rode in the ambulance with me. She stayed in the hospital room with me and nursed me back to health in her own bed. For weeks, she held together the pieces of a shattered man who blamed himself for his friend's death. I fell in love with her almost immediately, but I couldn't understand why she'd fallen in love with me, too. The closer she got to me, the more I kept telling her to walk away.

I'd made too many mistakes in life, too many bad choices. In my heart of hearts, I didn't think I deserved to have those bad choices lead me to someone like her. Sooner or later, I expected her to see who I really was, and that would be the end of us. When she slept with Scotty Ryan, I felt as if she'd finally proved me right. I didn't want any explanations. That whole weekend in the country, I refused to listen.

Until the last night. Until her last words.

As we were heading home, with our bags in the car and the rain pouring down and our marriage in ruins, she stopped me at the door and said with resignation in her voice: "May I say something?"

I didn't answer. I simply waited.

"Dylan, you never asked me what I saw in you after the accident, but if we're really done, I want you to know the truth. From the moment I met you, I realized that we were exactly alike—no, wait, let me finish. I know you don't believe that, because you have this strange, twisted vision of yourself. But we're the same. We both grew up in cages we built for ourselves. And when I met you, I thought, here was a man who could help me become the person I wanted to be, and I could do the same for him. I still think that's true. The thing is, I'm ready, Dylan. I can't wait anymore. I'm not happy with my life, not because of you, but because I need to be someone different. I'll do it without you if I have to, but I'd rather do it with you. And deep down, I think you want that, too. My question is, are you willing to try?"

That was a good question.

That was a very good question, and I knew what I wanted to say. I wanted to rise above the anger I carried—for the world, for her, but mostly for myself. Karly needed me to forgive her, and that was what I needed to do, too. Instead, I failed both of us. It was another of my mistakes, another bad choice. I should have kissed her right then, but all I did was walk past her and get in the car. That was how we drove out into the rain that night, with a bitter silence lingering between us.

You see, there are moments in your life you are desperate to take back as soon as they happen, but the clock ticks, and they're gone. You make your choice, and an instant later, nothing is the same.

By the time I was ready to tell her how I felt, we were already in the water.

I couldn't stay at the accident scene any longer. I walked down the side street toward the green fields of Horner Park, which I knew from my childhood. As I did, I learned that my life was still governed by Chance with a capital *C*, because in the next block, across from the park's basketball courts, I noticed a two-story house with a familiar red-and-black sign mounted in the yard. The house was for sale, and the listing agent was another woman at Chance Properties whom I'd met once or twice.

However, I didn't care about that.

Instead, I focused on the white pickup truck parked at the curb. The truck had a painted logo on the door for Ryan Construction.

Scotty Ryan.

He was inside the house.

I heard a roaring in my head, a thump-thump-thump as my heartbeat took off. I hadn't had a drink all day, so there was no excuse for making a foolish mistake. No good could come from seeing him.

It didn't matter. I couldn't stop myself. I walked down the sidewalk and stood in front of the white picket fence. The house was neatly put together, freshly painted, with flowers growing in the window boxes. The front door was open, and I could hear the whine of a power saw inside. My common sense sent me a very clear message to walk away, which my heart ignored. I let myself inside the fence and headed for the steps. I hesitated only briefly at the house's screen door before I ripped it open.

The interior had the sweet smell of cut wood. Plastic sheeting lined the living room floor. The noise of the saw deafened me, but then it cut off, leaving a stark silence. Scotty Ryan stood behind the saw, holding up a long length of oak trim to examine the cut. As he did, he saw me.

His whole body stiffened. When he recovered, he took off his noise-canceling headphones and his safety goggles and canvas gloves. He was dressed in jeans and work boots, with a loose Black Hawks jersey over his long torso. Sawdust made a film on his arms.

"Hello, Dylan," he said.

"Scotty."

We faced each other across the room. The standoff between us was like two tough dogs growling in an alley.

Scotty Ryan was forty years old, so nearly a decade older than me. He was half a foot taller, too, with a lanky, almost rubbery frame. He had wavy reddish-blond hair, and his face was sunburned pink from time spent in the sun. When he talked, he had an aw-shucks drawl in his voice, and his words always came out slowly, like honey from a jar. His casual good humor made him a difficult man to dislike, but believe me, I'd found a way.

"I'm really sorry," Scotty said, which covered a lot of ground. "You can't imagine how sorry I am."

"You should be."

My verbal blow rolled off him without causing any damage. He brushed his hand through his thick hair, and I could see the glow of sweat on his face. "I can't believe she's gone. I'm crushed. I'm sure you must be, too."

"Wow. You think?"

Scotty shrugged his wide shoulders. "Hey, it's hard to tell with you, Dylan. Karly always said you kept things locked up tight. You never showed her anything. That drove her crazy. No offense."

Because adding "no offense" made everything better, coming from the man who'd slept with my wife.

"I have a question, Scotty."

"Yeah? What's that?"

"How long were you in love with Karly? How long were you hiding that little secret?"

Scotty rubbed his jutting chin and took his time to answer, the way he always did. "Maybe we shouldn't do this now, Dylan."

"How. Long?"

"Oh, I don't know. Probably from the day I met her. I've known her a lot longer than you. I think she was only eighteen back then, but I never thought of her as young. She was so smart, confident, full of herself. I knew she was way out of my league, but yeah, I guess I had a crush on her from day one. Not that I ever intended to do anything about it."

"Or you were just biding your time. Waiting until she was vulnerable."

"That's not how it went down. I swear. That's not what happened."

"Then what did happen?"

I took a couple of steps toward him. The plastic sheeting crinkled under my feet. He watched me warily, like a fighter in the ring.

"Look, what else do you want to know? I'm sure Karly already filled you in. When she called me, she said she was going to tell you everything."

"You *talked* to her? Are you kidding me? When?"

"The day after," Scotty admitted. "She was upset, blaming herself, said she couldn't believe she'd made such a stupid mistake. She was going to tell you the truth, and she wanted me to know. For what it's worth, I told her to keep it to herself and not risk her marriage over this. Believe me, I knew she had no intention of leaving you for me. That's not what it was about. Whatever that night meant to me, it was just a drunken error in judgment to her. You should know what that's like. You've made enough of those yourself, am I right?"

I didn't take the bait.

"The details, Scotty. How did it happen?"

Scotty shook his head. "I don't know what to tell you, Dylan. Karly and I have been friends for a long time, and yeah, it's always been more than that for me. If she knew how I felt, she was classy enough not to let on and embarrass me. But the last few months, she started telling me things. Personal things. Confiding in me about her problems. She needed to talk to someone, because you weren't listening."

"And there you were, with a shoulder for her to cry on."

"You think Karly was the only one turning to someone else? She said you told your assistant Tai more than you ever told her."

I felt slapped. "There was nothing between me and Tai. There never was. Karly knew that."

"Did she?"

"Don't try to put any of this on me."

Scotty rolled his eyes and stared at the ceiling. "I'm not. Seriously, man, I'm not. I'm just telling you the way it was. You were running so fast in your life that you never saw that Karly wanted to slow things down. She was ready to quit, Dylan. To tell her mother that she wanted out of the real estate business. She was always more like her dad than her mom—you know that. A book type. A poet. Karly was ready to have kids. She wanted all of that more than anything, but she didn't think you'd ever go for it. It was eating her up inside."

"I never said anything like that to her."

"I don't care what you said. I'm telling you what she heard. That night? Her and me? She'd landed a buyer on that place in Schaumburg for Vernon Hotels, and the renovations were all done. I opened champagne for us, and yeah, we had too much. But if that's all it was, nothing would have happened. Except the more she drank, the more Karly started talking about wanting a different life and not knowing how to tell you. She didn't *blame* you for it, if that's what you're thinking. She was just upset, and she started crying. I hugged her. I wanted to comfort her, and one thing led to another. Neither one of us planned it, and Karly *hated* herself for letting it happen. You can believe this or not, but I'm sorry it happened, too."

I didn't need a drink now to be losing control.

"*You* killed her," I snapped. "It's your fault she's gone. We were out there in the middle of nowhere because of you."

Scotty's casual demeanor hardened into anger. Our nerves were both fraying. "Hey, you can blame me for the affair. I'll take that. But I'm not the reason she died. If you want someone to blame for that, look in the mirror."

"What the hell does that mean?"

"I mean, *what happened* in that river, Dylan? Explain it to me. Tell me the truth. Why are you here and she's not?"

"I tried to *save* her. That's what happened."

Scotty opened his mouth and then clamped it shut. His sunburned cheeks flushed even redder, like steam building up in his face.

"Do you have something to say?" I asked.

"No."

"Don't hold back, Scotty. Say it."

He pushed into my space, his scarlet face inches from mine. His voice became a snarl. "Fine. You want me to say it? I will. *You* should have died out there. If it was me in that car, I would never have come out of that river without her. Either we both lived, or we both died. But there's no way I would have let her die alone."

My left hand flew. I didn't even feel it happening. I never did when I lost control. My arm swung like a rocket left to right, and my fist collided with Scotty's mouth. The impact was like hitting a wall. Blood sprayed from his lips and nose, and I felt the shudder knifing through my forearm. I wondered if I'd broken my fingers. His head snapped sideways, and he staggered back, spitting out a tooth like a kernel of popcorn.

I tensed, waiting for him to charge me. He was big enough and strong enough to give me a beatdown if he wanted. A part of me hoped he would. I wanted to feel the pain of his fists until I was unconscious on the floor. I deserved punishment. I'd failed, and it felt as if I was doomed to relive that failure over and over. Whenever I closed my eyes, I was in the water, swimming through nothingness, searching for the car where Karly was trapped. I had to find her. I had to save her. I dove and swam and searched, but each fragile second dragged her farther away from me. Her voice stopped calling my name. Her cries vanished. All that was left was a terrible silence in my head, a silence of guilt and death. She was gone. My wife was gone.

I hit Scotty because I knew he was right.

I'd let Karly die alone.

When it was obvious that Scotty wasn't going to fight back, I left the house, nursing my bruised and bloody hand. I was consumed by a mix of adrenaline and despair. At the sidewalk, I met an elderly woman walking her Westie. She studied my face with suspicious eyes and noted the blood on my fingers.

"Is everything all right?" she asked me.

"Fine."

"I heard loud voices. An argument."

"Don't worry about it."

"Should I call the police?"

"Everything's fine, ma'am," I told her, continuing into the street.

"This is a nice neighborhood!" she called after me, with the reproach of a schoolteacher. "We don't like that kind of thing around here! People shouldn't fight!"

I didn't answer her. I crossed through the traffic to Horner Park and then into the wet, open grass of the park's baseball field. I used to come here as a kid. Roscoe and I would toss a football around and tackle each other in the mud. We'd talk about playing quarterback for the Bears, and believe me, they've had worse.

The drizzle had turned into showers, and the rain soaked me as I stood there. No one else was around. I winced, feeling the sharp burn in my hand. My fingers felt stiff as I tried to move them.

The sheriff called me a violent man.

You're not.

But my history said otherwise.

Ahead of me, I saw a lineup of trees where the park ended at the narrow ribbon of the Chicago River. A fence discouraged kids from hiking down the riverbank and falling into the water. Not that it worked. As teenagers, Roscoe and I had explored the banks on both sides of the river, playing spies, throwing rocks, hunting rats. Today, in the rain, I walked all the way up to the fence and took hold of it with both hands and closed my eyes. I leaned my forehead against the mesh.

Without Roscoe, without Karly, I didn't think I'd ever felt more alone. They'd gone on to other worlds, and I was still here. However, when I opened my eyes again, I realized that I wasn't alone anymore.

He was with me.

I can't tell you *how* I knew. I didn't hear footsteps on the trail. I didn't see anyone watching me. The trees were close in around me, and the gray sky made it seem like night. A stranger could have been six feet away, and I wouldn't have seen him. But someone was on the other side of the fence, hiding on the riverbank the way I used to do when I was a kid. Like he knew this was where I'd go. Like he'd been waiting for me to come here. I tried to be patient, to stand there like a statue in silence and see if he'd show himself.

He was back. *I* was back.

My doppelgänger.

I stared into the brush, watching for movement in the shadows. I could see the tree trunks like soldiers, and among them, I finally spotted a dark outline that looked out of place. A person. I hadn't been this close to him before. Only a few feet separated us. I also realized, as I had in the museum, that this wasn't just about me. He knew *I* was here, too. He was aware of me, just as I was aware of him. We were connected. And what I felt emanating from him was an aura of sheer sadistic rage. It was like I'd handed this shadow all my anger, all my bitterness, all my frustrations.

I looked around to be sure that no one else was nearby. Just him and me. My hallucination. My mental breakdown.

"I know you're there," I called to him in a low voice. Then I added for the hell of it: "Talk to me."

I waited for an answer, but I didn't expect to get one. Hallucinations didn't talk back. Even so, by speaking to him, I felt as if I'd taken a leap into a rabbit hole, and I had no idea where it would lead me.

"Who are you?" I asked.

I still got no reply. The silence around me was punctuated by the patter of rain on the leaves.

Then, like a statue coming to life, a voice spoke from the darkness. *My* voice, as if I were on the radio, when you can't believe that's how you sound to everyone else.

"I'm you."

I lurched back in disbelief. Did I really hear that? No, I couldn't have heard that. Alicia had told me: he's not real. This was my fevered imagination at work, all my memories playing tricks on me. My body twitched. I dug my fingertips into the top of my skull, as if I could squeeze out what my mind was telling me. My eyes blinked over and over. I rushed the fence and grabbed hold of it like a prisoner in a cell.

"What do you want?" I hissed.

Again the rain was the only sound for a long stretch of time. He dragged out my torture by saying nothing. I was starting to hope that I'd awaken and realize this had all been a nightmare. I'd be sane again. I'd be back in my bed, and Karly would be next to me, and all the preceding days would have been a dream. But as I stood there, soaking wet, chilled to the bone, the nightmare deepened.

It got blacker.

I shouted at him. "Why are you here? Tell me!"

This time, my shadow man answered. He whispered from the trees.

"To kill."

Chapter 6

I ran.

I ran without looking back at the river. I sprinted through the park's wet green fields, dodged through random side streets like a man being chased, and finally boarded the first bus that passed my way. I didn't care where it was going. It took me away, which was what I wanted. Eventually I got off and transferred, and then transferred again. A long time later, I made it back to the hotel. I hurried through the lobby without talking to anyone and twitched impatiently, waiting for the elevator. When the doors opened, I tensed, not sure what I would see inside. The same was true when I got to the floor where I was staying.

I expected to see *him*. Me.

Finally, back in my room, I locked the dead bolt. I even thought about dragging a chair to the door to make sure it wouldn't open. With my heart pounding, I paced back and forth between the walls, unable to stop, unable to calm down. When the phone rang, I jumped. I let it go, and eventually the ringing stopped, but only seconds later, it rang again. This time, I picked up the receiver without announcing myself. I waited nervously to hear who was on the other end, and I exhaled in relief when I heard Tai's voice.

"Hey," she said. "Are you okay?"

"Yes. Fine."

"I tried you several times and didn't get an answer. I was worried. I asked the desk people to keep an eye out for when you got back."

"I was out," I told her, without going into detail.

"Do you need anything?"

"No. Thanks."

Tai was quiet for a while, breathing softly into the phone. "Well, I'm almost done for the day. I'll be heading home soon. The team has everything under control for the Eve Brier event. Our Lady of Infinite Worlds. She's speaking in the ballroom tonight."

"I remember."

"You sure you're okay? You sound tense."

I was more than tense. My life was breaking down like the pieces of a jigsaw puzzle, but I couldn't tell her why. I couldn't even explain it to myself.

"I'm fine, Tai. You've had a long day. Go home."

"Okay."

But she didn't hang up.

"Do you want some company?" she went on after a brief pause. "There's nothing but Lean Cuisine and Prime Video waiting in my apartment. I still have that thank-you bottle of pinot the Walkers gave us. I could bring it up, and we could talk. Or not talk. If you want to just sit there and drink and look at the lake, we could do that, too."

"Not tonight."

"Look, I know you may feel like it's better to be alone, but that's not always the best thing. Sometimes it helps to have a friend there with you. Someone warm, someone who cares."

As if her meaning wasn't clear enough, she made it even clearer.

"I can stay all night if you want, Dylan. As a friend. That's all. I really have no expectations. But if you need to be close to someone, I'm here."

I was tempted. Not because I'd ever been attracted to Tai, not because I wanted sex, but because I liked the idea of having a real person with me, keeping me sane. I was afraid of being alone and of what would happen to me next.

Listening to her, I also felt like a fool for missing her intentions. Karly had been right, as she usually was. I'd been telling Tai my secrets for months because it felt safe, but there was nothing safe about it.

"I appreciate the offer," I told her over the phone, "but I wouldn't be very good company."

"Are you sure?"

"Very sure."

Her disappointment was palpable. "Well, the door is always open, Dylan. I mean that. If you change your mind, call me. Or come by my apartment. I don't want you feeling like you have to be by yourself."

"Thanks, Tai."

I hung up the phone. The hotel room was quiet, just the rumbling white noise of the fan blowing warm air. I'd turned up the heat, but I was still cold, because my clothes were soaking wet. I peeled them off and stood shivering in the darkness. I'd bought a bottle of bourbon in the gift shop earlier, and I opened it and poured a glass, neat. The amber liquid trailed fire down my throat into my stomach, and the warmth spread. I took it to the window and stared out at the city, where night had fallen. In the distance, I could see the gold lights of the fountain, the glow of waterfront condominium towers, and the kaleidoscope of the huge Ferris wheel out on Navy Pier.

Where was he?

Who was he, this man that my mind had conjured? Was he down in that darkness, staring up at my window?

I didn't know what was happening to me. I wanted my old life back the way it was. I wanted Karly, naked like me, her skin pressed up against me from behind, her chin on my shoulder. If I closed my eyes, I could feel her there. I could hear her whispering to me. I would turn around, and we would kiss, and our eyes would glisten with desire, and we would tumble onto the bed and melt into each other with breathless, urgent laughter.

We'd had so many moments like that.

We would never have them again.

I drank more bourbon, but my body was still cold. When my third glass was empty, I went into the bathroom and ran a scalding-hot bath for myself. As the tub filled, I slid down into it, the hot water lapping at my skin. I let it go as high as it could, and then I sank down below the surface. I immersed my whole body, and the hot, clean water became black as night, and the slimy mud oozed over my skin, and my wife screamed for me to save her.

Dylan, come find me! I'm still here!

If I drowned myself, I'd be with my wife again. But my body betrayed me. As I ran out of air, I threw myself upward. My face burst from the water, and I gasped for breath, gagging and coughing. I opened the tub drain and listened to the loud, sucking slurp as the water went down. When the tub was empty and I was cold again, I finally climbed out and went back into the bedroom.

I needed to talk to someone about all of this. About my grief and my hallucinations. I needed answers.

I realized there was someone in the hotel who could help. Dr. Eve Brier—author, philosopher, and psychiatrist—was downstairs, and according to Tai, she knew me, even though I didn't know her. I wanted to understand how that was possible.

"Don't you know her?"

"No."

"Well, that's strange. She told me she picked the hotel on your recommendation."

I got dressed again. I put on a navy blazer and black slacks, playing the role of hotel events manager. I made sure I was shaved, and I brushed my teeth and popped a few mints in my mouth to cover the smell of the bourbon. Then I headed to the elevators.

The hotel's gold ballroom had a narrow second-story balcony that made a U around the palace-like space. From up there, people could lean on the elaborately carved railings and watch the wedding parties dance below them, or pretend that they were in powdered wigs and part of the court of Louis XIV. I let myself onto the walkway through a staff entrance and stayed discreetly at the back. No one was up here tonight. The action was below, in the darkened ballroom, with several hundred guests paying rapt attention to the woman illuminated on the stage.

Dr. Brier was dressed completely in black. Black pantsuit, black heels. In the stark spotlight, her head looked almost disconnected from her body, and her hands fluttered like flying birds as she gesticulated to the crowd. Her highlighted hair swirled as she walked from one side of the stage to the other. I could see the reflecting glint of her golden eyes like two faraway jewels. Her voice, through the microphone, had a mellifluous quality, the kind of singsong sweetness that could hypnotize you or seduce you, depending on what she wanted. It worked its magic. I didn't think I'd ever heard our ballroom as drop-dead quiet as it was at that moment. Dr. Brier had these hundreds of people holding their breath.

"*Think* about what this means," she told them, drawing out her words with a pregnant pause. "If we accept the Many Worlds theory as true, then our universe is constantly replicating itself, atom by atom, moment by moment, choice by choice. Every possible outcome of an event exists in its own separate world. We are all inching along on a single, solitary, fragile branch of a tree that grows infinitely larger with each nanosecond. As I leave the ballroom tonight, I turn left, but I also turn right. I go home, and I don't go home. I kiss my husband, and I slap his face, and I have sex with him, and I stick a knife in his heart. In my consciousness, I only experience *one* of those outcomes, because I'm on one branch of the tree. But the Many Worlds theory tells us that *all* of those things happen in parallel universes."

She paused. "Of course, I'm sure my husband is hoping I'm in bed with him later and not wiping the blood off my knife."

Laughter rippled through the crowd.

"In fact, I'm not actually married," she said, "not in this life. However, in a myriad of other worlds, I am. In other worlds, I'm not a psychiatrist, I'm an actor, I'm a cop, I'm a homeless drug addict. In other worlds, I'm not alive; I'm dead. And so are you. There are infinite copies of you in infinite worlds, making all of the choices you don't make in this life. That's what the theory says."

Dr. Brier stopped in the middle of the stage.

"Is this crazy talk? The ravings of mad scientists trying desperately to explain why their elegant math doesn't work in the real world? Well, maybe. Or maybe our vision of the universe is simply limited by what we can see. Until we had microscopes and could look at a drop of blood, nobody would have believed that there were so many other worlds living inside it. Millions of cells inside a single drop of blood! Impossible! But now we know it to be true. So is the idea of the Many Worlds an absurd theory? Or do we just need a better microscope?"

There was something magnetic about this woman. She wasn't speaking to the audience as a whole. She was speaking to everyone in the room. Personally. Individually. Or maybe she was just talking to *me*, because that was how it felt. Standing on the balcony, I might as well have been alone with her in the giant ballroom. I felt her watching me. Staring up at me. Directing all her comments and thoughts to me. I expected her to use my name.

Dylan, you are not alone. You are part of many worlds.

You are infinite.

"Philosophers took this idea from the physicists and came up with their own theory," Dr. Brier continued. "They called it the *Many Minds*. Their theory is that all these endless choices, all these parallel lives, really do exist—not in the big wide universe, but inside our individual brains.

We're the ones who divide like amoebas over and over. Still sound crazy? Well, think about your dreams. A dream is an elaborate world that your brain creates *instantaneously*. All that extraordinary detail devoted to building a fantasy place that only exists for a few moments of sleep, never to be visited again. If the brain can do that night after night after night, then maybe it isn't so strange to think that it can build entire parallel worlds, too. No, for me, the important question isn't whether it's *possible*. The question is, What does this have to do with you and me and our actual lives? With our single little branch of the tree? Does any of this really matter if it's all just theoretical? Because physicists and philosophers don't agree on much, but they do agree on one thing. Whether it's Many Worlds or Many Minds, we're stuck on our own branch. Isolated. Powerless. Every version of yourself lives in its own separate world, and you can't visit those other universes."

Dr. Brier let all of that sink in. She took a sip of water from a bottle on the stool placed in the middle of the stage. Before she began to speak, I saw it again. Her eyes shifted to the balcony.

She stared directly at me.

"Or can you?"

After her speech was over, I waited in a long line to meet her. This whole event was about selling books. She'd written a self-help book, using the hook of the Many Worlds, Many Minds theories to give it a sexy twist. The idea was to teach people to lead better lives by showing them how to "visit" the alternate choices they'd made in parallel worlds.

Still wondering if you should have asked your college girlfriend to marry you? Imagine the version of yourself that's living in that world.

Trying to decide whether to take that new job? Somewhere in the universe, you will. What does that life look like?

I understood the appeal of the theory. I was drawn to the idea that there was a universe right now where I hadn't driven into that river. Somewhere, either in another world or buried inside my head, Karly was still alive, and I was still with her.

Believe me, I would have done *anything* to have that life for myself.

But that was a different Dylan. A Dylan who made better choices.

I could see Dr. Brier on stage as the guests trooped across one at a time to get her signature, along with a smile and a photo. She was attractive, eloquent, and persuasive, the way all cult leaders tend to be. I kept staring at her face and trying to remember where I could have met her, but I came up blank. It had to be a mistake. Somehow, Tai had misunderstood what she said.

Finally, it was my turn. I walked across the stage, leaving the line of people behind me. I had the copy of the book I'd bought in my hand. Dr. Brier's eyes watched me come closer. I reached the table where she was seated by herself, and I could feel myself enveloped by her aura. I stood over her and handed her the book to sign. She took it, but her smile looked forced.

"Hello, Dylan," she murmured. "I saw you in the balcony. I didn't think you'd come. It's not such a good idea, you and me being seen together."

Her words threw me off balance. "I'm sorry, do you know me?"

She froze before she signed the book. Her almond-shaped brown eyes bored into mine. "Is that a joke?"

"No."

"I don't like this game, Dylan."

"I'm sorry, Dr. Brier, but you must have me confused with someone else. As far as I know, we've never met."

"I see." She glanced at the people still in line on the other side of the stage, and then she swept her long hair across her head. She signed the book with a flourish, added a little note, and then handed it back to me across the table. As she did, her fingertips grazed mine.

"My mistake," she said. "Enjoy the book."

I walked away in a daze. I glanced over my shoulder to see if she was watching me, but she'd moved on to the next person. I left the ballroom and found a bench near the elevators, where I sat down and opened the book.

Below her signature, she'd added a note.

The fountain. 1:00 a.m.

CHAPTER 7

Three hours later, I walked into Grant Park with a cold lake wind blowing into my face. I kept my hands in my pockets and my head down. Every few steps, I looked back at the lights of Michigan Avenue to see if I was being followed. I didn't feel his presence now—*my* presence—but that didn't mean my doppelgänger wasn't here.

I crossed over the railroad tracks and continued beside the green lawns of the park. Traffic was light, and I jogged to the other side of Columbus to get to the Buckingham Fountain. Its water cannons had been stilled until morning. Beyond the fountain, the dark swath of Lake Michigan filled the horizon. I stood by the pond for a while, near the sculptures of the seahorses, and then I found a bench on the south side of the plaza to wait.

I wasn't alone. I saw a homeless man wrapped in a blanket on one of the benches near me. From behind me, I heard the sultry breaths of a couple having sex in the shelter of the trees. Near the fountain, two silhouettes whispered to each other, and I saw something pass from one hand to another. Drugs.

Dr. Eve Brier arrived exactly on time. I checked my watch, and it was one in the morning on the dot. I saw her coming, still in black, with a dark trench coat waving like a cape behind her as the wind blew. I stood up as she approached, and she came up and put her arms around me, an oddly intimate gesture that took me aback. Her perfume rose off her skin like a bouquet of roses. To anyone watching us, we must have looked like two lovers meeting, but I felt her hands exploring my back and then my chest, patting me down.

"What are you doing?" I asked her.

"Making sure you're not wearing a wire."

"Why on earth would I do that?"

"I don't know, Dylan, but none of this makes sense. I'd rather be careful."

We sat down next to each other on the bench. I could feel an incredible tenseness radiating from her. She was scared of something. Her head swiveled, surveying the shadows to see if we were being watched.

"What was all that about in the ballroom?" she asked me.

"What do you mean?"

"Pretending not to know me."

"I *don't* know you."

"Stop it, Dylan. You're scaring me."

"I'm serious," I told her.

She studied my face carefully, as if looking for a lie. "Say the word," she said finally.

"What word?"

"You know."

"I don't. I have no idea what you're talking about."

"*Infinite*," she said. "Say it."

"Why?"

"Say it," she repeated like an order.

I shrugged. "Infinite."

Dr. Brier eased back on the bench. I didn't know what she expected would happen, but nothing did. She crossed her arms tightly over her chest, as if the lake breeze was making her cold.

"Do you want to tell me what's going on?" I asked her.

"You seriously don't remember me?"

"Dr. Brier, I already told you. We've never met. The first time I heard your name was when I saw the poster for your event at the hotel."

"Call me Eve," she said. "Please. Anything else sounds strange. I need to ask you some questions."

"Okay."

"Have you been having blackouts? You wake up and can't account for where you were or what you did?"

"Not that I'm aware of."

"Even when you drink?"

"How do you know that I drink?"

"Just answer the question."

"No, I haven't gotten blackout drunk in years. Typically, I remember the stupid things I do."

Eve frowned. "Have you experienced any kind of trauma lately?"

"Yes. The worst trauma of my life, in fact. I lost my wife in a car accident."

"Your *wife*," she exclaimed.

"Karly. Our car went into a river. She drowned. I wasn't able to save her."

Eve inched away from me on the bench. Her voice grew frostier. "I'm very sorry for your loss. That's a terrible thing."

"Yes, it is."

"Is it possible you experienced some kind of memory loss after the accident?"

"If I did, you're the only thing that got erased," I told her. "Look, you obviously think I'm someone else. Are you going to tell me how I supposedly know you?"

Eve stood up from the bench and reached out a hand to me. I stood up, too, and we walked eastward, away from the fountain. We crossed the outer drive and then continued until we were within a few steps of the lake. I could taste the spray on my lips. Out in the harbor, sailboats bobbed, their ropes clanging. Beyond the piers, I could see whitecaps dotting the rough water. The skyscrapers glowed behind us.

She turned and faced me. In her high heels, she was taller than I was. The wind whipped her silky hair. "You're my patient. That's how I know you."

"What are you talking about?"

"You've been coming to me for therapy for several weeks."

I backed away from her. *"What?"*

"It's true."

"No, it's not. I don't even know you."

"Believe me, you do. And I know you, too. Of course, you never told me about being married, which is a surprise." She cocked her head, studying me like a clinician trying to get inside my brain. "This *must* be some kind of memory loss. Although I suppose there's one other possibility."

"What's that?"

Eve frowned. "You could be suffering from multiple personality syndrome. Your mind has split into different versions of yourself. One Dylan doesn't remember what the other Dylan has done. I never saw any signs of that, but other personalities can be very convincing. I guess it's also possible that my treatment made your condition more severe."

"Treatment?"

"Yes. You were my first patient in a new experimental protocol I developed. I call it my Many Worlds therapy."

"What the hell is that?"

"It's a way of breaking down barriers between the separate lives that our brain creates. Of *bridging* the parallel universes. It's similar to the concept of past life regression, but instead of going backward in time, it's like going sideways into your other worlds. That's why I had you say *infinite*. That's our code word, the signal that triggers your brain to end the session. Wherever you were, whatever world you were in, you could say that, and you'd be back with me. I wanted to see how you reacted to the idea of saying it."

"I didn't react at all, because it meant nothing to me."

"Yes, that's interesting. I'm not sure what to make of that."

I shook my head. "How does this *treatment* work?"

Eve glanced at the sidewalk near the water. We were still alone, but she obviously didn't want anyone to hear us. "Have you ever heard of a San Francisco psychiatrist named Francesca Stein? She was in the news a few years ago when she was found to be altering the memories of her patients using a combination of psychotropic drugs and hypnosis."

"If you say so. I don't know the name."

"Frankie and I are friends. We were in school together. We've talked a lot about the therapeutic possibilities behind the Many Worlds theory. She believed it might be possible to use a technique similar to what she used in altering memories to get people to 'experience' their other lives. I've been exploring the idea ever since."

"Jumping between worlds?" I asked cynically.

"That's right."

"Are you saying you did this to me?"

"Exactly."

"I would never have agreed to that."

"In fact, you volunteered. You pushed me to try it. You said you wanted to know the truth about yourself. So we agreed that you would be my guinea pig."

I felt as if all I could do was sputter out my protests. "Experimenting with psychotropic drugs? Is that even legal? Because it sure as hell doesn't sound ethical."

"You're right. I push the boundaries. Actually, you said that was something you liked about me, that we had things in common. I've made a lot of mistakes in my life. I was a drug addict for a while back in medical school and nearly got kicked out. If people found out what we did, I'd probably lose my license. That's why I was so cautious with you tonight. Yes, I gave you hallucinogenic drugs to alter reality for you, but believe me, it was with your full consent."

I shook my head. "Impossible. You're making a mistake. I don't know you."

Eve sighed at my denials. "You're Dylan Moran. Events manager at the LaSalle Plaza Hotel. Your father killed your mother and then killed himself right in front of you. You moved in with your grandfather, Edgar, after their deaths. You still go to the Art Institute with him every week. Your favorite painting is Hopper's *Nighthawks*. Edgar likes to say that if he hadn't accidentally bumped into the museum director when he was a boy and saved him from getting killed on State Street, that painting would be hanging in a totally different place."

My breath left my chest. I grabbed her shoulders and hissed in her face, "How do you know all that?"

"How do you think? *You* told me."

I stared at her face in the starlight and tried to make sense of this woman. She was a doctor and a psychiatrist, but she was something more, too. I didn't know exactly what it was, but she had an enigmatic quality about her, as if she could seduce people with her mind. I felt the spell she cast pulling me into her orbit. She was beautiful, sensual, unforgettable. A magician. I could picture being with her in her office. I could hear my own voice telling her secrets about myself.

But it had *never* happened.

"This therapy," I went on. "What did I experience?"

"You told me you saw other Dylans from other worlds. You interacted with them. You went into their lives."

"Do you really believe that?"

"*You* believed it."

"What did I see?"

"If you want to know that, you should go back inside your head. Try it and see for yourself."

"No thanks."

"Are you sure? You told me after one session that you wished you could stay in the world you found. You were tempted to take over that other Dylan's life."

"None of that is *real*," I said.

"How do you know? Frankly, I wasn't sure before we began, but your experience made me a believer. The Many Worlds theory is true. We really do take every road that's open to us. In some other world, you and I never met. We're passing each other by the lake right now like strangers. In another world, we're having sex. In another, you're holding me under the water and drowning me."

I flinched at the violent image. "Drowning you? Why on earth would you say something like that?"

"Because that's why you came to me, Dylan," Eve said. "You said you were having visions of killing people, and yet these people were still alive. But you could give me details, dates, descriptions, methods of how you'd murdered them. You wanted my help. You were afraid you were on the verge of becoming a serial killer."

CHAPTER 8

Have you ever looked at yourself in the mirror—I mean, really looked at yourself—and wondered who you were?

What kind of person lives behind your eyes?

That was how I felt at that moment. I no longer had any idea what to believe about Dylan Moran. Eve had told me things about myself that seemed impossible, and yet they also made sense in a crazy way. If my personality had split apart, if another side of me was living a different life that I knew nothing about, then maybe my mind was projecting that second Dylan Moran into my hallucinations.

I was seeing myself. Talking to the *other* version of myself. Somehow, my brain was bringing my second personality to life, and what I knew about that personality scared me. When I was him, I didn't know what I was capable of doing.

Why are you here?

To kill.

I needed something I could hold on to, some kind of driftwood in the sea that would keep me afloat. I needed Karly, or at least a reminder of her. So I took a cab north along the lakeshore toward the house where Karly's parents lived. There were faster ways out of the city, but I asked the driver to take the slow route along Sheridan Road, and I told him I'd make it up to him in the tip. Karly and I had taken this road many times when we were visiting her parents. She liked to see the neighborhoods

change, from the green fields of Lincoln Park to the academic neighborhoods of Loyola and Northwestern, and then to the lakeside mansions
of Evanston, Kenilworth, and Winnetka.

Personally, I just thought she wasn't in a hurry to see her mother.

Susannah Chance lived in a stone mansion that dated to the 1930s.
It looked like a Tudor castle, with bay windows, tall austere chimneys,
and sharp gables. Yes, Karly's father lived here, too, but this was the
House That Susannah Built. Karly's father, Tom, was a published poet
and high school English teacher who would have been just as happy
living in a one-bedroom apartment near Wrigley Field. Susannah,
however, was the force of nature behind Chance Properties, and her
Wilmette estate was the ostentatious symbol of her success.

I had the cab let me off on Sheridan Road, and I walked the last
hundred yards under the old-growth trees. I was white and wearing nice
clothes, which probably protected me from someone calling the cops.
The people in this neighborhood had itchy 911 fingers. When I got to
the Chance house, the lights were off, which wasn't surprising given
the late hour. I didn't want to talk to Susannah or Tom. Instead, I let
myself into the fenced backyard and made my way through the gardens
to Karly's dollhouse.

You can call it a dollhouse, but at more than a thousand square feet,
it was bigger than our Lincoln Square apartment. That tells you how
far down in the world Karly came to live with me. When she turned
twenty-two, she moved out of the main estate and into the dollhouse,
which was all the independence that her mother would allow her. She
was still living there when we met, so I'd spent a lot of time in this
strange fairy-tale world. I'd had a key for years, and I knew the security
code.

When I went inside, Karly may as well have been a ghost rattling
chains at me, because her presence was so strong. Her school pictures
were on the walls and her dance trophies and poetry books on the
shelves. She hadn't lived here in three years, but her mother still kept

it like a shrine, decorated with furniture she'd picked out for Karly at age sixteen. Susannah probably hoped that her daughter would eventually come to her senses, dump me, and move back home where she belonged.

I sat down in a beat-up leather chair that overlooked the garden. The chair came from Karly's father, and I think he gave it to Karly for the dollhouse rather than let his wife take it away to Goodwill. It was a man's chair, ugly and incredibly comfortable, and it looked out of place amid pink wallpaper and sunflower quilts. I'd spent weeks in this chair after Roscoe was killed. With my arm and leg in casts, I was essentially immobile, and Karly did everything for me. We barely knew each other, but she was my caregiver. And soon after that, my lover.

The last time I'd been here was six months ago, in January. She'd called me from the office on a Tuesday morning and said she needed to get away, and could I meet her in the dollhouse? I said yes, but I got there late. I was always late. Work always came first. As I came in from outside, I brought cold wind and snow flurries with me. Karly had made a winter picnic for us, spreading out a blanket on the floor and opening wine and laying out a Mediterranean lunch of hummus, grape leaves, and pita.

She stood on the other side of the dollhouse, where a fire in the fireplace warmed her bare legs. The chill had pinked up her face. Her breasts swelled with each calm breath. She stared at me with a kind of forever seriousness, just the barest smile on her lips. I swear, she was like a painting that way, frozen in her beauty. A Manet. A Vermeer.

"What's the occasion?" I asked.

"Nothing. I love you, that's all."

"I love you, too."

It was hard to imagine a more perfect moment, but looking back, I knew that very day was when things had begun to fall apart for us. I could draw a line from our lunch in the dollhouse to her foolish affair with Scotty Ryan to the last speech she'd given me that weekend in the country.

If I'd been paying attention, I would have noticed that Karly was unusually quiet. She was off somewhere in her own world, and she never took time off in the middle of the day unless something was wrong. I should have looked behind her peaceful smile, but instead, I was blind. I poured wine, and we sat across from each other on the blanket, with the fire crackling beside us.

"Susannah talked to me," Karly said, when we'd enjoyed our lunch quietly for a few minutes. She said it casually. No big deal.

"Oh?"

"She's giving me the Vernon Hotel account."

I put down my wine and realized this was a celebration. Except it didn't feel like a celebration. "Are you serious?"

"Yeah."

"That's like the biggest account in the firm."

"Yeah. It is. She says I'm ready."

"Well, of course you are."

"Thank you."

"This is huge," I said, trying to fill this moment with excitement, because the excitement in her face was strangely missing.

"Yeah. Pretty huge. It's way more money. That's good, huh? But a lot more time. Long hours."

"So neither one of us will ever be home," I joked, but Karly didn't laugh.

"Susannah thinks we should move. We should be up here in Highland Park or something. She says we need a place where we can entertain."

"What do you think?"

"I don't know."

The same flat monotone all the way through. So unlike her. So not Karly. Why didn't I see it?

"Well, congratulations," I said, leaning over to kiss her. "You're a star. I mean it."

Karly smiled at me, but her smile was hollow, like one of her dolls on the shelves. Then, just like that, she changed the subject.

"I bumped into a friend at Starbucks this morning," she went on. "A girl I knew in college. Sarah. I don't know if I've ever mentioned her."

"I don't think so."

"She's got four kids now. They were all with her. Her youngest is almost two. A Down syndrome girl. So, so sweet. While Sarah was chasing the others, her little girl sat in my lap. I fell in love."

"Of course you did."

Karly delicately brushed something from the corner of her eye, and then she closed her eyes altogether. "Anyway . . . ," she murmured.

I thought she was just basking in the warmth of the fire and in the glow of her success. She'd worked hard for it. I had no idea, no idea at all, that she was watching two trails diverge in the woods and thinking that she was on the wrong one.

"I'm really proud of you," I said.

"Yeah. Thanks."

You were running so fast in your life that you never saw that Karly wanted to slow things down.

Scotty was right. Karly had told me how she was feeling that day in everything but words. I never heard her.

"I wondered who was out here," Susannah Chance said from the doorway of the dollhouse. "I thought it might be you."

Karly's mother wore a satin robe tied at the waist over her nightgown, and I could have sworn she'd put on makeup to go check on an intruder. She came inside the cottage and went and made herself a cup of coffee at the Keurig machine on the counter. When that was done, she took the mug into her hands and sat down on the sofa across from me.

Physically, she looked the way Karly would have looked in another twenty-five years, although Susannah was still trying hard to look like Karly's older sister. She'd groomed her only child to be a carbon copy of herself, with the same ambition, same charm, same need for success. Karly had spent her twenties following that blueprint under Susannah's watchful eye.

"How are you, Dylan?" she asked.

"I'm lost."

"Yes, of course. Tom and I are devastated. I wake up each day, and I can't believe it."

"I'm sorry."

Susannah sipped her coffee. The steam rose in front of her face. She'd said she was devastated at the loss of her daughter, and I'm sure she was, but Susannah Chance didn't show emotions easily. Her husband was the poet, the one who wore his heart on his sleeve.

"You can stay here tonight if you like," she added.

"Thanks. That's nice of you. But I just needed to feel her again. That's why I came."

Susannah looked around at the dollhouse and gave me a numb smile. Maybe loss always brings self-reflection. "I don't know if this is the right place to do that. I think Karly felt like a doll herself when she was here. Artificial. Unreal. A plaything. That's my fault. The truth is, she was never really happy until she met you, Dylan. And if you sometimes felt that I didn't like you, maybe that was the reason."

I didn't know what to say to that, so I said nothing at all.

"She told me what happened between her and Scotty Ryan," Karly's mother went on. "She was inconsolable over what she'd done. It was a stupid, drunken, onetime mistake and had nothing to do with how she felt about you. I hope you know that."

"I do now."

"Did you forgive her?"

"I never got the chance."

"Oh, Dylan." Susannah drank her coffee and looked away, with a teary shine in her eyes. She got up and went to the sink in the kitchen, where she washed the mug carefully and dried it with a towel. Susannah was always neat and precise. She put it away in a cabinet and then tugged her robe tighter around her body. She went to the door and opened it as if she were going to leave without saying anything more, but with the night air coming in, she hesitated. "I should tell you something. I know what you did. I understand it, even if I can't condone it."

"What do you mean?"

"I know you confronted Scotty about the affair."

"Yes, I did."

"Dylan, why? Why couldn't you let it go?"

I shrugged, because I had no excuse for the assault. "I didn't plan to see him. It was chance. He was there, I was there. I should have walked away, but I gave in to my temper. I blamed him when I should have been blaming myself. That doesn't change what he did, though."

"Well, the police know," Susannah said.

"The police?"

"Yes, they called me. The house was one of our listings, so they called to see if I knew anything about it. They had a description of *you*, Dylan. They had a witness who saw you leaving the house. They knew about the fight. I'm sorry, I couldn't lie to them. I told them about the affair with Karly. I'm afraid it gives you a motive on top of everything else."

"Susannah, what are you talking about?"

"They know you killed Scotty," she replied. "They told me you stabbed him in the heart. He's dead."

CHAPTER 9

I expected to find the police waiting to arrest me when I got back to the hotel. Instead, at five in the morning, the lobby was quiet and empty. Apparently they didn't know I was sleeping here. I was relieved, because I needed time to think, to figure out what to do and where to go. Scotty Ryan was dead. The man who'd had an affair with my wife had been murdered. *I'd* killed him.

Except I hadn't.

I'd hit him in the face and left him alone, bleeding but very much alive. Yes, a part of me *wanted* to kill him. That was true, and I couldn't deny it. When I walked into that house, I'd been consumed with rage and out for revenge. But if I'd taken a knife and plunged it into Scotty's chest, I'd remember doing it.

Wouldn't I?

Or had a different personality taken control of my mind? A personality that was here to kill. Just like my delusion had promised.

I took the elevator upstairs and let myself into my hotel room. I was exhausted. When the door closed behind me, I leaned back against it and measured out my breathing, trying to relax. Trying to *think*. To grasp at some kind of explanation for what was going on. Except I noticed almost immediately that something was wrong. There was a foreign smell around me, a sharp, sweet fragrance that lingered in my nose. I took stock of the room, suddenly awakened by a rush of adrenaline.

The bed was undone. The blanket lay on the floor, the sheets tangled. That wasn't how I'd left it. The maid had done the room long ago, and I hadn't slept since then. When I'd left to see Eve Brier, I was certain that the blanket had been folded into crisp corners.

Someone had been here. In my room.

It was like a macabre joke: *Who's been sleeping in my bed?*

Slowly, my eyes filled in the details. I saw an empty bottle of Jim Beam on the window ledge, reflecting the lights of the city outside. That was the bottle I'd opened earlier. I'd had three glasses myself. Or was it four? Regardless, the bottle was *empty* now, and there were two lowball glasses beside it. I went to take a look at the glasses and saw water in the bottom. Melted ice.

Ice? I never put ice in my drink.

I picked up the second glass and saw a red smear on the rim. Lipstick. Two people had been here, a man and a woman.

I examined the room again. This time, I spotted clothes scattered near the bed. Women's clothes. A beaded, multicolored dress lay pooled in layers like an accordion, as if it had dropped straight down over bare shoulders and hips. Near it was a lacy bra. Lavender bikini panties. Black high heels, kicked off.

The sweetness I'd smelled wafted like a freshly opened flower from the clothes and the bed. I recognized the perfume now. *Obsession.*

Then the rattle of a doorknob startled me. I wasn't alone. I glanced at the bathroom door and saw a bright light go off under the crack of the frame. When the door opened, Tai emerged into the darkness of the hotel room. Chicago's glow through the window lit up her naked body, which had a sheen of dampness from the shower. She had a towel in her hands, drying her long hair, her face obscured. I could see the prominent swell of her collarbone, her narrow hips and bony legs, and everything else, too. Chocolate-brown erect nipples dotted her shallow breasts. The triangular thatch between her legs was black and full.

She dropped the towel and noticed me. Her bright-red lips made a sexy smile, and her dark eyes devoured me.

"Oh, hi. I thought you had to go. I'm glad you stayed."

I didn't have time to ask her what was happening. She crossed the space between us, laced her fingers through my hair, and molded her lips against mine. Her nude body pressed against me, soft and sensuous.

"You're cold," she murmured. "Did you go out and come back?"

I still couldn't find any words.

"Let me warm you up," she said, her hand traveling down my body, slipping inside my pants. As much as my hormones didn't want her to stop, I separated myself from her and backed away. She gave me a confused look.

"What's wrong?"

"I can't do this."

She smiled at me again. "Oh, I bet you can. I could already feel things waking up."

"Tai, it's not that."

"Then, what is it?" She tried to read my face, and something about my expression must have made her feel very naked. She sat down on the bed and wrapped the rumpled sheet around herself. Her smile fell away. "Ah. I get it. You feel guilty. You're sorry we did it, aren't you?"

I studied the bed, which looked and smelled of sex. Tai and I had made love here. In some part of my memory, I could feel her beneath me, feel her legs tightly wrapped around my back, feel myself deep inside her. But it wasn't really *my* memory. It wasn't *me*.

"It's okay," Tai went on. "I said no strings, and I meant it. I'm still glad you called. You turned to me when you needed someone, and that's what I wanted. But I know you're dealing with a lot of pain right now."

"Tai, I'm sorry—" I began.

"Don't apologize. I'll go. When you told me you needed to leave, to clear your head, I should have guessed."

I sat on the bed next to her and tried to figure out what to say. What she'd told me, what I saw in this room, was making my head spin.

"Tai, this will sound crazy, but I need you to tell me exactly what happened between us tonight."

"I don't understand. Why?"

"Please. Humor me. Did I call you?"

"Are you saying you don't remember?" she asked, with an irritated frown.

"Actually, that's exactly what I'm saying."

"Are you kidding? You don't remember what we just did?"

"I wish I could explain it to you, but I can't."

Her expression turned to concern. "Are you okay?"

"I have no idea. I just need to know what happened."

She hesitated. "All right. Yes, you called me."

"What time?"

"I don't know. Sometime after midnight, I guess. I wasn't asleep yet. I know it was one in the morning when I got here."

"One o'clock?"

"Yes."

"You're sure about that?"

"Yes."

I shook my head. "Is there any possible way you made a mistake?"

"Dylan, I saw the clock in the lobby. I'm telling you, I got here at one o'clock."

I checked my watch and then the clock on the nightstand. There was no mistake. Everything matched.

One in the morning. That simply wasn't possible.

I was meeting Eve Brier at the fountain in the park at exactly one in the morning. At the very same time, I was also having a rendezvous with Tai back at the hotel.

"What did I say when I called you?"

"You said you were lonely, upset. You didn't want to be alone. You asked if I'd come over. I said sure. I mean, we both knew what you wanted. We both knew what was going to happen. I dressed accordingly."

"You came to the hotel room?"

"Of course."

"And *I* was here."

"Well, obviously."

"So did we—?"

"Yes. We had sex. Twice, in fact, if you need the details. You don't remember that, either? Is this some kind of game to make yourself feel better? Are you trying to pretend it never happened?"

I didn't answer. "Tai, please, just go on. Then what?"

"We fell asleep. When I woke up, you were already awake. Dressed. You were staring out the window. I asked you to come back to bed, but you said you needed to go. Right away. And you left. So I went into the shower, and when I got out, you were back here again. That's all, Dylan. It was like ten minutes ago. You're freaking me out if you really don't remember any of this."

"I'm sorry."

I thought about what Tai had told me, but I had no way to explain it. Nothing made sense.

This was not a delusion.

Not a missing memory or a split personality.

No matter what games my mind was playing with me, I couldn't be in two places at the same time, and yet I'd been in the hotel room with Tai at the same time that I was in the park with Eve Brier and then in Wilmette with Karly's mother.

I could only come to an impossible conclusion.

Two.

There were two of us. I wasn't hallucinating. My doppelgänger was real.

There was a Dylan Moran out there stealing his way into my life. It was as if this other Dylan had decided to follow every hidden impulse in my head and unleash my darker soul. Kill Scotty. Sleep with Tai. He was my id come to life.

This Dylan Moran was *not* me, but even so, we were connected by some kind of shadowy line. Echoes of his memories, of what he'd done, were in my own brain, like ghost images in a photograph. I suspected that he could sense *me*, too. He'd felt that I was coming back to the hotel, and that was why he'd made a fast exit.

Tai spoke softly from the bed. "If this was a mistake, Dylan, just say so. You don't have to pretend."

"It's not that. I mean—okay, yes, what happened between us was a mistake. My mistake, not yours. The last thing I would ever want is to see you hurt."

"I'm a big girl," she replied. Then she looked down at her lap. "You know, I've been in love with you practically since the day we met."

I felt as if I'd turned a knife into her chest, and I realized again how horribly unfair I'd been to her. How I'd played with her emotions without meaning to do so. "I never meant to lead you on. I should have been more careful."

"Hey, you were married. I knew I was playing with fire."

I stood up from the bed. "I need to go."

"Okay. Go."

"I have one more question. Believe me, I know none of this makes any sense."

"What is it?"

"A few minutes ago, when I told you that I needed to leave, did I say where I was going?"

Tai looked at me as if I were a crazy person, and maybe I was. "Home," she said. "You said you were going home."

Home. Back to our apartment in Lincoln Square. Our apartment, where I kept all of my memories of Karly. I'd avoided the apartment for days, but this other Dylan was drawing me back there. Only a few minutes had gone by. It was still not even dawn. If I went quickly, I could corner him before he had a chance to run.

I needed to find out *how* he could possibly be real.

I headed for the door, but Tai called after me. "Can I ask *you* a question?"

"Of course."

"The sex. What was it like for you?"

"Tai, I wish I could tell you, but—"

"You don't remember. Right. Sure." She sounded cynical and angry, and I didn't blame her.

"Tell me what it was like for you," I said, because I knew she wanted me to ask.

Her face turned dark. "It wasn't what I expected."

"What do you mean?"

She tugged the sheet tighter around her shoulders, covering any hint of bare skin. "You weren't tender with me like I thought you'd be. You were so raw, so . . . I don't know . . . violent. Honestly, there were moments when it didn't even feel like it was really you."

CHAPTER 10

He knew I was coming. He could feel me. I was sure of that.

The neighborhood around River Park was dark, with only the occasional streetlight spilling a yellow glow on the ground. The cab let me off at the corner. I waited until it drove away before going anywhere, and I checked to make sure I was alone. I took the sidewalk beside the park, keeping an eye on the trees and empty benches.

If I was looking for him, then he was looking for me, too.

Halfway down the block, I stopped near one of the mature trees, its branches hanging down nearly to my face. From there, I could see my apartment. This was the place where I'd lived since I was thirteen years old. The building was two stories, tan brick, shaped like the rook on a chessboard. Upstairs, where Edgar lived, one large square of chambered windows faced the street. A matching set of windows was below, where Karly and I lived. I saw no lights anywhere, but I stayed where I was, watching for any movement.

It was a humid early morning, with a dank stench wafting from the river a few hundred feet behind me. The birds were starting to awaken and sing. A few traces of white fluff from the cottonwoods still clung to the grass, weeks after it had fallen. I wasn't far from a children's playground, and when the wind blew, metal groaned on one of the rusty swing sets. Parked cars lined the curbs on both sides of the street, but I saw no people.

I kept looking behind me, expecting him to stalk me from the rear, coming up on me with silent footsteps. I tried to embrace the madness of this situation, to listen to my senses and see the world through his eyes. I had to believe, had to accept, the reality that there were two of us. I needed to feel what he felt, receive the echoes of his presence as he was obviously receiving mine. I needed to connect with him, which was the same as connecting with myself.

Where are you?

Then I saw it.

A light came and went in our downstairs apartment. It lasted only for a moment, like a flashlight turning on and off, but it was enough to give him away. He was there. He was inside. Soon after, the shadows in the glass seemed to change shape. He'd gone to the window to look out. To look for me.

I backed away, still invisible. When I knew I was safely out of view, I ran to the corner of the street and down the block to the dead-end alley that led behind the buildings. Power lines dangled overhead. The concrete was riddled with cracks and weeds. I made my way slowly between the garages on both sides. A couple squares of light from early risers showed in the bedroom windows. One of my neighbors had a rottweiler that slept outside, and he must have smelled me coming, because he began to bark.

I reached my garage. My back fence. I let myself quietly into the yard, which was nothing but a strip of concrete patio with an old gas grill and a few plastic chairs stacked against the garage wall. Ahead of me, wooden steps climbed to our back door, then to the entrance to Edgar's apartment above. Two buildings away, the rottweiler kept barking. I took the steps slowly, trying to avoid the squeal of loose boards. At the landing, the rear door led into the kitchen. I expected the door to be locked, but when I turned the handle, it gave way under my hand, and I felt the door opening inward. I slipped into the kitchen and eased the door shut behind me.

The air felt warm and stale, shut in for days with no windows open. The room wasn't completely dark; a butterfly night-light cast a faint glow near the sink. I had to squeeze my eyes closed against a frontal assault of grief. Karly's scent perfumed the kitchen. I expected to hear her humming and singing. The kitchen faucet leaked—it always did— and with each slow drip, I felt water pouring over my head, as if I'd dived into the river and was swimming through blackness.

Dylan, come back to me!

I had to force away my wife's screams.

Where was he hiding? I listened, but wherever he was, he was frozen stiff, a statue, waiting for me to make the first move. Ahead of me was the unlit hallway. On the right was our bedroom, then the postage-stamp dining room that doubled as Karly's office, and finally the living room, which faced the street, with a fireplace where we would sit with wine on winter nights and kiss as we watched the flames dance.

Stop it!

I couldn't think about Karly now.

I needed a weapon. Something. Anything. I went to the kitchen counter and grabbed the butcher's knife from our wooden block, but when I slid it out, I hissed in shock. When I held the knife high in the air, I could see that the blade was bathed in dried blood.

I knew what it was. Scotty's blood. I was holding his murder weapon in my hand. Leaving my fingerprints. But wouldn't they be mine anyway?

The grip of the knife was slippery. That was sweat. I started down the hallway, my eyes adjusting to the darkness. In here, I could have made my way blindfolded, because I knew every square inch of the house. As I approached the doorway to the bedroom, I looked inside, seeing the queen-size bed unmade, the way my hotel bed had been. I might leave a bed undone, but Karly never would. I realized that while I'd been staying in the hotel, *he'd* been staying here.

I kept going. I crossed into the dining room, where the ceramic tile changed to a hardwood floor. It should have been replaced years earlier; it had water stains and warped boards. With each footstep, I announced myself, but it didn't matter. We both knew the score. We were both here. Strange glistening patches of wetness made the floor slippery. He was tracking water from somewhere. I continued past the dining room into the living room, all the way to the front windows. I looked outside, seeing no one illuminated under the streetlights. He hadn't escaped. There were no places to hide in the rooms I'd checked, so that told me where he was.

I squeezed the handle of the knife even tighter in my hand. I retraced my steps and went back to the bedroom doorway. This room, so normal and familiar, now terrified me. I had to fight away memories again. Karly and I had made love in that bed hundreds of times, but it had been weeks since our bodies had joined together. First I'd been busy at work, distant, hassled, the way I usually was. And then, after her confession about Scotty, we'd avoided each other for days. I didn't know the last time she'd been naked in my arms. I hated that I couldn't remember. I hated that Scotty had been the last one to hold her, not me.

Inside the bedroom, a closed door led to our small closet, and a closed door led to our small bathroom. He had to be behind one of those doors. I thought about calling out to him, but I simply listened, trying to hear someone else breathing above the wild pounding of my own heart.

I approached the bathroom door slowly, expecting it to burst open as he charged me. I waited outside, listening again, hearing nothing. Finally, with the knife poised, I threw the door open and leaped inside, jabbing the blade forward as I did. He wasn't there, but the shower curtain was stretched across the length of the tub. The floor was wet. Steam clouded the mirror and made the air in the tiny space close and damp. I pictured him, naked in the shower, dripping as he got out and ran to the front of the house. He could feel me coming.

I went to the tub and tensed as I threw the curtain back.

He wasn't there. The bathroom was empty.

Which left one more hiding place.

I went back to the bedroom and stood outside the closet door. It was an old, heavy wooden door with a metal knob. The closet itself was small, not much bigger than a couple of phone booths. Karly was always complaining that she had no room for her clothes.

There was no point in pretending anymore.

"I know you're in there," I whispered.

This time, unlike in the park, he didn't answer me. It made me think for a moment that I was wrong. That I was crazy. Then I slowly closed my hand around the doorknob, and with the knife ready in my other hand, I pulled hard.

The door didn't open.

I yanked again, but as I put pressure on it, someone on the other side responded with an equal pressure in reverse. I couldn't move the door. It stayed closed. He was every bit as strong as I was. In fact, if I thought about it, he was *exactly* as strong as I was. We were in equilibrium, with the door fixed like a wall between us. But he was inside, and I was outside. He had nowhere to go, no way to escape. I didn't understand the point of this game.

And then I did.

Standing outside the closet door, trying frantically to get it open, I heard a voice from inside. It wasn't *my* voice. This was a stranger's calm voice, slightly muffled and staticky. A woman's voice on a speakerphone.

"911. What's your emergency?"

A long moment of silence passed, and the dispatcher spoke again.

"911. Hello? What's your emergency?"

This time, the man in the closet replied, drawing out his words as if it were an echo in the canyon. I knew that voice. It was my voice. "Well, *hello* . . ."

He was speaking to me as much as to her.

"Sir? Hello? What's your emergency?"

"My name is Dylan Moran. You need to send the police here right away."

He rattled off the address—my address—and said, "You need to hurry."

"Sir? Can you tell me what the problem is?"

"I've been a bad boy," he told the operator, drawing out the adjective with a smirk in his voice that was meant for me. "I need to be stopped."

"Sir? Are you in danger? Is it someone with you who's in danger?"

"Everyone near me is in danger. I kill people. I murder them. I stab them. I *drown* them."

He put an emphasis on that last one, and I felt myself ready to be sick. I pulled at the door again, but it wouldn't budge. I wanted to shout, to say something, but my throat felt paralyzed with shock. I couldn't get out the words.

"Send the police," he said again.

"The police are on their way. Sir, are you alone? Is anyone with you?"

"No one's with me," he said, with an irony for me to savor. "I'm alone. Just me. Dylan Moran."

"Stay right there, sir. The police are two minutes out."

"I need to be punished," he said intensely.

"Sir? Stay on the line, sir."

"My evil is limitless. My evil is . . . *infinite.*"

He used the word.

Eve's word.

Infinite.

I was still pulling on the closet door, but all of a sudden, the counterpressure disappeared. The door flew open in my hand, and I lost my balance, stumbling backward. I could still hear the dispatcher speaking on the phone.

"Sir? Sir, are you there? Sir?"

I charged the closet, but no one was inside now. I yanked the chain on the bulb overhead and squinted at the bright light. The closet was empty, nothing but Karly's and my clothes hanging on hooks and a cell phone on the floor, still broadcasting the voice of the 911 dispatcher.

"Sir? Sir? Stay right there. The police are on their way."

I was alone, and my doppelgänger was gone. I was the only one here.

Dylan Moran, who'd just confessed to murder.

Dylan Moran, who held a bloody knife in his hand.

My fingers opened wide, and the knife clattered to the floor. I grabbed my head in wild despair and realized that I needed to get out of this house. To leave. To escape. To never come back. I ran from the bedroom, but as I did, I saw that I was already too late.

Sirens wailed. Flashing lights lit up the windows from the front and back.

The police were here.

CHAPTER 11

I met them at the building door.

Two burly Chicago cops stood on my front step, their squad car parked diagonally at the curb, its lights flashing. One had his hand close to the gun in his holster. The other was talking on a radio to another team of officers who'd obviously arrived at my house via the alley.

The cop who looked ready to shoot was six inches taller than me and about the size of a Hummer, with mottled black skin, a thin mustache, and hair trimmed on the top of his head to look like a skullcap. His eyes gauged whether I was any kind of threat.

"Sir? We received a 911 call from this address."

I did the only thing I could think to do. I lied.

"911? From here? I'm sorry, officer, it must be a mistake. I'm the only one here, and I didn't call about any emergency."

"Can you give me your name, sir?"

I hesitated, and the cop obviously noticed. "Dylan Moran."

The two officers glanced at each other. "Well, sir, that's the name we were given on the 911 call."

"My name? I don't know what to tell you. It must be someone playing some kind of trick. I've heard about that kind of thing—you know, where people send the police to somebody's house. What do they call it? Swatting?"

"Do you have some kind of identification, sir?"

"Of course."

I dug into my pocket and found my wallet. I pried my driver's license out of the slot and gave it to the cop. I'm sure he saw that my hand was shaking. When he handed it back to me, I needed a couple of tries to get the license back into my wallet.

"We'd like to take a look inside your apartment, Mr. Moran."

"I understand, Officer. I know you're just doing your job. But I don't know anything about a 911 call, and I'm afraid I'm not prepared to let the police search my home for no reason. I'm sorry."

I could see him looking over my shoulder through the open door, no doubt hunting for some kind of probable cause that would give them an excuse to come inside without my permission. Then he glanced at the stairs leading to the second floor.

"Is there another apartment upstairs?"

"Yes. My grandfather lives there. Edgar Moran."

"We'd like to talk to him," the cop said.

"Well, he's ninety-four, Officer, and not in good health, so I'd really prefer if you didn't bother him. As I say, this whole thing has to be some kind of weird joke."

"A joke," the cop said, chewing on the word like gum.

"That's right."

"The 911 caller said his name was Dylan Moran, and he was ready to confess to murder. That doesn't sound like a joke."

I didn't have any trouble summoning anger to my face, because I *was* angry. Angry and desperate and losing my grip on the world I was in. "Well, that's crazy, Officer. I'm not a killer. Obviously, I would never call the police and say anything like that."

The cop was silent for a while. He didn't believe me, but he also didn't have any evidence to back up the 911 call. On the other hand, a bloody knife was still sitting on my bedroom floor, and I wasn't going to let them inside to find it.

"Why would someone make an accusation like that against you, Mr. Moran? That's a pretty serious thing to do."

"I have no idea. All I can tell you is, it wasn't me, and it isn't true."

I tried to hide my impatience. I needed the police to *go away*, and then I could take the knife and find somewhere to dispose of it. I could wipe down the entire apartment, not knowing what other evidence my double had left behind.

The two cops exchanged nervous glances. I could see them wondering if they'd made a mistake, but my hope that they would leave me alone didn't last long.

On the street, a gray sedan pulled to a stop behind the squad car. A tall, emaciated man in his sixties got out and grabbed a bulging leather briefcase from the back seat. He wore a loose-fitting white dress shirt and pleated brown slacks, and I could see the gleam of a badge clipped to his belt. His thinning gray hair was as tangled as a bird's nest, and his face had a cadaverous appearance, sunken around his eyes and hollowed out under his cheekbones. He looked as if he should be lying in a hospital bed instead of walking around the Chicago streets. But his unblinking eyes sized me up like a hawk as he came closer, and his mouth bent into the tiniest cocky smile.

"Guys, I'll take over," he told the uniformed cops. "Stick around, though, okay? I may need you."

The two cops deferred to him as if he were a Mafia don. Without another word, they retreated to their squad car, where they leaned against the doors and watched us. The newcomer extended his hand, and I shook it. His grip was limp, and his skin felt as dry as dust.

"Mr. Moran? I'm Detective Harvey Bushing. I'd like to ask you a few questions."

"I'm not in much of a mood to talk, Detective."

"Well, when you made that 911 call, it sure sounded like you wanted to talk."

"That wasn't me," I told him.

"Really?" Detective Bushing grabbed a phone from his back pocket, pushed a few buttons, and let me listen to a recording of the 911 call from a few minutes earlier. "That's not you, huh? Because it sounds like you."

"I don't think it sounds like me at all."

"Well, I know what you mean. My wife tells me I sound like that Ben Stein guy. You know, like in the Ferris Bueller movie? I don't hear it myself. Anyway, here's the thing, Mr. Moran. My partner is getting a search warrant for your apartment. I'm going to stick around, and so are my friends out there, until he gets back. You can invite me in or not, but we're going to come inside sooner or later."

"A search warrant? Based on a fake 911 call?"

"And other things," the detective replied.

"Like what?"

"I'm happy to explain all of it to you, if you let me inside."

"Detective, I swear, this is a crazy misunderstanding. I didn't make that call."

"Yeah, I heard you say that. The thing is, if it's a misunderstanding, how about we clear it up? Because to be totally honest with you, Mr. Moran, I didn't show up here because of that 911 call."

"No?"

"No. I was already on my way. See, I've had a colleague of mine sitting in a car down the street all night, watching to see if and when you came back home. He got me out of bed a while ago to tell me you were here. And then, as I was driving over here from Glenview, what should I hear on my radio but a report about a really weird 911 call involving *you*. Funny coincidence, don't you think? Oh, and believe me, it takes a lot for a 911 dispatcher to consider a call weird."

"Am I under arrest, Detective?"

"Not at all. I just want to talk."

"Well, I told you, I'm not talking."

"That's okay, too. How about I talk, and you listen?" He held up his briefcase. "I've got some things in here you'll find pretty interesting, but it would be easier to do it inside. We don't have to go farther than the nearest chair. I had my hip done in the spring, and it's a bitch to stand for very long. Give me ten minutes. Any time you want me to go, I'll go."

I was under no illusions. I knew he was playing me, trying to lay out what he'd learned about me and Scotty Ryan and get me to talk. If he was being honest about the warrant, I also knew that I'd be under arrest as soon as they finished their search. The only thing I could do was *run*. But I couldn't do that with the police staking out the front and back of the building.

Without saying anything more, I backed away from the door and let Detective Bushing into my apartment. When we were in the living room, I gestured at the sofa near the front window. I took a chair opposite him. My eyes did a quick survey of the room to make sure I hadn't missed any other incriminating evidence that had been left behind. I noticed Detective Bushing's eyes doing the same thing.

Then he reached into his briefcase and pulled out a photograph of Scotty Ryan. "Do you know this man, Mr. Moran?"

"I thought you were doing the talking, Detective. Not me."

"Sure. Right. Well, of course you know him. He's the man who slept with your wife."

He was baiting me. I tensed and pushed my lips together.

"That's your wife in the picture there, huh?" the detective said, pointing at the mantel.

"Yes."

"Very pretty."

"Yes."

"I heard about your wife, by the way," he went on. "That's just awful. Talk about a coincidence, huh? Your wife dies in a car accident while you're driving, and then her lover gets killed a few days later, right after you get in a fight with him."

"If you think I killed him, you're wrong," I said, even though the knife used to kill Scotty Ryan was lying a few feet away on my bedroom floor.

"But you were there, right? A witness put you in the house with Mr. Ryan. She identified you right away. She heard shouting, and then you came running out with blood on your hands."

"If I'd stabbed him, I would have had blood on a lot more than just my hands," I pointed out, even though I was talking when I should have stayed quiet.

"I don't recall mentioning that he'd been stabbed."

"I talked to my mother-in-law," I said. "I know you did, too. She told me what happened."

"Ah, sure. Of course. But you admit fighting with Mr. Ryan?"

"I'm not admitting anything."

The detective nodded. "Sure. I understand. What about your wife? Did you fight with her about her cheating on you?"

I still said nothing, but I felt my heartbeat take off again.

"I mean, if my wife did that to me, I'd break a few windows and probably some other things," Detective Bushing went on. "And you've got a temper, right, Mr. Moran? I know about your assault arrests. People who mess with you get their faces bashed in, don't they?"

"That's not what happened."

"Yeah. They probably all had it coming. I get it. Say, you work at the LaSalle Plaza Hotel, don't you?"

My brow wrinkled with puzzlement at the shift in the conversation. "Yes, that's right."

"You handle their events?"

"Yes."

"Nice place."

"Yes, it is."

"I went to a wedding there a few years ago."

"We do a lot of weddings," I said.

Detective Bushing dug his fingers into his open briefcase and pulled out a photograph, which he laid on the coffee table in front of me. The picture showed a pretty twentysomething blond woman in a jogging outfit. In the background, I spotted Lake Michigan and the planetarium.

"Do you recognize this woman, Mr. Moran?"

"No."

He extracted another photograph from his briefcase. This one showed another young, attractive blonde, seated in a restaurant with a drink in front of her.

"How about her?" he asked.

"No."

He dug into the briefcase again. Another photograph, another blonde.

"This one?"

"No," I said again.

And once more. Again I told him I had no idea who the woman was. That was the truth. They were all strangers to me.

"None of these women look familiar?"

"No, they don't."

"It seems to me they all look a lot like your wife," Detective Bushing said.

I glanced at the photographs again, and I realized that he was right. There was no denying the resemblance. The hair, the look, the smiles—they definitely all had a touch of Karly in them.

"A little, I suppose. Who are they?"

"They're murder victims, Mr. Moran."

I began to feel dizzy. "Murder?"

"Yeah. All four stabbed to death in the past few weeks. We figured the cases were connected, because the method was the same and the

94

victims all looked so much alike. We couldn't figure out what they had in common, though. Their homes, work, background—all different. It was driving me crazy, because I couldn't find any overlap, nothing that would suggest how the same killer would have come into contact with them. Until very recently, that is."

"I hope you don't think the connection is that they look like Karly. Because they look like a million other blond women, too."

"True. That's true. No, that wasn't the connection. I mean, it's interesting, but only because of what else we found. Actually, I stumbled onto it mostly by accident. A witness mentioned something to me in passing, and that tied in with a restaurant receipt I remembered from one of the other victims. See, what links these women together is that they all attended an event in the ballroom of the LaSalle Plaza Hotel within a few days of when they were killed."

I couldn't stop myself. I gasped. *"What?"*

"That's right. So I'm sure you see the problem here, Mr. Moran. Four women who look an awful lot like your wife got murdered right after they went to your hotel. And now your wife is dead, and so is the man who slept with her. Stabbed. Just like my other vics. To top it off, today we get a 911 call from someone calling himself Dylan Moran and saying he's ready to confess to murder."

I bolted out of the chair.

"You going somewhere, Mr. Moran?"

"I need to use the bathroom."

I turned around and stumbled down the hallway. I went into the bedroom and closed the door behind me. My eyes were drawn to the knife on the floor. The faces of the women in Detective Bushing's photographs smiled at me in my head. I didn't know them. I had never met them. And yet, now that I was alone, something about them stirred echoes. I remembered them. Worse, the echoes in my head weren't of these women alive. I could see them dead. Their faces drained and pale. I could see *my* hands, covered in their blood.

They all looked like Karly.

My stomach turned over. I didn't need to fake it. I ran into the bathroom and locked the door, and I fell to my knees at the toilet and vomited, once, twice, three times. When my stomach was empty, I rinsed my mouth. I stared at myself in the mirror, but the man staring back was the stranger I had seen for days. Exhausted. Out of control, out of my mind. I didn't recognize who I was anymore.

From outside the bedroom, I heard a pounding on the door. "Mr. Moran?" Detective Bushing called.

"I'll be right out."

As soon as I said that, I went to the bathroom window. I slid it open silently and studied the walkway between my building and the neighbor's next door. I didn't see any police. As quietly as I could, I slithered through the opening and dropped to the concrete below me.

I grabbed hold of the adjacent fence and threw myself over.

Somewhere close by, the rottweiler began barking again. I heard voices, saw streams of light coming my way. A man shouted.

"Stop!"

I took off running and didn't look back.

CHAPTER 12

An early sunrise broke over the lake and made pink slashes in the clouds. I sat on a bench by the water at the far end of Navy Pier. The old brick pier building behind me was closed, and I had the boardwalk mostly to myself. On my left, overnight lights lingered in the downtown skyscrapers. The wind made whitecaps on the dark surface of the lake.

Physically, I was tired from running and from lack of sleep. I'd barely made it out of the neighborhood without being captured, but fortunately, I knew the area better than the police did, from my teenage days exploring the riverbank with Roscoe. I assumed they'd be looking for me throughout the city now. The serial killer, on the loose. Get him before he kills again.

A bus took me downtown. When I got off, I stopped at a twenty-four-hour convenience store to clean myself up. I assumed it wasn't safe to use any of my credit cards, but fortunately, my wallet was flush with cash. I shaved and washed my hair and sponged off the sweat. I bought a pair of sunglasses, but the whole effect didn't make for much of a disguise. From there, with my head down and my mind spinning, I walked the empty streets to the pier.

I'd been waiting for an hour now. I was getting nervous about staying in one place for so long. I'd called Eve Brier, but I didn't know if she would come, or whether she'd send the police after me instead.

But when I glanced down the pier, I saw her heading my way, her steps quick and determined.

She wore a knee-length navy-blue dress, which the fierce wind was playing with, plus the same dark trench coat she'd worn when we met in Grant Park. She had a beret tugged low on her forehead, and she had to keep it in place with one hand while her long hair swirled around her face. She sat down on the bench a couple of feet away from me, as if we were strangers, which we still were. At least to me. Her eyes were lost in the lake, but then she turned to stare at me with a passionate intensity.

"Tell me again what you said on the phone."

"Because you don't believe it?" I asked.

"That's right. I don't believe it, because it's impossible."

"Think that if you want, but there are *two* of me. Two Dylan Morans in the same world, sharing the same space. You brought him here."

"How do you know that?"

"Because he used your safe word to get away. *Infinite.*"

"My treatment couldn't possibly make that happen."

"I think you're wrong. I think your therapy opened the door, and somehow another Dylan Moran walked through it. He's a killer. The police showed me photographs of the women he killed. Four of them— all of them look just like Karly. Now he's gone somewhere else to do it again."

She reached out her long arm to stroke my hair, invading my personal space as if I were a pet. "I know you don't want to hear this, but maybe it's all *you.*"

"I'm not a killer. I'm many things, but I'm not that. Not in this world."

Eve took away her hand and looked off at the lake again. "If you're right about this, the implications are . . . disturbing."

"Why are you surprised? You said the whole point of this therapy was to create a bridge to other worlds."

"Yes, of course, but what you're talking about—"

"I'm talking about a Dylan Moran who is *dangerous*. Eve, you said that I came to you for treatment. If the Many Worlds theory is right, there are endless other Dylans going to you for the same treatment in other worlds. Imagine that this doppelgänger—this violent Dylan— became aware of what was happening. He interacted with one of your patients and followed him into a completely new world. Into a hunting ground. He could kill without worrying about getting caught, because all the evidence would point to the Dylan who really lived in that world. And he had an escape hatch whenever he wanted to leave. You. He's been using you to come and go, Eve. Who knows how many times he's already done this and in how many different worlds? It's the perfect crime."

Eve frowned. "What do you plan to do about it?"

"Follow him and stop him before he kills anyone else."

"Into the Many Worlds?"

"Yes."

She shook her head firmly. "You can't. The rules say that even if you find him, all the choices come into play. That means you can never stop him. There will always be a world where he gets away."

"Maybe, but the rules also say you can't jump between timelines. He's *breaking* the rules. For all we know, he's the only Dylan who has figured out how to do that."

"What if he stops *you*? What if you don't make it back?"

I stared at the city around me. My city. My home. "I'm done here, Eve. There's nothing for me anymore. Roscoe is gone. Karly is gone. When the police catch up to me, I'll spend the rest of my life in prison. It doesn't matter whether I come back."

"This won't work," Eve insisted. "You can't actually cross over to these worlds."

"Well, if I don't try it, some other Dylan will, right? You said that every choice comes into play. So it might as well be me. Did you bring the drugs?"

Eve glanced around the pier to make sure the two of us were alone. She reached into her handbag and extracted a small vial of clear liquid and a hypodermic needle. "This is what I use."

"How does this work?"

"Once I inject you, I guide you into the Many Worlds with hypnotic suggestion. You won't be aware of it happening."

"What are you giving me?"

"It's a cocktail of hallucinogens. I've been experimenting with the mix since college to find a balance that makes the brain most susceptible to alternate realities. That's the key, you see. We all grow up convinced that we know what reality is, and the only way to cross over is to break down that certainty. To open the mind to completely new possibilities."

"Lucy in the Sky with Diamonds," I said.

Eve gave me a tight smile. "In a way."

"What will it be like?"

"The first time can be overwhelming," she warned me. "Whatever it is you see with your eyes, what you're really doing is going to the inner depths of your brain. Like you're at a kind of Grand Central Station, where the various versions of yourself cross paths. I don't know what you'll see, but the sensory overload may well be too much for you. If it is, you know the safe word to get out."

"Infinite."

"That's right. If you say the word, it should break you out of wherever you are and end the session."

"And take me right back here?" I asked.

"It will take you somewhere. Beyond that, I don't know. I've always assumed that the Dylan I sent out into the void was the same Dylan who came back to me. But now I don't know if that's true. For all I know, some other Dylan will end up here on the bench with me in a few seconds. I won't be aware of it. And nothing else will seem to have changed."

"I hate to think that I'd be handing my bad choices to someone else," I said with a smile.

Eve's face turned severe. "Don't joke. You act like this situation can't get worse for you, Dylan. It can. It can get much worse. And remember, wherever you go, another Dylan is already there. It's *his* life, not yours."

"Meaning what?"

"Meaning you should remember what I said before. You might find yourself tempted to stay. You might want to kill that other version of yourself and take over his world."

"I'm not a killer," I insisted again.

"Are you sure?"

I didn't answer her. I stared at the sun, getting higher over the water. The city was coming to life. Soon people would be coming down the pier. Impatiently, I rolled up my sleeve. "Let's get on with it."

Eve readied the needle. She drew in the liquid from the vial and tapped the hypodermic with one of her fingernails. She slid closer to me on the bench and took hold of my wrist, pushing on the seam of my arm to find the vein. When she found it, she put the metal point against my skin.

"Last chance," she said.

"Do it."

I felt the puncture like the prick of a bee sting. She pushed the plunger down.

For a brief moment, the world stayed the same. Nothing happened. I was Dylan Moran, I was on Navy Pier, I was sitting on a bench with Dr. Eve Brier. A part of me was gripped by hesitation, wanting to hold on to this world, but it was too late to stop. My bloodstream carried the drug throughout my body, and it washed over me like a wave rolling across sand. I closed my eyes, and when I opened them again, I wasn't on the pier anymore. Wherever I was traveling, I was far away.

I heard a chorus, like a billion whispers, each one soft, but together so loud that I wanted to clap my hands over my ears. I saw nothing at first. Whiteness. Blackness. Then something took shape in front of me. Something physical. Something familiar. I saw a diner on a clean city street. It was late, and I could see bright lights through the window. A man sat alone at the counter, a lonely urban stranger. Suit. Fedora. His back was to me. Near him, but not with him, were two others, a man and a woman. He was in a suit like the first man. She had red hair and a red dress.

This wasn't real.

This was a painting that I'd seen thousands of times before.

I was in the Art Institute, staring at *Nighthawks*.

Chapter 13

"Sometimes I'll look at this painting for hours," a voice next to me said. "I don't know what it is, but it just sucks me inside. Funny story, actually. This painting wouldn't even be here if it weren't for my grandfather. When he was a kid, he accidentally bumped into the museum director and saved him from getting killed in a car accident. The director bought *Nighthawks* from Edward Hopper the next year."

I glanced at the man who was talking. He had a casual smile, which was not like my smile at all. He wore a gray collarless T-shirt with a few buttons at the neck. His stonewashed jeans were frayed. He had a full beard in serious need of a trim, and his brown hair was wildly messy, sticking up in a dozen places. I wouldn't have been caught dead looking like that, but regardless, it was me.

Me but not me. A double. A twin.

"I think I've heard that story before," I told him.

He looked at me, but his face showed no reaction, as if he saw nothing strange about encountering an exact likeness of himself. Or maybe he didn't even notice. "Oh, yeah? You've met Edgar? Well, he comes here a lot. He'll tell the story to anybody he meets."

"What about you?" I asked. "Do you come here a lot, too?"

"Me? Not so much anymore. I moved away from Chicago a couple of years ago. Too many people, too much winter. I tried to get Edgar to go with me, but he's a stubborn old mule, wouldn't leave the city. I'm on the sand near Cocoa now. Pick up odd jobs here and there, but it's all about the waves."

"Surfing?"

"Hell, yeah."

"Well, that's one way to live," I said, absolutely horrified.

"Yeah. Best thing I ever did." He stuck out his hand for me to shake. "Dylan Moran. Ex-Chicagoan turned beach bum."

"My name's Dylan, too," I replied.

"Small world."

"Very small."

I looked around at the rest of the museum. Every detail matched my memory, every painting looking as vivid as the original, every window in the skylight and every angled floorboard under my feet looking unchanged. It seemed impossible to me that my mind could replicate the entire museum in an instant, but here I was. Except where were all the other versions of myself?

Surfer Dylan and I were alone.

"I'm looking for someone," I said to him.

"Oh, yeah?"

"I was wondering if you'd seen him. Choppy dark hair, heavy five-o'clock shadow, mean smile. He likes to wear a beat-up old leather biker jacket with stains on it."

The other Dylan's smile disappeared. "Man, you don't want to find him. He's bad news."

"Yeah? Why is that?"

"Word gets around. That dude's trouble. Whatever you do, don't let him follow you out of here."

"Thanks for the advice."

I heard footsteps behind me. When I turned around, I saw another Dylan Moran walk into the gallery. This one had a completely shaved head, wore a black turtleneck, and had silver circular glasses on his face. Everything about him was neat and orderly. He wandered past us without a word to a nearby painting, Peter Blume's surrealistic *The Rock*. The centerpiece of the painting was a jagged sphere, like a pink geode cut open, around which men were laboring with hammers and stone slabs. A lone woman on her knees grasped for the sphere, as if worshipping it. Bald Dylan stood with perfect posture as he examined the painting, his hands folded together in front of him. Every now and then, he leaned forward to study a particular detail.

"This is a working man's painting," I said, joining him.

He studied me with a serious expression, but like Surfer Dylan, he showed no recognition that we were twins. "Yes, my father used to say this painting was about the ennoblement of the union man."

"I can't remember my father ever going to the museum."

"No? My father worked here until he retired. He was an art historian. Actually, the museum runs in the family in a way. *His* father was the reason we got *Nighthawks* here."

"Daniel Catton Rich? The car accident?"

"Oh, you've heard the story. Yes, that's right."

"Is your father still alive?" I asked.

"He is. We lost my mother last year, though. Cancer."

"I'm sorry."

"Well, her dying brought my father and me closer together. I don't think either one of us would have made it through that time without the other."

I tried to imagine a world in which my father hadn't killed my mother. A world in which they'd both been with me as I grew up, in which my father didn't drink and took me places and made me a part of his life. I knew nothing else about this Dylan next to me, but I already knew that I envied him.

I began to understand what Eve Brier had warned me about.

You might be tempted to stay.

Around me, more Dylans arrived at the museum. Half a dozen. Twenty. Forty. I soon lost count. They were all completely different and yet all the same. They wore different clothes. Some had beards; some didn't. Some were heavier than me, some skinnier. One was in a wheelchair. One had an artificial right leg. Some looked almost identical to me, just a few little changes to tell me that a part of their life was different from mine.

But I saw no Dylan wearing my father's leather jacket.

I wandered through the museum as it got more and more crowded. We kept bumping into each other, all the Dylan Morans squeezed into every wing. Near the *American Gothic* display, I saw one Dylan stop in the middle of the gallery as others streamed around him. He was dressed exactly the way I was, in a slightly rumpled blazer, dirty slacks, and loose tie. Tears streamed down his reddened face, and his chest heaved with despair.

"Are you okay?" I asked.

His mouth fell open. He unleashed a guttural cry that was pure agony. He stared at me, consumed by pain. "Karly's *dead*."

The words nearly knocked me over. "Yes, I know. I'm sorry."

"I can't live without her. I can't."

Tragic Dylan reached into the pocket of his suit coat and removed an automatic pistol, which he armed by racking the slide. Instinctively, I took a step backward and put my hands up.

"Dylan, put the gun away."

He shook his head and continued to sob. As I watched, he opened his mouth and closed his lips around the barrel of the gun. His hand quivered as he slid his finger onto the trigger. Mucus dripped from his nose, and drool leaked onto the barrel. His screwed-up face looked like a version of *The Scream*, as if he were one more painting in the museum.

"Dylan, *no*! No, don't do it!" I looked around at the others; there were hundreds of them now. "Somebody help over here!"

But no one stopped. No one even noticed the drama playing out.

The Dylan in front of me squeezed the trigger. The bullet blew out the back of his skull, spraying the Dylans behind him with bone, blood, and brain matter. They didn't react; they just kept walking with their clothes and faces covered with the remains of another man's head. Tragic Dylan crumpled to the floor in front of me. The others walked on top of him as if he wasn't there at all. Blood spread into a pool on the museum's wooden floor, getting on everyone's shoes.

I shoved through the crowd, because I had to get away from here. I needed air, but my surroundings grew claustrophobic as the room filled with more Dylans. I had to fight my way forward, wrestling people aside. All the Dylans around me did the same thing, each one seemingly oblivious to the others.

Finally, in the atrium near the museum's grand staircase, I found a railing where I could lean and catch my breath. The marble statue of *Samson and the Lion* loomed immediately behind me. Blinding sunshine poured through the skylights overhead. The atrium was filled with a strange sound, a susurrus made up of tiny noises—clothing brushing together, heels tapping on stone—that combined into a deafening assault on my senses. I wanted to shut it out, because it was simply so *loud*, but covering my ears did nothing to quiet the tumult.

Eve had warned me about this part of the experience, too. The first time was overwhelming.

I was tempted to say it. *Infinite.* Say the word, and this chaos would be over. I'd go back to my version of reality, where there was only one of me. But it was a reality where Karly was dead and I was wanted for murder.

Then I looked down.

I saw him.

Where the four staircases from the museum's top floor converged on a square landing below me, I saw a single Dylan among a thousand others, standing absolutely motionless. The others yielded to give him space. The sea of doubles parted around him.

He wore my father's jacket.

As I stared down at him, he looked up and saw me. His sea-blue eyes were clear and cold. His lips formed a smile of cruel, violent intent as he recognized me. We knew each other. A wave of sadism engulfed me, and I knew *this* was the man who'd whispered to me near the river, who'd hidden inside my bedroom closet and confessed his crimes to the police, who'd stabbed the hearts of at least four women who looked like Karly.

Not an endless number of killers named Dylan Moran.

Just one man. This one. The man who'd figured out how to break the rules.

I shouted. *"Stop him! Hold him!"*

No one did. He headed down the steps, as a new path opened up in the crowd ahead of him. I tried to run, to follow him, to chase him, but I was trapped and couldn't move. The crush of Dylan Morans held me where I was, and they showed no reaction as I screamed for them to get out of my way. The staircase, like the railing where I stood, teemed with doubles. I had nowhere to go. Below me, my doppelgänger disappeared from view. If I didn't get to him now, he'd be gone, out the door into another world, where I would never be able to find him.

I took hold of the railing with both hands. To free a tiny bit of space, I kicked hard to my right, driving the other Dylans back, and then I did the same on my left. When I had a few inches in which to move, I swung my legs over the second floor railing and jumped. It wasn't far, but far enough to feel as if I were diving from a cliff. My body accelerated, and then I landed hard on the crowd below me, scattering Dylans like bowling pins. They cushioned the blow. I fell, got up, lowered my shoulder, and charged down the last few steps like Walter Payton.

Over the heads of the others, I saw the museum doors. Through the glass, the sun let in a blinding light. I didn't know if the doors led to Michigan Avenue and the sculpted lions guarding the museum entrance, or to someplace else entirely. But the doors led out of here.

They were the gateway out of the many minds of Dylan Moran, and like a vast parade, my doubles were leaving one at a time. The doors opened. The doors closed. One by one, they headed to different worlds.

I could see *him*. Waiting for his moment.

He stood beside the doors, watching each person leave, studying them up and down, as if he were trying to judge the perfect Dylan for the next perfect crime.

I thrashed toward him, shouting across the mass of people who blocked my way. He saw me coming, but he made no effort to escape. He watched me with stoic, evil curiosity, a wolf puzzled by the charge of a dog. I got closer and closer. I didn't care about the others around me. I pushed, kicked, swung my fists, and opened up a trail like a pioneer chopping down one tree at a time.

When I was six feet away, with only a few bodies left between me and him, everything happened at once.

One of the Dylan Morans reached the glass doors. This Dylan looked a lot like me: same haircut, same blazer, as if he'd come to meet Edgar in front of *Nighthawks* and was now heading back to the LaSalle Plaza Hotel. The only real difference I could see between us, when he lifted his arm to open the door, was that he wore no ring on his right hand. Me, I'd worn Roscoe's high school class ring there ever since the accident.

I wondered where our choices had split.

I wondered what road he'd taken in life that diverged from the one I'd traveled.

I didn't have time to think about it. The door opened, and a wave of fresh air blew inside, along with noises of the city. Somewhere out there was Chicago. The Dylan without Roscoe's ring disappeared into the white light, and as he did, the Dylan in the leather coat winked and stepped across the threshold in the wake of the other man.

Whatever you do, don't let him follow you out of here.

The door began to swing shut behind them. I knew, somehow I knew, that when the door closed, the world on the other side of it was sealed off from me forever, just one universe among billions, and I'd never find it again.

I sprinted across the remaining space and left my feet in a desperate leap. My body tumbled through the door just as it closed, and the light around me got brighter and hotter, as if I were diving into the sun.

And then there was nothing. No city. No Chicago.

Nothing at all.

CHAPTER 14

"Hey, buddy."

I heard the words through a fog in my head, but I didn't want to wake up. I was caught in a dream.

"Hey, buddy, come on, get up. You can't sleep here."

My eyes blinked open slowly, and I tried to focus. Gradually, my senses caught up with my mind. I lay on my back, outside, with the summer sun high in the sky. Somewhere close by, I heard the screech of seagulls and a clamor of children's voices. The air around me had a strange, sick-sweet smell of body odor and cotton candy. As I turned my head and my face got close to my clothes, I realized that the source of the body odor was probably me.

A man leaned over me, blocking out part of the sky. "Up, up. Come on, let's go."

I pushed my stiff limbs until I was sitting up, fighting off a wave of dizziness. My muscles ached, as if I'd been motionless for hours. I winced as I massaged my neck, and I looked around with a terrible feeling of disappointment. Nothing around me had changed. I was still on the same bench at Navy Pier.

Even worse, the man standing in front of me was a Chicago police officer. He was medium height and stout, with wiry red hair and florid cheeks. "You got some ID, buddy?"

My mouth felt gritty. I tried to talk through the dryness. "Um, yeah. Yeah, sure."

I dug around in my pockets and found my wallet, and rather than fumbling for my driver's license, I simply handed him the whole thing. He opened it, and I tensed as he read my name. I didn't know if the search for Dylan Moran had made its way to every street cop yet.

The police officer made no effort to pull his gun or his handcuffs. His mouth mushed into a frown as he tried to make sense of me. I probably had the hygiene of a vagrant, but my wallet contained the identification and credit cards of a downtown professional. "Dylan Moran? Is that you?"

"Yes, that's me."

"You okay, Mr. Moran? You don't look like you're having a good day."

"You're right. I'm not."

"The thing is, parents don't like to see homeless people sleeping on benches when their kids are around here. You made them nervous. A couple folks thought you were dead."

I tried to smile. "I'm not dead."

"You need help or anything? A doctor?"

"No, thanks. It's just the aftereffects of a rowdy office party, I guess. I don't remember a lot of it."

"Well, next time you want to tie one on, party on the buddy system, okay? You get drunk, make sure somebody knows where you are. When you crash out on a bench down here, you're likely to get rolled, know what I mean?"

"I do. Thank you, Officer. I'll be heading home now."

"Good plan. A shower might not be the worst thing, either."

"Yeah."

I got to my feet, wobbling as I did, and offered the cop a weak smile. I wasn't really ready to move, and I didn't know where to go, but I didn't want to linger in case he got the idea of calling in my name and having it bounce back with a red flag. A few tourists on the pier looked at me curiously. Suspicious mothers tugged their children a little closer. I tightened my tie for whatever good it did, wiped some of the dirt off my sleeves and pants, and headed toward the city. When I checked my watch, I saw that it was already past noon. Several hours had passed since my early-morning rendezvous with Eve Brier.

As far as I could tell, having Eve inject me with her hallucinatory drugs had accomplished nothing, other than giving me a weird dream and a splitting headache. I didn't know why I'd expected anything else. In the harsh light of day, the idea of jumping between worlds inside my head sounded like what it was. Impossible. And yet if I was wrong about my doppelgänger, I also couldn't explain the murders of Scotty Ryan and four innocent women.

Meanwhile, Eve herself was nowhere to be found. She'd injected me and then left me alone, which made me wonder if she'd hoped that I would never awaken. I dug out my phone and dialed her number. I wanted to tell her I was still here, still in trouble. However, the call didn't go through. I didn't get her voice mail; instead, a recording told me that the number was out of service.

Eve had disconnected her phone.

Her message couldn't be more obvious: she didn't want me anywhere near her.

When I got to the end of Navy Pier, I stayed by the water, heading toward the downtown skyline. The trouble was, I didn't know what to do when I got there. Wherever I went, the police would be looking for me. A part of me thought about turning myself in, but I had no idea what to tell them. I had no way to prove that I wasn't what they thought I was.

A killer.

As I stared out at the water, debating my next move, my phone rang in my hand. When I checked, I saw Edgar's name on the caller ID. I answered the phone hesitantly—Edgar almost never called me—but I heard my grandfather's unmistakably raspy voice on the other end.

"Hey, where are you?" he demanded.

"Why, what do you need, Edgar?"

"I'm here at the Art Institute. Where are you?"

"Edgar, we just did that yesterday. We meet on Thursdays, remember?"

"It *is* Thursday."

I sighed. It wasn't uncommon for my grandfather to get his days mixed up. On the other hand, I was also suspicious that the police had arranged this call for me as a trap. "Stay put, I'll be there in twenty minutes," I told him. Then I added, "Was anything happening at home when you left?"

"Like what?"

"Like police in the neighborhood."

"Well, yeah, a cop said they were trying to find you."

"What did you tell them?"

"I told them I didn't know where you were."

"Did you say you were going to meet me?"

"No. What you do is your business, not mine. You've made that pretty clear over the years."

He wasn't wrong about that.

"Okay, Edgar. I'll be there as soon as I can."

I hung up the phone.

Meeting Edgar felt like an ordinary day in an ordinary life, but nothing about my world was ordinary anymore. I walked briskly toward the museum, along sidewalks I'd taken throughout my life. It would have been faster to take a cab, but I wanted to preserve my cash for when I really needed it.

When I was back in the heart of the city, I cut through Millennium Park, passing the Pritzker Pavilion, where the wide-open stretch of green grass was crowded with people eating picnic lunches. On the sidewalks, every bench was taken. I passed an old man who was reading a copy of the *Chicago Tribune*, and he'd left the front section on the bench next to him. My eyes went to the headlines automatically, and I spotted a notice on the very top of the page about the Cubs completing a three-game home sweep of the Phillies. That made me stop in surprise. Not just because the Cubs had swept anybody. No, if there's one thing I keep a close eye on, it's Cubs baseball, and I knew they weren't supposed to be hosting Philadelphia until next week.

Then I glanced at the date on the paper and saw that it *was* next week.

It was Thursday, just as Edgar had said. I didn't understand how that was possible. Somehow, I'd lost almost an entire week of my life after my encounter with Eve, and I remembered none of it.

I thought about her question: *Have you been having blackouts, Dylan?*

Up until that moment, I would have said no, but I'd sat next to Eve Brier on Navy Pier in the early hours of Friday morning. Now it was six days later, and I had no idea what had happened in between.

The old man on the bench looked up from the sports pages. "Help you?"

"I was wondering if you'd finished the front section of the paper."

His eyes narrowed as he studied the state of my clothes, but then he shrugged. "Yeah, take it. I'd just throw it away."

"Thank you."

I took the front section with me and kept walking until I found an empty bench. I sat down and ripped through the pages, not even sure what I was looking for. Somehow, I wanted to believe that I'd made a mistake. Or maybe I hoped I would see a news article that would trigger my memories of the past several days. Instead, the stories confirmed that events in the world had gone on without me. Nearly a week had passed, and I hadn't been here to see it.

With my headache getting worse, I closed the paper.

That was when I noticed an article in the lower left corner of the front page. The headline jumped out at me:

Woman Stabbed to Death in River Park

I didn't have to read far to discover that the murder had taken place two days ago, barely a hundred yards from my apartment. The body had been found in the dense trees on the riverbank by a couple of teenagers who were exploring the trails, the way Roscoe and I used to do.

The victim's name was Betsy Kern. Twenty-seven years old. She was an IT programmer who'd gone out for a nighttime run and never come back. The boys had stumbled upon her body the next day.

There was a picture of Betsy Kern accompanying the article. I didn't know this woman, but I spotted the resemblance immediately.

She looked just like Karly.

I felt a strange nervousness walking into the Art Institute. Part of me expected to find a seething mass of Dylan Morans inside, the way I had in my drug-addled dream. Instead, all I found was the usual crowd of visitors. Even so, when I climbed the grand staircase to the second floor, I had a vision of jumping from the balcony that felt so vivid it seemed like more than a nightmare. I even noticed that I felt a sharp pain in my ankle, as if I'd sustained some kind of fall in real life.

Upstairs, Edgar was waiting in the gallery. He had his hands cupped behind his back, holding his cane, his pants hiked high on his waist, in the way that old men do.

"Hey, Edgar," I said.

He harrumphed at my late arrival, and we both stared silently at the characters populating Edward Hopper's diner. After a while, Edgar's mood improved enough that he told me his usual story about Daniel Catton Rich, which I listened to as if I'd never heard it before. As we stood there, other people came and went to admire *Nighthawks*.

"So you said the police were looking for me?" I murmured when we were finally alone again. "Did they tell you why?"

"Nope. They just said that you were missing. I wasn't worried. I figured you'd turn up sooner or later."

"Did they say how long?"

Edgar shrugged. "Couple of days."

My brow furrowed. "That's all? Not like a week?"

"How could it be a week? We had dinner on Monday."

"You *saw* me on Monday?"

Edgar stared at me through eyes that were sunk into the bags on his face. "You got bats in your belfry, kid? Of course I did. You brought in fried rice and chop suey from Sam Lee's."

I shook my head. "Edgar, Sam Lee's closed six years ago."

"Well, wherever, some Chinese place. I thought it was Sam Lee."

"You're sure it was Monday? Three days ago?"

"I know you think I'm losing my marbles, but yeah, it was Monday. Shit, Dylan, what's wrong with you?"

I ignored his question, even though I was wondering the same thing. "Was I acting normal? Did I tell you about anything strange going on?"

"We didn't talk. You and me never talk, remember? We watched the Cubs beat up the Phillies and ate chop suey. I got a fortune cookie that said, 'Love is a four-letter word, but so is hell.' I laughed so hard I snorted."

I shook my head. Three days ago.

Three days ago, I was awake, conscious, and having dinner with my grandfather. If the police were looking to pick me up, why didn't they do it then? Why didn't I *remember* any of it?

And where had I been for the past two days?

I was quiet for another long stretch. More people came and went to stare at the painting. I thought about what Edgar had said: *We didn't talk. You and me never talk.* That was true. We'd been hostile strangers since I was a teenager.

"Can I ask you something?"

Edgar didn't say yes, but he didn't say no, either. So I plunged ahead.

"What happened to my dad? Did you see it coming?"

Edgar looked at me as if I'd started speaking a foreign language. We never talked, and we definitely never talked about *that*. He chewed on the question like it was a bad shrimp, and I didn't know if he'd actually say anything or just pretend that I'd never even brought it up.

"No," he told me finally. "No, I never saw it coming. Your dad was an angry drunk, I knew that. And things were bad between him and your mother. But I never thought he'd go that far. Definitely not."

"Do you hate him for it?"

Edgar sighed. "Hating my son's not in the rulebook for parents. No matter what he did."

"Well, I hate him. I hate that I've lived my whole life afraid of *becoming* him. Every time I get angry, I think, 'This is the moment when I snap.'"

"You? Snap?" Edgar snorted. "I'd like to see that."

"What do you mean?"

"I mean, a turtle's more likely to walk out of his shell than you."

"Are you kidding?" I practically laughed at the absurdity of that comment. I couldn't imagine Edgar saying something like that about me. The kid who'd argued with him at the top of his lungs practically every day of his teenage life. The kid whose fighting nearly got him kicked out of school half a dozen times. If I was afraid of my temper, it was only because it had gotten the best of me so often.

"Kidding?" Edgar retorted. "Hell, no. Yeah, it was awful what your father did, but I think the worst thing was that it turned you into a god-damn robot. Face it, Dylan, you run away from emotion before it has a chance to get anywhere close to you. I thought maybe you'd change when you got married, but you froze her out, too."

"That's not true. I only froze her out over the affair, and that's because I couldn't stand the idea of being angry with her."

Edgar shook his head. "Affair? What affair?"

I realized I had never told him what Karly had done. "It's not important. Not anymore."

"Look, Dylan, you feeling sick or something? You're not looking good."

"Yeah, I'm a little out of it. Sorry."

I shut up at that point. My experiment in opening up to Edgar hadn't exactly gone smoothly, and I didn't need to argue with my grandfather on top of everything else that was going wrong in my life. I let him go back to *Nighthawks*.

That was when I felt my phone buzzing in my pocket. A text had come in. I checked it and saw that there was no caller ID associated with the number. Whoever was reaching out to me was anonymous.

I read the message and didn't like it.

Meet me at the Horner Park house. We need to talk.

CHAPTER 15

The house across from Horner Park, where the police thought I'd killed Scotty Ryan, looked deserted. I stayed in the back of the park's baseball field, which gave me a view of the entire street. No one watched the house from any of the parked cars, and I saw no one who resembled an undercover cop. If this was a trap, they'd done a good job of concealing it.

There was no police tape around the house, which surprised me. Then again, a week had passed since the murder, and no doubt the owners wanted to get back inside their house. They'd also taken down the FOR SALE sign; there was no large poster for Chance Properties outside. Crime scenes didn't exactly fly on the Chicago real estate market.

I waited to make sure I was right about the lack of surveillance. Then I made my way across the street, still on the lookout for police, still ready to run. As I approached the house, I cursed silently, because of all the people I could meet, I spotted the same elderly woman walking her Westie who'd seen me after the fight. I doubted that she'd forgotten me or the blood on my hands. There was nothing I could do, so I gave her my friendliest I-am-not-a-serial-killer smile. We both stood outside the house's white picket fence.

She smiled at me with no obvious recognition. "Hello."

"Hi," I replied. "That's a sweet dog you've got there."

"Thank you, yes, he's a doll. Did you buy this house? Are you the new owner?"

"Me? No."

"Oh, well, we all heard it was a young man. I wanted to welcome him to the neighborhood."

"No, sorry, it wasn't me."

"All right. Well, you have a nice day."

"You too."

That was that. She waited while her dog lifted his leg at the boulevard tree, and then she continued down the street. I watched to see if she would look over her shoulder at me, but she didn't.

New owner? The house had already sold?

I didn't know what to make of that.

I let myself in through the gate. On the walkway, I studied the windows, but no one looked out at me. I checked the street again and then went up to the front door and rang the bell. There was no answer, even when I rang twice more and pounded on the door. With my apprehension growing, I turned the knob. The door was open.

"Is anyone home?" I called. "Hello?"

I got no reply.

The house still smelled as it had when I was last here, of sweet cut wood. A fine layer of sawdust coated everything. I went into the living room, where Scotty and I had argued. Somehow I expected to see a chalk outline marking the location of a body, with bloodstains dried on the plastic sheeting, but there was nothing like that. I saw no evidence that a crime had been committed here.

"Hello?" I called again. "It's Dylan Moran. I got a note to meet someone here."

Still no response. The house was empty.

I ventured deeper inside. There was no furniture. Everything had been removed. With each step, I listened for a noise to suggest that someone was hiding, but I heard nothing. I checked every room on the ground level, and then, with only the slightest hesitation, I went upstairs to the second floor.

The door to the master bedroom was closed.

I approached it with soft footfalls and knocked. "Is anyone there?"

I tensed, then opened the door. For some reason, I had visions of finding a body inside, but I was wrong. No one was here. However, the bedroom, unlike the rest of the house, showed signs of life. Someone was living and sleeping here. There were open moving boxes strewed across the floor, and a mattress with a rumpled blanket lay below the windows. When I glanced in the bathroom, I saw a towel bunched over the shower rod and a lineup of male toiletries on the sink.

It was time to go. I'd stayed here long enough.

I headed to the stairs, but before I got there, I heard the front door open below me. Seconds later, footsteps crinkled on the plastic sheeting in the living room. I tried to decide what to do. Announce myself, or slip downstairs and get away. I put a foot on the top step, but when I shifted my weight, a loose nail squealed, sounding loud in the quiet house. Immediately, I heard more footsteps heading my way.

The foyer below me was in shadow. A man emerged from the downstairs hallway, and I couldn't identify him at first, but when he got to the bottom of the stairs, he turned around. Seeing who it was shocked me into silence.

Standing at the base of the stairs was a dead man.

Scotty Ryan.

He didn't look at all surprised to see me, and his face broke into an easy smile. "Hey, buddy, you got my message? What do you think of the place?"

"Scotty," I managed to choke out from my chest. I thought about saying something stupid: *You're alive.* But I held my tongue even as my mind whirled.

"Come on down, I'll get you a beer," he said.

Whistling some kind of country song, Scotty disappeared toward the kitchen. I steadied myself and continued downstairs. I went back into the living room and examined it all over again. There comes a time in most dreams when you realize you're dreaming, but that wasn't how this felt. I almost said the word out loud to see what would happen.

Infinite.

But I didn't. I needed to see what came next.

Scotty returned with two bottles of Goose Island in his hand. He gave me one and clinked the neck of his bottle against mine. "Cheers. Good to see you, man. So where were you last night? I kept texting you from the bar. Hell of a game, huh? Ten to one. Suck it, Phillies."

I looked into Scotty's eyes to see why he was pretending that we were friends. Pretending that nothing had happened between us. Pretending he hadn't slept with my wife. I glanced at my hand and saw the raw bruises and scrapes on my knuckles where I'd swung my fist into his face. Then I realized: *His* face had no damage at all. His lips should be cut and swollen. He'd lost a tooth. I was sure I'd broken his nose. But there was no evidence of a fight.

Scotty swigged his beer and gestured around the house. "Can't believe it's all mine. Never thought I'd be able to afford a place in the city. I mean, it needs work, but it's nice to be able to remodel my own house for a change."

"It's great," I said, because I had no idea what to say.

"Isn't it? Total fluke that I found it. I was redoing a kitchen down the street, and I noticed the FOR SALE sign over here. Went in and looked around, and I thought, perfect. Love the location, love the park. With the money my uncle left me, I had enough for the down payment. So now we're neighbors, sort of. What is it, half an hour's walk to your place?"

"Yeah."

Scotty's face scrunched with puzzlement, as if he was noticing my condition for the first time. "Everything okay? You seem kind of out of it today."

"I'm fine."

"Why'd you miss the game last night?"

"I was pretty tired."

Scotty drank his beer and eyed me thoughtfully. "That all it is?"

"What else would it be?"

"I don't know, there's something different about you today. I can't put my finger on it. You're not acting like yourself. You and I have been friends a long time, Dylan. If something's going on, you can tell me about it."

"There's nothing to tell," I replied.

But I wanted to say: *No, we haven't been friends for a long time.* I barely knew Scotty Ryan. We'd met a handful of times when I was visiting Karly at one of her listings and Scotty was doing construction work for her. He and she went back for years, but he and I didn't. I didn't watch Cubs games with him at the bar. I didn't even particularly like him. In fact, at the moment, I had every reason to hate him.

There's something different about you today.

I thought about Edgar telling me that I'd spent my whole life with my emotions shut off, when in reality, the opposite was true.

I thought about the old woman with her dog on the street, who didn't remember me, even after telling the police that I'd killed a man.

Most of all, I thought about Scotty and the fact that *he was supposed to be dead.* But he wasn't. There had been no knife plunged into his heart. There hadn't even been a fight between us. I hadn't changed, but everything else had. I'd been slow to realize it, but the world around me *was* different. I wasn't in the Chicago I'd left behind. I was somewhere new.

I'd gone through the door at the Art Institute into the life of an entirely different Dylan Moran. A man the police were looking for. A man who had been missing for two days.

Where was he?

"What did you want to talk to me about?" I asked Scotty, remembering his message.

He put down his beer bottle in midswallow. "Oh, yeah. I finished up the drawings for the remodel on your bathroom. You're going to love it. Travertine tiles, body sprays in the shower, recessed lighting. All I need are some decisions on the cabinetry, and I'll be ready to get started."

"Oh. Okay."

"I pulled pages from the catalog to give you an idea of your options. Doors, knobs, roll-out trays, that kind of thing. I can do all the drawers with a soft close, too."

"Sure."

"Take it home and talk to the missus, and then let me know what you guys want to do."

I almost stopped breathing. "My wife."

"Right. I can start next week if you want. My job in Oak Park finished early."

I heard it in my head again: *My wife.*

"Dylan?" Scotty said, his voice sounding far away.

My wife, my wife, my wife . . .

"Jesus, buddy, you're white as a sheet," he went on.

"Scotty, I have to go."

"Sure. Okay. Let me gather up the plans and catalog, and you can take everything with you."

I pushed the bottle of beer into his hand and backed away. "No, I have to go now," I said again. "Right now."

"Dylan? Hey, what's up?"

But I was already out the door.

My head throbbed. I felt a tightness in my chest, and my breath came in sharp, ragged bursts. I kept repeating a mantra to myself that this was real, that this wasn't a dream, but I didn't dare allow myself to believe it. I didn't even want to blink, because I was afraid that closing my eyes would take me back to my old life.

I *wanted* it to be true.

I wanted that more than anything else I'd ever prayed for in my life.

I started walking, but the pace of walking felt glacial. I pushed past people who were going too slowly, ignoring their comments when I bumped into them. Soon I was running. I sprinted north past the park and then into the quiet, leafy streets of Ravenswood Manor. I ran full out all the way until Lawrence Avenue, where I finally had to stop and bend over, gasping for air. When I could breathe again, I crossed the river.

I was only a few blocks from home. This time, I didn't run. I measured out each step, because I wasn't sure what I would find when I got to my door. I didn't want to face the reality of being wrong.

My wife.

I walked through a neighborhood I'd known my entire life. Nothing looked different. The buildings were all the same. I could tell you the names of most of the people behind those doors, and I wondered if they'd led identical lives to what I remembered or whether they'd taken different paths in this world.

Ahead of me, I saw the green lawn of River Park, half a block from my apartment. *Our* apartment. Only one dark cloud passed quickly through my mind. I remembered the headline in the newspaper about a young blond woman on the trails there two nights ago, the last night of her life. Someone had put a knife in her heart and murdered her.

The Killer Dylan I was chasing was already here. My doppelgänger in the leather jacket had struck again. He'd killed a woman who looked just like Karly.

I thought: *Or was it me?*

I didn't remember this woman, but I remembered nothing from those missing days.

There was our building. I stopped, cupping my hands in front of my face, breathing hard. I walked up the sidewalk the way I had thousands of times, since I was a teenager. I wondered if I could simply use my key and let myself inside. Would the locks be the same? My phone still worked, so it seemed as if some of the little details followed me across worlds.

But I rang the doorbell anyway. I wanted her to come to the door. I wanted to see her face.

Seconds passed. Interminable seconds. Then I saw a shadow on the other side of the glass.

The door opened, and there was my wife.

It wasn't Karly. It was Tai.

CHAPTER 16

"Oh, thank God!" Tai exclaimed, throwing her arms around me. "Dylan, I was so worried. Where have you been?"

I tried to hide my crushing disappointment. My body was stiff as I hugged her back. She went to kiss me, and instinctively I turned my face, making her kiss my cheek instead of my lips. I saw confusion in her eyes, but she let it go, took my hand tightly, and pulled me into our apartment.

It looked nothing like I remembered. None of the furniture that Karly and I had bought was here. No more sleek grays and blues on the walls, no more gliders where we'd drink wine and coffee, no more plush rug by the fireplace to make love. The style now reflected Tai's taste, with enough ferns and hanging planters to turn the apartment into a rain forest. A handwoven mat with a geometric pattern lay in front of the hearth, looking hard and uninviting. The chairs were made of wood and wicker. If I hated anything when it came to furniture, it was wicker.

This was not my home. And yet it was. Photographs crowded the mantel, all of them showing me and Tai in places I couldn't imagine being. The two of us side by side in front of Cinderella's castle in the Magic Kingdom. The two of us wearing leis near the firepit of a Hawaiian luau. Me in a tux, her in a wedding dress. Husband and wife. Instinctively, I shook my head at the idea of any of this happening. Tai was smart and sweet, and she was a friend, and I wanted her to be happy. But I couldn't imagine a world where I'd fallen in love with her and married her.

Except I was in that world right now.

When I didn't say anything, Tai put both hands on my face. "Dylan, are you okay? Do you have any idea how terrified I've been? You've been gone almost two days."

"Yes, I know."

"Not a call, not a text, nothing. You didn't show up at work. Your phone was off. I've been trying to reach you. I had visions of you being dead somewhere."

"I'm sorry."

"Do you need a doctor? You look terrible."

"No, I'll be all right."

"Dylan, what *happened* to you? Where have you been?"

I didn't have time to formulate a lie. A knock on the door interrupted us. Tai kissed me quickly, on the lips this time, and then she hurried to the outside door. I heard voices, and when Tai returned, she was with a man I recognized immediately. I couldn't let on that I knew who he was, because in this world, we were strangers.

The tall skeletal man was Detective Harvey Bushing. He didn't seem to have changed. When he looked at me with those sunken eyes, I thought he could see right through me and guess everything that I was hiding. I felt like running, the way I had when we first met, when he accused me of multiple murders. I had to remind myself: *He doesn't know about any of that.* For him, in this place, none of that had actually happened.

Except for a murder a hundred yards away in River Park.

I was no fool. I'd been missing for two days, and a woman named Betsy Kern had been killed near my house two nights ago. Detective Bushing wasn't going to consider that a coincidence.

He introduced himself, and we shook hands again, his grip as dry and limp as it had been the first time.

"It's good to see you home safe and sound, Mr. Moran," Bushing told me. "I was just coming over to see if your wife had heard from you, and here you are."

"Good timing, Detective. Yes, here I am."

"I'm sure I don't need to tell you that your wife was pretty panicked."

"Of course she was."

He smiled at both of us, showing yellowed teeth that could have used a good orthodontist when he was a kid. "How about we all sit down? I'm very curious to know where you've been."

"I'm actually pretty tired, Detective, and I could use a shower. Could we do this tomorrow?"

"This won't take long, Mr. Moran. Please." He said it in a way that didn't give me any room to say no.

The detective took a seat on one of the wicker chairs. I sat uncomfortably on a sofa near the window, and Tai sat beside me and put her hand over mine. As she caressed me, her fingers rolled over Roscoe's ring on my hand, and I saw her glance at it with surprise.

"Since when do you wear that?" she asked.

I shrugged. "I found it in a drawer. It's from high school."

An unsettled look passed across Tai's face. She was the kind of woman who noticed things like jewelry and clothes; her eye for detail was what made her a good events manager. I'm sure she was thinking that she would have spotted that ring on my finger long before now.

"So Mr. Moran," Detective Bushing said. "Fill us in. Where have you been for the past couple of days?"

I needed to sound convincing as I made up a story, so I used a story that was at least partly true.

"To be honest, Detective, I don't know. I woke up a few hours ago on Navy Pier, and I have no idea how I got there. I was shocked to discover that I'd been gone for so long. I have no recollection of what happened in between."

"Navy Pier?" Bushing asked. "Really?"

"Yes. I was sleeping on a bench. Actually, a police officer woke me up. I'm sure he made a note of it."

"Navy Pier is more than ten miles from here. How did you get there? Did you walk? Take a bus? Did someone take you there?"

"As I said, I don't remember."

"Well, what's your last memory?" Bushing asked.

I hesitated, because nothing that had actually happened in this world meant anything to me. "Everything is pretty blurry. I remember I had dinner with my grandfather on Monday night. Chinese food."

"But nothing after that?"

"I don't think so."

Bushing focused on Tai. "When did you say your husband left home?"

"Tuesday evening around nine. He was going to take a walk in the park."

He turned to me again. "You don't remember that, Mr. Moran?"

"No."

"Do you remember anything at all from that evening?"

"Not a thing."

"Have you ever had a blackout like this before?"

"Never."

"Were you drinking that night?"

Tai interrupted. "My husband rarely drinks. The occasional beer or glass of wine, and that's all. On Tuesday, I made Filipino food for dinner, and we had salabat with it. That's ginger tea."

I was surprised to learn that, in this world, Dylan Moran had no problems with alcohol. He'd also shut down his emotions and his temper. And he'd married Tai. Different man. Different choices.

"Do you usually follow a particular route when you walk?" Bushing asked.

"No, not really."

"Did you see anyone?"

"I already told you, I don't remember. If Tai says I left the house to go for a walk, that's what I did. But after that, I have no memory until I found myself on that bench near the lake."

Detective Bushing dug into the inside pocket of his ill-fitting sport coat and extracted a piece of paper. He unfolded it and handed it to me, and I saw a photograph that matched the picture I'd seen on the front page of the *Tribune*. It was the woman who'd been killed in River Park.

"Do you recognize this woman?" he asked me.

I shook my head. "No."

"She doesn't look familiar at all?"

"No."

"Have you ever seen her around the neighborhood?"

"I told you, no. Who is she?"

Tai murmured near my ear. "She was murdered."

I pasted surprise on my face. "Murdered? That's terrible."

"In fact, she was stabbed to death in River Park on Tuesday night, Mr. Moran," Detective Bushing went on. "Her roommate said she went out for a run, right around the same time that you took a walk. Same time, same night, same park. Her body was found the next morning. You can understand why your disappearance was of considerable concern to us, Mr. Moran. Two people in the park, one dead, one missing. I can't help but wonder if whatever happened to you was somehow connected to the murder."

"I wish I could help you, Detective. I didn't know this woman, and I don't remember anything about Tuesday night."

The detective's eyes shifted to my left hand. He took note of the purplish bruises. "What happened to your hand, Mr. Moran?"

I wiggled my fingers, because they still hurt. "I don't know."

"You don't remember how you injured yourself?"

"No."

"It looks like you hit someone."

Next to me, Tai laughed. "Dylan? Hit someone? That's ridiculous."

"I wish I could tell you what happened, Detective, but I can't." Then I added impatiently, "Is that all?"

"Yes, that's all I have for now. If you do remember anything, please call me right away. Oh, and I wonder if you'd mind if I bagged the clothes you're wearing and took them with me for analysis."

"My clothes? Why?"

"Well, I'd like to run forensic tests that might fill in some of the blanks in your memory. For all we know, you may have seen the murder taking place and tried to intercede. If you were involved in some kind of fight in the park, perhaps the person you struggled with left behind traces of DNA on your clothes. Whoever that person is could be a killer."

His hawk eyes stared at me, and I knew what he was thinking. *Or maybe Betsy Kern left her DNA on your clothes.* I was pretty sure that he didn't believe my story of having no memory of the past two days. He thought I was lying, and he wanted me to know it.

"I'm sure my husband won't object to any tests you want to run," Tai said. "We both just want to find out what happened to him."

I interrupted her politely but firmly. "Actually, Detective, I do object. Sorry. No warrant, no clothes. I've read about too many innocent people who got railroaded by the police while trying to do the right thing."

"*Dylan,*" Tai said, her voice shocked.

Detective Bushing shrugged his bony shoulders as he got out of the chair. "That's all right, Mrs. Moran. Your husband is within his rights. The fact is, we already have a DNA sample for Betsy Kern's killer. He hit her while he was trying to subdue her, and he left some of his blood on her face. We'll find a match."

"He hit her?" Tai murmured, with an uncomfortable glance at my hand.

Detective Bushing curled his fingers into a fist and tapped it against his own chin. "Yup. Right in the jaw. You sure you don't remember how you hurt yourself, Mr. Moran?"

I stared back at him without blinking. "I have no idea."

I took a pounding shower to wash away days of dirt, but the water on my body was a kind of torture. Instead of clean, hot water from the tap, I imagined the slime of the river coating my skin like an oily film. When I closed my eyes, I was back in the blackness, assaulted by waves of debris whipped along by the swollen current. I held my breath as I dove to find Karly. Somewhere, lost in the river, was her voice. I swam hard, but her scream kept getting farther away.

Dylan, come back! I'm still here!

I shut off the water and crumpled into the shower wall. I pounded a fist against the tile in frustration, and the searing pain reminded me that my hand was probably fractured. The dripping water felt like cold fingers scraping down my back.

Outside the shower, I dried myself with a pink towel. Karly would have hated the idea of pink towels. I went back into the bedroom and stood in front of our open closet, which was now neatly organized to reflect Tai's OCD tendencies. As I looked at the clothes, I was reminded of the fact that they weren't mine. They belonged to someone else. Obviously, Tai had picked out my shirts, my ties, my pants. A few items matched things I'd bought in my single days, but Goodwill had apparently made out well after my marriage.

I wondered how long she and I had been married. How had I proposed? Where? What had led me to think that Tai was the one?

On my nightstand, I saw monogrammed cuff links, something I'd never owned. There was also a bottle of cologne, something I never wore. The Dylan who lived here had the same kind of computer tablet

I had in my other life, but when I opened it and tapped in my pass code, it didn't work. Of course not. My pass code had been Karly's birth date, and there was no Karly in this life. However, I knew Tai's birth date, and when I entered it, I found myself on the tablet home screen. I scrolled through a few photographs, staring at pictures of Tai, photos taken inside the LaSalle Plaza ballroom, and a few selfies of us near the lake. It was painfully obvious that the person in those pictures *wasn't* me. The expressions weren't the same: no joy, no anger, no life. There was a bland nothingness in my eyes.

I didn't think I'd like this Dylan Moran. He seemed like a sanitized version of myself, someone who'd learned the wrong lessons from the death of his parents. Not that I was proud of the things I'd done, the drinking, the fighting. But at least I'd lived. I'd fallen in love, head over heels in love with Karly. Even if I'd made mistakes, even if I'd lost her in the river, I'd still had her in my life. I found it hard to imagine that this Dylan even knew what love was.

At the same time, I also wondered: *Where is he?*

This was his home. He lived here with Tai. *He* was the one who'd been missing for two days, not me. He'd gone into the park on the same night as Betsy Kern, and he'd never come back. I realized that any moment, he might return home, and it would be matter and antimatter meeting face to face.

"Dylan, what's going on?"

I turned and saw Tai in the doorway. I was naked, and my first instinct was to cover myself. But she was my wife, so I let her see me that way.

"Nothing's going on," I said.

"I don't believe you."

"Tai, I wish I could explain, but I can't."

"Are you cheating on me? Is there someone else? Is that where you were?"

"I'm not cheating on you."

She was silent for a while, and then she came and sat on our four-poster metal bed, which was covered by a frilly lavender comforter. "Did you hurt that woman?"

"Are you serious? How can you even ask me that? *No.*"

Tai shook her head. "You're so closed off. Sometimes it makes me wonder what you're hiding. You're like a pressure cooker that's ready to explode."

"That's not me," I protested, but maybe it *was* me. The me who lived here.

"I just wish you'd open up, Dylan. You tell me you love me, you marry me, you sleep with me, but you never tell me anything. I've always accepted that you are who you are, and I loved you regardless. But now you're making me feel like I don't even know you."

"I'm sorry. I'm not trying to make you feel that way."

"Roscoe warned me about it, you know," Tai went on. "He talked to me before the wedding. Just him and me. He told me if I wasn't happy with who you were, I shouldn't go through with it. He said if I thought that getting married would change you, I was going to get my heart broken. The thing is, I was willing to take that risk, because I loved you. Now you have to be honest with me. Was I wrong?"

This was one of those moments where a relationship teetered on the brink and could swing one way or another depending on what you said next. By not answering her, I was at risk of blowing up this other Dylan's life with Tai. That was terribly unfair of me to do, but I couldn't focus on anything other than the name she'd said.

"Roscoe."

"I know he's your friend, but he was trying to help me. Even so, I never doubted my decision about marrying you. That's the truth."

I grabbed clothes and began putting them on. A burgundy dress shirt that I left untucked. Black slacks. "Tai, I have to go."

"Now? Dylan, no, don't walk away from me."

"I have to talk to Roscoe."

"You can see him anytime. You need to talk to *me*."

"I told you, it's hard to explain, but I have to see him right now."

I spotted car keys on the nightstand and put them in my pocket. I was on my way to the back door when I stopped at the noise behind me. Tai was crying. Her eyes were closed, her head down. I froze with indecision, then went and knelt in front of her. I caressed her cheek.

"I'm sorry," I said again. "I know you want answers. I wish I could give them to you."

"Do you love me?" she asked, looking up and wiping her face. "Have you ever loved me?"

I didn't say anything, which was the worst thing I could do. I wanted to tell her what she needed to hear, but I couldn't lie. In the silence, she hung her head again and kept crying.

"It's not you, Tai," I murmured. "It's me. Believe me, I've never known who I am, either. But I'm trying to find out."

CHAPTER 17

The South Side Catholic church where Roscoe served as a priest was a century-old redbrick building with a massive rose window built into its face. I'd been here many times to help him with raffles, book fairs, and food parties, but I hadn't been back since the day of his funeral four years ago. I wasn't a churchgoer anyway, and I found it hard to stand in the shadow of all those monuments to God after he had taken away my best friend.

It was early evening by the time I got there, with the summer sun barely hanging on above the trees. I let myself in through heavy double doors. The interior was cool, as it always was, and the tap of my shoes echoed from the high ceiling. As I walked down the center aisle, I was alone in this place, just me and the spectacle of the church. White columns soared over my head. The multicolored stained glass glowed darkly in the walls, and candles flickered in the shadows. Jesus was backlit on the altar, arms spread wide, welcoming me.

I took a seat in one of the pews near the crossing. This was where I'd been seated for the funeral, close enough that I could go up to the lectern under the watchful eyes of the saints and angels to give Roscoe's eulogy. I was on crutches from the accident then. Karly had helped me. I could still remember the things I'd said through my tears, about the utterly selfless man Roscoe was, about the many ways he'd tried to save his best friend even when I had no interest in being saved.

I missed him so much. He'd left an emptiness behind in my life that I could never fill.

And then, risen from the dead, there he was. I saw him. Roscoe came from the north transept in his black suit, a Bible and a small leather notepad in one hand. It was the first moment that I believed, truly believed without any doubts, that what was happening to me was real.

He crossed in front of the altar and knelt, and then he went to the pulpit, where he stood on a platform to give himself more height and began making notes as he flipped through tissue-thin pages in his Bible. No doubt he had a sermon to give that night. He had his head down in concentration, and he didn't see me. I tried to call to him, but my throat choked up, unable to form words. He'd barely changed from the man in my memory. Maybe he'd put on a couple of pounds and lost a little more hair, but that was all. His thick glasses were in the same black frames. His beard made a trimmed square around his lips and mouth. He hummed as he worked, the way he often did, a tuneless grumble that was easy to hear in the acoustics of the church.

As he considered his sermon, he tapped a pencil against his mouth and then looked up pensively. That was when he finally saw me sitting in the pew. His face broke into a warm smile, and I tried to hold it together, to not cry. To him, this was an ordinary moment, his boyhood friend paying him an unexpected visit. To me, it was a gift that only came for a few moments in the occasional dream. My companion, my anchor, my confidant, was here with me again.

"Dylan, what a nice surprise," Roscoe said, in a voice that was much deeper than anyone would expect from his size.

He came down from the pulpit. For a small man, he always walked quickly. I stood up, and he pulled me into a hug. His hugs were long, he said, because life was short. Then he took the back of my head in his hands and kissed both of my cheeks. It was a habit he'd picked up on a summer trip to Italy, and he never let go of it. That greeting from him was something I'd never thought I would experience again.

The two of us sat down next to each other in the pew. I stared at him like he was an old photograph come to life, and he stared at me with an equal intensity. His keen eyes narrowed with surprise as he took a close look at my face. Somehow, I'd known that I wouldn't be able to hide the truth from him. This man knew me better than anyone other than Karly, and like a parent with identical twins, he could tell immediately that the man in front of him was different from the man he knew.

I was not the Dylan Moran that this Roscoe Tate had grown up with. He couldn't explain why, but he knew that something was wrong.

"This is very odd," he said.

"What is?"

"Well, you've changed. I can't put my finger on how."

"It's just me, Roscoe."

He shook his head. "No. No. There's definitely something new."

"When did I last see you?" I asked.

"Two months, I think? Too long, for sure. But it's not that."

"Then, what is it?"

Roscoe stroked his neat beard and considered his answer seriously, the way he always did. "I have a one-hundred-year-old Chinese man in the parish. We've had the most amazing talks. I've learned some incredible things from him. I think he would say that your *qi* is different."

"Better or worse?"

"Neither. It's just not the same." Roscoe shrugged, as if some mysteries had no explanation. "Anyway, that isn't important. I'm glad you're here, but why *are* you here? What's wrong?"

"Does something have to be wrong? I just wanted to see you."

He chuckled. "Never play poker with me, my friend. I can always read your face. It's not just your *qi*. In addition to everything else that seems off about you, I can tell you're struggling with something. Talk to me."

I had no idea what to say.

I was still overwhelmed by the fact that I was really here, talking to my best friend, four years after he'd died next to me behind the wheel of a car. Part of me wanted to confess everything, because after all, that's what you do with priests, isn't it? Confess. But if I told him what was happening to me—or what I believed was happening—he'd think I had gone insane. I couldn't expect him to take me seriously with a story like this. And yet I also needed the counsel that Roscoe had always given me. When I veered off course in life, he steered me back. Right now, I felt like a stranger in a strange land, and even though I knew this was not *my* Roscoe, he was still my best friend.

I also knew that I could not, would not, lie to him. That was a pact we'd made with each other years ago. Never judge, never lie.

"I don't even know where to begin," I said.

"Well, are you okay? Is it your health?"

"No, I'm fine."

He leaped to the next obvious conclusion. "Is it Tai? Or rather, you and Tai? You've been married more than a year now. The two of you are past the honeymoon and into real life, which is much harder."

"Tai's not the problem," I replied. "It's me. Things are happening to me that are very difficult to explain. It has nothing to do with her, but to be honest, I have to know. Did it surprise you when she and I got married?"

Roscoe never pulled punches. "You mean because you didn't love her?"

"You knew?"

"Of course I knew. If you'll recall, I told you exactly that. I told you that she loved you fully and passionately, and she deserved a man who loved her just as much. Which you didn't. You said you'd grow to love her with time, and I told you that was about the stupidest thing I ever heard you say. On the other hand, let's not sugarcoat the truth. You've never been in love with anyone, Dylan. You don't feel anything. You're shut up inside a world that must be awfully dark and lonely sometimes.

I've tried to pull you out, and so has Tai, but ultimately, you have to make that choice for yourself."

I couldn't stay quiet. If I didn't say something, if I didn't let out the secret of what was going on, I'd drown.

"Actually, you're wrong. That's *not* who I am."

"Come on, Dylan. Let's not kid ourselves. We've talked about this many times. You're like a radio whose plug got kicked out of the wall when you were a boy. I'm not blaming you for that, or saying you don't have a right to be who you are, but you can't pretend with me."

"I'm not pretending, Roscoe. I'm saying I'm a different man than who you think I am. If anything, what scares me is how deeply I *do* feel things. I lose control too easily."

"You? Out of control? I can't remember a day in your life when I've seen you like that. And I know you pretty well."

"That's the thing. You don't know me at all."

"Dylan, what are you talking about?"

"You were right about what you said before. I've changed. I'm not Dylan. I mean, I am, but I'm not. Not the Dylan you know."

Roscoe shook his head. "What are you saying?"

I put my hand on his shoulder and squeezed. He was real; he was flesh and blood. "For starters, you're supposed to be dead."

It took me an hour to tell him the story. When I was done, Roscoe sat motionless in the pew, with nothing but his breathing to tell me he was alive. His face had no expression, and he hadn't said a word the entire time. People confided their worst sins to him every day, so he'd developed a stony poker face to hide his own feelings. If he thought I'd gone crazy, he was kind enough not to tell me.

"Parallel worlds," he murmured finally.

"That's it."

"And you come from a different one."

"Yes, I do." I added after a moment, "I know this seems impossible. I'm asking a lot for you to believe it."

Roscoe gave me a little smile, and I saw his eyes drift to the altar. "Dylan, my faith tells me that Jesus Christ rose from the dead. Many people consider that impossible, but the doubts of others don't shake what I know in my heart."

"Does that mean you think I'm telling the truth?" I asked.

"I'm saying it doesn't matter what I think. It's whether you believe it yourself. Obviously, you're convinced something extraordinary is happening to you."

"It is. I know how it sounds, but it's real."

"Well, I was the one who said you seem like a different man," he told me. "There's no doubt of that. Something has caused a profound change in you, whatever that may be."

I still felt the need to prove what I was saying. I reached for my right hand and slipped the silver class ring off my finger. "This is *your* ring, Roscoe. See the engraving? I've worn it ever since the accident. I'm telling you the truth about my world. I haven't seen you in four years."

Roscoe put the ring on the tip of his thumb and studied it. "Yes, you're right. I've never seen you wearing this."

"But?"

"But your Many Worlds must come with a sense of humor. In this world, I lost my ring to you in a bet the summer after our high school graduation. You've had it ever since. Apparently fate has a way of making even the smallest parts of our lives converge."

I shook my head as he gave me back the ring. "Roscoe, I'm not making this up. You *died*."

"I heard what you said. A car accident after I bailed you out of a police station. Dylan Moran in a bar fight—now that's truly a miracle. You're far too stoic and practical for anything like that. I don't recommend violence, but actually, it would be nice to think you're capable of losing control once in a while."

"That night changed my life," I told him.

"So I gather."

"I lost you, but I met my wife because of it."

Roscoe steepled his fingers in front of his chin. "I rather like the idea of me dying to help you find the love of your life. You must know that I wouldn't have hesitated over that kind of sacrifice."

"I do know that." Then I looked around at the church, which was like seeing Roscoe back home where he belonged. "But in this world, there was no accident. No bar fight. No car wrapped around the tree. You never died, and I never met Karly."

He gave me a strange look that I couldn't interpret. "I doubt it would have made a difference if you had. You don't believe in the idea of love at first sight."

"That's your Dylan," I insisted. "Not me. I fell for Karly as soon as I saw her."

"*My* Dylan," Roscoe murmured.

I could tell that he still had his doubts. Around us, night was setting in, which made the dangling lanterns overhead glow brighter. The stained glass deepened into shadows on the walls. We were alone, but even so, I felt a strange shift in the environment around me. The air changed, as if a door had opened and closed somewhere.

"I know you're humoring me," I told him.

Roscoe sat where he was, his lips pursed in thought. "Well, it's a lot to take in, I won't deny that. For the time being, let's assume this is really happening to you. That you're a different Dylan Moran, someone I haven't met before. If that's true, where is the Dylan that I grew up with? The one who belongs in this world?"

"I don't know."

"Did he somehow disappear when you arrived?"

"I have no idea. The other Dylan I told you about—the serial killer—he shared my world, so I can't understand where your Dylan is. He should be here, too, but he's been missing for two days."

"In which case, I'm worried about him."

"Yes, I understand."

"I love him. He's my closest friend. I'm sure your Roscoe felt the same way about you."

"He did."

Roscoe stood up from the pew and gave me one of his penetrating stares that meant he was going to say something that I didn't want to hear. "Dylan, can I ask you a question?"

"Of course."

"If you are who you claim you are, then *why* are you here?"

"I needed to see you again. To talk to you. I knew if anyone would believe me, you would."

"Yes, I get that. And I'm glad you came. What I want to know is, why are you here in this world and not your own?"

"I told you. I need to stop this other Dylan. He's a killer."

"That's a job for the police. In any world. It's not your job."

"The police don't know what's going on. They have no clue. Roscoe, this other Dylan has already killed again. The woman in the park, Betsy Kern. Another woman who looks just like Karly—"

I stopped.

Restlessly, I got up from the bench and paced back and forth in the aisle under the long sweep of the arched ceiling. My sharp footsteps sounded like the crack of bullets. I understood what was happening now, and my terror increased a thousandfold. My doppelgänger was here. He knew I was following him. By killing Betsy Kern, he was sending me a message.

"Oh, my God. *He's going to kill her.*"

"Who?"

"*Karly.* That's what this is about. That's his plan. I need to stop him before he finds her. I'm the only one who can save her."

Roscoe shook his head sadly. "Is that what you're trying to do? Save her?"

"Of course it is. Don't you see? I'm the only one who even knows she's at risk."

"I know that's what you're telling yourself. But it also gives you a convenient excuse to meet her again, doesn't it? You can meet her and make her fall in love with you. You can have the life you lost. That's what you really want."

"That's not what this is about."

"Isn't it? Dylan, whether or not your story is true really doesn't matter. You can't live two lives at the same time. No good will come of it. You've already hurt people. The longer you stay on this path, the worse it will get. If any of this is real, then the best thing you can do is say the word *infinite* right now and go back home. Let us worry about our own world."

I put my hands on Roscoe's shoulders. "I can't do that. I failed Karly in my other life. I let her die. I should have been the one who died, not her. I'm *not* going to fail her again. This time, I'm going to keep her safe."

"That was your responsibility in your own world," he replied firmly. "Not here. In this world, you have no connection to her at all. Wherever Karly is, she has her own life, and you don't belong in it."

Roscoe knew me well, but I knew him, too. The truth always showed in his face.

"My God. You know her, don't you? You know Karly. You know where she is."

"I don't."

"Well, you know something about her. What is it?"

"This is a mistake. You should let it go."

"Roscoe, please. You have to tell me."

My friend sat down in the pew again. He exhaled with a heavy sigh. "I can see you're not going to give up. One thing is consistent about every Dylan Moran. They disregard all of my good advice."

I waited impatiently, but Roscoe could never be rushed.

"Almost ten years ago, I set you up on a blind date," he went on. "Do you remember that?"

I thought back. "Yes. You had a married friend who was a religion major at Northwestern. I met her and her husband at Thanksgiving dinner at your mother's house. Afterward, she told you that she had a girlfriend who'd be perfect for me."

"Did you meet up with her girlfriend?"

"No. I said thanks, but no thanks. I had no interest in blind dates. Why?"

"Because in this world, you did go," Roscoe told me. "The two of you went out to some dance club, and she didn't like you. There was no chemistry. That was it. The two of you never went out again. Maybe it's just a coincidence, but so far, there don't seem to be a lot of coincidences in your worlds, Dylan. The thing is, I remember the woman's name, even after all this time. It was Karly."

CHAPTER 18

I drove to the north side of the city, where Karly's parents had their house. When I got to their upscale neighborhood in Wilmette, it was obvious that they'd never lived there. There was no dollhouse in the back of the estate where Karly had nursed me back to health after the accident. The mansion itself was unchanged, but it was no longer a testament to the real estate empire built by Susannah Chance. The woman who answered the door was a stranger who had never heard of the Chance family and who had owned the house since the 1980s.

When I did research on my phone, I learned that Chance Properties didn't exist. In fact, I couldn't find any indication that it ever had. Whatever Karly's mother had done with her life, she wasn't in the local real estate market. I searched for Karly herself, but I got listings for different women all over the country, and nothing gave me a clue about how to find the Karly I wanted. I didn't know where she was living or working or whether she was still in Chicago at all. In fact, I didn't even know whether Karly Chance actually existed in this world. The blind date I'd had ten years ago might have been with a different person who just happened to have the same first name.

But I didn't think so. I thought Roscoe was right. Fate had a way of making our lives converge across different worlds.

Finally, I called Roscoe's friend Sarah, the Northwestern alum who'd originally suggested I meet Karly. She was now a homeschool mom living in Elgin. As I dialed her number, I tried to think of a way to explain my interest in finding a woman with whom I'd had a single disastrous date nearly a decade earlier. The truth was clearly not an option.

When Sarah answered the phone, we exchanged pleasantries, which didn't take long. Roscoe was the only thing we had in common, so we talked about him and his parish work for a minute or two, and when that well ran dry, I explained the reason for my call. I hoped she'd believe the lie.

"This is a total fluke, Sarah. You may not be able to help me, but you're my only lead. I'm the events manager at the LaSalle Plaza Hotel, and my assistant took a call today from a woman named Karly Chance who was interested in booking our ballroom for an event next spring. Unfortunately, my assistant must have gotten the number wrong, because my calls won't go through. The thing is, I remembered that you set me up on a blind date with a woman named Karly Chance a long time ago. I have no idea whether it's the same person, but I figured it was worth a try. If you were still in touch with her, I thought you might know how I could reach her."

Sarah had no problem believing my story, but she didn't have much information to offer. "I'm sorry, Dylan. Karly and I lost touch after college. I haven't talked to her in years. I'm afraid I have no idea how to get hold of her."

"Sure. I understand. Am I right about the name of your friend, though? It was Karly Chance?"

"Yes, that was her."

"Do you know if she stayed in Chicago after school?"

"Well, if I remember correctly, she was planning to continue at Northwestern and do graduate work in English. I don't know if she did, but you could probably check with the university. They might have a way to track her down."

"I appreciate it, Sarah. I'll let you go. Roscoe says hi."

I hung up the phone. I did another online search—this time adding the word *Northwestern* to the name Karly Chance—and not only did I find a record for her, I discovered that she was a junior member of the Northwestern faculty. The idea of Karly teaching English didn't seem far fetched to me. Her father had been a poet and high school teacher, so it seemed as if she'd followed in his footsteps in this world rather than in the footsteps of her mother.

The online biography didn't include a photograph, but the website listed her office location on the third floor of University Hall. That was only about five minutes away from where I was.

I could feel my heart racing as I drove to the campus. It was late, but being so close, I couldn't wait until tomorrow to get an answer. My instincts all told me it was her. My Karly. My wife. She was leading a different life here, and for all I knew, she was married to someone else. The one time we'd met in this world had gone poorly. But none of that mattered. I needed to see her again.

At night, I had no trouble parking. I walked along Chicago Avenue toward Sheridan, and I shivered a little in my thin red shirt, because the lake breeze had cooled the air. The serene stone buildings of the university surrounded me. I crossed under the black arch that led into the heart of the campus and saw the clock tower of University Hall down the path in front of me. The closer I got, the harder it was to breathe. Just by seeing her, even for a moment, I felt as if I could get a little bit of my life back.

The doors of the white, rough-stone building were unlocked. Inside, I heard muffled voices. From somewhere nearby came the acrid smell of an illicit cigarette. The building stairs were ahead of me, and I climbed to the third floor. In the corridor, I passed a long lineup of offices, a few with doors cracked open. I could see a couple of faculty members tapping at their keyboards. Otherwise, the hallway was empty and museum quiet.

I found the room number listed on her online bio. The door was closed and locked. There was no window to see inside. But there was her name. Karly Chance. She'd posted no photograph on the door, but it was *her*. I saw a handwritten listing of her office hours pinned to a bulletin board, and the handwriting was unmistakably Karly's. I'd found her. She came and went day by day down this same hall. She worked on the other side of this door. I thought about breaking in, just so I could smell the fragrance inside, because I knew it would smell like her.

"May I help you?"

I turned around and saw a slight Indian man studying me suspiciously from behind a pair of red glasses. He was one of the faculty members I'd seen working in his office.

My mind was getting accustomed to lying. "Oh, I was supposed to meet Karly here, but we must have gotten our signals crossed. I tried texting her, but my messages aren't going through."

"Are you a student?" the man asked, even though I obviously wasn't.

"No, no, I'm her cousin. I'm in town from Seattle on business, and I was supposed to take her out for a late dinner. Do you know Karly?"

"Of course."

I took a chance that the world had only changed so much.

"I've been looking forward to seeing her," I went on, inventing a new story. "I don't get out this way very often. Her dad is my favorite uncle. I guess the apple doesn't fall far from the tree. Tom's a teacher, Karly's a teacher. I used to really like Tom's poetry, too. I loved listening to him read his poems when they'd come out to Washington for Christmas dinner."

The faculty member visibly relaxed. He was obviously protective of his colleague, but I'd passed the test by talking about her family. "Yes, Tom is an accomplished poet. As is Karly, of course."

"Yes, she's incredibly talented."

"Great trauma can bring that out in a person," he added.

I stuttered with surprise. "Yes."

Trauma.

It scared me to hear that word, and I wondered what it meant. He assumed I knew something about Karly that I obviously didn't. Something terrible. I realized that the more I said, the more it would become clear that I didn't actually know her. Not in this world.

"Well, there's not much I can do but head back to my hotel," I said. "Nice talking to you. I'm sorry I missed Karly. Hopefully she'll check her phone soon."

"You know, she doesn't live far away. She's the faculty rep in Goodrich."

"Goodrich? Is that one of the dorms?"

"Yes, it's just a few minutes' walk up Sheridan. If you go up there, one of the students can probably let her know you're outside."

"I'll do that. Thanks a lot."

I left the building and went back to the street. The wind whipped through the trees, and I shoved my hands in my pockets as I took the sidewalk north. As excited as I was at the idea that Karly was close by, I also found myself confronting an unhappy truth. I was trying to find a stranger. More than that, I was trying to find a stranger who'd gone through something dark in her past. Trauma.

In my mind, I couldn't escape the idea that Karly knew me. I'd see her, and she'd be my wife, and she'd be in love with me. But none of that was true. If I simply showed up at her door, a man who'd met her once on an awful blind date years earlier, she'd wonder why I was there and what I wanted.

What *did* I want?

Honestly, I had no idea. I needed to protect her, but I didn't know how to warn her of the danger from someone who was actually *me*.

When I got to the residence hall, I hesitated at the alley. A few lights were on inside the building, and I could see a handful of summer students through the open curtains and hear music through their windows. I debated whether to stay or just leave. What would I say if I found her?

Then, not far away, a door opened. A woman emerged from inside the dorm, lingered briefly under the lights, and then turned away toward the gardens in back. She was visible for only a moment, and all I could see was a hint of blond hair and the curve of her jaw.

The woman looked like Karly, but I couldn't be sure. Maybe I just *wanted* it to be her.

Even so, I followed. I took the alley to the back of the building, where the dormitories and fraternities came together in a kind of quad. It was almost impossible to see in the darkness back here. Trees crowded the open lawns and blocked my view. Ivy-covered walls butted up to the cobblestoned sidewalks. I didn't see Karly—if it really was Karly—but she couldn't have gone far. I heard the tap of her heels on stone, but the noise bounced between the walls and made it hard to tell where she was.

I crossed beside a building with Greek letters engraved over its doorway. Bike racks were crowded near the rear door, and I smelled weed through one of the windows. I stopped by the dense, overgrown hedges and listened again, hearing no footsteps this time. Then, on the far side of the lawn, I spotted a flash of her blond hair as she passed under the glow of a lamppost. She disappeared into a narrow corridor between two buildings. I changed direction to go after her, navigating between the trees. The branches dangled low to the ground, scraping my face as I hurried through the damp grass.

When I was halfway across the lawn, I stopped.

A stab of horror ran through my body. Ahead of me, a silhouette detached itself from the thick trunk of an elm tree. It was a man. He stood on the fringe of the grass, framed in darkness by the lamppost. I recognized the outline of his body, because I'd seen it in photographs throughout my life. That was how I looked, with my lean, small frame, with my shock of wavy hair. It was me. It was *him*. He headed after the blond woman with a determined stride, and as he crossed under the light of the lamppost, I saw the dirty leather of his coat. My father's coat. I also saw a glinting reflection of something metal in his hand.

A knife.

He was carrying a knife.

I tried to run, but the slick mud under my feet slowed me down. When I got to the walkway between the buildings, the corridor was already empty. I sprinted to the far side and found myself in a wooded area where four sidewalks met in a cross, with more ivy-covered walls on every side. My doppelgänger was gone. So was Karly.

Was it Karly?

Was I going to lose her again?

I didn't know which way to go—left, right, or straight. In front of me, the cobblestones led beneath an archway between two buildings, and I ran that way, finding myself in another dark quad where brick walls loomed around the square. The area was silent, except for the noise of the tree branches rustling together. I saw no one, and I turned around to reverse my steps.

There she was. Right behind me. Staring right at me.

She was fit, young, and attractive, with bobbed blond hair, but she wasn't Karly. They looked similar, but this woman was a stranger. In her hand was a small canister that she pointed at my face.

"Freeze, shithead. This is pepper spray. One more step, and you'll be choking on the ground, and I'll be kicking the crap out of you. Got it?"

I backed away and held up my hands. "Hey, I'm sorry. I saw someone following you, and I was just trying to help."

"Yeah, *you* were following me. And now you're done. I'm calling security, so unless you want to explain why you're on campus stalking women, you better get the hell out of here and not come back."

She didn't take her eyes off me. With the can of pepper spray still poised, she backed to the doorway of the nearest building and disappeared inside. I didn't want to be around when campus security arrived, so I walked quickly back the way I'd come.

Even so, when I reached the alley that led toward Sheridan, I stopped.

No one was in sight, but the shadows offered plenty of hiding places.

I waited to see if he would show himself, but he didn't. Regardless, I knew he was here. Our minds were linked, and I could feel him watching me from the blackness. I'd stopped him tonight, but this wasn't over. We both knew the stakes.

He was in this world, and he was hunting for Karly.

I had to get to her first.

It was after midnight when I finally made it back to the apartment near River Park. I had nowhere else to go. It occurred to me that the Dylan who really belonged here might have come home while I was gone, but I had to take that chance, so I let myself inside. Moonlight stole through the windows, giving me enough light to see. I made my way to the bedroom and saw that Tai was alone in bed. I took off my clothes, feeling a wave of tiredness. I slid under the covers next to her. She faced away from me, her breathing steady. I knew she'd heard me arrive; I knew she was awake. I lay on my side, and the room was quiet.

"Where were you?" Tai said softly from the other side of the bed.

"I told you. I needed to see Roscoe."

"You left the church hours ago. I called him. Where did you go?"

"I drove around."

Tai turned over, just inches away. We were eye to eye. Her long hair spilled across the pillow. I could see her bare shoulders and breasts where the blanket slipped down.

"What are you not telling me?" she asked.

"Nothing."

She stayed silent for a while, watching me. "I'm glad you're safe. Those two days without you were hell. I was worried about you."

"I know."

"Why don't we go away this weekend? We could drive to Lake Geneva, find a little B and B."

"I can't."

"Oh. Okay. Whatever."

I heard her disappointment and regretted the harshness in my voice. She didn't deserve that. She had no way of knowing she was in bed with another man. "Tai, I'm sorry."

She nudged closer and put her lips on mine. "You know, I can't fix something when I don't know what's broken."

"I already told you, it's not you. It's me. It's all me."

She kept kissing me. My lips. My chin. My eyes. Her taut nipples brushed against my chest, and her long hair caressed my skin. Her hand slid between my legs and began to tease an erection from me.

"Tai, it's not a good night for that."

"I don't care."

Her motions grew more urgent, her fingernails working on me with long, gentle strokes, and I responded to her touch despite myself. Yes, it felt good, but my body and mind were in two different places. I was thinking about the first time Karly had touched me, when I lay on the bed in the dollhouse, still in casts and mostly unable to move. She'd given me a sponge bath, and we made jokes to defuse the awkwardness of the effect it was having on me, which was impossible to miss. When we ran out of jokes, she giggled and said, "Oh, what the hell" and made me come harder than I ever had in my life.

That's what I was remembering when Tai took hold of my shoulder. "Make love to me."

I should have put her off, but I didn't. I rolled on top of her, and she spread her legs wide, and I sank inside her. She cried out a little, then moaned. I thrust in and out slowly, feeling the heat of her response, and I tried to be in the moment. I tried to take pleasure in this, but every touch and every sound she made reminded me that our bodies were strangers. Seeing her face below me, not Karly's, felt wrong, as if I were somehow cheating on both of them at the same time. I kept dreaming of making love to my real wife, but this wasn't her. I rushed to finish, and the more I tried to climax, the more my body betrayed me. My arousal vanished. Tai wrapped her legs around me and tried to coax me back to life, but we were done. I couldn't do this.

I pulled out of her and collapsed onto my back. "I'm sorry."

"What's wrong with you?"

"I have a lot on my mind."

"So tell me about it. Talk to me."

"I don't even know where to start."

She stared at the ceiling, and the dim light gave away the shine of tears in her eyes. "You've always been distant. I never blamed you for that. But I thought we were making progress. I thought you were learning to love me. Now you're going backward."

"I know."

"You can't go on like this," Tai said. "Something's wrong with you. If you won't talk to me, then talk to Roscoe, or talk to a shrink. You need help. Please, sweetheart."

She reached out a hand to me, but I pulled mine away. My body was damp with sweat, my heart still racing. I didn't say anything to Tai, but she was right. I needed help, and I could only think of one person who would understand what I was going through.

I had to find Eve Brier.

Chapter 19

I awakened before dawn. Tai was still asleep, or pretending to be asleep so she didn't have to deal with me. I stood over the bed and watched her silently, feeling guilty about what had transpired between us overnight. My instinct was to wake her up. Tell her everything. But I waited. Somehow I managed to convince myself that I was protecting her with my silence.

I showered in the darkness. The water brought me right back to when I was trapped in the river. It didn't matter what world I was in—that helpless sensation never left me. I struggled through the claustrophobia, then went back into the bedroom to get dressed. There wasn't much in the closet of this other Dylan that appealed to my own tastes. I looked for the blazer I'd seen him wearing when I followed him from the Art Institute, but I didn't see that coat on any of the hangers. Instead, I chose the least offensive patterned shirt I could find and a pair of Dockers.

It was too early to head downtown, so first I took a walk on the trails of the park to clear my head. I crossed the open grass, passing the jungle gyms and the community pool, and reached the path that led along the bank of the Chicago River. A strip of weeds and clover ended in dense trees, obscuring the fence that protected the steep slope over the water. The path was closed off by police tape here for at least fifty yards. I knew why. Betsy Kern had been found hidden in the brush near this spot, a knife in her heart. She was the latest victim in a chain of violence that stretched across the Many Worlds.

I walked north by the river. Ahead of me, the path descended under Foster Avenue, where graffiti marred the stone wall and the steel girders of the bridge. I walked beside the river's drab green water here. Beyond the bridge, the trail climbed into a new section of parkland. By that time, the horizon was brightening, but in the semidarkness, the trail lights hadn't switched off.

I came upon a weeping willow whose dangling branches swished against the sidewalk. As I passed the tree, I disturbed an enormous rat, which scampered practically over my toes into the dense undergrowth near the water. Seeing the rat made me freeze, although rats were a common sight along the river. I was still looking down at my feet when I spotted a fleck of gold reflecting the shine from the light post. It made me curious. I squatted and used my fingers to brush away the mud to see what it was.

What I found was a brass button. I picked it up and rubbed the metal to clean it, and then I used my phone to light up the button in my hand. The insignia showed a small crown and shield, with the initials HSM underneath. I knew that those initials stood for Hart Schaffner Marx, because that was the brand of navy blazer I'd been wearing yesterday, and my coat had identical buttons on the cuffs.

The Dylan who lived here, Tai's husband, owned the same blazer. I didn't think that was a coincidence.

I stared at the dark riverbank where the rat had disappeared. The weeds beside the trail grew particularly high here. Between the brush and the trees clustered tightly together, I couldn't even see the rusted fence on the riverbank. I looked up and down the trail to make sure I was still alone, and then I plunged into the weeds. When I reached the fence, I didn't even need to climb it. The mesh had been cut away from the post, leaving a gap where I could squeeze to the other side. Only a few feet separated me from the river at the bottom of the slope. A dense web of green branches leaned over the water. I heard the low slurp of the current. Birds chattered loudly, as if warning me away.

It was still night in here, dark and deep. Using my phone again, I lit up a small patch of the woods around me, watching a cloud of insects flock to the glow. When I turned the light to the ground, I caused a stir, as half a dozen more rats scattered from where they'd been feeding. When I looked at what they'd left behind, my stomach lurched. I held in the urge to vomit. I squeezed my eyes shut and took several deep breaths. Then I steeled myself to see what was below me.

A body.

A body with no face. That was partly because of the rats eating away what was left of the corpse and partly because someone had used a shovel or club to bash the man's face to a pulp. He was completely unrecognizable, but he was wearing a Hart Schaffner Marx navy blazer identical to the one I owned. I checked the cuff and saw a missing button, and below the cuff, the body was missing something else. His hand had been cut off. I checked and found that the other hand was missing, too.

No fingerprints.

It was an eerie feeling, staring at myself, dead. Because I knew this was Dylan Moran. Tai's Dylan Moran, who was never coming home to her. No one was likely to identify him in his current state, and that was assuming his body was found at all before the rats skeletonized him and gnawed away what was left of the bones. He'd simply ooze away into the ground.

What did I do next? I did nothing.

I left him there. I definitely wasn't going to call the police.

When I was sure no one else was nearby, I slipped through the fence again and headed toward home. His home. No one would be looking for him, no one would wonder if the body was his, because Dylan Moran wasn't missing. He was right where he was supposed to be. I was here in his place.

I had a strange, disorienting realization about what this all meant. If I wanted it, this man's life was mine.

Eve Brier had already warned me. *You might be tempted to stay.*

Roscoe had feared the same thing. They were both right.

I'd come to this world to stop a killer, but now that I was here, I found myself wondering: What if I really could find Karly?

Could we be together again?

Could I have what I'd lost?

I'd be lying if I said I didn't want that, but it gave me a sick feeling to think about rebuilding my life over the decomposing body of another Dylan Moran.

I didn't know what to do. I needed Eve's help. I needed to find out more about the Many Worlds and what would happen to me if I stayed.

She'd given me her business card when we first met. It listed the address of her office in the tapering black tower that Chicagoans would always call the Hancock Center. Her psychiatry practice was lucrative enough to afford her exclusive space along the Magnificent Mile.

I drove downtown, parked a couple of blocks away, and joined the morning chaos on Michigan Avenue. It felt normal to be here, as if nothing in my world had changed. I could head south to my favorite lunch places, and they would recognize me. I could walk into my office at the LaSalle Plaza and go to work, and no one would find anything strange about it.

This was Dylan Moran's Chicago.

I entered the building through the doors on Chestnut Street along with a sea of commuters. Inside the lobby, I found myself mesmerized by the sculpture that dominated the space. Called *Lucent*, it was a globe formed by thousands of blue lights designed to emulate the stars of the night sky. With a mirrored ceiling above it and a black pool of water beneath, the endless reflections made me think of the parallel worlds in which I was caught. Somehow, I didn't think that was an accident. Eve had picked this place for a reason, as if the artwork were the first step in opening a patient's mind to limitless possibilities.

I gave the guard at the security desk my name and the number of Eve's office on the twenty-ninth floor. While he tapped on his keyboard, I thought about what I needed to say to her. As far as I knew, she and I were strangers in this world, but she was also my ally, my coconspirator. She was the one who'd delivered me here, so it made sense that she could help me decide what to do next.

"Sir?"

The guard interrupted my thoughts. I watched a frown furrow his face.

"I'm sorry, sir, but that office isn't registered to Eve Brier."

I tried to focus on what he was telling me. "Who does have the space? Maybe she's part of a larger practice."

"Actually, no one's in that office right now," he replied. "The suite is vacant."

"Do you know for how long?"

"Almost a year."

"Was Eve Brier the previous tenant?" I asked. "Is it possible she moved?"

"Not according to my records. I ran the name, and there's no Eve Brier in any other space inside the building. It doesn't look like there ever was. I'm sorry, sir. She's not here."

I thanked him and walked away. Eve had no phone; she had no office in Hancock Center. I should have expected that her world had changed, just as everyone else's had, but I was genuinely shocked to realize that she wasn't here. Not just shocked—afraid. I was under the spell of *her* therapy, and she was gone.

I sat down in one of the lobby chairs and used my phone to run searches for Eve Brier.

For her psychiatric practice.

For her medical school and degree.

For her lectures.

For her bestselling book about Many Worlds and Many Minds.

For Eve Brier herself, with her swirls of highlighted brown hair and her distinctive, hypnotic eyes. If she wasn't in Chicago, where was she? If she wasn't living *her* life, what was she doing?

She had to be out there somewhere, but I found nothing. There was no record of Eve Brier, doctor, psychiatrist, philosopher, author. There was no record of Eve Brier *anywhere*, no one who even looked like her. She'd left no footprints in this world.

As far as I could tell, she didn't exist.

I got up from where I was sitting. As I stood in the lobby, the *Lucent* sculpture engulfed me again. I found myself lost in its thousands of lights and endless reflections, and then my eyes focused on a single star among the many. That was me, one insignificant point of light, lost somewhere in an infinite number of universes.

Infinite.

I heard the word in my head.

All I had to do was say it. That was my way out. Roscoe had told me it would be better if I just went home, but I hadn't finished what I'd come here to do. There was a Dylan Moran in this city who had already killed twice. Karly was alive and in his sights, and I had to save her.

Eve Brier couldn't help me.

I was going to have to navigate this world on my own.

CHAPTER 20

From downtown, I drove back to Northwestern.

I retraced my steps in the light of day to the residence hall where Karly lived, but like last night, I stopped before going inside. This wasn't the way to approach a stranger. All I would do was alarm her. Instead, I needed a meeting with her that was innocent and accidental.

I noticed a young man in shorts and sunglasses, reading an economics textbook on the building's back porch. It wasn't even eleven in the morning, but he already had an empty beer can tipped on its side and another one in his hand. Ah, college days.

"Hey, do you know where I can find Karly Chance?" I called to him. "I need her signature to add a class in the fall."

He didn't even look up from his book. "Try Norris. She hangs out there."

"Thanks."

Norris was the university's student center and gathering place. It was only about a ten-minute walk from where I was, and the path took me past a quiet inner lake formed by fill land that blocked the waves of Lake Michigan. Sunshine beat down on my head, but the breeze off the water was cool. I entered Norris in the dining area and checked the tables to see if Karly was there. She wasn't, but the building was a large space with several floors, and she could be anywhere. I strolled around the sprawling center, and everywhere I looked, I expected to see her. I tensed for that moment.

What would I do? What would I say?

When I passed the university bookstore, I glanced at the window display and saw at least three dozen books arranged under a sign for faculty titles. Among books on climate change, Sufi literature, and French cinema, my gaze landed on a slim paperback with a cover that showed the outline of a woman's face as she held up a mirror, creating an endless series of reflections vanishing into the center of the photograph.

The name of the book was *Portal*.

The author was Karly Chance.

I went into the bookstore and picked up a copy. The first thing I did was check the last page to see whether the publisher had included a photograph, but the only information was a brief biography. *Karly Chance is a lecturer and poet-in-residence at Northwestern University. This is her first collection.*

That was all.

I checked the listing of poems included in the book. The one-word titles unsettled me. One was called "Cut." Another, "Plaything." Another, "Jump." Another, "Candy." When I flipped through the pages, I was impressed but also horrified. Her poems used beautiful imagery to build a tableau of violent self-destruction, like Thomas Eakins painting the blood of a nineteenth-century surgical procedure in exquisite detail.

It seemed impossible to me that the Karly I knew could have written these poems. I'd never seen a side like that in her personality. But then again, this was not the Karly I knew.

I also thought about the word her faculty colleague had used in describing her background.

Trauma.

"You should read the book," a voice next to me said.

I looked around and saw a young woman no more than twenty, in a Northwestern T-shirt, with her brunette hair tied in a ponytail. Her name tag told me she was a bookstore employee. As I held the book in my hand, she tapped a purple-painted fingernail on the cover.

"The poems are really deep. I mean, some of them will turn your stomach, but if you want to know what depression can do to someone's head, it's all in here."

My finger caressed Karly's name on the cover. "Do you know her?"

"Sure. I've taken her class."

"What's she like?"

"She's amazing. So many of the profs around here are just talking heads, you know? But Karly lived it."

I smiled. "You've sold me."

I followed the young woman to the cash register. As she rang up the sale and took my money, I said, "You mentioned depression. Is that what the poems are about?"

"Oh, yeah. She spent years in the cave."

"Did something happen to her?"

"You don't know?"

"No, I don't."

"Well, Karly was in a car accident right after college. She talks about it in class and doesn't sugarcoat how bad it was. She had her mom in the car with her, and they were having some kind of big argument. The two of them didn't get along, like *really* didn't get along. Karly got distracted. She ran a red light, and they got T-boned. Her mom was killed."

I felt those words like a blow to my chest.

"She spiraled after that," the girl went on. "She spent a year in hell. Heavy into meth, abusive relationships, suicide attempts. The last time she almost succeeded."

I hesitated, but I needed to know. "What did she do?"

"She drove her car right into the river."

I had trouble standing. Waves of violent memories rolled over me. My mother, dead on the floor. My father, with the gun in his mouth.

Roscoe, dead in the seat next to me, his face shredded by broken glass. Dylan Moran on the riverbank, the rats eating his face.

Karly and I, swirling and tumbling in the black water.

Roscoe said: *Fate has a way of making even the smallest details converge.*

"Shit," I murmured.

"Yeah. When they pulled her out, she was dead. No heartbeat. No oxygen for like four minutes. They put her in a coma to give her brain a chance to recover, but nobody figured she'd come out of it. But she did. She says that was what finally turned her around."

I didn't know what to say, so I said nothing.

"Anyway, enjoy the book," the girl told me with a macabre smile.

"Yeah. Thanks."

I left the store, still devastated by what I'd heard. I took the stairs up to the next level, and I used a coffee coupon on my receipt to buy myself an iced latte. When a table opened up, I sat down and began reading Karly's book.

Knowing it was her, knowing what she'd been through in this life, made the words almost unbearable to me. All this naked emotion roared off the page. Fury. Lust. Savagery. Ecstasy. Coldness. Guilt. Despair. "Plaything" was about bondage with a series of strangers. "Candy" was about her overdose of pills. "Jump" was about standing on an eighteenth-story Marina City balcony, naked and high as a kite, hallucinating that her mother was shouting from the ground below that she should climb over the railing.

Jump, *she said to me.*

Jump, *she sang.*

I told myself that this was a different Karly, not my Karly, not the woman I knew, but I realized something as I read the book that made me impossibly sad.

This *was* my Karly.

I could hear her voice in the turn of a phrase. Little things she'd said when we were together, the words she'd made up about people, showed up here. The poems *sounded* exactly like her. All the pain, all the darkness, had been inside her when she and I were together. Same soul, same mind. Maybe it had taken a journey of shame to bring it to the page, but she'd had this identical wounded heart all along. I had never seen it, never asked her about it, never dived into the deep, deep pool of who she really was.

I had loved this woman and not known her at all.

How could I have missed it?

I was in tears when I put the book down, for everything I'd lost, for everything I'd failed to appreciate while I had her. I hadn't looked up from the pages for an hour. My vision was blurred, and I wiped my eyes. I hadn't touched the coffee at all, and the ice had melted away, leaving a drink as muddy brown as the flooded river. Trying to regain some sense of where I was, my stare traveled from table to table, person to person, spying on the lives of others.

Then my gaze froze.

My heart stopped.

Not even twenty feet away from me, a woman with jagged blond hair sat in profile, her graceful fingers tapping on the keyboard of a laptop. When she paused, which wasn't often, she sipped tea from a paper cup. Her face was absorbed in her work, and she didn't seem to notice the rest of the world.

She had no idea that a stranger at another table had seen her. That I had to plant my feet on the floor with heavy chains to stop myself from getting up and sweeping her into my arms.

That woman was Karly.

Perfect. Gorgeous. Alive.

That woman was my wife.

∞

Seeing her, I felt like a tongue-tied fool, with no idea what to do next. I could get up, go over there, introduce myself. But then what? Anything I would say to her felt completely insufficient to that moment. And yet if I offered even a glimmer of what was happening to me, she'd think I was crazy. I was the one whose world was turning upside down, not her.

Needless to say, I couldn't take my eyes off her. After a while, she felt it, the way you get that prick in your neck that someone is watching you. I saw her head turn, taking in the people around her, wondering where that odd feeling had come from. She stared at the others in the coffee shop one by one, and then, finally, she stared at me. Just for an instant, she looked right at me, before she moved on. I looked away, too, but the damage to my soul was already done.

I was crushed.

She didn't know me. There wasn't any recognition at all. Ten years ago, we'd had one date, and I'd come and gone from her life without making so much as a ripple. In my world, she'd found me bleeding in the car next to Roscoe, and we'd fallen in love with each other in the time it took for her to tell me that everything was going to be fine. But not now. Her gaze passed over me with no interest at all, no attraction, not even a physical curiosity. I felt *nothing* from her. Complete disinterest. That was worse than any other reaction she could have given.

The despair I felt made the reality of my situation very clear. Roscoe was right. I didn't belong in this world.

I got up from the table, took Karly's book with me, and left. I didn't even turn around for another glimpse of her. The risk of her looking back with those blank eyes was too painful. I went downstairs, anxious to get back outside. I knew what I should do. Go back to the lake, find a quiet place where no one could see me, and say the escape word simply and clearly. Say it out loud and hope that it would send me home.

But fate got in my way and reminded me why I was here.

As I walked back into the sunshine, I met a man coming the other way. He was old and slightly stooped, with salt-and-pepper hair. We were on a collision course, and I side-stepped to give him space. Instead, he blocked my path.

His weathered face studied me curiously. "Oh, hello again. Did you find her?"

"What?"

"Did you find the woman you were looking for? Karly Chance?"

I was about to say yes—but then I realized that I had no idea who this man was. We'd never met. I'd never seen him before. And yet *he* knew me.

"Why did you think I was looking for Karly Chance?" I asked, but the twisting sensation in my gut told me why.

His face screwed up with confusion. He squinted, looking at me again. "Didn't we meet last night? I could swear you were the man who asked me about Karly Chance. Sorry, it must have been someone who looked like you. These old eyes of mine aren't what they used to be. My mistake."

"No problem," I said, walking away.

I wanted to tell him his eyes were fine. He hadn't made a mistake.

My doppelgänger was still here. Still hunting. I couldn't leave this world until I'd found him.

Chapter 21

I spent the day consumed by thoughts of Karly. I didn't go to work, because the job at the hotel wasn't really *my* job. I didn't go home, because Tai wasn't really *my* wife.

But Karly? I couldn't stop thinking about her.

I went to the Bohemian National Cemetery, which is a couple of miles west of our apartment. That's where I go when I need to think. I usually visit one particular sculpture. Its true name is *The Pilgrim*, but people call it by other names. Death. Walking Death. The Grim Reaper. It shows an old woman covered by a cloak, walking with a staff toward a nearby mausoleum. Unless you get up close and look under the cloak, her face is invisible, just black shadow. However, the legend says that if you look at her face, you'll see a vision of how you're going to die. I'd never looked. It never seemed worth the risk. That day I was tempted enough that I stole a peek, but all I saw was the pilgrim mother's serene expression as she stared at the ground. She didn't give me any clues about what was coming next.

I spent the afternoon there, lingering even after the cemetery gates closed. I sat on the steps of the mausoleum, and I reread Karly's book of poems over and over. It wasn't just that I wanted to know the woman she was now, in this world. I wanted to know who she'd been. The wife I'd lost. The more I read, the more I fell in love with her all over again, as if I'd discovered an entirely new person. It killed me that we couldn't be together.

Eventually, the cemetery caretaker kicked me out. I had nowhere else to go, so the only thing I could do was head home to the apartment. When I got there, things got even worse.

Detective Bushing was waiting for me. He sat in the wicker chair where he'd been the day before, his face like a dry desert except for those sharp eyes. Tai sat on the sofa with her hands in her lap. She wouldn't even look at me.

"Mr. Moran," the detective croaked. "Welcome home."

I took a seat on the opposite end of the sofa from Tai. Her coolness gave a chill to the apartment.

"What do you want, Detective?" I asked.

Bushing pulled his briefcase into his lap and drew out a yellow pad, along with a stubby pencil in need of sharpening. "It's been a whole day since you got back. I was hoping you've started to remember things from when you were gone. Like what you did in the park that night when you went for a walk."

"I still don't remember anything."

"That's too bad."

"It is what it is, Detective. I can't help you."

Bushing nodded, seemingly unconcerned. "What about last night? You remember that, right? Where did you go last night?"

I saw the twitch of a smile on his lips. He knew something. I glanced at Tai, who was uncomfortably quiet.

"I went to visit a friend on the South Side. Roscoe Tate."

"Yes, your wife told me. She also said she called to check on you and found out that you left the parish where your friend works midevening. You didn't come home for several hours after that. Where did you go?"

"What business is it of yours, Detective? Why do you care?"

174

"I'm investigating a homicide, Mr. Moran. I care about everything."

"I don't see what that has to do with my whereabouts last night."

Bushing played with the pencil between his fingers. "Then let me explain it to you. The fact is, in this city, some murders are more equal than others. Ten black kids get shot on a holiday weekend, nobody seems to blink. But a pretty white girl gets stabbed in a park? People notice that. They see it in the paper; they remember it. It tends to generate a lot of tips. Most of them go nowhere, but every now and then, you find a needle in a haystack."

"You've lost me," I said.

"Well, see, a tip came in late last night. Someone in campus security at Northwestern called us. Seems a grad student reported a strange man stalking her near one of the residence halls. She gave a pretty good description of him, too. That kind of thing wouldn't typically make it onto our radar, but the security guy remembered the photo of Betsy Kern from the newspaper. He said the two women looked a lot alike."

Bushing removed two photographs from his briefcase. One was of Betsy Kern, the same photo I'd seen in the newspaper. The other was the young woman who'd confronted me near Goodrich Hall the previous night. The woman I'd thought was Karly.

"That security guard had good instincts," Bushing said. "These two women do resemble each other. Now, that in and of itself wouldn't really trip my trigger, but the security guy also sent along the description of the suspect. Figured it might help us. *That* got my attention. Short white guy, late twenties or early thirties, scruffy dark hair, heavy stubble. Sound like anybody you know, Mr. Moran?"

I didn't answer.

"The grad student also said the man who followed her was wearing a dark-red button-down shirt. According to your wife, you were wearing a shirt like that when you went out last night. Was that you on the Northwestern campus, Mr. Moran?"

He had me cornered, and we both knew it. All it would take was a photograph for the woman at Northwestern to identify me, if she hadn't done so already. I couldn't pretend that I hadn't been there.

"Yes," I admitted. "That was me."

"Why were you following that woman, Mr. Moran?"

"I wasn't. I saw someone else following her, and I was concerned. I was trying to intervene to make sure she was okay."

"She didn't see anyone else behind her. She saw *you*. She also said she was pretty sure you had a knife."

"I didn't."

"If we search your car, will we find a knife?"

"No."

"Because you got rid of it?"

"Because I never had one."

"Betsy Kern was killed with a knife."

"Yes, that's what you said."

"Did you kill Betsy Kern, Mr. Moran?"

"*No*," I hissed.

"Well, you say you don't remember anything from the night you disappeared. So how can you be sure?"

"I think I'd remember killing someone."

"Right. Or maybe this whole memory-loss story is nothing but a big pile of steaming dog shit on the bottom of your shoe."

"I'm telling you the truth. I don't remember that night. But I would never kill anyone."

"Then what were you doing up at Northwestern?"

I sighed, because I had no explanation that made any rational sense. I couldn't mention Karly. I had no connection with her, no reason to be looking for her. But even if I kept her name secret, it wouldn't take Bushing long to track down the calls I'd made and the people I'd talked to about Karly. He'd find a photograph of her and see the resemblance to the other two women.

176

They'd ask Karly about me, and as soon as they did, I'd be cut off from her forever. She would never talk to me, never trust me.

I could feel a web closing around my life, exactly the way it had in my own world. No doubt that was just what the other Dylan Moran wanted. I was running out of time.

"I drove up there to visit the Block Museum," I said, grasping for any kind of excuse.

"You went all the way from the South Side to the North Side to visit a museum? Why? When I talked to you, you said you were exhausted."

"I was, but I was also restless. I'd lost two days of my life, and I didn't know what had happened to me. I was trying to shut off my mind and see if anything came back. It's not like I really thought about where I was going. The Block had a photography exhibit I wanted to see, so I went up there."

"Did you see it?"

"No. The museum was closed by the time I got there. I had it in my head that they were open until nine or ten. I was wrong. They closed at eight. So since I was already up there, I decided to take a walk."

Bushing snorted. "Another *walk*, Mr. Moran? You took a walk on Tuesday, and Betsy Kern died. You took a walk last night, and a woman who looks a lot like Betsy Kern saw you coming after her with a knife."

"She made a mistake."

"Is that the story you plan to stick with?"

"It's the truth."

The detective stuffed papers back into his briefcase and stood up from the wicker chair. "Let me tell you what happens next, Mr. Moran. I'm going to tear your whole life apart. Everywhere you've lived. Worked. Gone to school. Gone on vacation. I'll be looking to see if there are unsolved murders around the time you've been there. Then I'll be back with a warrant to search your house, your car, your office, everything."

"You can search all you want. I'm innocent, Detective. I haven't done anything."

"Yeah? Well, if I were you, I'd get a lawyer." Bushing glanced at Tai. "And if I were *you*, Mrs. Moran, I'd think about sleeping somewhere else."

∞

When Bushing was gone, Tai stayed on the sofa, not saying anything. Her back was straight, with perfect posture, and she kept her hands neatly folded in her lap. She calmed herself with steady breaths, and then her head swiveled slowly to watch me. Her eyes didn't blink.

"Who are you?" she asked.

"Come on, Tai."

"I'm serious. Who are you?"

"You know who I am."

Tai shook her head. "No, I thought I did. Now I don't know. I'm beginning to wonder if you've been wearing a mask all along. Yesterday I was afraid you were having an affair, but this is a thousand times worse."

She got up from the sofa. As she passed by me, I grabbed her hand to stop her, but she made a violent twist to shrug me away. "Don't touch me! Keep your hands off me!"

"Tai, I'm sorry. I wish I could make sense of this for you."

"But you can't."

"No. The only thing I can tell you is that I am *not* a killer."

Tai's mouth pinched into a frown. Her eyes made it clear that she didn't believe me.

"Who were you having sex with last night?"

"What do you mean?"

"Who were you screwing in our bed last night, Dylan? Because it wasn't me. You were thinking of someone else, I could tell. Was it this girl at Northwestern?"

"Tai, please. This is all messed up."

"Yes, it is. It's very messed up. Sleep on the sofa tonight. I don't want you anywhere near me."

"Whatever you want. But I swear to you, you have nothing to fear from me."

Tai walked away. At the fireplace, she stopped and studied our wedding photo, then reached up and turned it facedown on the mantel. "I have nothing to fear from my husband," she told me. "You're not the man I married."

Chapter 22

The next day, I found Karly back in the coffee shop at Northwestern.

I had a decision to make. Talk to her, or let her go. I knew I couldn't get what I wanted from this world. I'd never have Karly back in my life forever. The walls were closing in on me, and soon I'd have to leave. But she was here now. Even a few minutes with her were more than I'd thought I would ever have again.

I walked over to her table.

"Karly?"

She brushed her hair from her blue eyes and looked up at me. Her gaze was far away. I'd distracted her in the midst of a thought. "Yes?"

"You are Karly Chance, aren't you?"

"Yes."

I tried to be myself and not to choke on my words. "I'm sure you won't remember, but we went out on a date a long time ago."

She gave me a smile. It wasn't a Karly smile, but a smile of polite disinterest. "Did we? I'm sorry, but you're right. I don't remember."

I shook off the blow to my ego and replied with a joke. "Don't worry about it. It went so well you've probably blocked out the entire experience."

Her eyes reviewed my face, trying to place me in her memory. It was excruciating, because to me, she looked exactly the same. Her face, the pale lips, the firm confidence in how she held her jaw. Her voice, soft and musical, making you lean in close to hear her. The uneven blond-brown ends of her hair. I was madly in love with this woman, and she didn't know me at all.

"Your friend Sarah introduced us," I added. "I'm . . . Dylan Moran."

At the sound of my name, something changed in her expression. She blinked; her pupils dilated. Her eyes reappraised me with an odd curiosity. She looked uncomfortable, and I wasn't sure why. Had something happened on that date that I didn't know about?

"*Dylan*," she murmured. "That was you? The blind date?"

"That was me."

"I'm sorry. I do remember now. It's just that my life is sort of Before and After, and that was Before."

"We went to a club that night, didn't we? I don't even remember which one."

"The Spybar," Karly replied without hesitation.

"Right, of course. Well, I'm sure that went really well. I have a reputation for being the world's worst dancer."

"You're probably being hard on yourself," she said generously.

"Oh, I doubt it. Anyway, I'm ten years late in apologizing."

"That's not necessary. I went into it with the wrong attitude. I hate blind dates."

"Same here."

We'd had our exchange of pleasantries. Now it was time for me to walk away. But there was still so much to tell her.

I'm your husband.

I love you.

You're in danger.

I couldn't say any of that, but I also couldn't let meaningless small talk be my last conversation with Karly.

"I've read your poems," I added.

"Oh?"

"Your book. *Portal.* In fact, after I bought it, I read it four times in a row."

"Four times. Are you a masochist?"

I smiled. That was such a Karly thing to say. "Actually, your poems are very eloquent, but they made me sad."

"Sad? I don't hear that very often. I hear disgusting. Gross. Satanic. But sad is a new one."

"They made me sad because when I read them, I realized what I missed," I told her.

"I don't understand."

"I had a date with someone who was obviously very deep, thoughtful, complicated, and talented, and I didn't get to know her at all."

Karly took a sip of tea as she reflected on what I'd said. I wasn't trying to flatter her. I was being sincere. If she was still the woman I loved, she'd recognize that.

After a moment's hesitation, she said, "Do you want to sit down?"

"I would. Thank you."

I took a seat and had to restrain myself from reaching over to caress her face, which would have felt so natural. Her gaze flicked to my left hand, where I still wore my wedding ring. White gold, with an inlaid Celtic knot over black titanium. "That's a beautiful ring," she said.

"Yes, it is." I wanted to tell her: *You gave it to me.*

"So you're married."

I didn't know how to answer her. My wife was sitting at this table, and she didn't even know it.

"I was."

"Divorced?"

"She died."

"Oh, I'm so sorry."

"Thank you. I still haven't been able to take off the ring."

"I understand."

"It's hard enough that I lost her, but our last conversation was an argument. She made a mistake, and I couldn't get past it. I let it ruin us."

"What was her mistake?"

"It doesn't matter. She was talking to me, but I wasn't listening. Now it's too late for me to make things right. There's so much that I wish I could tell her."

Karly's eyes drilled into mine. "What would you say?"

I thought about that. My wife was sitting right here, and I could tell her anything I wanted. It was easy now to say what I couldn't say before. *I forgive you.* But I was so far past that. If I could have my wife back, I wanted her to know that things would be different.

"'*Don't give up on me,*'" I said. "That's what I'd tell her."

"Maybe she felt the same way. I mean, it was her mistake."

"Maybe. We'd both gone down the wrong path and ended up somewhere we didn't want to be. I just wish we could get a do-over. A second chance. I want that more than anything in the world."

"Yes, it would be nice if life worked like that. I think about that a lot."

"I'm sure." I frowned and then said, "I heard what happened to you. Your mother. And everything after."

Karly nodded. "I don't run away from it. Not anymore."

"I probably didn't tell you about this when we met. The Dylan from back then didn't like to share personal things. My parents died when I was a kid. My father shot my mother, and then he killed himself. I was there to see it happen. It changed me. I had to make a lot of choices in my life after that, and believe me, I didn't always make the right ones."

She sipped her tea, but her eyes never left mine. To me, it felt unbelievably intimate. "That's an interesting way of phrasing it."

"What's that?"

"'The Dylan from back then.' Almost as if you're not the same person."

"I'm not. Not really."

"I'm well aware of that feeling," Karly said.

"I imagine so."

"Why are you telling me this, Dylan?"

"I guess I want you to know who I am."

"No offense, but why does that matter?"

"Because I learned who you were from your poems, and you never got a chance to know me."

"It was only one date," she reminded me. Then she said something extremely strange. "Wasn't it?"

I wanted to say: *No. No, it was so much more than that.* But I didn't.

"You're right. It was just one date."

She almost looked disappointed at my reaction.

I realized that my coffee cup was empty. I picked it up and crumpled it in my hand. She smiled; I smiled. Two nervous, awkward smiles. I checked my watch, and she checked hers. We'd swayed on the edge of being something other than strangers, but that was all we could be here.

"Well, it was good seeing you, Karly."

"You too."

"Take care of yourself. Be safe."

"I will."

"Maybe—" I began, then stopped.

"Maybe what?"

"I don't know. It's foolish. I was thinking, maybe sometime we could try a do-over. On our date, I mean."

She hesitated. "Maybe."

I got up from the table, but then sat down again immediately. I couldn't let go of her so easily. I couldn't let this be nothing more than a vague promise of seeing her again sometime in an uncertain future. I needed more than that. "Actually, do you mind if I ask you one other question?"

"If you like."

"It's about your book. Why *Portal?*"

"What do you mean?"

"There's no poem by that name in the book. And the cover, with the endless mirrors. I didn't see any connection in the poems. What did any of that have to do with what you wrote?"

An answer rolled smoothly off her tongue, as if she'd said it a million times. "I tell people that the book was a portal from who I was to who I am. I was leaving my relationship with Susannah, and my guilt over what happened to her, in the past. I was stepping through a door to somewhere else. Does that make sense?"

"Yes, it does." But somehow I thought she was testing me, so I relied on my instincts and plunged ahead. "Except I feel like that's not the real reason. Is it?"

She hesitated. "Actually, no. It's not."

"What is?"

Her fingers twisted strands of her hair in a gesture I knew very well. "If I tell you, you'll think I'm crazy."

"Trust me, I won't."

"I have no idea why I'm saying this to you, Dylan. I don't know you, and I've never admitted this to anyone."

Because we're still connected, I thought.

"I'll keep your secret," I told her.

Karly stroked her cheek as she stared at me, studying me, evaluating who I was. A stranger. I could feel her debating with herself. When she spoke, even before she formed the words, I knew she was going to say something that changed absolutely everything. "Have you ever heard of something called the Many Worlds theory? It's from quantum mechanics in physics."

I wanted to scream, but I could barely breathe. All I could say was, "I have."

"Do you know what it says? About the idea of living other lives? About parallel worlds?"

My voice was almost inaudible. "Yes."

"Do you believe it's possible?"

"Actually, I do."

"I tried to drown myself," Karly went on. "I nearly died."

"I know."

"I was in a coma for almost a month."

"Yes."

"The thing is, while I was in that coma, I went somewhere. I didn't even recognize the place. It was some kind of—some kind of dollhouse. I know that sounds weird, but it was a huge dollhouse. There were other Karlys there. Endless numbers of them, all like me, as if they were passing through on their way to somewhere else. It was like I was *inside* those Many Worlds, at a kind of crossroads."

She stopped. Embarrassment filled her face. "See, I'm crazy."

"*No.* Go on."

"I met one of the others there. I know how it sounds, but this woman was another *me*, living a totally different life. I told her everything that had happened to me, about Susannah, about how bitter she was about her business failures, about how we never got along. And then how I lost myself after she was gone. This other Karly understood my dark side, even though she had a much happier life. She was in love. She was married to—"

Karly stopped.

"Who?" I asked urgently. "Who was she married to?"

She looked down. "It doesn't matter. I told you, she had a different life. Anyway, she wasn't a poet, but she was talented and funny. We sat in a corner of the dollhouse, watching the other Karlys coming and going, and we wrote poems together. We wrote *Portal*. Her and me. We sifted through all that dark matter together and came out the other side."

"That sounds like an amazing experience."

Karly shook her head with something like wonder. "It was. Except none of it was real."

"Are you sure?"

"Of course it wasn't. It was me talking to me. All I know is, when I came out of my coma, most of the poems from that book were already in my head. I knew what I needed to do with my life. I was finally ready to let go of the past and become a different person." Suddenly, Karly pushed her chair back and stood up. "God, what am I doing? This is nuts. Please don't tell anyone I said this."

"I won't."

"I need to go."

"No, wait, stay. I want to talk more. There are things I need to tell you."

"I'm sorry, I really have to go. I'm meeting a student in my office. I don't know how you found me, Dylan, but I'd rather not discuss any of this again. I shouldn't have said what I did."

She gathered up her laptop and her papers, but I put my hand gently on hers. The hand where I wore my ring. "Meet me tonight," I said.

"I don't think that's a good idea."

"Please. I want to tell you a story."

"It's better if you and I don't share anything more. We don't know each other."

"Karly."

She stopped. I saw a faint tremble in her whole body. "What is it?"

"Don't give up on me."

Her hand covered her mouth. She didn't say a word. Instead, she stared down at the table and hugged her laptop to her chest.

"Meet me tonight," I said again.

Without looking up, Karly nodded. "Nine o'clock. Right here."

Then she hurried away.

After she left, I was flying.

I was so high I couldn't see any way back down, which is a dangerous thing. The higher you go, the farther you're likely to fall. Even so, I allowed myself to dream that I could tell Karly the truth, and she might believe me. I began to wonder if she and I could really start over in this world and rebuild what we had. That was the first moment of happiness I'd had since the accident.

Then I went to see Roscoe, and he sent me plummeting back to the ground.

I told him everything that had happened in the past day—including finding the body of *his* Dylan by the river—and when I was done, he bowed his head in grief. When he finally looked up again, his eyes were as cold as I'd ever seen them. This was not Roscoe the priest. This was Roscoe the friend, and I'd disappointed him.

"I told you that you didn't belong in this place," he snapped at me. "I told you to go back home before more people suffered. Now look what you've done. Look at the wreckage you've already caused."

"What happened by the river wasn't my fault," I protested.

"Is that true? Can I believe anything you tell me? You arrive out of nowhere with this story of parallel worlds, and now you tell me my real friend is dead. Murdered. How do I know that you didn't decide to do this yourself? Get him out of the way, take over his life, all so you can find a way to be with Karly again."

I shook my head. "Roscoe, you know me. I would never do anything like that—"

"Actually, you made it clear that I *don't* know you. And you're right. Yesterday you promised me that your only interest in Karly was to protect her from this so-called killer. Now here you are, telling me you think you can get her back, just as I predicted. I'm sorry, Dylan. Haven't you done enough damage?"

"How is it damage if she and I are meant to be together?"

Roscoe exhaled slowly and loudly. He took off his black glasses and wiped them on his sleeve. Then he positioned them on his face and focused his hard eyes on me. "Do you know what I spent an hour doing just before you got here? I was talking to Tai. She's devastated.

Confused. Afraid. She thinks she's lost her husband, a man she deeply loves, and from what you tell me, she's right. I don't care whether there really is a dead man by the river or not. I don't care whether your story of parallel worlds is true or a delusion. What I care about is seeing my friend—a man *I* love—turn his back on his wife and pursue a relationship with someone else. That is not who you are."

"Roscoe, I feel bad for Tai, but I don't love her. She's not my wife."

"In this world, she is!" Roscoe shouted, his voice echoing off the high ceiling of the church. He closed his eyes, then spoke more softly. "I'm sorry. If you're going to live in this world, you have responsibilities to this world. You can't come in here and expect things to be the way they were. You made decisions here. You made choices here. You have to honor them."

I clenched my fists. "Roscoe, try to understand my situation. I love Karly, and I *lost* her. I never believed there was any way to have her back again. But now I realize she went through something similar to what's happening to me. It's not a delusion. She'll listen to me."

"Really? How do you think that goes, Dylan? You're the suspect in the murder of a woman who looks just like her. You told her that your wife died, but pretty soon she'll discover that your wife is actually alive and you've lied to her. You think she's going to ignore all of that and fall in love with you? You think there's any way this ends well?"

"Roscoe—"

My friend shook his head with the sharpness of a door closing. "No. I'm sorry, Dylan. You can't simply undo the choices you regret from another life. That's not how it works. All you can do is learn from them and become a better man."

"I'm trying to do that. I swear, I'm trying to change."

"Change requires *sacrifice*. Change requires *acceptance* of your sins. Is that what you're doing? Or are you still pursuing your own selfish desires? I'm telling you, walk away. Walk away from Karly. If you think you can't be with Tai, then walk away from this world altogether."

"You don't know what you're asking."

"I do. Believe me, I do."

"Roscoe, I came to you as my friend. I need your help."

"Yes, I know. Believe it or not, help is what I'm giving you. I know you think I should be loyal to you, and I've told you many times that I'd always be there for you. But you've also made it clear that you're *not* the man I know. *My* friend is dead. Don't you understand? The longer you stay here, the worse it's going to get. You are a trespasser, Dylan. You need to leave."

Chapter 23

When I got home, Tai was packing. Grabbing clothes by the handful, she stalked back and forth between our closet and a pink suitcase on the bed. Her long black hair was mussed, her golden face streaked with tears. I stood in the doorway, and she pretended to ignore me, but I could feel the depth of her hurt. Watching her, I knew that Roscoe was right about everything. I'd come to this world and ruined her life. She deserved better.

Her husband, her real husband, was gone. He was dead by the river, and he was never coming back. Meanwhile, the husband who was living in her house was in love with another woman.

"Who is she?" Tai asked, as if she could read my mind.

"What?"

She stopped in the middle of the bedroom and let the dresses she was carrying fall to the floor. "I followed you this morning. I saw you talking to that blond woman at Northwestern. Who is she?"

I hesitated, but there was no point in trying to hide it. "Her name is Karly Chance."

"Are you having an affair with her?"

"There's no affair."

"Don't lie to me. I *saw* you. Do you think I can't read your face? Do you think I haven't looked for that expression when you stare at *me*?

But I've never seen it. Not once. You've never looked at me the way you were looking at her."

"It's impossible to explain," I told her. "You wouldn't believe me if I told you."

"Save your explanations. I don't care. I'm leaving. I'm going to stay with a girlfriend."

"Tai, I'm sorry."

She shook her head. "No, you're not. That's the worst thing. You say the words, but you're not sorry at all."

"That's not true. I hate that I've hurt you."

"Everybody warned me. My family. Roscoe. Hell, even Edgar warned me. They said I was making a mistake by marrying you. I should have listened."

There was nothing I could say to that.

"Is it love?" Tai went on. "Are you in love with this woman? Or is it something worse?"

"What do you mean?"

"I'm not an idiot, Dylan. I see the resemblance. She looks like the woman who was murdered across the street from us. She looks like the woman you were stalking behind the dorm at Northwestern. What kind of man are you? Who did I marry?"

"You have it all wrong," I insisted.

"Do I? Well, I guess we'll see about that. I gave Detective Bushing the clothes you were wearing when you came back on Thursday. I told him to get your DNA and test it. If you killed Betsy Kern, they'll find out."

"I don't care what the test shows. I didn't kill anyone."

"In other words, you already know the DNA will match."

"I'm telling you, this is *not* what it looks like."

She started packing again. "Go away, Dylan. Leave me alone. I don't want to be in the same apartment with you."

"Tai, please—"

"Go!" she screamed at me. "Get out! If you don't go, I'll call 911 and have them drag you out."

I held up my hands in surrender. "Okay. Whatever you want. I'll go."

I left the apartment, because I didn't want her to get any more upset. She was wrong about me, wrong about who I was and what I'd done, but then again, she wasn't wrong. No, I wasn't a killer, but the DNA would probably say that I was. No, I wasn't having an affair, but I was in love with Karly and would take her back in my arms if I could. I'd been cruel to Tai in this world, but it's not like I'd been a saint to her in my own world. I'd led her on and told myself it was innocent, because I had no bad intentions. But it wasn't innocent at all.

After I left the apartment, I took the stairs to Edgar's place. My grandfather and I didn't have a great relationship in any world, but I was running out of people to talk to. Roscoe and Tai had both thrown me out. I was feeling increasingly isolated by my mistakes.

Through the door, I heard the blare of a game show on his television. I had a key, so I let myself in. He was asleep in a recliner, his snores blowing like a trumpet. Seeing him like that, alone, gave me a shiver. Despite the six decades between us, I can always see the family resemblance. It's not just him and me. I can see my father in both of our faces, too. His ghost is never far away.

When I shut off the television, the sudden silence jarred Edgar awake. He blinked with surprise, seeing me sitting on the sofa opposite him.

"You're up here?" he growled. "Am I dying or something?"

I gave a sad smile. "No."

"Then what's going on?"

"I just wanted to see how you were."

Edgar reached for a warm open can of Budweiser. "You're going to have to do better than that."

"Okay. Well, if you want the truth, Tai is downstairs packing. She didn't want me around."

"She leaving you?"

"Yes."

"You cheat on her?"

"It's complicated. Mostly, I think she just figured out that I wasn't in love with her."

Edgar snorted. "I'm pretty sure she knew that from the beginning."

I thought about the Dylan whose life I'd taken over and the choice he'd made to be with Tai. I still didn't understand it. "She said you told her not to marry me."

"That's right."

"Sounds like everybody told her the same thing."

"Yeah, so? Were we wrong?"

"I guess not."

"So what are you going to do?" Edgar asked.

"What is there to do? She's leaving."

"Yeah. Give up. That sounds like you."

"I don't love her, Edgar. According to you and Roscoe, I never did. The best thing I can do is let her find someone who really does love her."

Edgar laughed so hard he nearly spat out his beer. "That's the best thing? For who, you or her? Aren't you forgetting something? That girl was nuts about you from the beginning, and I assume she still is. Everyone told her you were damaged goods and she should run away, but she didn't. That takes some balls, I'll tell you. It's not like she didn't know what she was getting, but she saw something in you that you didn't see in yourself. I gave her a lot of credit for that. Honestly, I gave you credit, too. I expected you to bail on her, but you stuck it out, at least until now. You worked your butt off to make a life with her, and it seemed to me like it was paying off. This past year, you were as happy as I'd ever seen you."

I hadn't heard that word very often in my life. "Happy? Tai made me happy?"

"Sure looked that way to me. I was beginning to think the two of you would go the distance. That would be a first in our family. I screwed things up, and your father—well, we both know about him. But you and Tai seemed to click. Made me glad to see it. I don't know what the hell happened to ruin that, and I'm not judging anything you did, because I'm sure no angel myself. But it's a shame. That's all I'll say. It's a shame."

Edgar's admonition hit me like a punch to the gut.

Since I'd been here, the only thing I'd processed was the idea that the Dylan Moran who was married to Tai didn't really love her. Not the way I loved Karly. That was all I needed to know. I saw a man who was nothing like me in any way other than our bodies. He was without fire, without passion, without a wife who was his soul mate. I looked into his closet and saw clothes that I hated and cuff links and cologne I'd never wear. It had literally never occurred to me that he was actually satisfied with his life. That he was wearing that cologne because his wife picked it out for him. That he went to Disney World and Hawaii because it made him happy to be with her. That he was trying hard to rise above his past and build a marriage that worked.

He was not me, and their relationship was not mine. But I'd taken that away from them. I'd destroyed their lives by coming here. Tai was about to walk away with her dreams shattered and her faith gone, and she had no idea *why*. She'd question herself and find it impossible to trust again. The man she'd loved had proven himself to be a total stranger, someone she didn't know at all.

Because of me. Because I *was* a stranger.

Son of a bitch. What had I done?

"I have to go," I told Edgar.

I knew what to do. Whether it was crazy or not, whether she believed me or not, I finally had to tell Tai the truth. I couldn't let her walk away thinking that her Dylan had changed. The mistake wasn't hers. I had to lay it all out and explain why her life had been turned upside down in a few short days. I also had to give her the hard truth that her real husband wasn't coming back.

I left Edgar. I ran back downstairs and let myself inside our place.

"Tai!" I shouted.

She didn't answer.

"Tai, I need to tell you something!"

And still there was only hurt silence.

"Please. Listen to me."

I glanced out the windows. Her car was still at the curb; she hadn't left. I went into the bedroom and saw her pink suitcase still on the bed, half-packed. The bathroom door was half-shut. The light was on inside. I went over and tapped my knuckles against the door.

"Tai? I'm sorry—I know you told me to go, but I really need to explain. It's important."

Still she ignored me.

I listened at the door, expecting to hear quiet tears, but all I heard from the other side was the noise of water running. When I looked down at my feet, I saw a stream of water creeping under the crack beneath the door, growing and spreading across the bedroom floor. My heartbeat took off with fear. I pushed the door open and went inside. Water flooded around my feet. When I glanced to my left, I saw the tub overflowing, cold water running down the fiberglass wall like a river overflowing its banks.

I took two steps and looked into the tub, and I wailed in disbelief. From under the crystal-clear water, Tai stared back at me, eyes wide open, mouth wide open. She wore the yellow dress she'd been wearing a few minutes ago, its sunny fabric now pasted to her skin. I knew she was dead, but I turned off the water and grabbed her torso and pulled it toward me. Her body was a limp weight, unmoving, her skin already frigid. Her face never changed; her fixed eyes stared at me with the same terrified expression.

"Tai," I murmured, shaking my head. "Oh, my God, Tai."

I knelt on the wet floor and held her. Water dripped and sloshed around me. I shook her and kissed her forehead, and I gently closed her mouth with my hand and used my fingers to shut her eyes. She looked peaceful that way, but I was caught in a storm. My mind struggled to catch up to what had happened. It took me until that moment to realize that someone had killed her.

Someone had grabbed her and overpowered her and run the water and held her down where she couldn't breathe.

Someone. Me.

I heard a footstep behind me. Tai's body slipped from my arms, and I spun around. I tried to get up quickly on the wet floor, but I was too late.

He was there, looming over me. *I* was there.

Dylan Moran stared down at me, his mouth bent into a hard frown, his blue eyes as implacable as a stormy ocean. The leather jacket he wore was wet, where Tai had soaked him as she fought for her life. He had a dirty red brick from the back patio in his hand. Before I could get to my feet and put my hands around his neck, he swung the brick toward the side of my head. I saw it coming, heard the rush of air. I tried to duck, but I wasn't fast enough.

A white-hot eruption of pain went off inside my skull like fireworks, and then I was gone.

Chapter 24

I awoke to a raging headache and the coppery taste of blood. My eyes blinked open. At first, I saw only the ceiling fan rotating slowly above me, making a low rattle. Then I shifted my head and saw that I lay in bed. When I tried to move, I found that I was tied down, spread-eagled, my wrists and ankles tightly bound with silk neckties to the four corners of the bed frame.

Night hadn't fallen yet, but the room around me was dark. The heavy curtains were closed. In the dense shadows, I could barely distinguish a kitchen chair that had been pulled into the corner of the bedroom. Someone was sitting in it. A dark shape watched me. I could hear his breathing and the rustle of his clothes as he moved. He knew I was awake now. With the scrape of a match, I saw a tiny flame illuminating the skin of his hands. Then the sting of cigarette smoke made its way to me.

"Hello, Dylan," my doppelgänger said.

He pushed himself off the chair and came and stood over the bed. I stared into a black mirror, his face identical to mine. He had the collar of my father's leather jacket pulled up, framing his neck like the wings of a crow. Under it, he wore a collarless olive-colored shirt, untucked and misbuttoned. He had wild, messy dark hair, and he hadn't shaved in days. The bones of his face jutted out in angles that looked sharp enough to make you bleed. He was the same as me in every physical way, but we were two different people. His mouth had no expression, whereas Karly had always told me she could read my mood by my lips. Given the things he'd done, I expected to see cruelty shining in his blue eyes, but his fixed gaze offered no evidence of his sadism. The bubbling cauldron inside him had to be at the bottom of a deep well.

"You didn't have to kill Tai," I said.

He didn't answer right away. He examined me with the same intensity I'd given him. With two fingers, he freed the cigarette from his mouth, tilted his chin, and exhaled gray smoke. Then he said with a shrug, "I do what I want."

The other Dylan retrieved the wooden chair. He put it next to the bed and sat down, folding his legs with the black heel of his dress shoe balanced on his other knee. He took the cigarette and offered me a drag with a flick of his eyebrows. I shook my head.

"I'm glad to finally see you up close," he said.

"Why?"

He shrugged. "Most of the Dylan Morans out there are dull little people. Frigid, depressed, beaten down. Look at this one, letting his wife dress him up like a Ken doll. It's hard for me to respect someone like that. But you fought back. You came after me. It makes me think you're more like me than the others."

"I'm nothing like you."

He gave me a quick, cynical laugh. "Oh, come on. You want to kill me, don't you? That's why you're here. That was your plan. If I let you, you'd wrap your hands around my throat and choke the life out of me. Admit it. We're not so different."

"I'm trying to stop you from killing anyone else. That's the difference."

"Yeah, you're a hero, and I'm the devil. You have no innocent blood on your hands." He leaned close, engulfing me in the smoke of his cigarette, and whispered in my ear. "But then why is Roscoe dead in your world? Why is *Karly* dead? You killed them, not me."

I flailed against the bonds but couldn't free myself. I stared at him with murder in my eyes. He was right. I would have strangled him then and there if I could.

He grinned, as if he'd made his point. Then he got up from the chair and went to the closet and began taking out men's clothes, which he draped across the bed piece by piece like a fashion show. "Relax. I'm just baiting you. I don't apologize for who I am. Unlike most of our other twins, I accept it. So should you."

"I can't imagine becoming someone like you. Doing the things you've done."

He shrugged, as if we were talking about the ethnic foods we liked and didn't like. As he reviewed the clothes he'd taken from the closet, he held up a Hawaiian shirt from the bed and rolled his eyes. Then he sat down in the chair again.

"Really? You've spent your whole life afraid of turning into your father. Why is it so strange to meet a Dylan Moran who did?"

His one cigarette was done, so he took the time to light another. Every motion he made was unhurried. When he'd savored a few puffs, he leaned close to me, with curiosity in his voice.

"Let me ask you something. If you could go back to that day, what would you do? You know what I'm talking about. Dad took the gun and fired. Mom was dead. You're sitting in the corner. What would you do differently?"

"I was a kid," I said, trying to make myself believe it this time. "There's nothing I could have done."

"Not true. I did something."

Oddly, I found that I had to know. "What did you do?"

"I killed him. I charged him, knocked him over, took the gun, and blew his head off. I got revenge for our mother."

"I don't believe you."

"Why not? Because you were a coward, and I wasn't? Because you wish you'd done the same thing as me?"

"I don't wish that."

"No? Then why do you keep getting into fights with men who abuse their partners? It's because when the chips were down, you didn't stand up for our mother. You did nothing, and it eats you alive."

I felt myself breathing hard. I wanted to scream a denial, but he wasn't wrong. Yes, I'd dreamed about doing what this other Dylan had done. This mirror of myself, this serial killer, knew me better than I knew myself. A little smirk of triumph crossed his face as I looked away.

"See?" he announced, easing back in the chair and sucking on his cigarette. "I'm the ultimate Dylan Moran. I do what all of you wish you could do, and I get away with everything. Killing my father? They let me off. I was just a traumatized kid. In high school, I kept beating kids up, but they didn't do a thing to me. Oh, that poor boy, he had such a tough upbringing. They'd send me to detention, or send me to a counselor, and then I'd do it again. Sound familiar?"

I frowned. Yes, it did.

"So I just kept raising the stakes. I wanted to see how far I could go. But I already knew where I was headed. I knew the line I wanted to cross. It's how I'm wired. Somewhere inside you, you've got the same code, whether you like it or not." He shot me a look that said he was familiar with all my secrets. "Who was the first girl you slept with? Diana Geary, right?"

There was no point in lying. "Yes."

"How'd you meet her?"

"We met on a train," I said, because it was obvious the same thing had happened to him. "I was seventeen. She was older, twenty-two. We started talking and went back to her place, and then she got me drunk on tequila, and we ended up in bed. She was feeling bad because her boyfriend had dumped her, and I was the consolation prize."

"I met Diana Geary on a train, too," the other Dylan replied. "Same as you. We had sex."

He stopped. He waited for me to ask, and I couldn't stop myself.

"Then what?"

"Then after we were done, I suffocated her with a pillow and cut off her head."

"Oh, shit." I struggled against the ropes that held me again, but I couldn't move.

"And do you know what happened after I killed her? Not a damn thing. No one found out. No one knew it was me. Once I figured that out, once I knew I could do anything, I tried different methods, different victims. The violence itself wasn't really the high. The thrill was knowing I could get away with it. By the time I turned twenty-six, I'd killed fourteen people. The police had no idea."

"You're a sick son of a bitch."

He shrugged off my loathing, as if moral and immoral were just mirror images of each other.

"I could have kept going like that for a long time, but everything changed on my twenty-sixth birthday. Do you remember what you did that day?"

Actually, I did. It was a memorable thing to do on my birthday. "I saw a shrink."

"That's right. Court-ordered therapy for anger management. After a bar fight."

"Yes."

"Who did you see?"

"Her name was Vanessa Kirby."

Dylan nodded. "Yeah, I was supposed to see Dr. Kirby, too, but she was sick that day and didn't show up. So I saw someone else. There was a shrink with an office on the same floor, and I figured, what the hell? All I needed to do was check off a box on my court papers. Guess who I saw?"

My brow furrowed. "Who?"

"Eve Brier."

I swore under my breath.

"Yeah, isn't it funny how things work out? Eve was smart. She really got me. She told me that I felt guilty about killing my father and getting away with it. She said I felt an intense need to be punished, so I kept putting myself in situations that proved I was a bad person. Of course, I hadn't told her about any of the other people I'd killed, but I guess that would have just proved her point."

Dylan got up from the chair again. He grabbed a skinny-fit dress shirt in deep purple, with a checkered design. He held it up on the hanger. "What do you think of this shirt? Can I pull it off?"

I stared at him. "What?"

"Is it stylish? Maybe with a button vest? There's not a lot to choose from here."

"You want fashion tips? Are you kidding me?"

He shrugged and took off the leather jacket and unbuttoned his olive shirt. When he slipped it off, I noticed a pattern of scars all across his bare chest, like cuts made with a razor blade. It was obvious they'd been self-inflicted. I understood why Eve thought that this Dylan felt a desire for punishment. He'd been taking out his self-hatred on his body for years.

"Anyway, that was when she told me about the Many Worlds thing," he went on. "Did you think it was bullshit?"

"Yes."

"Yeah. Me too. But Eve wanted to try it on someone, and I thought, what the hell? She said experiencing other worlds would help me deal with the bad choices I'd made. So I let her inject me with her little cocktail. That was a ride, huh? There I was in the Art Institute, surrounded by all of these other versions of myself. Except I was the only one who knew what it meant. The others were oblivious. Knowing what was going on made it even worse. The more of them I saw, the more I felt like I was cracking up. Is that what it was like for you?"

I didn't want to answer, but I did. "Yes, that's exactly how it was."

He nodded, as if it made him happy to hear that. Then, without saying anything more, he turned around and went into the bathroom. With his back to me, he found a razor and shaving cream in the medicine cabinet, and he began shaving his face with slow, measured strokes. He was doing that with Tai's body still in the tub, where he'd drowned her. We could see each other in the mirror, and he smiled a little as I kept struggling to free my hands and feet. But I couldn't.

Eventually, he finished, washed his face, and came back, drying his now-smooth skin with a towel. He sat down and continued his story. "I didn't try to go anywhere that first time. I just got the lay of the land, you know? Then I said the word—you know the word—and boom, there I was back with Eve. She asked if the treatment helped me, and I told her it did. That was true, but not in the way she was thinking. I was already starting to wonder if I could really go into one of these worlds. So I said I wanted more sessions. The next time, I followed one of the other Dylans out the door. I had no idea what to expect, but holy shit. I was totally lost. When I woke up, it was days later. I was on the can in a men's room in Woodfield Mall in Schaumburg. It made no sense, right? Except when I got out into the mall, I spotted my double, and I followed him. I never let him see me, but I got to know his whole life. I stayed there for a week or so, and finally I said the safe word to get the hell out of there. Same thing, there I was, back in Eve's office, and like half an hour had passed on her end. I told her I wanted to keep doing it. I wanted to go back. Only this time I knew what to do."

"Kill," I murmured.

"Oh, yeah. I followed another Dylan into his life, and I watched him. Studied him. Figured out his routines. Then I did an experiment. I went into his job at the hotel while he was at a meeting somewhere else. Nobody knew. Nobody suspected a thing. I mean, why would they? So then I slept with his wife. She thought it was the best sex they'd ever had. I loved that. And then on a night when I knew he was home alone, I picked up a girl at a bar and went to her place."

I closed my eyes. I knew what was coming.

"And then I cut out her heart."

I swore, over and over and over.

"The next day, I watched from the park as the police arrested this other Dylan Moran. They had him on camera at the bar. He'd given his name to the bartender. They had his fingerprints in her apartment. They took him away, screaming that he was innocent. I'd never had a high like that. The thrill of killing wasn't even close to the thrill of watching Dylan Moran suffer for *my* crimes. Of all things, it turned out that Eve was right about me. I really did want the punishment. I wanted everybody to know that Dylan Moran was an evil, terrible person who should be put away forever. But the best thing was, I could do it over and over and never stop. There was always another world, another Dylan to destroy."

"The perfect crime," I said.

"The perfect crime," he agreed. "You're right."

He put on the checked purple shirt he'd found earlier, and then he went back to the closet and grabbed a gray vest. He changed pants, too, switching from jeans to black slacks with tapered legs. He slipped his feet into loafers. He took one of the cologne bottles from the nightstand, opened it, and winced as he inhaled. Even so, he dabbed a little on his face. I could smell the musk. He sat down again and checked his watch and obviously concluded that he had time for one more cigarette. He was loosening up, enjoying himself now as he blew smoke up into the blades of the ceiling fan.

"Then there was you," he went on. "I've done this so often now that I try to make the crimes fit the punishment. And with you, well, once I got to know you, I knew what to do. I started killing women who looked exactly like your wife. Sooner or later, Detective Bushing would show up, all the evidence in hand, your pretty wife shocked to realize she was married to a killer. But after Karly died in the river, I decided to make things more interesting. I decided to let you *see* me. I'd never done that before.

I wanted to watch you disintegrate as you lost your mind. It added a nice little twist. But you surprised me. You figured it out. And then you used Eve to come after me. Knowing you were on my trail forced me to improvise. I had to move fast. I also couldn't have *two* other Dylans in this world, so I took care of one by the river. Now it's just you and me."

"So what happens next?" I asked. "Do you kill me, too?"

"It's not about the killing. Remember? It's about the *punishment*."

He left the bedroom, and I could hear him opening a drawer in the kitchen. When he came back, he held two serrated knives in his hand. He slipped one into his pocket and then put the other on the bed just out of the reach of my fingers.

"It may take you a while, but you should be able to figure out how to get hold of the knife and free yourself," he said.

"Then what?"

"Then you can come after me, and we'll see who wins."

"Or maybe I'll just wait here and take my chances," I replied. "The police are going to have a hard time charging me with Tai's murder if they find me tied to the bed. They'll know I didn't do it."

"You won't wait here," my doppelgänger replied with a strange degree of confidence.

"No?"

"No." He calmly smoothed the sleeves of his purple shirt. "You have a date with Karly tonight. Remember?"

Suddenly, I understood.

Suddenly, the horror of what he was doing became clear. The dress clothes. The smooth shave. The musk cologne. My body wrenched against the bonds that held me, making the entire bed frame rattle on the floor. *"Stay away from her! Don't go near her! Don't do this!"*

He took the knife from his pocket and dangled the blade in front of my eyes.

"You couldn't save Karly in your own world," Dylan told me. "So this should be very interesting. Do you think you can save her in this one?"

CHAPTER 25

Karly.

I was going to lose her again. This predator with my face was going to meet her and kill her.

I had to stop him, but I had almost no time. Night was falling fast, which meant the time of our rendezvous wasn't far away. Meanwhile, I was alone and trapped in the apartment. Alone with Tai's body haunting me from the bathroom. Another woman I'd failed to rescue.

I shouted for Edgar, but he could barely hear the television even when it was turned up to full volume. I called for help at the top of my lungs, hoping to hear the thud of movement on the wooden floor over my head, but I heard nothing. Edgar was asleep in front of his game shows.

I needed to do this myself.

Dylan had left the kitchen knife just outside my grasp near the headboard. I jerked my body straight up, trying to jiggle the knife toward me. It moved a tiny bit toward my outstretched fingers, but it also slid dangerously close to the edge of the mattress. Where the knife was now, I could just touch the bottom of the handle with the tip of my middle finger. Another fraction of an inch, and I would be able to slide it into my hand.

Again I thrust my body fiercely upward. All four posts of the bed clanged up and down on the floor. The vibration bounced the knife closer, but the blade rotated, and the black handle crept over the side of the bed. I saw it falling in slow motion, and I was able to pinch the point of the sharp metal between two of my fingers, but it cut me, and I lost my grip. The knife dropped to the floor.

Now I had no way to escape.

For several more minutes, I struggled uselessly. However, I noticed that as the bed shook, a lamp on my nightstand kept moving. The lamp had a heavy base and a delicately fluted glass column rising to a conical shade. Glass could break. Glass could cut. I jolted the bed again, and the lamp wobbled. If it fell, there was no way to predict the direction it would go, but I had to take the chance. I hurled myself up and down one more time, watching the marble base of the lamp nudge over the side of the nightstand. Another shudder, and the thing would topple.

My fingers were ready. I heaved my left side upward. The lamp swayed, then fell like a tree, thudding onto the mattress next to me. Immediately, the weight of the stone base began dragging it to the floor. All I could do was cling to the shade with my fingertips. If I let go, it was gone. I held my breath, then snapped my fingers shut like a mousetrap. The lamp jumped closer to me and immediately began to slide back down, but my hand wrapped around the slim glass column and held it firmly.

With a quick twist of my wrist, I smashed the lamp backward against the brass headboard behind me. The glass broke and left jagged edges. It was fragile glass, but sharp, and I used it to saw at the fabric that secured me to the corner of the headboard. The process was frustratingly slow, but the silk began to come apart in threads, and when I'd opened up a small tear, I yanked hard and heard the tie rip apart and felt my right arm come free.

I swung my body over and repeated the process to free my left arm. When the silk tore away on that side, I pushed my body up and cut through the knots that held my ankles. I bloodied myself in the process as I rushed to get free, but when the last knot separated, I leaped off the bed.

Karly.

We'd agreed to meet at nine o'clock on the Northwestern campus. Outside the window, darkness had fallen in the time it had taken me to get free. When I checked the clock, I saw that it was nine thirty. *He was already with her.*

Using my phone, I found the contact number for the Norris center and waited through what felt like two dozen rings before someone answered. It was Saturday night. I was sure the place was busy. I asked to be transferred to security, and this time a gruff voice answered immediately.

What to say?

"One of your faculty members, Karly Chance, is meeting someone in the coffee bar on the second floor. You need to get up there and get her away from him. He's dangerous."

"Dangerous? How do you know?"

"Please, just go talk to her and tell her she isn't safe. Karly Chance. Do you know who she is?"

"No, I don't. You need to tell me what's going on, sir."

"Karly Chance. She's on the English faculty. Blond hair, ragged cut down to her shoulders, fair skin, blue eyes, about thirty. She's with a man named Dylan Moran. Messy black hair, lean, not very tall. He's wearing a checked purple shirt and gray vest. You need to hurry."

"I'm heading up there right now, sir, but you need to tell me what this is all about."

I needed a story he'd believe. I needed something. Anything.

"Look, Dylan's my roommate. He's obsessed with this woman. He read her book, and now he won't stop talking about her. He was on campus the other night stalking a girl near Goodrich who looked just like her. He's unstable, takes a lot of meds. When he left the apartment tonight, he took a *knife*. Search him. You'll find it."

"A knife? Are you sure?"

"I'm absolutely certain."

"Okay, hang on."

The sound on the phone grew muffled. I could hear the background noise of a large crowd of people, and then I heard the man's voice again, talking to someone else. I couldn't make out what they were saying. The length of time felt excruciating, and I squeezed the phone impatiently.

Finally, he came back on the line.

"Karly Chance? English professor?"

"Yes, that's her."

"She hasn't been in here tonight."

"She must be. We were supposed—I mean, Dylan told me that he was meeting her there at nine o'clock."

"Well, she didn't show. The coffee guy knows her. He hasn't seen her. He's been here all evening."

I squeezed my eyes shut and tried to think. "Okay. Okay. Can you put out a security alert to the rest of the campus? Have them look for her. She lives in Goodrich. Somebody needs to check her apartment."

"First you better tell me *your* name, sir."

I hesitated. You really can't hesitate when somebody asks you your name.

"What's this all about?" the guard went on, a new shadow of suspicion in his voice. "Who are you? How do you know Ms. Chance?"

"Just look for her! Please!"

I hung up the phone. I paced in the bedroom, overrun by panic. *Where were they?* Maybe Karly had skipped the date, but my ego told me that wasn't true. She wouldn't have stood me up, not after the conversation we'd had today. But if it wasn't Karly, then it was *him*. He'd changed the place where we were supposed to meet. He'd assumed I would get free and alert the campus police, so he'd reached out to her to pick a new location away from the university.

Where did they go?

They were out among millions of people on a Chicago Saturday night. They could be anywhere.

I tried the office number I'd found on Karly's faculty profile. It went straight to a generic voice mail message. I tapped out a short e-mail to her university account: *You're in danger. Get away from Dylan now.* But I had no idea whether it would reach her.

Where?

Where would they meet?

Then I remembered a fragment of our conversation. We'd talked about wishing for a do-over in life for our worst mistakes, a chance to go back and change whatever we'd done wrong.

Wasn't that what tonight was for Dylan and Karly?

A do-over for a disastrous blind date?

If Dylan asked the Karly of this world where she wanted to go, I was willing to bet she'd go back to the beginning. She'd suggest we try our first date over again and see if we could get it right this time.

"We went to a club, didn't we? I don't even remember which one."

"The Spybar."

The entrance to the basement dance club called the Spybar was down an alley off Franklin in the artsy River North neighborhood. By the time I got there, a line of twenty-something club hoppers stretched around the corner from the black-draped entrance. I stood under the rusted steel beams of the L tracks, and one of the trains thundered like a roller coaster over my head.

From across the street, I studied the people in line. Dylan and Karly weren't there. That meant they were already inside. Or it meant I was completely wrong and they weren't here at all. I needed to get into the club and find out. I had no time to wait, so I found two Hispanic girls in skintight outfits near the front of the line. I gave them each fifty dollars and paid their covers, and five minutes later, I was down the stairs and inside the club.

The synthesizer beat of techno music wailed like a siren. I felt it deep in my chest, making it hard to breathe. The house was packed, bodies crammed shoulder to shoulder, arms and hips writhing as people danced. I moved slowly through clouds of fog. Strobe lights blinked, twisting around the floor in cones of white, red, yellow, and green.

A girl in a black bra, see-through top, and pink skirt blocked my way and grabbed my face. She had dreamy dark eyes that were high on something. "Buy me a drink?" she shouted.

"Sorry."

"Hey, come on. One martini."

"I can't."

I tried to squeeze around her, but she pressed her body hard against me and stuck out her tongue between her teeth. "I'll make it worth your while."

I made up an excuse. "I'm with someone."

"Yeah, so? She can join the party, too. I saw her. She's hot."

It took a second for my distracted mind to catch up to what she'd said. Then I took hold of her shoulders with both hands. "You saw me tonight? You saw a woman with me?"

"Sure. Blond, classy."

"Where?"

"What are you talking about?"

"*Where* did you see her? Where in the club? Show me!"

She wriggled in my grasp. "Let go of me, you freak!"

"Tell me! Where did you see the woman I was with?"

"Get *off!*"

She twisted away from me and shoved a middle finger in my face. With an irritated toss of her hair, she swayed on high heels toward the bar. I saw others watching me curiously. Two men who were probably bouncers started my way. I melted into the crowd, losing myself among the seething bodies. I couldn't afford to be tossed out, not when I knew Karly was here.

The relentless pulse of the music thudded in my brain. The swirling lights dizzied me. I pushed through the club, bouncing off people like a bumper car. No one knew what was happening; no one understood my panic. They laughed. They screamed. Drunk girls did shots and kissed each other on the lips. All I could see around me was a kaleidoscope of skin and sweat, in which faces appeared and disappeared in a fraction of a second.

Blink on. A face. Blink off. The face was gone.

Hundreds of them pressed in around me, constantly moving, constantly changing places. I tried to isolate them in my head one at a time. Men. Women. All strangers.

Then I saw him.

Blink, blink, blink, went the multicolored lights.

His face flashed on and off under the strobe, but it was him. My double, my alter ego, my doppelgänger. He balanced a drink in one hand and danced with a slow, sinuous energy, as if riding some kind of adrenaline high. His head undulated like a snake while the beat taunted me: *find her, find her, find her*. But Karly wasn't with him. I looked among the nearby faces and didn't see her. I tried to shove my way toward him, so I could wrap my hands around his throat, but the dancers made an unbreakable chain. I was trapped where I was. The beat grew louder, like a boxer punching me in the chest.

Find her!

His head stopped moving. He felt my presence in his brain. His body ground to a halt, and his smoky gaze landed on me. There we were, the two of us, staring at each other across the frenzy of the dance floor. I shouted at him, but the music drowned out my voice. He raised his drink to me, a toast. His grim lips bent into a grin, and I knew in my heart what that awful smile meant.

I was too late.

I shouted again. No one paid any attention. No one heard me.

The lights went off and on. In that split second, Dylan disappeared. He vanished from where he was, and I didn't see him again. But Karly was still here somewhere. Dying. I knew it. I fought my way through the crowd. When I got to the building's brick wall, I headed for the back of the club, where people hid from the tumult and noise. I pushed past couples making love in the dark. I slipped on spilled drinks and God knows what else. As the strobes flashed—blink, blink, blink—I spotted someone on the floor. A woman. She sat in the corner with her knees against her chest and her arms wrapped around them.

"Karly!"

I scrambled to her and got down on my knees beside her. Blond hair covered her face. When I pushed it aside, her stare was empty, seeing nothing. Her head turned, but when she looked at me, I don't think she saw me. I watched her lips move; she said something, but in the chaos of the club, I couldn't hear what it was. I put my arms around her. As I did, my hand sank into a river of blood. When I pulled away, my fingers were covered in crimson red that blinked on and off in the lights.

"Help! We need help! Over here!"

No one heard me.

I put my lips to her ear and whispered. "Karly, hang on. Please hang on. Stay with me."

Her head sank against my shoulder, the way it had a million times before. At the movie theater, in the car, in front of the fireplace, on the pillows in bed. It felt so warm, so good, so familiar, as if it should last forever. But she was leaving me again. She was getting farther away, dragged from me by a river of blood that pulsed between my fingers. I put my palm to her chest, feeling her ragged, rattling breath go in and out.

"Karly, I love you."

In.

Out.

"You're my wife. I love you."

In.

Out.

"I should have saved you. I failed you. I'm sorry, God I'm so sorry."

In.

Out.

And then nothing.

"Karly."

Nothing. She was gone. I'd found her again and lost her again.

"Karly."

All I could do was say her name and hold her limp body.

Inches away, people danced. The electronica pounded into my heart, louder and louder. We were invisible on the floor. For the longest time, the partiers in the club were oblivious to us, the beautiful woman dead in the corner, and the man who'd let her die twice.

Chapter 26

Finally, someone saw me. Saw her. Saw the blood. A piercing scream cut through the noise, and several more followed like a chain reaction, triggering bedlam. The music shut down, and a moment of shocking silence gave way to panic. People called for help and ran to get away. Half the crowd pulled out their phones, some dialing 911, some filming me as I laid Karly gently on her back. I couldn't stay, not with the police on their way. I got up and headed for the club stairs. I needed to get out of here.

The people parted for me like some kind of sordid celebrity. Look, there goes OJ. One man tried to be a hero by stopping me, but I planted my foot and delivered a hook across his jaw that sent him reeling. Don't get into a bar fight with Dylan Moran; he's been there before. Other men closed in on me, but as they did, I bolted for the steps and escaped into the cool night. Not far away, police sirens blared, heading for the club from multiple directions.

I ran. So did other club hoppers dispersing from the alley. I sprinted below the L tracks, which loomed over my head like a metal centipede. For four blocks, I ran full out, and then I stopped, slumping against a wall to catch my breath. My head snapped up as I spotted the lights of a squad car speeding toward me, and I quickly spun around the corner into an empty alley. When the police car passed, I went back to the street. I knew I needed to get out of the neighborhood before the cops cordoned off the area, and my car was parked several blocks away. But I found it hard to move. I squatted down, my elbows on my knees, my face in my hands as I endured a new wave of grief.

When I finally looked up, I saw him.

Diagonally across the street, near the stairs that led to the Brown Line L station, Dylan Moran stared back at me. He was in his leather jacket, a cigarette dripping from his mouth. He leaned against one of the yellow concrete impact poles off the curb. His grin was gone; he was emotionless again. Her blood was on him, the way it was on me. Seeing him, I felt a rage like nothing in my life. I erupted from where I was and charged toward him. He watched me come, not even moving at first. Then he flicked his cigarette to the street and walked unhurriedly up the stairs to the train station.

It took me no time to cross the street. Like an animal, I bolted up the stairs after him, but when I got to the top, the station was already empty. No one was there. I used my fare card to spin through the turnstile, and when I got to the platform, I ran along the tracks in both directions. There were no hiding places, no way for him to escape.

Even so, Dylan was gone. I could almost hear the echo in my head. *Infinite.*

He was done with this world, and he'd left me behind to take the fall. It was another perfect crime.

After I made it back to my car, I drove aimlessly through the downtown streets until I was nowhere near the club. Then I pulled to the curb. There was only one thing I could think to do. I called Roscoe. In every world, when I needed him, he was there to rescue me.

We agreed to meet near the sandy shoreline of North Avenue Beach. It didn't take me long to get there, and I sat in the car with dried tears on my face and my clothes soaked in blood. The midnight beach in front of me was empty. A stiff cold breeze blew into the car and sent spray over the windshield. I lowered the window, listening to the rhythmic roar of the surf, which went in and out like my wife's last breaths.

This was my catastrophic reward for trying to be a hero.

The Dylan who owned this life was dead. So was Tai. So was a woman named Betsy Kern.

So was Karly.

I'd destroyed all of them, and the man I'd chased here had already moved on to kill again.

As I sat there, the waves lulled me with a kind of hypnosis. I wasn't even aware of time passing, but when I looked up, I saw the glow of headlights in my mirror. A car parked beside me, and Roscoe got out. He wore a light-blue windbreaker and casual clothes rather than his priest's collar. Standing next to the car, he shivered a little and watched the lake, with his hands in the pockets of his jacket. He was probably thinking about all the times we'd biked here as kids and hung out on summer afternoons by the water.

Roscoe climbed into the passenger seat next to me. With a single glance, he took note of my condition.

"Are you hurt?"

"No."

"So I take it that isn't your blood."

"It's Karly's."

He adjusted his black glasses and spoke softly. "I'm sorry, Dylan."

"Thanks."

"I brought the fresh clothes you wanted," he added.

I just nodded.

"I heard on the radio about a murder at the Spybar. They said a suspect was on the loose. Was that you?"

"Yes, it was me, but it *wasn't* me. Not that it matters. The killer had my face, so what will anyone believe? But I didn't do this, Roscoe.

I know it's hard for you to accept anything I've told you, but I hope you'll have faith in me. I did not do this."

This would have been the time for Roscoe to point out that he'd warned me about the dangers of being in this world, but he was gracious. His deep voice soothed me, the way it always did. "You're my best friend, Dylan. I've said you could always call me for help, and I mean that. As for having faith in you, that goes without saying."

"That means a lot."

"So what happens now? What are you going to do?"

"I don't know. He won. I lost. Now he's gone, and here I am." I pushed open the car door, because I needed to breathe in the fresh air. "Do you want to take a walk on the beach? Like in the old days? We may never have another opportunity to do that together."

"If you like."

We crossed to the sand and then to the rolling edge of the surf. It was a clear night under moon and stars, and the waves made white ribbons as they broke toward shore. We wandered north, not talking. Around us, I could see a few beach dwellers huddled under blankets, hoping to avoid the park security. When I looked over my shoulder, I saw the city skyline awash in light. Where we'd walked, the lake was already wiping our footsteps clean.

I stopped, confronting more memories.

"When we were about sixteen, we came out here on a summer afternoon," I said. "We saw a little kid flailing in the water. His mother was distracted because her youngest was crying. The two of us plunged in and saved him. Did that happen here, too?"

"Yes, it did."

"His mom bought both of us new bikes."

"I remember."

"I always felt good about what we did. The strange thing is, now I know there's also a world out there where we didn't save him. We failed, and he died."

Roscoe put a hand on my shoulder. "I prefer to look at how hard God worked to put us on that beach at the exact moment when the boy was drowning. We almost missed the bus going down here—do you remember that? We were complaining because we were going to have to wait another twenty minutes for the next one. But as it turned out, the bus we wanted was running late. So we made it. If that hadn't happened, we wouldn't have been here to save that child."

"Yes, but there's also a world where we *missed* the bus," I protested. "So what's the point? There's no meaning to any of it. There's no plan."

"Not at all. It simply means in a different world, there's a different plan."

A sad smile creased my face. "I've always envied the strength of your beliefs, Roscoe. I wish I shared them. If there's been one good thing about being here, it's seeing you again. I'm going to miss you."

"Are you saying you have to go?"

"You were right all along. I don't belong here."

"Will you follow this other Dylan again? And stop him this time?"

"No, it's time for me to go back to where I came from and face what I left behind. That's what you said I should do, isn't it? Say the word and go home. I was a fool to think I could change the world."

Roscoe squatted in the sand and let it run through his fingers. Then he spoke to me softly. "Actually, I've changed my mind about that."

"What do you mean?"

"I don't think you're ready to go home, Dylan. That's not who you are. If you believe in what you're doing, the worst thing you can do is give up. The fact that you failed doesn't mean that you should quit. The friend I've known my whole life would never give up."

"You really think I should try again? After everything that happened here? What if I make it worse wherever I go next?"

He shrugged and looked up at me. "What if you make it better?"

"I appreciate the vote of confidence, Roscoe, but even if you're right, it's a moot point. The only thing I can do is go back home. I have no way to go anywhere else. I can't chase him, even if I wanted to."

"Why not?"

"I have no way back into the portal without Eve Brier."

He flinched at the sound of the name. "Eve Brier?"

"She's the therapist who sent me here. The idea of trying to bridge the Many Worlds was her idea. But as far as I can tell, she doesn't exist in this world. There's no record of her anywhere."

Roscoe dipped his hand in the cool water and shook his head. "God really does work hard to make things come together."

"What do you mean?"

"I know her," he replied.

"What?"

"Well, I don't know if she's your Eve Brier. She's not a therapist, that's for sure. But I do know an Eve Brier, and I'm not surprised you wouldn't find any record of her online. She's a drug addict. Homeless, has been for years. She comes into the parish sometimes when we're preparing meals."

"An addict?"

"Yes, she's very smart, but she went off the rails a long time ago and never made it back. Actually, I think she was in medical school once upon a time. She got thrown out over theft of prescription drugs. It's only gotten worse since then. She's been hospitalized for overdoses multiple times."

"That's got to be her," I told him. "How can I find her?"

"If she's still alive, you'll probably find her sheltered under the train tracks west of my church. That's where she usually hangs out. But I wouldn't count on her being able to help you, Dylan. Eve doesn't live where the rest of us do. She spends most of her time in other worlds."

CHAPTER 27

The streetlight near the railroad tracks had been shot out, leaving the tunnel ahead of me pitch black. I parked near a fence that guarded a vacant lot overgrown with weeds. Using my phone for light, I walked down the middle of the road. Spiderwebs of cracks ran through the pavement, and loose gravel crunched under my feet. Where the asphalt had chipped away completely, I saw layers of red cobblestone. Above me, dense trees leaned over the railway bridge. Retaining walls supported the overpass on both sides, and ribbons of ivy and green mold ran along the concrete.

Inside the tunnel, brown water dripped from the low ceiling. The I beams were connected by round archways, where the white paint had mostly flaked away. I wasn't alone here. The night people were with me, and I was conscious of being watched by a dozen sets of eyes. The smell of weed hung in the air, thick enough to make my head spin. I saw a lineup of old blankets, sleeping bags, and pole tents crowded against the walls. The broken glass of a tequila bottle glinted in my light. A feral cat sniffed among the debris for food and rats. Someone near me talked to himself incessantly, stringing together random words that made no sense. I heard the splatter of someone urinating against the wall.

I stopped near a kid no older than twenty, who skipped rope with nervous energy in one of the archways. The snap of the rope echoed in the tunnel. I waited until he missed a step and then approached him. I dug out a ten-dollar bill from my wallet as an incentive.

"I'm looking for Eve Brier. Have you seen her around here?"

His jaw pumped as he chewed tobacco. I could smell it on his breath. He spun the jump rope in his hand like he was Will Rogers with a lariat. "Who wants to know?"

"I'm a friend of Roscoe's. Roscoe Tate from the church."

"Yeah, everybody knows Roscoe. What you want with Eve?"

"I need to talk to her."

He snorted out a laugh. "Talk, huh? Lotta people like to talk to Eve. Best wear a sleeve when you talkin'."

"I swear. Just talk. Do you know where she is?"

"Yeah, sure. Couple blocks up. Alley behind the cemetery. She takes her little rides up there."

"Her rides?"

"That what she calls 'em. Seems like some crazy trips. When she goes away, she gone."

I pushed the ten-dollar bill into his hand. He took off his baseball cap, put the cash on his head, and slapped the hat back on. Then he started skipping rope again.

On the other side of the overpass, most of the houses had barred windows. I passed a couple of late-night bars and some empty storefronts. Two blocks down, I found the cemetery, which was protected from grave robbers by concrete walls topped with barbed wire. A narrow alley ran adjacent to the cemetery wall, and I walked into the darkness, kicking garbage out of my way. In a small yard of mud and grass behind one of the buildings, I saw a woman slumped on a blanket.

I shined my light on her face.

It was Eve Brier, but this was a very different Eve than the one I knew. She wore a soiled gray sweatshirt and no pants, only frayed purple underwear. Her long legs were riddled with bruises. She had one sleeve pushed up, displaying the track marks of numerous injections. The long, elegant nails I remembered on her fingers were chewed down, her cuticles bitten and bloody. She lay on her side, her body wrapped in the blanket. Her almond-shaped eyes were closed. I didn't know if this was sleep or unconsciousness. I knelt next to her and gently brushed the long hair from her face. She had no elegant highlights, just brown hair that matched the mud.

"Eve," I called softly, getting no reaction.

My hand stroked her shoulder. "Eve?"

She moaned, a guttural protest through her closed mouth. Her limbs twitched as she stirred. Her eyes blinked open, failed to register her surroundings, and sank closed again. I patted her cheek.

"Eve, wake up."

This time, she did. She opened her golden eyes as she rolled onto her back. When she focused on my face, her eyes widened in shock. Inhaling, she let out a primal scream and skittered away from me. I came off my knees and followed, but she beat at me with her fists, her throat wailing without forming words. She bumped into the brick wall behind her, and her hands flew at me as if trying to wave off a cloud of bees. I had to wrap her up tightly in my arms to stop her.

"Eve, it's okay, it's okay."

She wouldn't stop screaming. I was afraid the people in the houses nearby would call the police. I put my hand over her mouth, trying to quash the noise, but she bit down hard on my palm, drawing blood. When I drew my hand back in pain, she wailed again. One word.

"Dylan!"

She knew who I was. She'd seen me before.

"Don't hurt me! Please don't hurt me! Dylan!"

I grabbed her shoulders, with blood dripping down my wrist, and pushed her against the wall.

"*Eve*," I hissed urgently. "Eve, listen to me."

"Don't hurt me, please!"

"Eve. Try to focus. I'm Dylan, but *I'm not him*."

"You are, you are! Go away, leave me alone!"

"Look at me!" I backed away and shined the light of the phone on my face. "Look at me, Eve. You can tell, can't you? We're the same, but we're different. I'm not him."

I put my hands up, a gesture of faith that she wouldn't run. That she should trust me. She summoned the courage to look at me, and I had the chance to look at her, too. I had no idea what she was on or how far gone she was, but when her animal instincts receded, I saw a little bit of the Eve Brier I remembered. Somewhere in there was the brain that had started all of this.

She was the portal.

"See?" I said quietly. "I'm not him."

She touched my face, like a blind woman getting to know me. "You're right. You're different."

"Yes, I am."

"How? How did you get here?"

"Through you," I said.

She didn't look surprised. "You mean a different me? From somewhere else?"

"That's right."

Eve exhaled with relief. "So you know about the worlds. You know they're real."

"I do."

"People don't believe me. I tell them I go on rides, and I tell them what I see. They think I'm crazy. They think it's nothing but the drugs."

"I don't think you're crazy. Tell me about the rides, Eve. Where do you go? What do you see?"

"There's a place where we all meet," she replied dreamily, looking over my head at the sky. "There are so many of them. So many of *me*. I'm not like this everywhere, you know. I'm smart. Rich. Beautiful."

"Yes, I know."

"Sometimes I follow them. The other Eves. Just to see what it's like to live like that. I hide, and I watch them, but I never stay. I couldn't live in those worlds. I'd still end up just the way I am now. We all end up back where we belong sooner or later. Except for *him*. He goes wherever he wants."

"Tell me about him."

Her face darkened. "He's evil."

"You've seen him on your rides?"

"Yes."

"I've seen him, too. That's why I need your help."

"Look at me. I can't do anything."

"You can send me after him," I told her.

Eve stared nervously into the shadows. On the street behind us, headlights came and went in the alley. "I wasn't always like this, you know. In college? I had a 4.0. University of Chicago, *summa cum laude*. Totally clean. No alcohol, no weed, no nothing. I went to medical school, and I was good, really good, but you can't imagine the stress. You're exhausted all the time. I needed something to keep me going, and a guy in the lab hooked me up. It was just supposed to be the one time, to get me through a rough patch, but the pills sucked me in. I tried so many times to stop, but I wasn't strong enough."

"I'm not blaming you, Eve."

"Except you know a different me, don't you?" she said. "One with a better life."

"Yes."

"How do you know her?"

"She wrote a book about the Many Worlds."

"And why do you care about that?"

"Because of the other Dylan," I said. "He came to my world and destroyed my life."

"He destroys everything."

"How do you know him?"

"I saw him on one of my rides. I do it a lot, you know. Ride. I was spying on one of my doubles in the park, and I saw him talking to her. I could see there was something wrong about him. Something bad. I don't know how I knew, but I knew. So after they split up, I followed him. I saw him go into the park that night, and he met this woman and—oh, my God."

She wrapped her arms tightly around her chest.

"Since then, I've seen him half a dozen more times in other worlds. I see the things he does. It's always the same. He's a killer."

"I know."

"The last time, he spotted me watching him. He *recognized* me. He knew I'd seen him, and he came after me. I had to say the escape word to get away." Eve shivered. Her fingers twitched. "Since then, I'm afraid that wherever I go, he'll find me. But I need to ride. I can't stay here. I have to get away from this life, you know? It's too much. I can't take who I am."

I grabbed both of her hands. "Eve, I want to stop this other Dylan. I never want him to hurt anyone else. I came here to do that, but I failed. He got away. Now I want to go after him again, but I need your help. I need you to get me to the Many Worlds again."

She shook her head. "I only have one dose left. I don't know when I can get more, and I can't be stuck here. Not like this. I'll go crazy."

"Eve, I can't do this without you."

"What if you go after him and you fail again?"

"I'm not going to fail."

"You might not be able to deal with it. The stuff I get isn't always pure. When it's laced, sometimes strange things happen to me when I ride. Weird, scary shit."

"I'll take that risk."

Her face softened. She put chapped hands on my cheeks and leaned forward, and I was surprised when she kissed me. Her lips were gentle and submissive, craving any kind of human connection. I didn't stop her. I let her kiss me for a while, and then she sank back against the brick wall. She lifted up her sweatshirt, exposing her flat stomach and the slopes where her breasts swelled. A capped hypodermic was taped across her skin.

"Take it."

I reached forward, peeling off the tape and taking the needle in my hands. I removed the cap and studied the clear liquid in the barrel. For all I knew, I was about to kill myself. OD.

"Where do you go?" she asked me.

"What do you mean?"

"When you ride. Where do you go? The crossroads."

I understood now. "The Art Institute. The painting *Nighthawks*."

"I'll talk you through it," Eve said, "but I don't know what will happen. I'll try to guide you there, but if it's a bad batch—"

"That's okay."

I stared at the needle and then rolled up my sleeve. When the moment came to inject myself, I hesitated. I rolled it around in my fingers and couldn't bring myself to put the metal tip to my vein.

"Do you want me to do it?" she asked.

I saw a steadiness in her eyes. "Yes."

She took my arm in hers with surprising skill and gentleness. But then I realized that once upon a time, she'd been on her way to becoming a doctor. She pressed the point of the needle into the seam of my arm.

"Are you sure? Once it's done, it's done."

"I'm sure."

I watched the clear liquid disappearing through the needle as she injected me. The cocktail flowed like a cool river into my body, and the last thing I heard was Eve whispering in my ear.

"Kill him."

Something was wrong. I knew it immediately.

I could see other Dylans coming and going, hundreds of them shuffling back and forth in front of me, but they were in a different place, separated from me by a window. I tried to get up from where I was, but

I was paralyzed. I couldn't even feel myself breathing. Glancing down, I saw the sleeves of a navy-blue suit and the brim of a fedora dipped low on my forehead just above my eyes. My arms leaned forward against some kind of counter. But I couldn't move at all. All my limbs felt frozen.

"More coffee?"

I saw another Dylan. He wore a white uniform, a paper cap on his head. He leaned over the counter where I sat motionless.

"What?"

"I said, more coffee, buddy?"

There was a white mug in front of me. "Yes. Sure. Okay."

He took the mug and went to a large coffee urn near the wall and refilled it. Then he put it in front of me. "How about the lady?"

I couldn't turn my head, but out of the corner of my eye, I saw a beautiful woman in a red dress sitting next to me on the adjacent stool. Like me, she sat stiffly, not talking, not moving, as if she were some kind of mannequin. Her face was intimately familiar to me. Pretty. Vivid red hair to match her dress. I knew her well, but I had no idea what her name was.

Then I understood.

I was inside *Nighthawks*.

I was trapped *inside* the painting. The man I'd dreamed of being for years, the one sitting next to the woman in the red dress, was me. All the other Dylans were outside, in the museum gallery, moving back and forth on their way to their next destination. I had nowhere to go.

Then I heard a laugh.

My eyes shifted. To my right, I saw the other man in the painting, the one whose back is always to the watcher. The mystery man. It was another Dylan. It was him. Instead of a suit and fedora as he should have been wearing, he was dressed in my father's leather jacket, stained with blood. His blue eyes, appropriately enough, were the eyes of a night hawk, out for prey. He sipped his coffee and chuckled.

"You don't give up, do you?"

I heard myself saying, "I'm going to kill you."

"Yeah? Well, we'll see about that."

He finished his mug of coffee. Unlike me, he had no trouble moving. He had a lot of experience at the crossroads of the Many Worlds, and I was still a novice. He got up from the stool, threw down a dollar bill on the counter, and headed for the door of the diner. In the painting, there was no door, just a long glass window and the city street, so when he got to the end of the painting, he melted away like fog. A moment later, I could see him inside the museum.

I had to go after him, but I was trapped here. I stared at my painted hands and arms, which were no more than color on canvas. Instead of two dimensions, I needed to become three again, but how could I move? How could I change what I was? Then I realized that the change was all in my head. If I could see and think and talk, I could do everything else, but I had to *believe* it.

I had to accept that this was real. If it was real, then I could control it. The only prison we can never escape is our brain, and yet our brain is what sets us free.

It happened slowly. A moment at a time. I willed myself to move and felt my mind bend to my commands. One of my fingers bent. Then another. My shoe tapped on the rail of the counter. My head swiveled. I was nearly there. I tensed my muscles and pushed, and like glass shattering, I felt my entire body break out of its bonds.

I was back in the gallery, surrounded by hundreds of other Dylan Morans. The painting hung on the wall again where it was supposed to be. The characters were strangers, not reflections of me.

I felt a surge of confidence. In this next world, everything would be different. I didn't run. I marched calmly, sure of where I needed to go and what I needed to do. This time, the other Dylans parted for *me* as I took off after my doppelgänger.

I was finally ready.

It was time for my second chance.

Chapter 28

The wail of a horn blared in my ears. Air brakes screeched. I looked up to see a semitruck shuddering to a stop inches from my face. The truck was so close that I could see dead bugs squashed on its grille, and I'd very nearly become one of them. Around me, Chicago traffic roared through the intersection in both directions. I was in the middle of Michigan Avenue, crossing against the light.

The truck driver barked at me through his open window. "Shit, man, where did you *come* from? Are you blind? Get out of the street!"

He added several more obscenities to make sure I got the message.

I raised my hands in apology, then waited for a gap in the cars and hurried to the opposite side. I steadied myself against a light post and took a few deep breaths. I couldn't help but think about the irony of almost dying as a truck ran me over. In my head, I could hear Edgar's raspy voice telling me the story of Daniel Catton Rich, director of the Art Institute, who would have died the same way in 1941 if my grandfather hadn't accidentally tackled him.

It made me think again that Roscoe was right. Fate had a way of making the elements of our worlds converge. What I called fate, he called God.

Standing at the corner, I got my bearings. I was on the park side of the street, across from the Hilton, a few blocks south of the LaSalle

Plaza. I had no idea why my exit from the Art Institute had taken me here, but a moment later, I heard someone calling my name.

"Dylan?"

Looking toward the lake, I saw Tai heading my way from Grant Park.

Seeing her gave me a shiver of disorientation. My last nightmarish memory of Tai was of seeing her face under the water in our apartment. Now she was back, alive and unharmed.

She walked up and gave me an awkward kiss on the cheek. "Dylan, it is you. What a nice surprise."

She said it in a way that told me it really wasn't such a nice surprise. We were definitely not married in this world.

"Hello, Tai."

"How long has it been? I mean, it must be four years."

I tried not to blurt out my surprise: *Four years?* How could I not have seen Tai in four years?

"It's been a while," I said, stumbling over my reply. "How are you?"

"I'm good. Really good. Things at the hotel are fine. I mean, not the same without you, of course."

"Sure." I had no idea what she meant. Then I added, "You look good."

"Thanks."

She really did look good. She'd chopped off her long hair, now sporting a modern androgynous cut. She wore a tailored burgundy suit, with a skirt that didn't quite reach to her knees, which showed off her legs. Her stilettos matched the suit. She'd always been pretty, but now she radiated confidence to go with it. She didn't look young anymore.

"You look good, too," she added, mostly as an afterthought.

"Still the same."

"No. No. Definitely different. But I like it."

"So the job's okay?" I asked, trying to understand why I'd left the hotel years earlier.

"It is. I mean, believe me, I did *not* want to take over the way I did. And without you, I felt like I was jumping into the pool to learn how to swim. For months, I didn't know which end was up."

"I doubt that."

"Oh, no, it's true. It really is. But enough about me. What about you? How are you? Are you okay?"

"Yeah."

"Seriously? You're doing all right?"

"I'm fine," I told her.

"Well, good. That's good to hear. Look, I really need to apologize. I should have done a better job of keeping in touch. I felt like a shit that I sort of cut you off. It wasn't because I didn't care. I mean, yeah, I felt a little weird about things, but it's just that I was so busy. We were shorthanded, and I was trying to learn the ropes. And after that, I don't know. I wasn't even sure you'd want to hear from me."

"It's okay, Tai. Don't worry about it."

"What are you doing downtown?" she asked me. "Are you trying to find a job? I mean, I'd help if I could. Truly. I'd hire you myself, but the hotel wouldn't go for it. I could put in a few calls if you'd like, but I think most of the hotel managers in the city know what happened."

"I'm not looking for a job."

"All right. Well, it really is such a nice surprise to see you again. You probably don't want to talk about it, but was it rough for you? Hell, what am I saying? Of course it was. But maybe it was for the best, you know?"

"Maybe so," I replied vaguely.

"I suppose that's a stupid thing to say." Her golden skin actually blushed. "Nobody thinks prison is for the best."

"Prison," I exclaimed, not able to stop myself.

"But you made it through okay?"

"I'm fine," I said again.

"Good." Tai checked her watch to give herself an excuse. She looked uncomfortable, as if she wanted to get away from me as quickly as she could. "Anyway, I need to go. Big event tonight, eighteen million details. You know how it is."

"I do."

"Of course you do."

Tai went to cross the street, but then she took a breath and turned back to me. She grabbed my hand. "I really am sorry, Dylan."

"It's not your fault."

"I know, but I always felt like I should have been able to reach you back then. Like I could have changed how you were. Made the anger go away. I mean, I probably shouldn't tell you this, but I always had kind of a thing for you. I never said anything about it. Maybe I should have. I always had this idea in the back of my head that if we'd gotten together, it would have helped you become a better person. That sounds arrogant. I'm sorry."

"It's okay. I appreciate the sentiment, but it doesn't work that way, Tai. You wouldn't have been able to change me."

"I guess. Are you doing better? You were always so hard on the whole world, especially yourself. I hoped you'd find some softness, you know? I wanted you to have peace."

"I'm getting there."

"I'm glad." She put her arms around me in a quick, awkward embrace, and then she bowed her head in embarrassment. "Take care of yourself."

"You too."

The light changed. She started across Michigan Avenue toward the Hilton. My eyes followed her, but then I looked beyond her to the crowded sidewalk on the opposite side of the street.

He was standing right there.

My Dylan. The Dylan in the leather jacket. The Dylan I was here to kill.

He stood on the corner and eyed me with his own steely resolve. Tai must have seen him, too, because she stopped in the middle of the street. Her shoulders spun around so she could look behind her. Finding me where I was supposed to be, she began to look back to confirm the impossibility of what her eyes were seeing.

As she did, a Chicago tour bus blocked our view of the Hilton. When it passed, the other Dylan had already vanished. I was sure he was in the crowd of pedestrians now, but as far as Tai was concerned, he was just a momentary trick of her imagination. She continued to the opposite corner and gave a little wave as she headed south for the LaSalle Plaza.

I didn't bother chasing after my doppelgänger. Not yet.

I knew that when the time came, he'd find me.

Obviously, the Dylan Moran who lived in this world had made mistakes even worse than mine.

I wanted to know who he was, what had happened that sent him to prison, and whether Karly was a part of his life. There was one person who could always give me answers. Roscoe. That was assuming there had been no car accident in this world that had taken him away from me.

I headed for Roscoe's South Side church, but when I went inside, I noticed a poster on the bulletin board with photographs of the church staff. My heart fell when I saw that Roscoe wasn't listed among them. I wondered if he was gone, as he was in my own world, but when I asked one of the priests about him, I was relieved to learn that no one named Roscoe Tate had ever been associated with the church.

So where was he?

I retraced my steps to the medical clinic on Irving Park where Roscoe's mother practiced. Fortunately, this part of the world hadn't changed. As I approached the building, I saw Alicia Tate coming out the front door, and her face broke into a broad smile as she spotted me on the sidewalk.

"Dylan, what a nice surprise."

Unlike Tai, Alicia sounded genuinely happy to see me.

"Do you need to talk to me?" she went on. "I was just on my way to the hospital to make rounds, but if something's wrong, I can fit you in."

"No, actually, I was trying to find—"

I stopped without saying his name. If Roscoe was dead, I didn't want to sound like a fool. However, Alicia leaped to the correct assumption.

"Oh, you're looking for Roscoe. Of course. Well, he's inside. You know him, that boy works too hard."

"Look who's talking," I said.

Alicia squeezed my shoulder affectionately. "You're sweet. Go on in, he'll be happy to see you."

I continued into the clinic, where several patients were waiting in the lobby. I didn't have time to ask the receptionist about Roscoe before the inner door opened, and my friend emerged, stooping slightly to help an elderly black woman who was using a walker. He wore more stylish, expensive glasses than he'd worn as a priest, and his face was smoothly shaven, but otherwise, he hadn't changed. Like his mother, Roscoe wore a white doctor's coat, which made me smile. Apparently, in this world, Alicia Tate had gotten her wish by having her son follow in her footsteps.

As Roscoe straightened up, he saw me. He wore the same sober expression I'd known since we were boys. "Dylan, hey, what are you doing here? Everything okay?"

"Fine, but I need a minute if you can spare it."

He glanced around the crowded waiting room and at the watch on his wrist. "I'm a little slammed, but sure, come on back."

I followed him down the inner hallway. We turned into a small office, where he sat behind a beat-up desk, under a wall that included a framed copy of his medical degree from the Pritzker School at the

University of Chicago. Alicia had gone there, too. On his desk, I saw pictures of him with his parents, along with a small photo of the two of us, back when we were kids playing football in Horner Park.

He followed my stare. "Long time ago, huh?"

"Very. And now look at you. That little kid's a doctor."

"I know. It's still hard for me to believe."

"I always thought that you would become a priest."

Roscoe chuckled. "Yeah. That was a tough call, but I've never looked back. Plus, I get to work with my mom. Most days, that's a blessing. Other days . . . well, you know how she is."

I smiled.

Back in high school, Roscoe had gone in the opposite direction. He'd decided that going into the ministry would allow him to do more good for people than medicine, by helping them find meaning in the losses and setbacks of their lives. He'd also rolled his eyes in exasperation at the idea of ever being able to work in a clinic with his mother.

"So what's up?" Roscoe asked.

"I have something to tell you."

"What is it?"

"It's hard to explain and even harder to believe."

"Try me."

I took a breath and considered what I would say. I'd thought about trying to pry my life's history out of him without telling him what was really going on, but Roscoe was my best friend, and we still had a pledge of never lying to each other. On the other hand, I wasn't sure if a doctor would take a leap of faith about unseen worlds as readily as a priest. Somehow, I had to prove that what was happening to me was real.

"Where should I be right now?" I asked him.

"What do you mean?"

"If I wasn't here in the clinic with you, where would you expect to find me?"

"I don't know. At your office, I guess."

I leaned across his desk, picked up the phone, and handed it to him. "Call me."

"What?"

"Call my office. Ask to talk to me."

"Why?"

"Please, Roscoe. Just do it."

With a look of confusion, he punched a button for the speakerphone and then pressed a speed dial number. The phone buzzed on the other end, and after several rings, a young woman answered.

"Chicago Housing Solutions."

"Dana, it's Roscoe Tate," he said, his foghorn voice as deep as ever.

"Oh, hey, Dr. Tate. Are you looking for Dylan?"

"I am. Do you know where he is?"

"Sure, he's on the other line. Do you want me to tell him you're holding?"

Roscoe didn't say anything for a long time. He stared across the desk at me, and his brow furrowed, like a mathematician confronting an insoluble problem. He stayed silent for so long that the woman on the phone finally broke in again.

"Dr. Tate? Are you still there? Do you want me to get Dylan for you?"

His eyes never left me. "Dana, are you saying that Dylan's in the office with you? Are you sure about that?"

"I'm looking right at him," she replied. "Actually, he just finished up his call. You want me to put him on?"

"Yes, please."

A few seconds passed. Then we both heard my own voice on the other end of the phone. There was no mistaking it.

"Roscoe. Hey, buddy."

"Dylan," Roscoe murmured. He opened his mouth to talk, but seemed unable to decide what to say next.

"What's up, Doc? You need something?"

Roscoe propped his arms on the desk and then balanced his chin on his hands. Our faces were barely a foot apart. He didn't have the look of a man who thought he was in the midst of a prank or an April Fool's joke. His eyes were serious, the same as mine. He spoke into the speakerphone, but he stared at me as he did.

I knew he was talking to both of us.

"Listen, I have a strange question for you," Roscoe said. "It came up with a patient today, and I thought you might remember. There was an old woman who used to work behind the counter at Lutz's bakery for a while. I think they found out her husband was some kind of Nazi. We used to make fun of her name while we were eating our pastries. Do you remember what it was?"

On the phone, Dylan answered immediately in a singsong chant.

So did I, mouthing the same words silently to Roscoe from the other side of the desk.

"Friedegunde, Friedegunde, face like die Hunde."

Roscoe closed his eyes in disbelief. We'd both passed the test, and neither one of us could have faked it. A long time passed before he said softly, "Yes, that was it. Now I remember."

"We weren't very nice back then, were we?" Dylan said with a laugh.

"Well, we were nine," Roscoe replied, opening his eyes and considering me like an alien come to earth. Which, in some ways, I was.

"So why did you want to know about old Friedegunde?" the other Dylan asked.

I put my finger over my lips and shook my head.

"I'll tell you later, buddy," Roscoe said into the speakerphone. "Gotta go for now."

"Okay, catch ya later," Dylan replied.

Roscoe stabbed the button on his phone to end the call.

"All right," he said to me, his voice a block of ice. "Who the hell are you?"

CHAPTER 29

I'd barely begun telling Roscoe the story when he shut me down. At the first mention of the Many Worlds, he put up his hands, unwilling to hear more. He had patients to see, and they came first. What it really meant was that he needed time to process the idea in his head. Roscoe never leaped to judgment about anything. He thought about things. He evaluated all the factors and made plans. He was cautious. In other words, he was everything I wasn't.

He told me to meet him at six o'clock at a bar just off the Kennedy on Montrose. The location he picked felt like another test. This was the bar where I'd gotten drunk and wound up in a street fight with a man who was abusing his girlfriend. Roscoe had come to collect me from the police station, and he'd never made it home alive.

The fact that Roscoe *was* alive meant that evening had gone differently in this world. And yet the fact that he chose the bar as our meeting place told me that the location still had some kind of special significance for Dylan Moran.

When I got there, I didn't recognize the bartender, which was probably a good thing. If anyone knew me here, I doubted they would serve me. I sat at the end of the bar and tried to hold back the flood of memories from that night. Me confronting the man four seats down, his girlfriend telling me to mind my own effing business, him throwing a drink in my face. It was a karaoke bar, and I could still hear someone doing a painful rendition of "Coma" by Guns N' Roses as the soundtrack to the fight.

"You want a drink?" the bartender asked me sullenly. She was an Asian girl with cherry-red hair.

"Vodka rocks," I said. Then, as she walked away, I stopped her. "Hang on. Forget that. Just club soda."

She shrugged. "Whatever."

When she brought me the drink, I sat and nursed it with a clear head, and then I ordered another. I tipped her like I'd ordered Grey Goose. The bar began to fill up as the after-work crowd arrived, and people came and went over the next couple of hours. By six fifteen, Roscoe hadn't shown up, and I began to wonder if he was planning to pretend that I'd been a figment of his imagination.

However, at six thirty, he slid onto the seat next to me. His eyes took note of the club soda, but he didn't offer to join me in my sobriety. Roscoe had always been a Southern Comfort man, even as a priest, and he still was. He ordered it on the rocks and said nothing until he had it in his hand and had taken the first sip.

"I drove by your office," he said. "Although I guess it isn't really *your* office, is it?"

"No, it's not."

"Dylan was inside. I saw him. Then I drove straight over here, no stopping, and here *you* are. I needed to see it with my own eyes, know what I'm saying?"

"I do."

He shook his head. "Many Worlds, Many Minds. I looked it up. The whole thing sounds pretty crazy to me."

"That's how I felt about it, too. But that's what's happening to me."

"You're a *different* Dylan. I mean, you're the same, but you're different."

"That's right."

He eyed me as he sipped his drink. "It's easier to believe when I really look at you. You've got a different edge, no doubt about it. It's in your face, your eyes, how you hold yourself."

"I met another Roscoe who told me the same thing."

"You're more like my Dylan was a few years ago. He's changed since then. You? Not so much. You haven't found yourself yet, not the way he did. Although I like the not drinking part. That's a start."

"You've changed, too," I told him.

"Let me guess. In your world, I'm a priest."

"You were."

He laughed to himself. "Sometimes I wonder what my life would be like if I'd taken that path. Maybe we all do that."

"Believe me, I've been obsessed with that idea recently."

Roscoe nodded as he looked around at the bar. "I asked you here for a reason, you know. This place right here is where *my* Dylan's life changed."

"Mine, too."

"So tell me what happened to you here," he said.

I picked up my club soda and swirled the ice, watching it clink around the glass. "Four years ago, on the anniversary of the night my parents died, I came here. I got drunk, and I got into it with a guy who was calling his girlfriend names. The cops came and arrested me. When they let me go, I called you, and you came to pick me up."

Roscoe knew there was more. "And? What happened next?"

"There was a car accident. You died."

A blink was his only reaction. He took another sip of Southern Comfort. "Oh."

"I blamed myself."

"Of course you did."

"There's more. I met a woman that night. It was a coincidence, a weird twist of fate—or at least, that's what I thought at the time. Now

I don't know. She rescued me. She helped me recover. We got married. Then very recently, I lost her, too."

"I'm sorry to hear that." Roscoe glanced at me from over the top of his drink. "What was her name?"

"Karly. Her name was Karly."

"Did you love her?"

"Yes, I did. I can't imagine my life without her. I finally had everything I ever wanted, and I let it all slip through my hands. I screwed up my whole damn life, and now I can never get it back."

I slammed my glass down on the bar. Ice and club soda sloshed over the side. I shook my head and dabbed at the spill with a napkin, and I waved away the bartender, who was looking at me with concern.

"You still have that temper, I see," Roscoe murmured.

I drank what was left of the club soda. "So that's my story. What happened here? In this world."

My friend sighed. "Four years ago, on the anniversary of the night your parents died, you came here. You got drunk, and you got into it with a guy who was calling his girlfriend names. You started beating the hell out of him on the street."

"And? What happened next?"

"The guy hit his head on the pavement. He died."

"*Shit.*"

"You pleaded guilty to involuntary manslaughter. Your lawyer argued for probation because of your family background. He said what happened to your mother triggered a kind of psychological fixation with defending a woman who was in danger, and that the man's death was accidental. The judge wasn't impressed. You'd been in fights before, so he said you were aware of the risks. He gave you a sentence of two to five years."

"Sounds like I deserved it."

"Yes, that's what you said. You didn't even appeal the sentence. You went to prison and did eighteen months before you got paroled.

It was rough for you. I know it was. But honestly, you became a new man. When you got out, you turned your life around. You went to AA and haven't had a drink since. You go to counseling every month. You found a job at a nonprofit focused on affordable housing, and within a year, you were running the place. You even managed to come to terms with Edgar. You apologized for all the crap you'd dealt him over the years. You thanked him for taking you in as a kid. The two of you had breakfast every morning during his last three months."

"Edgar died?" I asked.

"Yeah. Heart attack in his sleep."

I felt an unexpected wave of grief. Edgar. My grandfather. My last family member. Dead.

In my own world, Edgar was still alive, but I didn't know whether I'd ever see that world again. For the first time, I confronted the idea of him not being there. I had a vision of myself standing in front of *Nighthawks*, wishing Edgar was there to tell me the story of Daniel Catton Rich. Roscoe was right. There were things I should have said to him when I had the chance.

Even without knowing the Dylan Moran in this world, I realized he was living his life better than me.

I had to know more about him.

"Am I married?" I asked quietly.

He didn't answer right away.

"I mean, in this world, there was no accident. You didn't die. Karly didn't find me in the car."

Roscoe stared into his drink and wrestled with what to tell me. "After Edgar died, you brought in a contractor to work on the upstairs apartment so you could rent it out. The two of you became friends."

"Scotty," I guessed. "Scotty Ryan."

"That's right. He did a lot of work for a realtor he thought would be perfect for you, so he set the two of you up on a blind date. You hated the idea, but I pushed you to go. You went dancing at the Spybar, and it was love at first sight. Six months later, you were married."

I closed my eyes and found it hard to breathe. Under my fingers, the bar was still wet where I'd spilled my drink, and the barest sensation of water made me feel as if I were drowning. "Her *name*, Roscoe. What's her name?"

"Karly."

I still couldn't open my eyes. I was too angry with myself, too frustrated with my mistakes. The Dylan in this world had learned his lesson before it was too late. He'd changed. Not me.

"Am I happy?" I asked.

"Yes, you are. For the first time I can remember, you're at peace. Plus, you've got—"

He stopped.

"What?"

"I've told you everything you need to know."

"There's something else. What is it?"

Roscoe shook his head. "I'm sorry. There are things that belong only to Dylan, not you."

"*I'm* Dylan."

"No, you're not. Not here."

I dug in my wallet and put money on the bar. "I have to go."

"Where?"

"Home," I said.

I began to get off the barstool, but Roscoe grabbed my wrist. For a small man, his grip was like steel. "Do *not* interfere in his world. He's come too far to have it ruined for him. You had the same chances he did to turn your life around, and if you regret the choices you made, that's on you."

I looked into Roscoe's eyes, which was a gift I never thought I'd have after I lost him. We'd known each other since we were kids. We'd grown up together, gone through all my struggles together. He was the most decent man I knew in any world, whether as a doctor or a priest.

Somehow I knew this was the last moment between us. I'd had one final little bonus, and now it was over. One way or another, alive or dead, I'd be gone from this world before the night was done. I would never see him again.

At least I had the chance to hug him and kiss him on both cheeks and say a proper goodbye this time.

"I'm not going to interfere in Dylan's life," I promised my best friend before I left. "I'm here to save him."

Chapter 30

I stood among the trees of River Park in the twilight. It would be dark soon. The Dylan I needed to kill was here, not far away from me. I could feel him on the other side of a milky cloud. In the same way that he could read my thoughts, I was beginning to read his, too. The last time, he'd been waiting for me inside the apartment, but I saw nothing to suggest that he was there now. Neither was the Dylan who really lived here, and neither was Karly. That worried me.

Whenever they came back, they'd both be targets.

From my vantage in the grass, I could see the whole street. As I stood there, I noticed a gray sedan easing down the block, its lights on. This wasn't the first time I'd seen it. The car reached the corner and turned, but I had the feeling it would be back. I was right. Less than ten minutes later, I saw it again, retracing its route down the street. This time, it pulled onto the park sidewalk near me and stopped.

A tall man with a skeletal appearance got out. He wore a wrinkled tan trench coat over a white shirt and baggy black pants. He had a casual, stooped walk, but he wasn't out for a stroll. He headed straight for me.

It was Detective Harvey Bushing.

"Excuse me," he called, pulling out his badge and introducing himself. "Do you mind if I ask you a couple of questions?"

"If you like."

"Do you live around here?"

I nodded at the building across the street. "Yes, that's my apartment right over there."

"And your name is?"

"Dylan Moran."

"Got any ID, Mr. Moran?"

I thought about arguing with him, but I pulled out a driver's license and gave it to him, and he studied it with careful eyes. When he handed it back to me, he said in his monotone voice, "I'm just curious, Mr. Moran. If you live right over there, what are you doing in the park?"

"Enjoying the evening air," I replied.

"Well, I've been down this street three times, and you haven't moved. You just keep watching the building. Are you waiting for someone?"

"No."

"Well, it's just that most people go for a walk, or sit on the bench, or light up a smoke, or something like that. Not too many people stand there and stare at their own house."

"Is that a crime?"

"Not at all." But he was clearly waiting for an explanation, and the longer I made him wait, the more questions he'd ask.

"Look, Detective, I've lived in this area for most of my life. My grandfather owned the building, and he used to live in the upstairs apartment. He died a couple of years ago. We didn't exactly have the best relationship, and sometimes I like to come out here and think about him. Is that okay with you?"

"Absolutely. I'm sorry for your loss."

"Thank you."

Bushing reached into his trench coat and pulled out a photograph. "Since you know the area, maybe you can help me out here, Mr. Moran. Do you remember seeing this woman around the neighborhood?"

I didn't need to squint in the diminishing light to see who it was. I recognized the picture from the headline in the *Tribune*, but that was in another world. It was Betsy Kern.

"No, I haven't."

"You sure? She only lives a couple of blocks away."

"Sorry. I'm sure."

"Well, she's missing. She went out for a run in the park last night and never came back home. Her family's pretty worried about her."

"I wish I could help, but I haven't seen her."

"What about people hanging around in the park? Have you seen anyone who looked suspicious?"

"We get strange characters around here all the time, Detective. But lately? No one comes to mind."

"Okay. Well, if you see anyone, please give us a call, Mr. Moran."

"I'll do that."

Detective Bushing retraced his steps to his car. He got back inside but didn't drive away, and I knew he was waiting to see what I would do. I couldn't really wait outside any longer. I headed across the street toward my apartment building. When I got to the door, I was relieved that my key worked, and I went inside and closed the door behind me. On the street, Bushing's gray sedan cruised past the building and disappeared.

I didn't turn on any lights. I stayed in the shadowy hallway, looking across at the park, which was now sinking into the grip of night. Finally, I let myself into the downstairs apartment. It had a different smell, not like my place and not like the apartment where a different Dylan had lived with Tai. I couldn't place what the aroma was. The only word that popped into my head to describe it was *creamy*, which wasn't a smell at all. It reminded me of how our home used to smell when I was growing up with my parents.

The building itself was dead quiet. I didn't feel the presence of my doppelgänger or the aura of menace that followed him. The only sensation here was that strange creaminess, which I didn't understand. Even so, I couldn't afford to linger. I needed to make sure the apartment was empty, and then I needed to leave before the other Dylan and Karly came home. I didn't want to risk leaving any footprints in their lives. I'd promised Roscoe I wouldn't do that.

But I was too late.

I had just started down the hallway when the front door rattled behind me. I froze where I was, and there was no time to hide. The living room lights went on, blinding me.

When I could see again, there she was. Karly.

I captured that moment in my head like a photograph, because I knew it wouldn't last. She wore a striped T-shirt and blue capris that hugged her willowy body. Heeled leather boots made her taller than me. Her hair was blonder and longer than my own Karly had kept it, and even her breasts seemed to swell larger from her torso than the woman I remembered. But her face was the same. Her blue eyes gravitated to mine like a magnet. Her mouth broke into a wide smile, and in that heartbreaking smile was everything I'd lost.

She was my wife. She loved me.

"Hey, sweetheart," she said, with happy surprise in her voice. "I thought tonight was your night to work late."

I tried to say something, but I couldn't. I simply stared at her, enraptured. I wanted to run to her and sweep her into my arms. We stared at each other for no more than a beat or two, and then instead of closing the front door, she kept it open with her foot and pulled something inside the apartment behind her.

A stroller.

Karly closed the door, then bent down and carefully lifted a baby into her arms, holding it like the treasure at the end of a rainbow. "Look, Ellie," she cooed to her child. "Daddy's home early. Don't we love that?"

Ellie. Eleanor. My mother's name.

My child. My daughter. *Our* daughter. That was the creaminess of this place. It was the smell of a baby, of life, of innocence, of freshness and beginnings. Staring at the two of them, I felt something tightening in my chest, as if there weren't enough oxygen in the world to let me breathe. I could not love this woman more, and yet suddenly, I did. I had never dreamed of what it would be like to have a child with her, but in that moment, I knew my life was empty without one.

"Are you okay?" Karly asked, studying me with a crinkle in her forehead.

I struggled to speak. "Fine. You look beautiful. Both of you."

"Well, you don't look so bad yourself." She crossed the space between us and casually deposited our little girl in my arms. "Here, can you take her? I need to feed her, but I want to change first."

She kissed my cheek and headed for our bedroom. I had held few babies in my life, but holding Ellie felt utterly natural. I wondered how old she was, but she looked new to this world. Her face, her hair, her eyes, they were *me*. And Karly. And Edgar. And my mother, even my father, too. My entire family lived in that child, free of anything bad, of anything that wasn't good and perfect. I wanted everything in my life to stop where it was right then and there. I wanted that moment to last forever.

Then Ellie began to cry. Her little face screwed up as she realized that her mother was gone and a stranger was holding her. With her cheeks red, she wailed for Karly and squirmed to get away from my arms. That was when the reality of this situation truly hit me.

She was not mine.

She belonged to someone else.

Nothing in this world was mine.

Karly returned moments later, wearing a loose Cubs jersey and sweats. "Aw, what's wrong, Ellie?" she murmured as she retrieved her baby and took a seat in the living room near the fireplace. She lifted her shirt and offered up her breast, and Ellie settled immediately, making soft suckling noises. "Could you dim the lights, honey? She likes it better when it's not so bright."

I did.

"And some music?" she asked. "Something mellow."

"Sure."

When the piano music was playing, I took a chair opposite her. I needed to go, because the real Dylan could return home at any moment, but I found it impossible to drag myself away. Watching Karly, watching Ellie, I felt in awe of the amazing life this other version of myself had built. To be honest, I was jealous. Envy ate me up inside. This man, whoever he was, had made bad choices like me—he'd *killed* someone with all his pent-up frustration—and yet here he was with this beautiful wife and child. He'd gone through hell and come out in heaven on the other side.

It was almost too much for me to bear. Everything here felt so good, so natural, so right. And none of it belonged to me.

"I saw Susannah for lunch today," Karly told me, using her mother's first name.

"How is she?"

"I think having a granddaughter may turn out to be a reasonable trade for me getting out of the real estate business."

"She didn't try to get you back?" I asked, because I knew what Susannah was like in any world.

"Well, she didn't put her heart into it. She brought it up once and then dropped it. She did remind me that with you working for a nonprofit, and me being a stay-at-home mom, we have practically no money."

"What did you say?"

"I said you have a ten-minute walk to work, and I don't mind Hamburger Helper."

Karly's eyes drifted to Ellie, and I watched her face glow with love.

"Are you really okay with this?" I asked her.

She looked up from Ellie, and her eyes were as serious as I'd ever seen them. "Life's about making choices, Dylan. This was my choice. I don't have a single regret."

I wished I could say the same. At that moment, I was consumed with nothing but regrets. I told myself again: *You need to go.* I needed to leave this house and give it back to the people who belonged here.

But I couldn't.

"I was working on another poem today," Karly went on.

"That's great."

She rolled her eyes. "Yes, because we're not poor enough, I want to get a useless graduate degree and write poetry. I haven't shown any of them to my dad yet. He keeps pestering me, but I'm not ready. They're really dark. I don't know where any of it comes from. I'm so happy with my life, but I start writing, and it all comes out like a nightmare."

"I think that's the sign of a deep soul."

"Oh, yeah, right," she replied, but she had the twinkle that told me she liked hearing that.

"Can I see what you wrote?"

"Sure. I'll read it to you later when we're in bed."

I covered my disappointment, because I wouldn't be here for that. "Okay."

"Would you get me a cup of tea, sweetheart?"

"Of course."

I stood up from the chair. I wanted nothing more than to spend the evening like this, in the dim glow, with music playing. Then I would put my daughter in her crib and go to bed with my wife. My hunger to stay in this life overwhelmed me, but all good things had to end. Like a jumper on a bridge railing, I finally took the plunge, but I regretted it as soon as I fell.

"I think I'll stretch my legs outside," I told her. "I need to clear my head."

"Are you all right?"

"Fine. I just want to get some air. Do you mind? Are you okay here?"

"I don't mind, but please stay out of the park. Did you hear about that woman disappearing? I don't like you walking home that way at night. I know the park is a shortcut, but I want you to stay on Foster."

"Okay. Whatever you want."

I went into the kitchen to make her tea. I knew the kind Karly liked: mandarin orange with a hint of cinnamon. It was too sweet for me, but she loved it. I could do this one last thing for her, but then I had to go. While the water boiled in a mug in the microwave, I got myself ready. I grabbed a light jacket from a hook near the back door, and I slipped it on.

Then I took a long, sharp knife from the butcher block on the counter and tucked it into the jacket pocket.

Chapter 31

Despite Karly's warning, I headed straight for the park. It drew me into its darkness. There was no one around, just empty sidewalks and shadows where the glow of the light posts didn't reach. The night hid me, but it hid *him*, too. I walked across the wet grass to the dense trees lining the riverbank, where my gaze couldn't penetrate the wall of tangled brush. The sewery dankness of the water intensified as I got closer, like the blooming of a corpse flower. The wind was dead still, letting the smell hang in the air.

I thought about calling out to him. I was sure he could hear me. *Let's end this now. You and me.* But I didn't think he'd show himself yet. He was like a virus, stalking his victims silently and only coming into the open when he saw that they were vulnerable.

In the quietness, I listened to the chirp of a lone cricket, like a spy issuing a warning. A mosquito whined in my ear, and I batted it away. Keeping my eyes on the riverbank, I returned to the trail and headed north. As I walked, I curled my fingers around the handle of the knife in my pocket. Every few steps, I looked back, trying to pick out a silhouette in the trees.

No one was there.

I kept looking for the Dylan who lived in this world, coming home from work. I wasn't sure what emotions I would feel when I saw him. We'd have the same face, the same body, the same walk, but he had so many things I didn't. Karly and Ellie were waiting for him. When he was back in our apartment, he'd kiss his little girl and sleep next to his wife. I had no one waiting for me in my own world. They were all gone.

All I could do was make sure that this Dylan Moran got home safely to his family.

At least, that was what I told myself I was here to do.

Ahead of me, the trail split. One way led up to Foster Avenue. The other way led down into a tunnel beside the water. I took the tunnel, where lights illuminated rust, swirls of graffiti, and a swarm of bugs. The last time I'd done this, I'd found Dylan Moran's body in the process of being consumed by rats. It made me wonder if I was already too late. Maybe the Dylan of this world was never coming home from his job. Maybe my doppelgänger had left his body beside the river, his decomposing flesh contributing to the rotting smell in my nose. But I couldn't let myself think that way. I had to keep going.

On the other side of the tunnel, I climbed the wet grass to the north side of Foster. A few cars lit me up with their headlights. I walked several blocks to the neighborhood of North Park University. My mother, Eleanor, had gone there. I walked as far as Kedzie and saw a one-story office building across from the entrance to the university campus. I could see white lettering stenciled on the tall windows.

Chicago Housing Solutions.

This was the nonprofit run by Dylan Moran.

The lights were on inside. I could see a few workers, but I couldn't make out individual faces. All I could do was wait for Dylan to head home and then follow him. I was near a McDonald's, and I was hungry, so I took a minute to get myself an order of fries. I brought them back out and ate them one at a time as I perched on the top of a low fence that ran along Kedzie.

I'd been there about twenty minutes when a voice behind me said, "Mr. Moran?"

It hadn't occurred to me that I'd be recognized here. I looked back, thinking about how to explain myself. A plump black woman in her sixties stood next to the door of an old Camry in the McDonald's parking lot, with a brown takeaway bag in her hand. A boy no older than ten held her hand. Seeing my face, she gave me a wide, gap-toothed smile.

"Oh, Mr. Moran, I knew that was you. You taking a little dinner break?"

"Yes, that's right."

She looked down at the boy who was with her. "William, you go shake that man's hand, all right? Do it right now. He's a very special person."

The boy looked nervous as he came up to the fence, but his grip was strong as he reached up to shake my hand. "My name's Bill," he said.

"Nice to meet you, Bill. I'm Dylan."

The woman approached the fence, too. "You don't remember me, do you?"

I began to apologize, but she waved it away.

"No, no, don't you worry about that. With all the people you meet every day, I'm not surprised at all. I'm Cora-Lee Hobart. You helped my son Lionel last year. Saved him is what you did. You saved all of us, including me and my grandson here. Lionel fell behind on our rent when he was out of work for a couple of months. I needed looking after when I had my heart attack, but do you think the landlord cared about that? He was going to kick us out on the street. You wouldn't let that happen. You made calls and wrote letters and got lawyers and people from the city on our side, and the landlord, he backed right down. Let Lionel catch up on the rent again when he went back to work. Without you, heaven only knows where we would be right now. God bless you, Mr. Moran."

I smiled at her, but I felt envy again.

Envy that no one had ever spoken to me with that kind of gratitude in their voice. Envy that I'd never changed someone's life like that.

"Well, it's good to know you're all doing so well," I told her.

"That we are." Cora-Lee looked around the parking lot and low-ered her voice. "I'm not sure if you realize this, Mr. Moran, but people around here know your story. You made mistakes, and I'm sure you feel bad about what you did, and I know you paid a price for it. All I can tell you is, I thank God for your mistakes. They're what brought you to us. Ain't no accident, that's for sure. You're here for a reason."

I shook my head with a kind of wonder. "That's very nice of you to say."

"It's the truth."

Her grandson shook my hand again. The two of them got into her Camry, and Cora-Lee waved at me as she pulled out of the parking lot. They drove down Foster toward the river, and I was alone again. When they were gone, I crossed the street to stand outside the offices of Chicago Housing Solutions. I hoped the darkness would keep me invisible on the other side of the windows. I needed to see this Dylan Moran up close—not just his face, but who he really was inside.

It wasn't a big-budget operation. All the furniture looked second-hand. The yellow paint was dirty, with posters that read "Housing Is a Human Right" stuck crookedly on the walls with masking tape. The gray industrial carpet was worn and stained. Despite the late hour, almost a dozen people worked the phones and computers as if it were the middle of the day. A couple of them wore business clothes, but most wore blue T-shirts with the CHS logo, identifying them as vol-unteers. I saw two Lou Malnati's pizza boxes on one desk, several liters of Mountain Dew, and a beat-up coffee machine with an oversize red tub of Folgers next to it.

My stare went from face to face. Then I saw him.

With his feet up on a desk and a phone propped on his shoulder, Dylan Moran drank Folgers from a paper cup.

He looked just like me. He hadn't cut his hair or shaved. His clothes were similar to mine, a dark slim-fit button-down shirt and khakis, and leather shoes that had been through a war. As he talked on the phone, I saw a range of expressions that I regularly saw on my own face in the mirror and in photographs. We smiled alike; we frowned alike. Our blue eyes had the same heat. If you stood the two of us next to each other, we'd look like twins you couldn't tell apart. Even Karly had accepted me as him. We were the same person.

But to my eyes, he was a completely different man. Our similarities were skin deep, and underneath all of that, we were strangers. Even the killer wearing my father's leather jacket resembled me more than this Dylan Moran did. I couldn't decide what it was that made him so foreign to me. I tried to unlock the riddle in his face, but I found myself unable to decipher it.

As I watched, he hung up the phone. I could see that it had been an intense, difficult call. I knew those calls—when I dealt with suppliers who were bucking deadlines, or with clients who kept changing their minds about their events. Those calls kept me up at night. But as soon as this Dylan put down the phone, a relaxed smile returned to his face. He called out something I couldn't hear to two of the volunteers, and one of them tossed a foam football his way. They passed it back and forth for almost a minute. Then he got out of his chair, clapping his hands like a coach. He went from desk to desk, checking in on each of his volunteers. They joked. They argued. An old man showed him something on a computer screen that obviously made him happy, and Dylan kissed the top of his head. He finished his coffee, poured a little more from the pot, and drank it all. He found part of a doughnut in a pink box, and as he took bites of it, he sat on the edge of a desk and checked messages on his phone.

There was nothing special or unusual about any of it. It all looked so casual. So normal. This day, this evening, must have been like any other day for the man who worked inside these walls. That was when it hit me. That was when I understood what made him so different from me.

This Dylan Moran wasn't running.

All my life, I'd been hurrying to get somewhere, without the slightest idea where that was. But this Dylan was already there. He looked at peace with the ground he was standing on. He would go home to his family tonight, and wake up tomorrow, and his life wouldn't have changed at all. That was just the way he wanted it.

I felt a malevolent emotion grip my heart again.

Envy, as deep as a well.

Dylan checked his watch and realized what time it was. He was late going home. He looked up with a start, and in doing so, he stared out the windows toward the street. Among the reflections, he saw me. His face did a double-take, and he pushed himself off the desk. Before his mind could truly reconcile the idea that there were *two* of us, I backed up into the darkness and turned from the window. I crossed the street and took shelter behind the North Park sign, where I was invisible. The door to the building opened a few seconds later, and Dylan came outside. He looked long and hard both ways down the street, but when he saw that the sidewalks were empty, he shook his head and went back into the office.

He didn't stay there for long.

Just a few minutes later, he reemerged, calling goodbye to the people inside. The incident in the window was obviously forgotten, because he didn't check the street again. Instead, he turned left, heading toward the river.

Heading toward home.

I followed on the other side of the street. When the traffic cleared, I crossed and fell in behind him. We walked in tandem, half a block apart, but he never looked back. I knew, somehow I knew, that he would take the shortcut home through the park, despite the warnings from Karly that it wasn't safe. He'd go through the tunnel beside the river, and he'd cut across the open grass where it was pitch black.

The three of us would be together. Dylan. Me. And the killer who was waiting for both of us.

I knew my job. I had to stop that killer once and for all. His journey ended here. This was why I was in this world. I swore to myself that I had no other motives in my heart.

Except I was lying.

I couldn't hold back dark thoughts bubbling out of that well of envy and desire. Everything this man had, I wanted. His wife. His child. His job. My perfect life was right there in front of me, and all I had to do was take it for myself. If this man disappeared, no one would know. No one would miss him. I'd *become* him. I would go home and wrap Karly up in my arms, and this world would go on just as it had before. The only price to pay was one sin.

A life for a life.

Eve Brier had whispered to me when this began: *You might be tempted to stay.*

And not just stay. She'd seen this coming. She'd known that sooner or later, a serpent would dangle an apple in front of me and encourage me to take a bite. *You might be tempted to kill that other version of yourself.*

Yes, I was tempted. In fact, I couldn't think about anything else.

Ahead of me, Dylan reached the bridge over the river. He crossed to the east side, still unaware of my presence only a few steps behind him. If he stayed straight, he'd remain on the brightly lit city streets, but the park was immediately below him, beckoning with its solitude and darkness.

I knew that's where he'd go, because that's where *I* would go.

And he did.

He turned onto the park path and skidded down a grassy slope. The empty tunnel led beside the river. For a brief moment, the hill blocked me from his view, and I used that moment to close the distance between us. When I got to the tunnel, Dylan was a shadow moving toward the light, only steps ahead of me.

I should have noticed immediately that the tunnel was dark. The lights had been on when I came this way before, but now they were off. I didn't realize what it meant. I was too focused on catching up to the man in front of me. I plunged ahead, practically running beside the river, and the noise of my footsteps finally made him aware of me.

He stopped, turning around slowly to see who I was. I stopped, too.

We confronted each other. He stood at the end of the tunnel, lit by the light post and the glow of the street above him. I was still in darkness, my face obscured. We weren't far apart. If I leaped for him, I'd be on him. He had nowhere to run.

Dylan raised his arms with the fingers of his hands spread wide. He knew that I was a threat, but for now, I was just another Chicago mugger shaking him down. "I'm not armed," he called. "I'm not going to fight back. What do you want? Money? I don't have much, but you can have whatever's in my wallet."

I spoke to him from the tunnel. "I don't want money."

"Then what do you want?"

I tried to speak, but my throat choked up with guilt and indecision. We were alone, no one around but the two of us. It was the perfect moment. Everything I wanted was right in front of me, standing on the trail. All I had to do was *take it*.

"Talk to me," Dylan went on. "Are you in trouble? Do you need help? Tell me what you want."

I couldn't hold it in. What I said made no sense, not when he couldn't see my face and see who I was. But I told him anyway.

"I want your *life*. That's what I want."

Fear widened his eyes. He flinched and took a step backward, ready to bolt. I wondered if he was thinking about that earlier moment, looking through the window, seeing his mirror image on the other side of the glass. Did he realize that was me? Could he hear himself in my voice?

"Don't run," I warned him sharply, grabbing the knife from my pocket and holding it up in silhouette. "Don't try it. You won't get far."

"Listen to me. I have a little girl. A baby."

"I know."

"You *know*? You know who I am?"

"I know everything about you . . . Dylan Moran."

"Then what do you want with me?"

"I told you. You're leading the life *I'm* supposed to have. And I want it back."

"What does that even mean?" He narrowed his eyes, trying to see me in the darkness. "Who *are* you?"

I almost stepped into the light and gave him the answer. *I'm you.* If I came at him, he'd know who was taking away his world. Before he died, he'd look into my eyes and see the truth. I tightened my grip around the knife handle, feeling it slip in my sweaty fingers. My mouth was dry with desire for what this man had. My legs tensed, ready to move.

But I couldn't do it. This wasn't me.

I was trying to take things that belonged to someone else. I'd lost my Karly; he'd kept his. I'd waited to have a child with her; he'd said yes. I could take those things for myself, but in the end, they still wouldn't be *mine*. I hadn't earned them, and this man had. He deserved to keep them, not to have them ripped away by a stranger. I couldn't steal his life.

I stayed in the tunnel, where I was invisible. The silence between us dragged out.

"It doesn't matter who I am," I told him finally. "Go home. Get out of here. Go home to Karly. Go home to your little girl."

He backed away, unsure whether this was a trick. I stayed in the darkness without moving, watching my one chance at happiness leave me behind. When Dylan got to the top of the slope, he turned his back on me. I knew he would run now, disappearing into the park.

"*Dylan*," I called after him sharply.

He stopped, although he was far enough away that I wasn't a threat anymore. "What is it?"

"Not that way."

"What do you mean?"

"Don't go through the park. Stay on the street. If you never want to see me again, stay out of the park at night."

There was something in the sound of my voice that convinced him. He went the other way. He clambered up the grass away from the trail, and when he was out of sight, he ran. I heard his footsteps pounding above me, as he joined the lights and traffic and people on the street.

He was safe. He'd make it home now.

My grief tasted bitter in my mouth. I felt hollowed out inside. I'd come a long way and ended up back where I started, with nothing to show for the journey. The guilt, the loss, the shame, all distracted me. I wasn't thinking about where I was, or the darkness of the tunnel that had been lit up when I came this way before. I'd missed the clues I should have seen immediately. I'd forgotten why I was in this world.

I turned around and saw my own shadow.

He buried a knife in my stomach.

Chapter 32

The blade sliced through tissue and muscle and severed my intestines. I felt an electric shock of pain and then a strange flowing warmth. My doppelgänger was right in front of me, his breath on my face. He cut through my abdomen with the practiced hand of a butcher. The damage was done in seconds, and then he put his other hand flat on my chest and pushed me away. I stumbled backward. The knife slid out of my body. I clutched at my stomach and felt blood oozing between my fingers. I staggered out of the tunnel into the light, with a wet red stain growing on my shirt. The river slurped along the bank beside me, sounding loud inside my head.

Shock overwhelmed me. With my fingers numb, my own knife clattered uselessly to the sidewalk. I tried to hold the blood in, but I couldn't. It pulsed out of my body.

Dylan followed me out of the tunnel, wiping the bloody knife on his leather jacket.

"I thought you were different," he sneered. "When I saw you take out that knife, I really thought you might have the balls to kill him. But no. You had your chance, and you let it slip away."

I fought down the dizziness in my head and charged at him. He saw me coming. Smoothly, he eased his weight onto his left foot, turned sideways, and lashed out with a jab of his right leg. His foot kicked like a piston into the wound in my stomach, and my brain turned upside down with agony. I stumbled, moaned, then collapsed to my hands and knees. My mouth spat up vomit. Blood dripped from my belly onto the trail, a constellation of cherry-red spatter.

I tried to forget about my panic. My fear. My pain. I needed to function, at least for a while longer. The blood on the ground became a kind of Rorschach test, centering me. I stared at the blood, and then my gaze shifted to the weeds and cracks in the bridge's retaining wall, and then to the shadows thrown by the light post overhead, and then finally to the long steel blade of my knife. It still lay on the trail where I'd dropped it. The black handle was inches away. My body blocked it from the view of the Dylan standing over me. I could feel him there, like a boxer crowing over the adversary he'd knocked to the ground.

My fingers inched closer to the knife like the legs of a spider. In one jerky motion, I grabbed it and pushed off my knees. I slashed at him with the blade, and my knife landed in flesh, driving four inches deep into his thigh.

He howled with pain and twisted away, ripping the knife handle from my hand. Grimacing, he yanked the knife out of his leg and threw it like a boomerang into the river. I could hear the splash. He lifted his own knife high over his head, and his eyes boiled with fury. I expected him to bury the blade in my neck, cutting through arteries that would erupt in fountains of blood.

Instead, slowly, he brought his arm back down. I was on my knees on the sidewalk, and he limped toward me and slid the sharp edge of the blade under my chin. He pressed hard enough that I could feel the sting. Then he lowered the knife and jabbed it into the fabric of my shirt and tore away one of the sleeves. He backed up and tied the sleeve tightly around his leg. The cloth was crimson in seconds.

With his wound bandaged, he jerked me to my feet. Another shock wave of pain radiated through my body. I had trouble standing. He threw me against the railing at the riverbank and pushed the point of the knife against my rib cage, where my heart was beating wildly. Below me, I could smell the brown sludge of the river.

"Do you want me to end it?" he asked.

"Do whatever you want."

"Sorry, I won't make it quick for you. You get to sit here and die slowly, knowing what I'm doing on the other side of the park. Listen carefully. Maybe you'll be able to hear Karly scream."

My lip curled into a snarl of rage. I dug my fingernails like claws into his wounded thigh. It felt good to see him suffer, but my victory was short lived. He scored the knife in a bright-red line across my chest and hurled me to the ground. I landed hard on my side as he delivered a vicious kick into my stomach with the toe of his shoe. Fireworks blew up in my head, white hot and blinding. I was barely conscious.

He knelt beside me, and his voice made a sadistic whisper in my ear.

"I'm going to kill all of them, Dylan. Do you want to watch? Sorry, but I don't think you'll make it that far. You'll see it through my eyes, though. We're connected, you and me. You'll know what I'm doing. You'll watch each one of them go. Dylan. Karly. And the little girl, too. I won't forget her."

"Don't."

It was the only word I could drag from my throat. He just laughed at me.

"It's too late. You had your chance. Once I'm done, I'll go back to the Art Institute and start over. I have more worlds to conquer, and you won't be around to chase me. You failed again, Dylan. I'm stronger than you are. Face it, I always have been."

He pushed himself to his feet and limped away.

I tried to focus, but my eyes spun in circles and then blinked shut. I lost consciousness. When I opened my eyes again, I didn't see *him* anymore. Inside the spinning kaleidoscope of my mind, I saw my father instead. I was a boy huddled in the corner of the bedroom, and my mother's gun was on top of the dresser, and my father was reaching for it, cocking it, aiming it, pulling the trigger.

I should have been able to stop it.

All my life I'd looked back on that moment and wondered why I'd let it happen. *I should have been able to stop it!*

If only I'd reacted faster. If only I'd seen him going for the gun, if I'd screamed, if I'd warned my mother, if I'd leaped off the floor and run to him, if I'd put myself between him and her. I could have done something. Instead, I sat there and watched my father pick up the gun and shoot my mother in the head. I did nothing.

I let her die.

I let Roscoe die.

I let Karly die.

Losing them was all on me, one failure after another.

Never again. I heard myself shouting somewhere in my head, trying to jolt myself awake. *Never again!* I wasn't going to let it happen to anyone else. I'd come here to set myself free, and that was what I had to do.

The blur of my memories faded away. Somehow, I came back to life. I was still in the park. I'd passed out, but I had no idea for how long. The other Dylan was gone. I was alone on the sidewalk in a river of blood, but I was still alive, and that meant I had one more chance. I grabbed the railing on the riverbank and pulled myself up. When I was standing, I tried to swallow down the pain. I pushed a hand against my abdomen to stanch the bleeding, and I staggered up the trail.

Where was he?

I didn't see him.

The trail crested a hill beside the trees. With each step, I dragged stale air in and out of my chest. Bugs swarmed around me, as if smelling that I was close to collapse. No, it was my blood they wanted. I felt them landing on my fingers, beating their sticky wings, drinking their fill from my wounds. I didn't have the stamina to swat them away. Let them feed.

Faster, I thought to myself. *You have to go faster.*

My legs carried me down the dark trail at a pace that was almost a run. I was in a race now, not just between me and my doppelgänger, but between my mind and my body, to see which one would give up first.

Where was he?

There. I could see him ahead of me now. He limped in and out of the glow of the light posts. He'd slowed; he was losing blood, like me. I dug into my reserves and pushed aside pain, and breath, and blood, and memory, and I stumbled ahead like a marathon runner with the finish line looming at the end of one more long block.

I was nearly there. I had him within reach.

Then, from the middle of the park, I heard something that sent a shudder of terror through my soul.

"Dylan?"

It was a voice from the darkness, calling my name. A voice I knew so well.

Karly.

No, no, no, no, it couldn't be her, not here, not now. But the Dylan I was chasing heard her, too, and he stopped on the trail. The unmistakable silhouette of my beautiful wife broke from the trees and joined him. She wrapped him up in an embrace and kissed him. It was dark, and she could barely see him, but she showed no fear.

Why should she? He was her husband.

Relief filled her voice. "Dylan, where were you? I was so worried when you didn't come home. I left Ellie with the neighbors and came out to find you. Sweetheart, I told you not to go through the park."

I saw him smile. There was nothing but evil in that smile. I heard him say, "I'm sorry, my love."

Then I saw his hand disappear into his leather jacket for the knife.

He was just like my father, reaching for the gun.

I should have been able to stop it!

271

I summoned everything I had left in my body. I threw myself across the last few steps and launched into the air, colliding hard with his back and knocking him to the ground. Pain exploded in my gut, tearing open my wound, unleashing a sea of blood. I took Dylan's head into both of my hands and slammed his skull against the concrete. Then I did it again, and again, hearing the bone crack. When his eyes finally closed, I wrapped my hands tightly around his throat and pushed my thumbs into his windpipe. I cut off every atom of air that would keep him alive.

Above me, Karly screamed.

Of course she did. She couldn't see my face. I was a stranger attacking her husband. She grabbed my shoulders to pull me off, and when I hung on, she kicked and scratched and got on the ground and clamped her teeth around my forearm. I couldn't take it. Finally, I let go, and she dragged me backward into the grass.

We were still in the dark. She couldn't see my face.

"Karly, stop!" I screamed.

But all her primal instincts had taken over. She hammered my body with her fists. Her knee sank into the bloody mess of my abdomen, causing waves of agony that left me struggling to breathe. I put up my arms to fend her off and shouted again.

"Karly, it's me!"

My familiar voice, my words, slowly seeped into her mind. She began to perceive that something impossible was happening here, but it was already too late.

Rising above her like a ghost under the park light, I saw my doppelgänger. He was on his feet again, the knife in his hand. Blood from his fractured skull ran in ribbons down his face. He jumped toward my wife. With a surge of adrenaline, I shoved Karly away, but Dylan kept coming. He landed on top of me, and we rolled together, battling for control of the knife. My strength was waning, but so was his. Both of us were dizzy, drained, desperate. The park became a whirling gyroscope inside our heads, and I could feel our minds coming together. I saw his face and my face through my own eyes. As we rolled, as our bodies intertwined, we were becoming one person. We'd always been one person, trapped inside endless worlds.

There was only one way to stop him. I had to sacrifice myself. I let go of the knife and took hold of his throat again, choking him. With his hands free, he thrust the knife into my back, and pulled it out, and thrust it in again. I held on through every lightning bolt of agony. I ignored the pain and weakness and blood and kept my fingers wrapped around his windpipe. Below me, his face turned purple. His eyes bulged. His tongue swelled from his mouth. He stabbed me over and over, but the shock waves rippling through my back belonged to someone else, not me. My mind shunted them aside. I had no wounds, no feeling, no body at all. I was nothing but two hands locked around a killer's neck.

He reared back to stab me one more time.

This time, the blow never came. His arm stiffened in midair. The knife slid away from his fingers and dropped to the grass. His stare grew fixed, the whites of his eyes ruby red with exploded blood vessels. His body went limp.

It was done.

Dylan Moran was dead.

It took time for me to unclench my knuckles and peel my fingers away from his neck. When I was finally able to let go, I rolled off him. We lay in the park next to each other, two twins. One dead, one dying. I turned my head, watching him, still not able to believe I'd killed him. Exhausted, I let my eyes blink shut—not for long, only for a few seconds. When I opened them again, he was gone. The ground was empty, as if his body had never been there at all. He was an intruder who didn't belong in this world.

Neither did I.

I had to go, too.

Every breath had become torture. I dragged in air and tasted blood as I exhaled. It wouldn't be long. And yet I felt free.

Karly knelt by my side. Her blue eyes were full of confusion and fear. "*Dylan.* Oh, my God, Dylan, what's going on? That other man, he was *you.* He had your *face.* Where is he? Where did he go?"

I whispered to her as my brain floated. "Go home, Karly."

"No, you need help. An ambulance."

She took her phone in her hand, but I found enough strength to hold her wrist down. "Don't."

She put her hand softly on my cheek. "I can't lose you. Ellie can't lose you."

"You won't lose me. Go home. I'm there."

"What are you talking about?"

"I'm not your Dylan. I'm not him. Your Dylan is safe. I promise you."

"I don't understand!"

I felt black clouds encroaching. I didn't want her to see the end. "Please, Karly. Go."

"How can I leave? How can you say that?"

She bent down, and her hair swished across my face. Her lips found mine. I could barely feel them, but the barest sensation of softness was enough to take away some of the pain. She held on to me, our faces pressed together. I smelled her perfume, but my five senses had begun to shut down, and only the sixth was left.

"Do you love me?" I asked her.

"You know I do."

"Then trust me. Go home."

She pushed herself up on her hands, her face over mine, only inches away. "Are you really there?"

"Yes."

"How can I possibly believe that?"

"Because I would never let you go."

She stared down at me, trying to find answers in my face. I felt her kiss me again, slow and soft, like a fairy touch. She got to her feet and stood over me, memorizing the look of me, the way I'd memorized her.

"Come find me, Dylan," she murmured.

I tried to speak, but I couldn't.

"Come find me," she said again. "I'm still here."

Then she walked away, not looking back. I followed her with my eyes until the darkness of the park enveloped her. She was in her world; she had her husband and her child. I was alone again.

I lay on my back, staring at the sky. Stars ran across the heavens in limitless numbers. There was no more pain at all. My blood was on the ground, but I doubted it would be here for long.

My chest swelled with one last breath.

It gave me the strength for one last word.

"Infinite."

CHAPTER 33

"Welcome back," Eve Brier told me.

I still lay on my back, but instead of a field of stars above me when I opened my eyes, I saw the white foam tiles of an office ceiling. Beneath me, the damp grass of River Park had been replaced by a leather sofa. Instinctively, my hands went to my abdomen, where I expected to feel blood gushing from an open wound. Not anymore. I was completely uninjured.

With a jerk, I sat up, trying to orient myself. A little bit of nausea lingered, as well as a splitting headache. "Where am I?"

"Hancock Center," Eve replied. "My office."

She sat across the room from me in a cushioned roller chair near a row of floor-to-ceiling windows. Behind her, I could see the expanse of Lake Michigan, a view that was interrupted by one of the building's huge diagonal crossbeams. On the horizon, the blue of the water met the blue of the sky.

Eve cocked her head over her bony shoulders. She had an enigmatic smile on her face. Her almond-shaped eyes still looked alien. She had a pen in her hands that she stroked in an oddly suggestive manner. Her lush blond-and-brown hair swept messily across her shoulders. She pulled her chair close to the sofa and leaned forward, looking at me with an intense, curious expression.

"Did you go there?"

I knew what she meant. "The Many Worlds? Yes, I did."

"Was it what you imagined?"

I didn't know how to answer her. I got off the sofa and had to brace myself, because my legs were unsteady. I crossed to the windows and stared at the vista. Chicago looked the same. "Why are we not at Navy Pier? How did we get here?"

"Navy Pier? I don't understand."

I turned away from the windows. "That's where you gave me the injection."

Eve shook her head. "No, we've been in my office the whole time."

"I've never been to your office before."

"Actually, you've been here half a dozen times. We've been working through your grief over Karly. But today was the first time we tried my new therapy."

I sat down again and tried to puzzle out what was happening to me. By saying the escape word, I should have gone back to *my* world. The *real* world. And yet my surroundings all felt brand new.

"How long?" I asked.

"What do you mean?"

"How long have I been here?"

"Today? About five hours. That's quite a bit longer than most of my patients experience in their sessions. I was starting to get concerned. If it went on much longer, I was debating how to bring you back. But I assume you finally said the escape word."

"I did," I said, after a moment of silence.

She sensed my hesitation. "Dylan, it may feel strange, but you really are back where you belong."

Was I?

Then why did everything feel different?

"I don't remember any of this," I told her. "Your office. The sessions we've had. I don't remember the past few weeks at all, other than being in the Many Worlds."

"That's not surprising. Short-term memory loss is a common side effect of the treatment."

"Because of the psychotropic drugs?" I asked.

"Psychotropics?" she replied with surprise. "Where did you get that idea? All I gave you was a simple muscle relaxant to put you in a receptive frame of mind. The rest is hypnotic suggestion, and then . . . well, it's up to your brain to take it from there. However, the intensity of the experience can leave patients extremely disoriented. Your memory typically comes back after a while. It may take a few hours, or even up to a few days. Given how long you were under, I'm not entirely sure what you can expect."

I squeezed my eyes shut and tried to remember my recent past, but the only experiences that were vivid were what I'd been through in the other worlds. I could still remember the violence and death I'd seen there. I could *feel* it. My hands were raw where I'd squeezed them around Dylan's neck. I could taste Karly on my lips.

"This hypnotic suggestion you gave me," I said. "How did that work?"

"Before we began, you picked a place that you wanted to use as your 'portal.' The place where the various versions of yourself would intersect."

"And that was . . . ?"

"The Art Institute," Eve replied with another curious smile, as if she knew I was testing her. "So that's where I told you to go."

I got off the sofa again, feeling restless. Everything she said made sense, but I was having trouble leaving the experiences of my hypnosis behind. "This will sound like a strange question, but are the police looking for me?"

Surprise creased her face. "The police? For what?"

"Murder. Four women were stabbed to death. They'd all attended events at my hotel."

"*Murder?* God, no, there's nothing like that. I'm so sorry, you must have gone through horrific things while you were under. That's very unusual. Most patients don't have experiences that are nearly so . . . violent. In fact, most of them never make it out of their portal. But I take it you did."

"Yes."

"You actually went to other worlds?"

"I went to several worlds, but the first time—"

"Yes?"

"The first time felt like it *was* the real world. That's how I remember it. I don't recall getting there through the Art Institute. You even had me say the safe word for you in that world, and nothing changed. I didn't come back here. I don't understand how that could be."

"The safe word only works if you're aware of what's happening to you," Eve replied. "Your brain may not have been ready to process the experience yet."

I thought about that world and everything I'd experienced. The insanity. The violence. The doppelgänger breaking into my life. Of course, none of it was real. Of course, I was already deep inside Eve's therapy.

So why did being here feel wrong?

"I'm distressed if this was traumatic for you," Eve went on. "That was definitely never the point of the therapy."

She sensed my disorientation and tried to reassure me with a smile.

"Look, we obviously need to talk about everything you experienced," she went on, "but it's better if we don't do that right now. You need time to process. We can set up another appointment in a few days, and you can fill me in on what you went through. In the meantime, hopefully your short-term memory will begin to come back, too."

I nodded. "Okay."

"It might be better if you don't drive yourself home."

"No, I'm fine. I'm starting to feel better. But I do have some questions. With my memory gone, I need to know—well, I need to know
more about who I am. I'm a little lost about what's real and what's not."

"Certainly. Ask anything you want."

I paced back and forth in her office, trying to gather my thoughts.
Eve's desk was on the opposite wall, and I ran my hand along the oak
surface. She had a copy of her book there: *Many Worlds, Many Minds*. It
matched the book I'd purchased in the hotel ballroom, at a time when
I still thought I was in the real world. When I picked it up and turned
it over, I saw the same photograph of Eve that I'd seen in the poster for
her event.

"Dylan?" Eve asked. "Are you okay?"

I put the book back down on her desk. "I guess so. You called me
Dylan. That's my name, right? Dylan Moran."

She smiled. "Yes."

"What day is it?"

"Wednesday."

"Where do I work?"

"You tell me," she replied. "It's easier to get your memory back if
you let your brain help you. Where do you think you work?"

"I'm the events manager for the LaSalle Plaza Hotel."

"That's right."

"I live in an apartment across from River Park. My grandfather,
Edgar, lives upstairs."

"Yes."

I thought about everything else that had changed in the other
worlds. "Have I mentioned a woman named Tai Ragasa during our
sessions?"

"The coworker with a crush on you? Yes."

"But that's all she is to me? A coworker? We're not involved?"

"No."

"My best friend, Roscoe Tate. He's—he's not alive."

"No. You lost Roscoe in a car accident several years ago. It was a devastating event for you. He was the one stable influence in your life after the deaths of your parents."

"That was also the night . . . ," I began, but I couldn't go on.

Eve waited, but when she saw me hesitate, she filled in the blanks. "That was also the night you met Karly."

"Eve, *why* did I come to you?"

"You know the answer to that question, Dylan. Why don't you tell me?"

"Karly," I said. "I lost her in the flood."

"See? You do remember."

"But I don't remember coming to *you*. I don't remember any of this."

Eve shrugged. "Three weeks ago, I had an event at your hotel. I gave a lecture about my Many Worlds, Many Minds theory. Afterward, you came up to me. This was only a few days after the accident. You were still devastated, still in deep grief. You said you normally didn't have much time for shrinks, but everyone had been telling you to get help. My theory intrigued you. You said that ever since the accident, you'd been obsessed with your bad choices. You thought Karly had died because of the man you were and the mistakes you'd made in life. You wondered whether there was a Dylan out there who'd made better choices, and you wanted to know what that world might look like. That's how it began."

"I suppose that makes sense."

"But you still don't remember any of it."

"No."

Eve stood up from the chair. "Don't worry too much about that. I told you, it will take time. For now, it's better if you go home and rest."

I crossed the room and shook her hand. "I guess I should thank you."

"You should only thank me if you experienced some kind of epiphany. The whole point of my Many Worlds therapy is to help you understand the world you're in by seeing the alternatives. Did you learn anything about yourself?"

"I think so."

"What?"

"There was a part of me I had to kill. So that's what I did."

She frowned. "Literally?"

"Yes."

"Well. That's extreme. I've never heard that before. Do you feel like a different person as a result of it?"

"Actually, I do. I just wish I'd figured it out a long time ago. I've lost the things that matter most to me, and now it's too late to change my life."

She gave me a reassuring smile. "It's not too late. As long as you're breathing, there's still time. I'll see you again soon, Dylan. Things will start feeling better, you'll see."

"I hope so."

I headed for the door, but as I reached to open it, I stopped. I glanced around at the office again, which was completely unfamiliar. Even so, I told myself that everything here was solid. Normal. Real. So was Eve Brier.

And yet.

"Dylan? Are you all right?"

"I don't know. Something still feels *off* to me. I can't put my finger on it."

"It's the aftereffects of the therapy. That will pass. Trust me, Dylan, you're back now."

I had no reason to disbelieve anything she'd told me, but I'm sure my face broadcast my doubts.

"You still don't think this is your own world, do you?" Eve asked.

"I'm not sure. To tell you the truth, I'm not sure I *want* this to be the real world."

"Why is that?"

I hesitated, trying to understand it myself. I could still feel those last moments in River Park as I lay dying. "Something happened to me right before I came back."

"When you had to kill your other self?"

"Yes."

"Try not to think of the violence as real, because it wasn't. You were right here in my office the whole time."

"Yes, I know, that's what you said. But it's more complicated than that. I saw Karly in that world. She was there, too."

Eve frowned. "Ah. That must have been very emotional."

"It was."

"Sometimes an experience like that is part of letting go," she told me. "It's how you deal with grief."

"Maybe so, but I can't stop thinking about what she said to me."

"What did she say?"

I could hear Karly's voice, as clearly as if she were standing over me again. Looking down at me and whispering her last words. It didn't feel like goodbye. It didn't feel like what she would say if we were about to be parted forever.

It felt like a message.

Something to carry with me wherever I was going.

"She told me to come find her. She said she was still here."

CHAPTER 34

I left Eve's office and passed the *Lucent* sculpture in the lobby of Hancock Center. Its thousands of lights, reflected in the black pool of water, taunted me like an echo of what I'd been through. Each flickering light was another world, another life, among an endless number constantly multiplying in my mind. I'd visited some of those places, and now I was back in my own world.

Except, according to Eve, I'd never actually left. All this time, I'd been lying on her sofa on the twenty-ninth floor.

As I got back to Michigan Avenue, nothing felt out of place around me. The city looked and smelled the same. The water tower was where it was supposed to be. The shops, people, and traffic hadn't changed. When I checked my wallet, I found a parking ticket for a garage on Chestnut. It was dated early that morning, just as Eve had told me. The key fob in my pocket led me to a used Ford in the garage, and the documents in the glove compartment told me I'd purchased the car three weeks ago. That would have been shortly after the accident.

Everything fit. So why could I remember nothing between then and now?

Why did I feel like I didn't belong here?

I drove from the garage into the city. Eve had told me to go home and rest, but I wasn't ready to do that yet. I was still struggling to decide if I could trust what my senses were telling me. I kept looking for a flaw, a clue, a telltale sign that this world was an illusion like the others. At every stoplight, I checked faces in the cars and crosswalks, hunting for another Dylan Moran. If I saw one of my doubles, then I would know that my brain was lying. But the only Dylan in this world seemed to be me.

My first stop was near Horner Park where Roscoe had died. I needed to see the scars on the ash tree at the corner. They were still there, marking the collision that had killed my friend. Nothing was different. When I was done there, I walked two blocks and found the home listed for sale by Chance Properties. Scotty Ryan's truck was outside. He was doing renovations; he was still alive. I had no memory of whether I'd gotten into a fight with him over his affair with Karly, but it was obvious that no version of myself had come to the house and stabbed him to death.

What I remembered of the past few weeks wasn't real.

What I didn't remember *was* real. I still found that hard to accept.

My next stop was at Alicia Tate's clinic. I needed to see someone I'd known for years, someone who would never lie to me. The last time I'd been in this clinic, which felt like only hours ago, I'd seen Roscoe, alive. I still expected him to come through the door, even though I knew that was impossible.

Alicia hugged me when she saw me. She looked normal; she looked the same. When she took me back to her office, she asked me how I was, and I told her very honestly that I didn't know.

"Alicia, this is an odd question, but when did you last see me?"

She gave me a quizzical stare. "What?"

"I'm having some short-term memory issues. When did we last talk?"

"You came in for an appointment a few days after Karly's funeral."

"Was anything wrong with me?"

"Only the things I'd expect. Depression, anxiety, sleeplessness. Your blood sugar was elevated, which can happen as a result of stress, and so was your heart rate. You were grieving, and that takes a physical toll as well as an emotional and psychological one. Now, tell me about these memory issues."

"I will, but first things first. When I saw you, did I say anything about . . . seeing things?"

"Seeing things? Like what?"

"Like my identical twin. A doppelgänger. Someone who looked exactly like me."

Her brow wrinkled in surprise. "No, you didn't say anything like that. Why, are you having hallucinations?"

I ignored her question. "Did I mention a psychiatrist named Eve Brier?"

Alicia frowned. "Yes. You told me you'd heard her speak at the hotel, and you'd read her book. You were planning to see her for therapy. I told you I wasn't sure that was the right thing to do. Not therapy itself—I strongly suggested you talk to someone. But I looked up this Dr. Brier, and based on what I found, I had concerns about the kind of treatment she offered. Something tells me you went to see her anyway."

"I think I did."

"You think?" Alicia asked. "What does that mean?"

I ran my hands through my hair in frustration. Then I told her everything. The whole story. What I remembered and didn't remember. What I'd experienced in the other worlds. What Eve had told me when I'd awakened in her office. Alicia took it all in and didn't say anything for a while.

"You saw Roscoe?" she asked finally.

"Yes. In one world, he was a priest, but in another, he was a doctor, practicing here with you."

Alicia glanced at the pictures of her son. "Well, I can see the appeal of what Dr. Brier is offering her patients. I can also understand your being reluctant to leave those worlds behind, if you were able to be with Roscoe and Karly again."

"That's the thing. I'm not sure I *have* left them behind."

"What do you mean?"

"Those worlds felt every bit as real to me as this one does. How do I know this isn't just another part of the illusion? I don't trust what I see, Alicia. I look around, and everything in my life looks and feels right. But then again, it doesn't."

"Well, I remember your whole life, Dylan. If you're asking me, this is the real world, but I don't know if that helps you. I probably would have told you the same thing in those worlds, right?"

"No, it does help. I appreciate it. Eve says the procedure can be disorienting, and that's probably what's happening to me. Somehow I have to turn off that experience and turn this world on again."

Alicia got up from her chair. She came around and sat on the front of the desk. "If these worlds were as vivid as you say, that will take time."

"I know. I just don't understand how I could *lose* three weeks of my life. If Eve's right, I've been getting up, going to work, living my life this whole time, right up until I went to her office this morning. Now it's like those past few weeks have been erased and replaced by the worlds she sent me to. How can that happen?"

"I can't tell you that without knowing more about her therapy. But I think there's more going on here than just Eve Brier."

"What do you mean?"

"Trauma can affect memory, too, Dylan. You've been through a singularly traumatic event."

"Karly."

"That's right." Alicia put a hand on my shoulder. "Let me ask you something. Forget about today. Forget about the past few weeks. What's the last thing you *do* remember?"

I closed my eyes and rewound the clock in my head until the seconds started ticking forward again.

"I remember being in the river," I told her. "I was under the water. That was when everything stopped."

∞

Finally, I went home.

In the foyer of our apartment building, I could hear the buzz of Edgar's game show on the television upstairs. I thought about going to see him, but he was probably asleep. Tomorrow was Thursday, and I'd see him at the Art Institute.

Inside my apartment, I saw the things I'd expect to find for a man who'd just lost his wife. Flower arrangements were beginning to wilt. Dozens of sympathy cards lay on the table, some opened, some still sealed. Laundry was piled in baskets, and dishes that needed to be done were stacked in the sink. This was the apartment of someone who'd been in a kind of Alaska for weeks, frozen in place, unable to move on. Seeing it all triggered fresh memories, too. The last three weeks didn't come back, but everything that had happened before Karly and I left on our weekend trip was still here in the apartment, waiting for me.

We'd argued in the living room that night. She'd lost an earring as she tore at her hair in guilt over the affair. There, on the floor near the fireplace, I saw the glittering diamond stud where it had fallen.

I'd packed carelessly for our trip, letting a pile of winter sweaters tumble from the upper shelf in our closet. I'd kicked them angrily across the floor. All the sweaters were still there, exactly where I'd left them. Obviously, in the time since then, I hadn't bothered to pick them up.

Karly had been playing Ellie Goulding songs before I got home late that night. She'd stopped the music in midsong when she saw me. I remembered what she'd been listening to, a song called "Figure 8." I started the music again, and the same song took up right where she'd paused the disc.

There was no way around the truth.

This was my apartment. This was my world. No other Dylan Moran lived here, just me.

I went to the kitchen to pour myself a drink. When the lowball glass was full, I stared at the ice rattling around in the vodka like diamonds and then drained it all out into the sink. I did the same with the rest of the bottle. We had an unopened bottle of Absolut in one of the cabinets, and I got rid of that one the same way. I kept going until all the alcohol we had in the apartment was gone.

Dylan Moran no longer drank.

While I was in the kitchen, I heard the front doorbell. I had no idea who would be coming to see me, but I went through the apartment and pulled open the door. Detective Harvey Bushing stood on my front step. He was as emaciated as he'd been in the other worlds, and his eyes had the same wily intelligence. In my own life, I didn't remember him at all.

Even so, he knew me.

"Mr. Moran? Detective Harvey Bushing. We met a couple of weeks ago. You called 911 after finding the body of a young woman near the riverbank."

"What can I do for you, Detective?" I replied, although two weeks ago was inside the fog that I couldn't remember. I had no memory of finding a body or calling 911.

"Well, I wanted to give you the news personally that we've arrested the man who murdered Betsy Kern. It was an ex-boyfriend of hers who'd been stalking her for some time. He confessed."

"I'm glad to hear it."

"I just wanted to apologize to you. I was a little harsh when I first interviewed you in the park. The fact is, it's not uncommon for the person who reports a crime like this to be the actual perpetrator."

"You were just doing your job, Detective."

"I appreciate your understanding. Anyway, the case is closed. I figured you'd want to know that."

"Thank you, Detective."

"Good night, Mr. Moran."

"Good night."

I watched the detective retreat down the sidewalk in the darkness. He got into his gray sedan and drove away. On the other side of the street, I could see the trees of River Park, where so much had happened to me in those other worlds. In the horizon sky, over the river, I saw a distant flash of lightning, followed by an extended roll of thunder that made the ground shake. A storm was coming in from the west.

I closed the door.

Inside, I sat down in a chair by the fireplace, feeling utterly empty. I bent down and picked up Karly's diamond earring and rolled it between my fingertips.

Oddly, it was Detective Bushing's visit that finally convinced me of where I was. I felt as if one last little mystery had been solved. I'd stumbled upon Betsy Kern's body during my missing weeks, and that experience had worked its way into my explorations.

It was over now. The Many Worlds were behind me.

This was reality, just as Eve Brier had said.

As that thought struck me, I realized what it meant. I'd never see Karly again. She was really gone. No matter what I'd learned about myself, I was too late to change the past. Once you lose someone, you've lost them forever.

I sat in the chair, cupped my hands over my face, and spent the rest of the night crying for my wife.

CHAPTER 35

In the morning, the rain came.

There was nothing for me to do but start living again, so I drove through the storm to the LaSalle Plaza downtown. Black clouds hung over the city and refused to move. A deluge poured across my windshield, making it almost impossible to see where I was going. The streets became lakes under my tires, and streams ran along the curbs and sidewalks, carrying Chicago debris.

I got to the office before anyone else, as I usually did. There was no dawn outside, just darkness. My desk was neat, the way I always left it, and I saw new contracts with my signature on them, reminder notes taped to my monitor, catering orders I'd placed in the past week, and phone messages with customer names for callbacks. I'd been working here for days, even if I remembered none of it. Yesterday, in Eve's office, appeared to be the only day of work I'd missed.

There were a million things to do, which made it a typical morning. This was my job; this was my life. I tried to get on with it, but as the early hours slipped by, I found I couldn't concentrate on any of the details. I picked up the phone and put it down. I turned on the computer and switched it off. The responsibilities that had kept me up nights and forced me to stay late so many times now felt insignificant.

Something had changed for me. *Everything* had changed. I had to face the fact that I was not the same Dylan Moran who had worked here for years. The Many Worlds had killed him. He was gone, and he was never coming back. I needed to become someone new, but I still had no idea how to do that.

Outside, the rain continued to fall, as heavily as it had since it began. I stood up from the desk and leaned against the window frame, watching the drops run down the glass. The city and the lake were hidden from view behind a gray curtain. Despite the raging storm, I felt restless inside. A compulsion or obsession in my mind drew me to leave this place, to drive away into the rain, to find something I'd lost. I was supposed to be somewhere else.

But where?

"There's a flood."

I heard a voice behind me and turned around. Tai stood in the doorway of my office, her clothes soaking wet. Her words made me shiver. "What?"

"Half the downtown streets are flooded. That's why I'm so late."

"That's okay. No problem."

"Good morning, by the way."

"Yes, good morning."

"How did yesterday go? You were going to try Eve Brier's new therapy. What happened?"

Tai showed no reluctance about asking me to share intimate confidences. Once upon a time, I would have done that, but not anymore.

"It went fine."

"That's all? Just fine?"

"That's all, Tai."

"Oh. All right."

I watched her hesitate, trying to understand why I was acting so distant. She took a step into the office, as if she were debating whether to come closer. Talk to me. Touch my shoulder. Tell me that if I needed anything, she was here for me. If I felt lonely, I could come by for a drink tonight and for anything else that might happen.

But she saw the dismissal in my face. I couldn't hide it. When I looked at Tai now, I saw all my mistakes with her come to life. I knew what it was like to sleep with her and share a bed together. I'd seen a world where we were husband and wife, and it was one more bad choice. None of it was real to her, but it was real to me, and I couldn't get past it.

"We should talk about the Seaton wedding," she said, her voice turning cool.

"Let's do it later, okay? I have to go out for a while."

"Okay. Whatever you want."

I turned away toward the window, shutting down our conversation. There was a long pause behind me, and then I heard her footsteps as she left.

As she did, a voice called from the doorway.

"Come find me. I'm still here."

I spun around. "What did you say?"

Tai was halfway out the door, and she stopped. "I said, when you get back, come find me. I'll be here."

"Sure. I will."

She gave me a confused look and walked away.

When she was gone, I wasted no time getting ready to leave. I couldn't get away fast enough. I turned off the lights and closed the office door. My coat and umbrella were in my car in the garage, but I didn't bother going to get them. I went to the lobby, ignoring the people who tried to talk to me. I had to get outside. I needed space, oxygen, light. I felt as if I were running out of breath, trapped underwater. A beast sat on my chest, weighing me down.

Tai was right about the streets. They were flooded. The rain on Michigan Avenue flowed six inches deep. Buses and cars plowed through the water, throwing up waves. My drenched clothes clung to my skin, and my hair was pasted down. I had to squint, because the wind drove the torrent hard into my face. Even the summer rain felt ice cold. I headed into the park, which I had virtually to myself, because everyone else was sheltered inside.

What was I doing here?

Where was I going? I didn't know.

I made my way to the bench near the fountain where I'd met Eve Brier. Except I hadn't met Eve here. Not really. Not in this world. I sat down and thought: *Say the word.* That was what she'd told me to do when we were together. *Say the word.* I said it out loud to the storm, as if I were somehow still locked away inside my head, a doll inside a doll inside a doll inside a doll.

"Infinite."

I held my breath, *hoping* that my world would transform, but the rainy Chicago day went on exactly as before. Whatever had happened to me was over and done. Why couldn't I accept the fact that this was the end of the road?

Why did I keep looking for something more?

I sat there in the park, a solitary man with the city all to himself. My city. Then I checked my watch, and I remembered with a curse: *Edgar.* He was waiting for me. Storms, blizzards, and tornadoes wouldn't keep him from the Art Institute on Thursday. I got off the bench and walked past Buckingham Fountain, which jetted water into the air despite the water pelting it from the sky. I splashed along cobblestones, the city skyscrapers going in and out of low clouds ahead of me. Around me were flowers, trellises, and topiaries, all drowning in the storm.

When I got to the museum, I hurried up the steps past the stone lions. Inside, tourists escaping the rain crowded the lobby. The smell of wet people got in my nose like the wormy stench of the river. I climbed the grand staircase to the upper level and squeezed through the busy galleries. When I passed *La Grande Jatte*, I found myself looking for Dylan Moran in a leather jacket. I expected to see his face—*my* face—eyeing me with a steely blue gaze. I expected *all* the faces around me to become my face, as if I were back inside the portal.

Instead, it was an ordinary day at the museum.

I found Edgar in the wing where he always was. He wore a raincoat and a fedora that had to be decades old. From the back, he looked a little like the mystery man in *Nighthawks*, whose face you never saw. I navigated the crowd, and he shot me an impatient stare as I came up beside him.

"You're late," he said, his breath engulfing me with its tobacco smell.

"I know."

"I hauled my ass halfway across the city to get here. You're, what, four blocks away? The bus took forever, and the streets are flooded. My feet are soaked."

"Sorry, Edgar. I'm having a bad day."

"Well, try being ninety-four, and then tell me what a bad day is."

I didn't want to argue with him. For all our battles over the years, I owed him a lot—for opening up his life to me, for putting food on the table, for taking shit from me as a bitter teenager and not kicking me to the street. He'd played the cards he was dealt, and yes, he complained about getting a bad hand until I didn't want to hear it anymore. I still loved him. I hadn't said that to him nearly enough.

"Why don't you tell me the story?" I said, putting a hand on his bony shoulder. "That'll make you feel better."

"What story?"

"You and *Nighthawks*."

Edgar gave me an impatient look. "What are you going on about, Dylan?"

"The man you saved on State Street when you were a boy."

My grandfather clucked his tongue in annoyance. "Saved? I watched a guy get flattened on the street when I was a kid."

"What?"

"Killed right in front of me. I still get nightmares about it."

I turned away from Edgar, and for the first time, I stared at the gallery wall.

That was when I realized that *Nighthawks* wasn't hanging in front of us.

I took a couple of steps in surprise, assuming we were in the wrong location, but then I looked around at the rest of the wing and realized that we were in our usual place. All the other paintings were exactly where they were supposed to be. But *Nighthawks* was gone.

"Where is it?" I asked, more to myself than Edgar.

"Where's what?"

"*Nighthawks.*"

"Huh?"

"It's missing. *Nighthawks* is missing." I pointed at the wall, which now featured a painting of the Harlem jazz scene by Archibald Motley.

"Same painting's been in that same spot long as I can remember," Edgar told me with a shrug.

I shook my head. "No, this isn't right."

I looked around the gallery and found a museum docent on the far wall. I went up to her and asked, "Where's *Nighthawks?*"

She gave me a polite smile. "*Nighthawks?* You mean the Edward Hopper painting?"

"Yes, where is it?"

"I don't know, sir. I assume probably the Whitney or MoMA in New York."

"Is it on tour?"

"I really have no idea."

"It's supposed to be *here*," I insisted. "Right on that wall."

"Here at the Art Institute?" she said with surprise. "No, I'm sorry, you're mistaken. You must be thinking of a different painting. We've never had *Nighthawks* on display here."

"What are you talking about? Daniel Rich acquired it from Hopper himself in 1942. It's been here ever since."

"Daniel Catton Rich? The former museum director? Mr. Rich died in 1941, sir. He was killed in a traffic accident here in Chicago."

I turned away from the docent and bumped into the people around me. I rubbed the dampness on my face; this was sweat, not rain. A tingling went up and down my skin like the fingers of a ghost. I came up next to Edgar again and found myself staring at Motley's painting, but all I could see in my head was *Nighthawks*. The lonely people at the diner. The empty city street. I could remember every brushstroke.

This was all wrong.

This wasn't how the world was supposed to be.

"Edgar, I have to go. Can you get back home by yourself?"

"I can with twenty bucks for a hot dog and a beer."

I dove into my wallet and found a twenty-dollar bill, which I pressed into his hand. Then I turned and retraced my steps through the pulsing museum crowd. Their overlapping voices made a deafening noise in my head, like the crash of a waterfall. I stumbled down the grand staircase and made my way out the doors onto the museum steps. Rain continued to flood from the sky, even harder than before, its impact as painful as pellets of hail. The black sky made it practically night. Traffic came and went on Michigan Avenue with lights on, horns honking, spray kicking up from the tires. People huddled under the overhang and ran through the downpour.

I needed to find Eve Brier.

Then I saw that she had already found me.

Eve was waiting at the base of the museum steps. She was dressed all in black like a mourner at a funeral, a black long-sleeve top, black slacks, and black heels. She held a black umbrella over her head, and she wore black lace gloves on her hands. Her face bore a teasing smile, and her glittering eyes latched onto mine. The pedestrians ignored us, as if we were both invisible. Somehow, Eve got brighter and clearer in the midst of the dark day, and the rest of the world blurred into gray shadows.

I ran down the steps and stood in front of her. I was strung out, breaking into little pieces. The rain poured ferociously over my head, but Eve was completely dry, not a drop of rain on her.

"This world isn't real," I said.

"No, Dylan, it's not."

"None of it. Nothing I've seen. It's never been real."

"No."

"Where am I?"

"You tell me. Where are you?"

"I don't know! All I know is that I don't belong here. I'm supposed to be somewhere else."

"Where?"

"I don't know! Tell me! Tell me the truth! You lied. You said it was over."

"I lied because you needed to figure out the truth for yourself."

"You put me through hell!" I shouted at Eve. "I watched people die. I've had to lose everyone I care about, over and over and over. And for what? So you can play games with me? So you can send me to world after world? I'm done with this. I quit."

Her eyes never blinked, not even once. "Quit? When you're so close?"

"Close to what?"

"To what you want more than anything."

"Stop with the riddles! Tell me what's happening!"

"You don't need me for that. You already know."

"I don't! I don't know what's real anymore!"

"Where did your worlds split apart, Dylan? Where did it all begin?"

"Here," I said. "It happened right here at the Art Institute. I saw that other Dylan in the leather jacket. That's why I went to your event at the hotel that night. That's why I found you."

Eve shook her head. "No, you were well on your way by the time you came to me. You didn't have to go looking for the Many Worlds. They'd already found you."

I tried to let it come back to me. I pushed on my temples to think, but my brain felt starved of oxygen, unable to process. Then I realized she was right. To get to the beginning, I had to go further back. I had to return to the one place that my mind didn't want to go.

"Wait. No. I was in the water. I made it to the surface, and I saw him on the riverbank. *Me.* That was the first time."

"Then what happened?"

"I dove down for Karly, but I couldn't get to her."

"How did you get out of the water?"

"What?"

"How did you get out of the water, Dylan?"

"I don't—I don't know. The police asked me that, but I don't remember."

"Why are you here, and Karly isn't?"

"I don't remember!"

"What *do* you remember?"

"Nothing! Nothing at all! I was trying to get to Karly, but I couldn't find her. That's when—that's when everything stopped."

"Yes."

"That's when everything else began."

"Yes."

I backed away from Eve, feeling an electric charge travel through my whole body. I looked up at the sky, which poured down a flood of rain over my head. I felt a tightness in my chest again, and I couldn't breathe. Blackness darkened my eyes. Something briny and dank filled my senses.

"Oh, my God."

"See? You know."

I did know. A curtain parted, and I saw through all the illusions. It was as if Eve were a magician, and I finally understood the trick. I knew where I'd been, while my mind passed from world to world to world. I had traveled in a circle so I could go back to the place where my story began.

"What do you want, Dylan?" Eve asked me. "What do you want more than anything else in life?"

It was a question that had only one answer. "A second chance."

"To do what?"

"To save Karly."

Eve twirled her umbrella with a flourish. "Then you need to hurry."

I ran. Yes, I ran. I ran like a madman through the Chicago streets, because I finally knew where I needed to go. I knew where my life was. I knew where I was supposed to be. I heard Karly calling out to me. She'd been calling to me ever since this began, and I hadn't listened. Her voice was muffled. The sound had to reach me through the thickness of water, because that's where she was.

In the river.

"Come find me. I'm still here."

CHAPTER 36

I had no map to guide me back, but I didn't need directions. The river drew me with the irresistible pull of a magnet. With each mile I drove, the storm intensified, as if this final world knew I was trying to escape and didn't want to let go of me. It threw up a maelstrom in my path. Angry branches of lightning shattered the sky, and thunder growled at me in a deep voice to turn back.

Chicago disappeared like a dream into the fog behind me. So did the suburbs. Soon I was in terra incognita, heading past open fields and deserted towns, where it felt as if I were the only person alive. I started out in daylight, but as the hours passed, night fell. No lights came on, leaving me blind as I headed deeper into the middle of nowhere. The only relief from the swath of darkness came from blinding shock waves that speared like tridents between the clouds. With each orange burst, I saw emptiness around me. Silhouettes of cornstalks in the fields. A few lonely farmhouses, devoid of light. The leafy crowns of oaks and maples. A rippled layer of clouds in the charcoal sky.

I drove and drove and drove, through flat mile after flat mile. I was a man in a bubble, hearing nothing but the drumbeat of rain and seeing only the cramped silver glow of wet pavement through the headlights in front of me. I lost track of time and distance, but eventually, the heaviness in my chest told me the river was close. I slowed down; I peered at the road ahead. I felt the way a soldier must feel when he's about to meet the enemy.

There it was.

I was back where I started.

Among the cornfields and trees, the flood monster loomed ahead of me, rolling, tumbling, like a dragon unleashed. I stopped in the middle of the road and got out into the teeth of the storm. The pavement ended just ahead of me, and the wild river began where the bridge should have been. The mud and water had become a kind of lava, whipping debris from the fields and roads in its teeth. I saw a highway sign making cartwheels like a circular saw. An electrical pole, dangling wires. Then an entire tree, its branches grasping for the surface like the crooked fingers of a skeleton.

I ran to the fringe of the water and followed it off the road into sodden fields. I kicked off my shoes, took off my belt and my shirt, anything that would slow me down. The wind gusted with a roar, nearly pushing me over. Rain stung my eyes, and another huge branch of lightning turned night to day. Barely a second passed before thunder exploded like a bomb. The storm was right on top of me now, not moving, firing all its weapons at me. I wiped my face and tried to see where I needed to go.

Where was the car?

Where was Karly?

I couldn't be far, but the river covered everything under a blanket of deep, frenzied rapids that wound over the land in both directions. Debris rolled past me, floating up and down on the waves, as if all the animals on the merry-go-round had been set free. I looked for some clue, something, anything breaching the surface to let me find her. A tire. A fender. The car was near me, trapped under the water along with my wife, but there was nothing to tell me where she was.

I stood there, needing help. *Please!*

That was when the Many Worlds sent me . . . myself.

Dylan Moran burst from the river right in front of me. We weren't even ten feet apart. He rose up like a sea creature, covered in mud and slime, spitting out water and gasping for breath. It was déjà vu in reverse. I was him. He was me. This was the moment when it had all started, but now we'd changed places.

He was in the water, and *I* was the man on the riverbank.

When the lightning flashed again, Dylan spotted me across the surging flood. It took a moment for him to register what he was seeing. I knew the feeling, because I'd already been through it. His face twisted with confusion, just the way mine had, because the man on the riverbank couldn't be real. But I was.

"Help me!" he shouted. My words.

The lightning faded to darkness, and he called out again: "My wife is drowning! Help me find her!"

Then he was gone, diving down into the water. With a kick of his feet, Dylan disappeared, but I knew he wouldn't find Karly. I'd been where he was, and I'd failed. He would search and search and come up empty. He would swim into nothingness. He would swim into other worlds.

Saving her was up to me now.

I waded into the water, where the wild current knocked me sideways. My feet spilled out on the slippery ground beneath me. I landed hard on my back, and the river sucked me into a whirlpool before I even took a breath. In an instant, the rapids spun me downstream in crazy circles. I choked, rising and falling, and finally, I fought back to the surface, where I gagged out water and desperately inhaled. The river swept against me like a speeding truck, but I kicked furiously with my hands and feet to fight the flow and stay where I was.

The car had to be submerged close by, but I couldn't see it. Once I was down below, I would be swimming blind. I was running out of time. I only had one last chance.

I swelled my lungs with a series of deeper breaths. In. Out. In. Out. I forced myself to go slowly, taking in more air each time as I got ready to dive. On the last one, I held my breath with my chest full. For a split second, I bobbed on the surface in the tumult of the storm, and then I shot deep down below the water and was immersed in blackness and silence.

The river was my enemy. Invisible debris swept from miles of fields shot through the narrows and assaulted me. Tree limbs punched my stomach, trying to drive the pent-up air from my lungs. Sharp objects flayed my skin. My eyes were wide open, but I saw nothing. I cast my arms as wide as a skydiver and felt a strange, slick sensation of speed as the current whipped me along. I didn't fight it. Wherever the flood had carried the car, I wanted it to carry me, too. Any second, we would collide in the channel, this huge obstacle in my path, like running full speed into a brick wall.

It happened so fast that I almost sailed right by it.

I felt myself bumping against the mud and jagged tree roots of the riverbank. One second, there was nothing, and an instant later, cool, slippery metal glided under my fingers. The car was right there, stuck in place against the bank, but I felt the river stripping me away from it. I grasped for any kind of handhold to keep me where I was, scratching at steel and glass, digging into the dirt of the riverbank with my nails.

Then something banged into my palm. By instinct, I snapped two fingers around it and held on. The river began to carry me away, but my body jerked to a stop. I struggled with my knuckles bent back and the water prying away my fingers. I thrust out my other hand and grabbed whatever had rescued me. With a solid hold, I felt the metal under my hand and recognized what it was. A side-view mirror.

I was there. I was at the car. The current dragged me sideways like a flag in a strong wind, but I clung to the mirror and used my free hand to thump on the windshield of the car. To alert her. To give her hope.

To tell her that I was here. Through the black, dense water, I heard something that made my heart soar.

Karly thumped back from the other side of the glass.

I beat on the windshield again—*Hold on!*—and then urgently, I felt my way along the car door. The glass was unbroken. The window I'd used to escape was on the opposite side, buried in mud. My only hope was to get the door open. With the current fighting me, I stretched out my hand to find the door handle, and I curled my fingers around it.

I pulled hard. The door swung open a couple of inches, then slammed into an obstruction and refused to move. There was no room for Karly to escape. I yanked repeatedly, trying to get it loose, but the car was trapped against the riverbank, with a wall of dirt and stone blocking the door from opening farther.

The chassis of the car seesawed as the river assaulted it. A solid shock would set it free. I wedged my foot against the side of the bank and pushed. Again. Again. And again. The car shimmied drunkenly but stayed where it was. I thrust hard with both feet, feeling each effort screaming in my lungs. My chest was on fire, and I was running out of time. My air was almost gone, and I needed to breathe or die. Those were the only two choices.

My whole body coiled into a tight spring. I bent both knees, levered my feet against the mud, and snapped every muscle, every atom of energy I had, into one last ferocious kick. The car lurched in the water. The frame rose up. Something shifted hard, and the entire vehicle floated free. Almost instantly, the current grabbed hold of it and shot the car downstream. Suddenly unobstructed, the door swung wide open, nearly ripped from my hand. I spun wide and felt the car pulling me behind it, like a rider unsaddled by a horse. The wheels hit the riverbed, and as the frame somersaulted, I heard a groan of metal bending, threatening to tear. I reached out for the interior of the car.

Karly reached back to me.

We had one instant together. Just one.

Our hands met. Her fingers laced with mine. I felt the touch of her skin. As I pulled hard, her body spilled out of the car, and then I released her. Like a rocket, she rose upward toward the surface of the river inches away. Somewhere above me, she broke into the night air, rain on her face, sweet oxygen filling her lungs.

I let go, too. I had no time left.

I kicked hard to follow her, but just as my arms broke through the surface, I jerked to a stop and felt my body pulled downward again. I tried to rise, to get free, to float, to swim, but an incredible weight held my leg in its grasp and wouldn't let go. I pulled hard, but I was caught.

The seat belt.

My ankle was trapped in the seat belt. The vast beast of the car dragged me with it downstream. I bent over, trying to free myself, but as the current spun us around, the knot wrapped itself around my leg. I pulled desperately, but I could feel the car and the river laughing at my efforts.

The air in my lungs began to leach into the water. Bubble after bubble escaped from my nose and mouth. Black clouds descended on my consciousness, and my heart began to beat crazily, an uneven rhythm. Unable to hold it back anymore, my chest gave way. I exhaled with a rush, feeling the last of my oxygen seep away.

I needed to inhale now. I couldn't stop myself.

I took a breath, knowing there was no breath there. I opened my mouth, and my lips formed a last soundless word.

"Karly . . ."

Then the river swam hungrily into my lungs.

CHAPTER 37

"Dylan?"

"Dylan?"

"Dylan, are you there? Talk to me."

"Dylan, come back. I'm still here."

I knew that voice.

I didn't know where it came from, but even in the depths of darkness, I could picture the face that went with that voice, like a speck of light at the end of a long, long tunnel. There was a woman waiting for me there, if only I could find her. If only I could find my way out.

"Dylan, I'm holding your hand. Can you feel me holding your hand?"

I did feel it. Something warm squeezed my fingers, and the touch felt familiar and good. It brought memories that floated in my head like dreams. There had been times when I would lie in bed in the middle of the night, and the only sensation I felt would be that hand holding mine. As long as I held that hand, life was worth living. With that hand in mine, I wasn't alone.

"Dylan?"

"Dylan, open your eyes."

"Dylan, please, open your eyes."

"Dylan, come back to me. I'm here."

I wanted to do what she said. I would do anything for her. To open my eyes, I had to break free from the darkness, but I didn't know how to do that. The darkness had held me in its arms for a long time, and it was hard to say goodbye and let go. There was a strange comfort in nothingness. But I also felt an ache, a longing, a need to see the woman who was talking to me, who was holding my hand, who was waiting for me at the end of the tunnel. I felt as if I'd been searching for her forever.

I knew her name. It was Karly.

I tried to do what she asked. I tried to let go of where I was and go back to where she was. I began to be aware of my body. Sensations slowly came back to life. I was conscious of being warm. I was aware that it hurt when I breathed. I had muscles I could move and control if I thought hard about how to do so. As Karly squeezed my hand, my fingers squeezed hers back.

I could hear, smell, touch. I was awake now. My eyelids fluttered.

Above me, I heard a sharp gasp, an intake of breath.

I opened my eyes. Closed them. Opened them. Even the dimness made me squint, and I struggled to make sense of what was around me.

At first, all I saw was a halo of light, but inside it, I recognized a face that made everything better. Karly stood over me. Slowly, as if not believing what she was seeing, she put her hands against her cheeks, her fingers trembling. Her lips moved but made no sound. As I stared up at her, her face dissolved into uncontrollable tears. She sobbed, and then she fell to her knees and threw her arms around me and held me tighter than anyone had ever held me in my life.

"Dylan."

Three weeks, Karly told me.

She waited until my disorientation had mostly gone away, which took several hours. By then, I was aware of being in a hospital room.

Three weeks, she told me.

Three weeks I'd been in a coma.

It was what they called a medically induced coma, in which they kept me sedated in order to give my brain and lungs a chance to heal from my lack of oxygen under the water. Nobody had known whether I would ever wake up.

"You got pneumonia in the early days," she told me, sitting with me by the bed and not letting go of my hand. "You could hardly breathe. They thought you were going to die. God, I was so scared."

"My chest hurts," I said, in a raspy voice.

"Try not to talk. Your lungs still need to heal. Let me talk."

"Okay."

"The doctors weren't sure about—about whether you'd come out of this with your brain functions intact. They said I needed to prepare myself for bad outcomes. But Alicia said the scans showed your brain activity was strong the entire time. In fact, she said the activity was hyperintense, like your mind was going through some kind of frenzied experience. She was sure you'd come out of it okay. She said Roscoe was looking out for you somewhere."

I smiled without saying anything. Part of it was gratitude, for surviving, for Karly being there for me, for coming through the experience of nearly drowning with my awareness and motor skills intact. Part of it was also the thought of Roscoe watching over me.

I'd seen him again, and that was a gift. Everything I'd been through was a gift.

The nurses called it a miracle. They didn't throw that word around lightly. I'd been without oxygen for nearly four minutes, which was dangerously close to the point at which brain damage would be irreversible. The day nurse had already been in after I awakened, asking me questions, testing my cognition. What's your name? What year is it? What city are you in? Apparently, I passed the test.

However, she was puzzled by the one question I asked her.

"Where is *Nighthawks?*"

I asked it several times, and finally, she called in Karly for help. My wife gave me a strange look, but she answered the question. "It's in the Art Institute, where it always is. Thanks to Edgar, of course. He's been by to visit you several times. Every time he was here, he told you the story again."

That was what I needed to hear. All was right with my world. With that, I was able to sleep.

I recovered for another full day before Karly said, "Do you remember what happened at the river?"

I shook my head. What I remembered I didn't trust.

"Do you want me to tell you about it? We don't have to do this now. We can wait until you're stronger."

"Please," I murmured.

"Okay. Well, we were driving home from our weekend away. The river had overflowed the highway, and we—we drove right into it."

"I'm sorry."

Karly put a hand on my cheek and stared at me with a deep regret in her eyes. "Don't use that word. That's my word. Dylan, there's so much I need to say to you, but let me get through this first."

"Go on."

"The car submerged. We were both trapped. I've never been so terrified. A tree came through the car window and nearly took our heads off. You were able to get out, but as you pulled me with you, the river ripped the car away. We were separated."

She described the experience in a monotone, as if it had happened to someone else. I think that was the only way she could talk about it.

"I was alone. You were gone. I was running out of air in this little pocket near the windshield. I tried opening the car door, but it was blocked. I realized I was going to die. I was trying to make peace with it. And yet—I don't know—I knew you would never leave me. I knew you'd come back and find me and save me. I just knew it. I don't know how much time passed. Probably only a few seconds, but it felt like forever. Then you were thumping on the windshield to let me know you were there. Somehow you dislodged the car and got the door open, and I was able to get out. I swam to the surface and made it to the riverbank. I thought you were right behind me. But then I realized you weren't coming up. You were still under the water. Thank God someone was there. A man from a nearby farm had seen the accident, and he'd already called 911. I could hear the sirens. I screamed to him that you were still down there, that you must be trapped. He went in after you. He found you by the car, with the seat belt wound around your ankle. He had a knife and was able to cut you free, but by the time he got you out, you weren't breathing. The ambulance was there, but I could see in the faces of the paramedics that they didn't think you were going to make it."

I brought her hand to my lips and kissed it. "The farmer who cut me loose. What did he look like?"

"Look like?"

"Did he look like me?"

A curious smile crossed her face. It was an odd question. "A little bit, I guess. You'll get to meet him. Once you have your strength back, we'll drive down there and thank him together. His name is Harvey Bushing."

I laughed, which made me cough.

"What's funny?" Karly asked me.

"Life. Fate. God."

She was still holding my hand. We sat silently, as an echo of horror rippled over both of us and slowly receded. I watched Karly open her mouth to say something more, then close it again. Her eyes filled with tears. It was a dam bursting, letting out guilt and shame and remorse. I knew how she felt, because I'd felt all the same things.

"Dylan, what happened before—what I did—"

I squeezed her hand. "Stop."

"I'm just so sorry. Please, please, say you can forgive me. If I hadn't been such a fool—"

"Stop," I said again.

"I love you. I love you so much. You're my world. What I did, how I betrayed you, I can't believe that was me."

"Karly."

She clamped her mouth shut and wiped her face. Her messy blond hair dangled across her cheeks.

"It wasn't you," I told her, struggling with the words.

"Don't talk. You shouldn't talk."

"I have to. Listen to me. This was my fault. I almost lost you, because I couldn't let go of my past. You saw something in me the day we met, and I've never been able to live up to it. I've spent my life angry and bitter and frustrated with the whole world, instead of treasuring what the world gave me. *You.* Well, that other Dylan is gone. I killed him. I just hope it's not too late for the two of us."

Karly started crying again. "It's not. Believe me, it's not."

"You married one Dylan Moran," I told her, "but I swear to you, I'm not the same, not anymore. I'm not him. I'm a different man."

Later that day, Karly went home to shower, and I slept in the hospital bed. My sleep felt absolutely dreamless, which was just what I wanted. Then I opened my eyes and recoiled, seeing a woman in a white hospital coat looking down at me. Underneath the white coat, she was dressed in black.

All at once, I felt as if I'd jumped down the rabbit hole again.

"Mr. Moran? I'm Dr. Eve Brier."

It was her. She hadn't changed at all. She gave me that mysterious smile that was all too familiar. Her eyes had the same seductive quality that I remembered from—

From what?

From a dream?

Or from other worlds?

"I know who you are," I said.

That made her hesitate. "You know me? Well, your wife probably mentioned that I'm the doctor who's been monitoring you while you were in your coma. You had us all very worried. It's a great relief to see you doing so well."

"Thank you."

I kept looking for a sign in her face, for some kind of recognition that she *knew* what had been happening to me. I wanted her to admit that she was still my conjurer. My magician.

Instead, she checked my vitals, and that was all.

"We'll still need to monitor you closely for a while, Mr. Moran, but right now, everything looks extremely promising."

"Good."

"You may find you have memory lapses," she added, as if I were lying on her couch in Hancock Center, twenty-nine floors above the endless lights of the *Lucent* sculpture.

"Not so far," I said. Then I added pointedly, "I remember *everything*."

"I'm pleased to hear it, but you may still experience side effects from the oxygen deprivation. You may become aware of cognitive difficulties that require some relearning and rehabilitation. I also suggest that you think about getting counseling after you're released. The physical implications of what you've been through are serious enough, but there are likely to be emotional and psychological ramifications, too. Don't feel that you have to manage those things alone."

"If I have Karly, I'll be fine."

"I understand, but you may want to consider professional counseling, too."

I said nothing. Dr. Brier looked disconcerted by my attitude. She checked my pulse, which she'd already done, and the touch of her fingers was warm. Her nails were long, and they pressed slightly into my skin. Then she bent over to check my lungs with her stethoscope and asked me to breathe as deeply as I could. While she was close to me, I caught a faint aroma of perfume, like roses, which took me back to the embrace she'd given me near the Buckingham Fountain.

"Your lungs are clear," she said. "That's excellent."

"Good."

"Are you in pain? I can give you something."

"I don't want anything."

Dr. Brier stood up and slipped the stethoscope out of her ears. Her eyes narrowed as she looked at me in bed. "You know, Mr. Moran, patients who are in induced comas often have disturbing experiences."

"Really?"

"Yes. Extremely vivid nightmares are common. Some patients describe them as hallucinations or phantasms. They experience terror, paranoia. Elements of the real world can creep into their dreams, albeit in distorted fashion. The sensations can feel quite real, and they can linger for a while once you regain consciousness. Did you go through anything like that?"

"I'm still processing what I went through," I replied.

"Of course. Well, I'll let you rest."

She gave me that strange intimate smile again, and I thought to myself: *You know, don't you?*

When she got to the door, I called after her. "Dr. Brier?"

"Yes?"

"Say the word."

She came closer to the bed. "What?"

"Say the word."

We stared at each other. Doctor and patient. Illusionist and fool. Puppet master and doll. I expected her to let the truth slip. I thought she'd put up a finger to remind me to be quiet and then soundlessly invite me to read her lips.

She'd mouth the word and wink.

Infinite.

But no. She played her part to the end. "I'm sorry. I don't know what you mean, Mr. Moran."

"It doesn't matter," I replied. "Thank you for everything. I mean that."

"You're welcome."

"You changed my life, and I'll always be grateful. Eve."

"It was my pleasure. Dylan."

Then she was gone.

And me? I was home.

EPILOGUE

"Is Ellie still okay?" I teased my wife. "It's been at least twenty minutes since you checked."

Karly flushed with embarrassment as she slid her phone back into her purse. She'd already called her parents four times to make sure that our daughter was fine. Which, of course, she was. But this was the first time we'd gone out on our own since Ellie was born, so I understood why Karly was nervous.

"Oh, yes, everything's perfect. Just like you said it would be. If you can believe it, my dad says that my mother is on her knees squawking and making duck noises to entertain her."

"Susannah? Please tell me he took video."

"He did. He's sending it to my phone. You know, I'm beginning to think this grandparent thing may buy me a free pass for having quit the real estate business."

I smiled at my sudden sense of déjà vu. "Do you miss it?"

"No. What about you?"

"The hotel biz? Not a bit. I prefer the nonprofit world. Well, except when I see my paycheck."

"We do okay," Karly said.

She slipped her hand into mine as we stood by the lake. It was a clear July evening, late, with the day's blue sky giving way to darkness. Only a handful of stars outshone the lights of the city. Crowds surrounded us up and down the lakeshore. Other couples walked hand in hand, children squealed, and joggers ran along the waterfront sidewalk. Behind us, we could hear the strains of rock music blaring from the band shell in Grant Park. Polish, Mexican, Greek, barbecue, and a hundred other ethnic food aromas mixed in the air. The Taste of Chicago festival was going on, and thousands of people were squeezed into downtown on a Saturday night. We'd come here to join the party.

And to mark an anniversary.

"Two years," Karly said, because she could see we were thinking about the same thing. "Two years ago tonight, we nearly died in that river."

Despite the warm air, she shivered with a memory of being under the water. I tilted up her chin and kissed her soft lips. "But we didn't die."

"No."

"Do you want the truth? I wouldn't change what happened even if I could. That night made everything better."

"I know it did."

"Look at me now," I added, smiling. "I'm married to the poet laureate of River Park."

Karly rolled her eyes. "It's one book. We'll be lucky if we make five hundred dollars."

"That doesn't matter. I'm incredibly proud of you."

She shoved me away playfully, but I knew she was pleased. We'd spent a lot of sleepless nights while she was pregnant and after Ellie was born, and sometimes Karly would sit by the fire and murmur poems into the voice recorder on her phone. She said she didn't know where the words came from; it was almost as if they just sprang into her head from someone else's mind. To her surprise, when she let her father read them, he said they were good. He sent them to his publisher, who thought they were good, too.

I wasn't surprised at all.

Karly inhaled the atmosphere of the park. She still had some pent-up energy. We'd already been here for hours, walking, kissing, talking, sampling foods, but Karly wanted to make the most of our one night of freedom. Her parents had Ellie until morning, so this was our time to be lovers again.

Her face glowed as she spied on the people around us. That had always been one of her gifts, to glory in the happiness of others. The older woman on the bench, with her head on her husband's shoulder. The two ten-year-olds kicking a soccer ball back and forth on the grass. A street performer juggling bowling pins for tips. A woman in a purple sports bra, jogging toward us, caught up in whatever music she was listening to on her earbuds.

Different people, happy lives.

My happiness was seeing the light in my wife's face. I saw that light when she was holding our daughter. And when she was lying next to me in bed. I saw that same kind of light in my own eyes, too, whenever I looked in the mirror. That was a new experience for me.

Peace.

"Do you want to go dancing?" Karly suggested.

"I want to do absolutely everything with you. Where should we go?"

Karly kept watching the people in the park come and go, her eyes traveling from face to face. "How about the Spybar? We can pretend we're still young and hip."

"The Spybar," I murmured darkly.

I looked away at the lake, where the water glistened with reflected lights, and I tried to swallow down a moment of anxiety. Karly was too preoccupied to notice my hesitation. I didn't spend a lot of time thinking about my coma dreams anymore, but the very mention of the Spybar took me back to that night when music pounded in my ears and my beautiful, beautiful wife was bleeding to death in my arms.

Some moments you just can't shake. They are with you forever. I had to remind myself that, as vivid as it was, that moment had never actually happened. It was a fantasy played out inside my head while I was lying in a hospital bed.

"Sure," I replied. "The Spybar. Let's go."

Karly didn't answer. Her stare followed the blond jogger who had passed us on the grass. The woman disappeared at a steady run toward the bright arena lights of Grant Park. I could only see the jogger's back as she went in and out of the shadows.

"Karly? Are you okay?"

My wife came out of her trance and gave me a dazzling smile. "I'm fine."

"Is something wrong?"

"No, nothing's wrong. That was just weird."

"What was?"

Karly shrugged. Her head swiveled again. From a distance, she eyed the jogger in the purple sports bra, who was nearly out of sight now, one more runner among hundreds in the Chicago night.

"That woman over there," she said. "The blonde who ran past us. It was the strangest thing. I saw her as clear as anything as she went by, and I swear, she looked exactly like me."

ACKNOWLEDGMENTS

I've published more than twenty thrillers in my life, but *Infinite* is the most unusual story I've ever told. I hope you enjoyed following Dylan Moran on his incredible journey.

When I was a teenager in the 1970s, one of my favorite novels was *The Magus*, by British writer John Fowles. It's the story of a schoolteacher who winds up enmeshed in surreal erotic mysteries on a Greek island, at an estate owned by an enigmatic "magus," or magician. Ever since I read that book, I've had in the back of my head the idea of writing a thriller that pushes the boundaries of reality, much as Fowles did with his literary novel. *Infinite* is the result. Fowles died in 2005, but I remain grateful to him for the inspiration he gave me as a boy dreaming of being a writer.

I also appreciate the support of my agent, Deborah Schneider, and my editor at Thomas & Mercer, Jessica Tribble Wells, both of whom saw the potential of this concept from the very beginning. Their excitement and enthusiasm for the book really helped me bring my vision to life. I'm also grateful to Charlotte Herscher for her great work in the editorial process, to Rex Bonomelli for the amazing cover, and to Gracie Doyle, Sarah Shaw, Laura Barrett, Susan Stokes, and everyone on the team at Thomas & Mercer who has helped get this book into your hands.

My longtime readers know that my wife, Marcia, gets the first read on every new novel. She's my editor, my sounding board, my psychology expert, and my proofreader—and her insights and feedback make every book better long before I ever submit it. My other advance reader is the wonderful Ann Sullivan. Together she and Marcia challenge me to make sure that the words on the page deliver what was in my head.

Of course, I want to give a big thanks to all of my readers, too, for joining me on this ride for more than fifteen years. You can write to me with your feedback at brian@bfreemanbooks.com. You can also "like" my official fan page on Facebook at facebook.com/bfreemanfans or follow me on Twitter or Instagram using the handle bfreemanbooks. For a look at the fun side of the author's life, you can also "like" Marcia's Facebook page at facebook.com/theauthorswife.

If you enjoyed *Infinite*, be sure to check out all my other thrillers, too. Visit bfreemanbooks.com to join my newsletter mailing list, get book club discussion questions, and find out more about me and my books.

Finally, I hope you'll post your reviews online at sites like Amazon, Goodreads, Audible, and other sites for book lovers—and spread the word to your friends, too. Publishing is still a word-of-mouth business from reader to reader! Thanks!

ABOUT THE AUTHOR

Photo © 2019 by Malyssa Woodward

Brian Freeman is an Amazon Charts and *New York Times* bestselling author of psychological thrillers, including the Frost Easton and Jonathan Stride series. His books have been sold in forty-six countries and translated into twenty-two languages. His stand-alone thriller, *Spilled Blood,* was named Best Hardcover Novel in the International Thriller Writers Awards, and his novel *The Burying Place* was a finalist for the same honor. *The Night Bird,* the first book in the Frost Easton series, was one of the top twenty Kindle bestsellers of 2017. Brian is widely acclaimed for his vivid "you are there" settings, from San Francisco to the Midwest, and for his complex, engaging characters and twist-filled plots. Brian lives in Minnesota with his wife, Marcia. For more information on the author and his books, visit http://bfreemanbooks.com.